THE IN CROWD

Also by Charlotte Vassell

THE OTHER HALF

The In Crowd

CHARLOTTE
VASSELL

Doubleday
New York

Copyright © 2024 by Charlotte Vassell

All rights reserved. Published in the United States by Doubleday, a division of Penguin Random House LLC, New York, and distributed in Canada by Penguin Random House Canada Limited, Toronto. Originally published in hardcover in Great Britain by Faber & Faber Ltd, London, in 2024.

www.doubleday.com

DOUBLEDAY and the portrayal of an anchor with a dolphin are registered trademarks of Penguin Random House LLC.

Jacket design by Evan Gaffney
Jacket photographs: hand based on a photo by Magdalena Russocka / Trevillion Images; London © Elena Pueyo/Getty Images; water © Guido Cavallini/ Getty Images

Library of Congress Cataloging-in-Publication Data
Names: Vassell, Charlotte, author.
Title: The in crowd / Charlotte Vassell.
Description: First edition. | New York : Doubleday, 2024. |
Series: Detective Inspector Caius Beauchamp
Identifiers: LCCN 2024010767 | ISBN 9780593685976 (hardcover) |
ISBN 9780593685983 (ebook)
Subjects: LCGFT: Detective and mystery fiction. | Novels.
Classification: LCC PR6122.A77 I5 2024 | DDC 823/.92—dc23/eng/20240318
LC record available at https://lccn.loc.gov/2024010767

Manufactured in the United States of America
1 3 5 7 9 10 8 6 4 2
First American Edition

For Uncle Nick

This land of such dear souls, this dear dear land,
Dear for her reputation through the world,
Is now leased out – I die pronouncing it –
Like to a tenement or pelting farm.
England, bound in with the triumphant sea,
Whose rocky shore beats back the envious siege
Of wat'ry Neptune, is now bound in with shame,
With inky blots and rotten parchment bonds.
That England that was wont to conquer others
Hath made a shameful conquest of itself.

Richard II, William Shakespeare

THE IN CROWD

THE LAST SATURDAY
IN AUGUST

Prologue

The Thames at Richmond

Eight men with respectable professions and long vowels. Eight men wearing Lycra all-in-ones with stripes down the side that match the blades of their oars and their boat club's badge. Their striped blazers match too. Matchy matchy, even though the colours clash. They proudly wear them at Henley every year. Once they inevitably get knocked out, which happens embarrassingly early on, they spend the rest of the week drinking themselves into a stupor and failing to pull university students. Eight grown men who for varying reasons – a desire to avoid high cholesterol, a release from their stressful jobs or just plain boredom – get in a boat every Saturday for an outing on the venerable Thames. Eight muscular, lean men all move in time with the calls of their coxswain. They all fantasise about fucking this small woman in the boat house over a rowing machine whenever their wives tell them to pick their towels up off the floor, so they don't get all mouldy. The towels were a wedding present from Great-aunt Nancy, a snip in the Harvey Nichols sale or in a discontinued colour, after all. These eight men keep their hands – blistering or already calloused from hours of gripping their oars – at the exact same height, all of them dropping their blades into the water at the exact same time at ninety-degree angles. They push back their legs, putting all the power they've gained into propelling them further.

Something's wrong. The bow, a junior doctor with sandy hair, is thrown backwards. He's caught a crab. Not a real one that you can cook and eat with butter, cracking its claws to slurp out its sweet meat, but rather his blade has hit the water at the wrong angle, and the oar flipped round and hit him square in the face. The boat stops.

'I hit something,' he says through a mouthful of blood. The oar has taken out his front two teeth, so he lisps those words. Blood dribbles down the side of his mouth and onto the white front of his Lycra.

The stroke, an investment banker desperate for a hobby that means he doesn't have to spend time with his family, peers over the boat and sees something bobbing about. 'Guys, there's a fucking body. Jonno hit a corpse.'

1

A large Georgian villa in Richmond

The tinkling of crystal and the tedium of small talk drifted in on the early evening breeze through the wide-open French doors. The summer would not die – it kept going on for what felt like forever and ever. The sky had taken on a lilac tinge against the tangerine of the coming sunset; the bristling lavender peeking through from the garden seemed to have permeated the light. Harriet, the newly engaged hostess, had with a deft hand plastered her recently landscaped garden with tasteful cloth bunting, the drinks were served in vintage cocktail glasses, and miniature pastel-coloured cakes from a fashionable patisserie in Fulham were elegantly arranged on china stands. The bunting had been handmade by a woman whose name Harriet was guarding like a national secret, the glasses had been bought en masse from an antiques dealer who was known to overcharge, and the cake stands had been purchased in bulk from an overpriced boutique on Hill Rise. These accoutrements were destined to be neglected after that afternoon, banished forever to cardboard boxes in the attic. Cards, flowers (none of which were from a supermarket) and good wishes were piled up on a table in the entrance hall.

Callie was wearing a sleeveless, buttermilk-coloured linen sundress that fell to the floor with a tight waist and a balcony bust – a revelation compared to the other female guests' aggressively ditzy floral prints – and a broad-brimmed straw hat with silk flowers pinned to the band. She was standing at the marble island in the middle of the kitchen slicing up mint, cucumber and strawberries. Fresh offerings to the god of English garden parties. Callie was being careful not to get any strawberry juice on her dress. Harriet, who was Callie's best friend from childhood, had severely underestimated the amount of Pimm's her guests would desire, and yet she was not the one in the kitchen remedying the oversight, dutiful Callie was. Callie was trying to be helpful, to be the best maid of honour possible. She could smell the mint on her fingers. Callie tipped the offending herb, cucumber slices and strawberry quarters into a couple of waiting jugs and chucked in satisfying glugs of neat Pimm's. She rooted around the freezer for ice cubes and threw a tray in after the booze.

'I bought four bottles from the corner shop,' said Inigo, Harriet's fiancé, as he barrelled through the door carrying bottles of cheap lemonade in flimsy blue plastic bags. 'Do you think it's enough? This was all they had. They're warm.'

'Yeah, that's plenty,' Callie said, taking a bottle from him, removing the cap and pouring some into the jugs. 'I've put a lot of ice in and everyone's already half-cut so they won't notice.'

'Do you like what Harriet's done with the house? You've not been since the renovations were completed.'

'It's so lovely,' Callie said, looking around at the maximalist interior.

Inigo worked in private equity. He made obscene money but couldn't really explain how. Something about how as a fund manager he was paid a fixed-rate fee on the assets they managed. It was just sounds to Callie, but it meant that he'd bought a beautiful Georgian house in Richmond for Harriet to play dolls in. Although Callie did wonder if the Bank of Harriet's Mum and Dad was actually responsible.

'Harriet has done such a lovely job decorating. I love the

wallpaper in the living room. One of her designs, I take it? She's always had such good taste,' Callie said.

'Unlike you,' Inigo said, giving Callie a friendly knock on the arm. Years ago Inigo had asked her out – this was before he'd asked Harriet – and she'd turned him down for a sexy but quite dreadful man whom she had since blocked on all social media channels. Inigo liked to joke about it every now and then, and Callie liked to pretend she hadn't heard him. She did not regret turning him down.

'Ha, well. Yes,' Callie said. While Harriet's material comfort was enviable, Callie could think of nothing worse than waking up next to such a boring man every day. He only ever wore grey or blue. She could never be in a relationship with someone with such a limited colour palette.

'God, that was rude. I'm so sorry.'

'It's all right. I've got to start finding it funny at some point too.' Callie picked up a jug in each hand and turned to go back to the party.

Inigo grabbed her arm to stop her without thinking. Pimm's sloshed onto the floor. 'I was just joking.' He realised he was tightly holding her arm and let her go as he began feeling ashamed. 'I meant nothing by it.'

'No harm, no foul,' Callie said, before looking to see if her dress had been spared. It had. 'You might want to mop that up before someone slips.'

'Darling, there you are,' Harriet said, coming into the kitchen. 'Everyone's been asking for you.'

'Callie was just saying how much she likes the wallpaper in the living room,' Inigo said.

'Yes, it's lovely. So lovely,' Callie said.

'Isn't it just?' Harriet said, turning to face Inigo squarely. 'I

9

think you should make a little speech to our guests, darling. It's only polite. Some of them have even trekked all the way over from St Reatham.'

'Oh, if I have to,' Inigo said, strolling out of the kitchen. 'You know I love an audience.'

Harriet turned to Callie but couldn't quite look her in the eye. Harriet let her gaze wander for a moment, flitting between Callie's right ear and her chin, before settling on the spilled Pimm's on the floor. Trust Callie to make a mess. She knew she should have hired caterers like Mummy had suggested rather than have a more 'pared down' party with a homemade, cutesy feel.

Harriet remembered herself and started speaking far too quickly, as if the words leaping from her tongue were themselves desperate to put Callie in her place. 'I've asked my cousin Emily to be my maid of honour. I know you thought it would be you, we've known each other for so long, but I . . . Well, family, eh . . . It's a tradition on my mother's side . . .'

Harriet's voice tailed off. She hadn't actually asked Emily yet, but she had seen Inigo's face when he looked at Callie just now, and she'd seen the last moments of his grip on her arm. Her mother, a subtle woman (although she had demanded that after her marriage to Harriet's father they not so subtly double-barrel their names) and a master of the dark art of the back-handed compliment, had seeded the idea not long after Harriet's engagement. She'd been flicking through a copy of *Tatler* and pointed out a picture of such-and-such's wedding and said, 'What a shame that no one warns these brides not to give too prominent a position to their prettier friends. They'll regret that bitterly when they are my age and looking over the photos. This poor girl has a rather buxom friend who is terribly distracting.' Harriet knew she had nothing to worry about. If anything, Inigo was merely flexing his ageing muscles and Callie was far too loyal, but still. Harriet had a ridiculous engagement ring that she was slightly afraid to wear in public. Harriet was going to marry him. Harriet was going to be happy, and if that meant that her plain cousin Emily was going to be maid of honour, then so be it. Harriet was choosing fucking happiness.

'Hey, you're the bride.' Callie smiled, gripping the jugs tightly. 'Whatever you say goes.'

'You're still a bridesmaid, of course you are. How could you not be. And I'm desperate for you to make me a headpiece to wear.' Harriet felt it keenly that there was no family tiara and that the Simpson-Bamber fortune had been made much too recently to have neither acquired the historic material trappings of grandeur nor totally lost the stink of lower middle-/upper working-class mannerisms.

'Of course, Hat. For you, anything.'

'Goody.' Harriet relaxed and started speaking at a normal pace. 'I've started a Pinterest board especially. It's going to be my "something new".'

'Send me a link and I'll knock up a sketch or two.'

Harriet opened the freezer, took out a solitary ice cube and started chewing on it. She was hungry, but she also had to drop a size before she even started trying on dresses. 'Do you remember Henry Chadwell?'

'Name rings a bell.'

'The headmistress of St Ursula's son.'

'Oh, just about. Gave me a Yorkie bar once and tried to be funny about me being a girl.'

'He's here. He works with Inigo now. It's so funny, we all had such crushes on him when we were fourteen, he was so much older and cooler. Remember how we used to obsess over his

11

floppy hair? And yet, he looks like nothing now. He's going grey and not in a sexy way.'

'Time is kind to no one.'

'Even you, darling. Callie, sweetie. I want you to have what I do. I want you to be this happy too, but you need to get a move on. Maybe you should come to hot yoga with me next week.'

Callie was stunned into a polite grinning silence until Inigo started braying for attention in the garden and Harriet trotted out after him. Callie followed moments later, putting the jugs of Pimm's on the table at the back as Inigo reeled off a fairly boring anecdote about Harriet. Callie in turn looked up at the sky and watched a flock of escaped parakeets land in a tree in a neighbour's garden. A man, whom Callie vaguely recognised from her childhood, was intently looking at her. Yes, Harriet was right. That was Henry Chadwell. He was tall and broad-shouldered still, time hadn't robbed him of his stature, but the charm that all of the girls in their year swooned over was definitely gone. Callie smiled at him in that distracted and yet deflective way that said you'd noticed their attention yet cared not to reciprocate it.

'Cheers!' the partygoers all called together. The attention of seventy people drifted away now to their stomachs. The jugs of Pimm's that Callie had made went down quicker than half of the crowd's tax bills after a few cheeky tweaks. Dainty sandwiches were passed around and more and more bottles of champagne paid for by Harriet's hideously rich father were uncorked. Peter Simpson-Bamber, né plain old Simpson, the Right Honourable Member for some godforsaken patch of Lincolnshire that he visited three times a year – and Harriet's long-suffering father – appeared by Callie's side.

'Is this what everyone young is wearing now? What are we

calling this look?' Peter Simpson-Bamber asked. This wasn't just the idle chat of a middle-aged man. He had ruthlessly made his fortune in clothing retail and still had a fondness for the rag trade.

'Forsterite. It's very Margaret Schlegel.' Callie turned to him. '*Only Connect*.'

'I don't get that show.'

They smiled at each other. Neither of them connecting with the other.

'How's your old mum?' Peter asked.

'Fine. I think.'

'Peter,' came a man's voice.

'Arthur,' he said, turning to face the gentleman who had appeared. Arthur Hampton was a handsome man in his mid-to-late fifties who carried himself with the sort of ease that cannot be learned, only bred. 'Oh. Hello. How are you doing?'

'Not too shabby, and this must be your daughter. Congratulations, young lady.'

'Oh no, this is Callie, the maid of honour. Harriet is the blonde girl in the blue dress over there. No, not that one, the one by the roses.'

'Ah yes, of course. She is the exact image of your lovely wife.' He held his hand out to Callie. 'Arthur Hampton. Putting my foot in my mouth has been my party trick since 1962.'

'Nice to meet you,' Callie said, shaking his hand and noting the exquisite cut of his jacket. 'Excuse me, I think Harriet said she needed my help with the napkins.' She left and went back into the house. There was no napkin crisis – she just didn't want to get stuck talking about share prices or whatever men like that talked about when they were alone. She lingered about the kitchen for a few respectable moments with the intention of going back out into the garden and talking to Jim, the best man, whom she'd spotted lurking near the cakes.

All of the other guests by now were somewhere between half-cut and fully plastered and yet the two Members of Parliament – colleagues, comrades, bitter enemies perennially masked by joviality – receded into a quieter corner of the garden shrouded by a rose bush from the eyes of anyone who might care a jot.

'Did I invite you to this?' asked Peter Simpson-Bamber. He pursed his lips – he hadn't intended to be so rude. Every time he spoke to Arthur Hampton, he became petrified of dropping his aitches or a stray glottal stop, of letting his cockney heritage show. And because he was worried about it, he always did it.

'Yes, in whichever parliamentary bar you frequent on some idle Thursday. You'd had four pints of beer subsidised by the public purse, so you may not remember it.'

'Ah.' Peter raised his eyebrows. Arthur always had to say something smart to Peter. A quip to belittle him. Or perhaps Arthur knew that gatecrashing an engagement party was rude even for a man as entitled as he was.

'Congratulations anyway.'

'Why are you here?' Peter asked, wanting to get whatever bollocking he was about to receive over with quickly.

'I was in the neighbourhood.' Arthur smiled. They both knew he hadn't been anywhere near Richmond until twenty minutes ago. 'The PM suspects you've been briefing the press against him, so I said I'd yell at you in person rather than over the phone. Much more personal that way.'

'How preposterous.'

'That's exactly what I said.'

'Probably that idiot upstart Singh in Transport,' Peter said, trying to brush it off.

'Yes, perhaps.' Arthur paused for a moment to watch Peter squirm. 'Whether it's him or not, I said that there's no way that you'd be fucking stupid enough to end your career by mouthing off to *The Times* about the "softening" of our drugs policy before the PR groundwork has been laid.'

'Softening, is that what you call it? I've seen that report you're bandying about. I don't care how much taxable revenue your sordid little "pilot scheme" could have generated or how safe you claim it is. And your plans for exportation are just bizarre. Do you honestly think other countries are going to just let you sell their population cheap party pills? You can't rock up to Hong Kong with a destroyer these days.'

Arthur looked at Peter, looked him square in the eye. Peter Simpson-Bamber, righteous neophyte, dilettante, inept career politician and mild xenophobe, had shown his hand. 'We've managed it before,' Arthur said, as he watched Callie come back out of the house and start talking to Jim, a politico whose face Arthur knew from around. He liked the look of her. She seemed sensible, yet there was a lightness behind the eyes, and her outfit was refreshingly simple. 'Pretty girl that, and she knows when to leave a conversation. Is she attached?'

'You're married,' Peter said, bristling.

'And to a man at that. I have a young family friend, actually, and I think they may well get on. He's recently single and not built for it.'

'Don't you have better things to be doing than play Cupid?'

'Most likely, but I am getting sentimental in my dotage. We should set them up.' They were both keenly aware that Arthur Hampton was pretty much the entirety of the British government these days, at least the functioning bits, and yet here he was matchmaking. Peter on pain of death would pass on the invite to Callie.

'My goodness, is that the time? I best be off. Oh, before I forget, I didn't arrive empty-handed.' Hampton gave Simpson-Bamber a bottle of Bollinger. Arthur Hampton did not like Simpson-Bamber, nor anyone who double-barrelled their surname willy-nilly, but at least he didn't despise him enough to threaten him at his daughter's engagement party without bearing a gift. Or rather, his manners dictated that he should arrive at a party with a bottle of something potable even if he hated the host's guts. He had good breeding. The Bollinger was the worst vintage he kept at home.

As Arthur Hampton turned to leave, he stopped and said goodbye to Callie and Jim. He'd since remembered that he'd had a good laugh with Jim at the bar during last year's party conference. They joked for a minute about the opposition leader's latest gaffe – opening his gaping maw to eat a huge slice of Victoria sponge at a church fete in his local constituency. Then he turned to Callie, ignoring Jim entirely.

'What's Callie short for? Not California, I hope?'

'Actually . . .' she said.

'Oh God.'

'No, I'm just teasing. It's Calliope. My mother had artistic pretensions.'

'"Achilles' wrath, to Greece the direful spring, Of woes unnumber'd, heavenly goddess, sing!"'

'Exactly so.'

'And are you a poet?'

'No, God no. I can barely string a sentence together. I'm a milliner.'

'How charming, and I take it this is one of your creations?' He nodded at the straw hat she was wearing. 'Is that a sprig of monkshood in the band?'

'It is. You have a good eye.'

'Delightful.' Arthur Hampton checked his watch. 'Lovely to meet you, Callie. Jim, see you in the trenches.'

They watched him leave. Jim raised his eyebrows at her, and Callie went into the house. There was a queue for the downstairs loo, so she slipped away and headed up the stairs. She freshened up her make-up afterwards and came down to find Jane Simpson-Bamber loitering at the bottom of the staircase.

'He's an odd fish, Arthur Hampton,' said Mrs Simpson-Bamber. She ran her finger over a marble-topped sideboard, collecting dust as she went. She stared disgustedly at her finger, covered in dead skin cells and other human detritus. She couldn't bear how inept Harriet's cleaner was and more pertinently she couldn't bear to look Callie in the eye lest she give too much away. 'Hates Peter. Always has. Can't bear that he's a self-made man and not one of the old boys. He's suppressed his career. I'm sure it was him who blocked Peter's knighthood. Jealous of his talent, I suppose.'

'Oh, really? They seemed friendly enough.'

'Don't mistake friendliness for actually liking someone.' She looked Callie up and down, noting the cut of her dress but refusing to betray any complimentary feelings she might have had. 'I wonder what he wanted.'

'I don't know.'

'He barges into Harriet's engagement party, doesn't even congratulate her and yet spends ten minutes joking about with you.'

'He knows Jim from work.' Callie wasn't sure what else to say to that, so she changed the subject. 'Hasn't Harriet done a wonderful job with the renovations? This staircase had practically rotted through when they bought the old wreck and now look at it.'

'Yes, she has.' Jane looked at her. She didn't say it out loud, but Jane's eyes said something like 'I know you can't help being the centre of attention, but you could at least try', or a plain old 'fuck off'.

Callie smiled back at her with all her teeth and walked out into the garden.

★ ★ ★

'Callie,' came a voice from behind her as she walked down the hill towards the station. 'Wait up.'

She stopped as Jim caught up with her. He had been Inigo's flatmate many years ago when Inigo was a mere business analyst and Jim was Peter's researcher. That was how they had all met. Jim was a good sort. The sort of man that sensible women were friends with and often tried to set up with their equally sensible female friends to no avail.

'So?' he asked.

'So?' she replied.

'What's this nonsense about plain old cousin Emily being maid of honour?' Jim took a drag of his cigarette. He offered one to Callie, but she declined.

Callie shrugged. 'Harriet lied to me about a family maid of honour tradition rather than be honest and say she didn't want me to do it. Classic Hat the Brat.'

'I only give them eighteen months anyway. No marriage can take that much cheating.'

'Inigo?' Callie was surprised, she didn't have him pegged.

'Oh, God no. Little Inigo stays very much where he's supposed to be. He's desperate to get married, he's worried about getting old and dying alone. You can't tell a soul. I don't even think Inigo remembers telling me that Harriet had a "thing" with one of the guys from that flower company. Oh, what are they called? You know, the ones with old-fashioned bicycles who loiter on street corners. They employ very handsome young actors and then send them knocking in all the wealthy neighbourhoods to convince the lady of the house to set up a subscription. Sound business practice if you ask me. Anyway, Harriet said she only did it because she wasn't sure that Inigo was committed to her because he hadn't proposed yet. He rang me drunk after his work's Christmas party last year and I had to rescue him from a disabled toilet that he'd locked himself in at a Marylebone pub. He was hiding from that prick called Henry that he works with. Actually, he was here today. Gives me the ick. Inigo felt obliged to invite his whole team. Fancy a swift half? There's that pub on the river. We can watch the boats go by.'

'Only if you have any more titbits like that.' Callie, who had been so sure of her position as best friend two hours ago, was no longer confident. Who doesn't tell their best friend about their affair with a twenty-one-year-old recent theatre studies graduate who hawked flowers? That's exactly the type of thing you do tell them.

They arrived at the pub, but rather than finding a spare table overlooking the Thames, they found a police boat and two police divers carrying a body out of its murky depths.

'How Victorian,' Jim said.

'How very sad.'

They stood on the riverbank and watched the police boat bobbing in the water as a crew of eight rowers in very revealing

Lycra was being interviewed by police officers nearby. One of them was bloody.

'Let's go to the pub on the green instead. The blue flashing lights are disrupting the ambiance,' Jim said.

'Sure,' Callie said.

They set off into the town and away from the crime scene, shrugging it off like a splash of rain.

'Hampton liked you,' Jim said.

'It's the hat, you know. Always attracts a certain type of old boy. Is he important?'

'Very. He's a kingmaker. The PM wouldn't stand a chance if he lost Hampton's support. They were at school together. If anything, I'd say the PM is his flesh puppet. He's like a medieval courtier – the power behind the throne. I like him, he's always good for a pint down the bar. It's funny, the grander someone is the more fun they usually are and less concerned with hierarchy.'

'Grand?'

'Yes, his brother is a duke.'

'Grand in the extreme.'

'I wonder what he was doing at the party. He's in a different faction from Peter. They aren't easy friends. They even had a slanging match in the lobby a couple of years ago. Peter is the de facto leader of a little fringe group of free-market nutters and Hampton is the leader of the gentlemen farmers.' They arrived at the pub. 'What can I get you?'

'I'll have a fruity cider.' Callie sat down at a bench outside the pub. Her phone pinged.

Harriet S-B added you to Cluck Cluck Cluck – it's a hen!

Harriet S-B added +44 . . ., +44 . . ., +44 . . .

Harriet S-B
Let the wedmin commence!!!

You

Jim came out of the pub with their drinks and sat opposite Callie. He'd bought himself a regular pint. 'Can I have a sip of yours?'

'Is it too pink for you to buy yourself a whole pint?'

'Yeah.'

'Go on then,' Callie said, handing him her drink to try. She scrolled through Instagram and saw that she had a message request. It was Henry Chadwell. She ignored it and turned back to Jim.

'How are you keeping?' he asked, passing back her cider.

'Me, I'm good.'

'I bumped into he-who-shall-not-be-named last week in the bogs in Quaglino's. He was very drunk.'

'You mean Max.'

'I do. That was rough, mate. He's a knob.'

'You know, I'm glad he broke up with me a month before the wedding rather than a month after it. Counting my blessings et cetera, et cetera, et cetera.'

'He asked after you. I think he regrets it.'

'Bully for him.'

'That's the spirit.'

THE FOLLOWING FRIDAY

2

Central London

Caius was pacing up and down the lobby of a reputable and just-anarchic-enough-to-be-respectable fringe theatre off Leicester Square. It had the faintest smell of spilled beer and dripping sarcasm that stopped it from becoming too establishment, too dull. In one hand he precariously clutched two rather vinegary-smelling Pinot Grigios in small, flimsy plastic cups while he repeatedly checked the time on his new watch (he'd found it in a vintage store on a recent day trip to Brighton and was very smug about it) as if there were some chance that time wasn't linear after all. That the rules of the universe might just bend for him this once. They did not, of course. The usher called for the last remaining audience members to take their seats. A woman with an impressively wide straw hat, and the sort of curves that Caius couldn't help but notice, was also lingering in the theatre foyer. The usher kept eyeing the pair of them up.

Caius walked over to the box office attendant who agreed to take his date's ticket from him after Caius wrote down both of their names on the top of it. There was a tube strike on most of the lines and Caius's date was stuck on the upper deck of a stationary bus on Euston Road. His phone buzzed. She said she'd hopefully get there for the interval at least. He handed his ticket to the usher at the door to the house who directed him to his seat. Everyone else in the row stood up and he apologised profusely as he squeezed past them to take one of the four empty seats at the other end. A man in a panama hat was sitting on the very end seat next to the wall. His head was bowed as he studied the programme. The theatre was small and already warm and sweaty-smelling despite the strike causing poor attendance. There were two seats between him and the man – who he thought must be getting quite hot wearing a hat indoors – and one between him and the studenty type on the other side. He put one of the cups of wine on the floor and took a sip from the other. It was warm. His phone buzzed.

Laura – Tinder
19.28
Someone's just been knocked off there bike by a van.
Luckily UCLH is just their. Lots of panic though. I think
I'm going to be stuck here for quite some time. Sorry! Let's
reschedule. I'm free next weekend x

Caius put his phone in his pocket as the woman with the hat from the foyer sauntered along the aisle that ran down the middle of the theatre and stopped at his row. Everyone stood up again, and she squeezed past them, taking the seat between Caius and the older man reading the programme. She took her hat off, put it on her knees and checked her phone.

'Let's get this over with then, shall we?' She looked him in the eye, so directly it felt as if she had hit him, and wryly smiled. Pursing her lips and rolling her eyes but not enough to extinguish their impishness. He looked bewildered; she liked that.

'Get it over with?' Caius asked, slightly shocked that first she was striking up a conversation with a stranger and second she could say that when she hadn't even given the play a chance yet.

'I've been forewarned that it's terrible, but my friend is in it, and we have to turn out for our old pals, don't we?'

'Oh.' Caius glanced quickly at the empty seat next to him

26

that was supposed to be filled by Laura, a woman with a love of fell-walking and a profile picture in which she was surrounded by friends attractive enough to make a casual swiper pause, but not so attractive they'd be a distraction. He wondered whether Laura was stuck on the bus or if she had just thought that his idea for a date was rubbish. 'How bad are we talking?'

'I'm going to drink through it.' She took a can of M&S pre-made margarita that she'd smuggled into the theatre out of her bag. She smiled at Caius. It made him feel weak. And almost immediately it felt like they were in an exclusive club of two, that they had known each other forever and were in on it, in on the joke that was their collective failures that had led them to be there in the front row. It was impossible for Caius not to like her.

'I like your hat,' Caius said, admiring the silk flowers sewn onto the burgundy band. He'd found the nerve to keep speaking to her from somewhere.

'Thank you very much.'

'You don't see many people our age wearing proper hats that often. I think it's a shame. Much more elegant than a baseball cap or a beanie.'

'Well, one tries. I'm a milliner. If I don't wear hats everywhere I go then the trade is doomed. I like to think I am a walking advert for the virtues of habitual hat-wearing. I have to prostitute my talents so I can keep paying my mortgage.'

The lights in the house dimmed and one lucky cast member was backstage, primed and ready to go. They had already been subjected to the show's gimmick: performing drunk. They were three tequila shots, a sambuca and two rum and Cokes down before the first line was even uttered.

'I'm hoping for a discussion between high art and low habits,'

Caius said, trying to rescue his pride. He hadn't realised that the show was generally poorly thought of.

'How pithy of you, and how hopeful. I'm Callie, by the way.'

'Caius. Nice to meet you.'

The curtain came up to Wankered Wilde presents *The Importance of Beering Earnest*. The actor playing Algernon came on stage. He was tall and handsome and dashing in his Victorian costume. There was also a hint of that steely determination to plough through this shit that Caius had seen in many underpaid workers before.

★ ★ ★

Caius had survived the first half and drunk both piteous cups of lukewarm Pinot Grigio without trying to taste them. He settled back into his seat after popping to the gents and continued chatting to his charming new acquaintance.

'I want to leave, and yet I feel compelled to stay and watch Lady Bracknell put away another pint of Guinness,' said Callie.

'I know. I'm mesmerised and I hate myself for that,' Caius said. Callie offered him a chocolate button from the bag she'd just bought from an usher, and he took one. 'Where's your milliner's then?'

'Oh, I've got a little hovel off the unfashionable end of the King's Road. Most of my work is for society weddings or Ascot, so it makes sense to be in that part of town. What do you do?'

'I'm a police officer.'

'Now I wouldn't have guessed that. You're wearing architect glasses.'

'I can't draw, I'm afraid.' Caius was flattered. He'd agonised over these specs.

'Oh, that is a shame, but it's a skill. It can always be learned.' Callie took out another tinny from her bag like she was a slightly alcoholic Mary Poppins. Caius couldn't work out where they were all coming from. 'Were you supposed to be on a date tonight?'

'No, yes. Maybe. Just meeting a new friend. I'm not sure. We matched on Tinder, but she keeps saying how she wants to make new friends first and foremost and see where it goes from there.'

'Cheers to whatever ambiguity you're feeling,' Callie said, raising her tinny.

The lights came up and the house fell silent, but before Lady Bracknell could even get anywhere near the haaaandbaaaaaggg-based denouement, the actor projectile vomited all over the man sitting next to Callie who was luckily just out of the main splash zone. The audience was aghast. The smell, horrendous. The man did not react.

'I've got some tissues,' Caius said, standing up and fiddling about in his pocket for a packet of Kleenex. They were for his hay fever. Still nothing from the man.

Lady Bracknell started sobbing as the rest of the cast recoiled. 'Three years at RADA for this, for this. I should be at the RSC. I gave everything in my audition. I should be playing Beatrice.' A sympathetic Miss Prism trotted out of the wings and helped her off the stage, for she had trained at LAMDA and had always dreamed of playing Ophelia.

'Are you all right?' Caius asked the man. He moved closer as he looked at the man's lifeless, ashen face. 'OK, everyone. I need you to remain in your seats. DI Caius Beauchamp, Met Police.' He flashed his warrant card and looked at the manager. 'Call an ambulance.'

★ ★ ★

'You smell nice,' said Matt, Caius's DS, who had just arrived at the theatre. 'Especially considering the general smell of vomit in the air. New cologne?'

'What?' Caius asked.

'Nothing.' Matt looked Caius up and down. 'Look at you in city shorts and loafers. You look smart but not too smart as your knobbly knees are out. What were you up to?'

'What have we got, Barry?' Caius said as he looked at Barry, his favourite forensic medical examiner. The three of them were standing over the body in the now empty theatre. An underpaid junior doctor from the audience had performed CPR for thirty minutes, before the man was pronounced dead by the underpaid paramedics.

'So far so natural,' Barry said, standing up. 'Stroke I'd say. You'd probably have noticed if he was having a heart attack. The post-mortem will confirm it.'

'Any idea who he was?' Matt asked.

Caius put on a pair of gloves and searched the man's pockets for any identification. There was nothing but a hotel key for The Ephesian Hotel on the Strand, a wallet with cash but no driving licence or bank cards of any kind, and a one-way train ticket from St Ursula in Cornwall from two days previously. Barry held a clear plastic bag open for him and he placed the items in it for safekeeping and one of his technicians came with a body bag to remove the corpse.

'I hate theatre people. I just hate them. Just no. They can all go in the bin.' DC Amy Noakes came into the house from the lobby barely containing her frustration. She'd been busy corralling the annoyed audience members in the foyer. 'One woman keeps on complaining about not being allowed to come back in to see the end of the play. A man died and was vomited on mid-performance, and she doesn't care. And then one man had the cheek to ask whether this was part of the performance, muttering something about "immersive theatre". What do you want me to do with them?'

'Well, it sounds like you want to obliterate them all from the face of the earth,' Caius said.

'Is that an option?' Amy took a deep breath to calm down, like she'd learned from her meditation app, but then the smell hit the back of her throat and she abruptly remembered where she was. This was not her happy place. 'The box office manager said the guy bought his ticket at the door and paid cash. Do we need to start taking statements, Caius?' she asked.

'No, I think we're good. Just get uniform to take everyone including the staff's contact details just in case, but there's nothing suspicious here,' he said, taking his gloves off.

'Already done it,' she said, turning and leaving to check that uniform's note-taking was in order.

'You're just that good, Amy. Let them all go then,' Caius said, looking at his watch. 'Matt, do you want to come to the hotel with me?'

'Look, mate, I like you but not like that,' Matt said.

'So that we can identify John Doe here,' Caius said, rolling his eyes.

'But tonight's your evening off,' Matt said.

'I don't have a life, we're short-staffed and you're doing over-time tonight anyway. We should try and find his next of kin as quickly as possible.' Caius glanced back around him at the scene and thought again about Callie and hoped that her hat had been spared the torrent of Guinness, sambuca, tequila, gin and shame.

★   ★   ★

The Ephesian Hotel was a grand Victorian establishment that had willingly succumbed to bright but inoffensive contemporary art devoid of any greater meaning on the walls and a 'riotous and challenging' afternoon tea menu to drag in adventurous day-trippers from beyond the M25. Matt made a mental note to come back and try it – he'd bring his mother for her birthday. His interest had been piqued by a chilli and satay-flavoured macaron.

After speaking to the manager, they had been shown up to the dead man's room. They said he'd booked as M. Hartley, but Caius wanted to be sure that it wasn't a false name. Caius, as respectful as he could be, started by going through the man's drawers. He was a Marks & Spencer man. Solid colours. Navy. Grey. Clothes no one would notice. Matt checked the wardrobe – all it contained was a grey suit, a striped red-and-navy tie and two white shirts. They both checked any pockets they found and still they did not know the man's name. There was a toothbrush and a can of deodorant – Boots' own brand – in the bathroom.

'This guy is so normal,' Caius said, wondering if it was possible to really be this ordinary. 'He had to have money to book himself in here rather than a Holiday Inn.'

Matt turned away from the wardrobe and towards Caius. 'So, the theatre, eh? You're not usually one for such things.'

'I thought I'd expand my cultural horizons.'

'Fair enough.' Matt then looked in the fridge just in case the man had left any medication with his name on in there but found nothing.

'It was pretty bad. I guess. I didn't know anything beyond the Wikipedia entry about the original play, so I don't have much to compare it to. The drunk actor kept purposefully trying to sabotage the others. It would've been funnier if they'd tried hard to get it right. It all kept aggressively going wrong.'

'Who were you going with?'

'Just a friend.' Caius straightened himself up. 'Sort of.'

'Do you think he might have used the room's safe?' Matt asked as he opened the wardrobe again, but the safe was unlocked and empty. He knew when to leave well alone. Caius, for a man as tightly wound as he was, was usually very open about the state of his love life. It had been obvious to Matt and Amy since Monday that something had gone wrong in Caius's personal life after he ate a carrot cake meant for six for lunch. He did use a fork rather than eat with his hands though. It was well mannered as well as sad to watch.

'Very few people don't have mobile phones any more. And who doesn't carry at least one bank card?' Caius tilted one side of the mattress before doing the same again on the other side to no avail. Then he pulled the bed's headboard away from the wall. 'His clothes are really, really boring. They're clothes to blend into the background in. You wouldn't pick them out of a line-up. Who is this guy?'

'The type of guy to hide an old-school Nokia in a shoe,' Matt said, brandishing his find.

'Does it have Snake?' Caius took the phone from Matt, turned it on and tried the last number John Doe had called. 'It's a land-line and it just keeps ringing through. He last rang it two months ago. Who is this guy?'

'What if he's a private investigator? It could be a burner for a particular client.'

'But what is he investigating?' Caius moved the bedside table away from the wall and he heard a 'thwup' as a folder full of newspaper cuttings hit the floor.

★ ★ ★

33

Matt took out two cans of Coke from his desk drawer in the incident room and handed one to Caius who was eating strawberry laces and glancing over the papers they'd found in John Doe's room. It was getting late and they needed the sugar.

'What have we got then?' Matt asked.

'They're press cuttings about a disappearance from a girls' boarding school in Cornwall on Halloween 2004,' Caius said, turning to his computer screen. His phone buzzed, but it was just a push notification from the *Guardian*: 'Change to Aristocratic Primogeniture Passes House of Lords'.

Matt picked up one of the articles and then sat down at his computer. 'I've got the record here – no body was ever found, and no one ever charged. Initially they assumed that the girl, Eliza Chapel, had run away: there were reports of terrible bullying in the school and a few girls had left already because of it. Plus, there was a rumour about some boyfriend who lived locally, but that all proved to be unfounded. Her parents live in Jersey.'

'They're the obvious people to hire a private investigator.' Caius took a sip of his Coke. He reached into his drawer and took out a couple of biscotti that he'd been saving. It was the only biscuit he could keep safe from Matt, who wouldn't eat it for the sake of his teeth. Caius picked up a sheet of paper from the desk. Ever-efficient Amy had asked the box office to print out a list of the tickets sold with email addresses by seat for that performance. John Doe had paid in cash, so that didn't confirm if he was M. Hartley. 'The only potentially solid thing we know about him is that he went to St Ursula in Cornwall recently. Probably as part of his investigation.'

Matt got St Ursula up on Google Maps and looked at people's tagged pictures of the harbour and the squat stone-built town. 'It's beautiful.'

Caius googled it. 'It's also got a high number of retirees. I'm not sure why. The town is built into a hillside, and it looks pretty steep. There's also a lot of second homes. Matt, get onto the local constabulary, mention the booking under M. Hartley and find out if they've had reports of any missing men over the age of sixty.'

Caius's phone buzzed.

Amy – Personal
23.08
Forgot to say that the woman with the hat who you were sat next to, passed me her business card to give to you . . . And I quote, 'in case he wants to question me about anything'. Then she said that she also drank fruity booze that didn't come out of cans. I think even by the rules of heterosexual dating that you're in there
(Picture)

You
23.08
Thanks mate

Amy – Personal
23.10
🫠

★   ★   ★

Amy was curled up on her sofa with her girlfriend Fi who was trying to convince her that they should rescue a fur baby. She was fighting the impulse to ask Caius what he'd do with the phone number. Amy had seen how disheartened he'd looked over the last week. She knew that Caius and Héloise had sort of got back together in the summer, but that it wasn't a solid thing, and she was still coming and going between Paris and London. She also knew that Héloise wasn't right for him. As noble as Caius's personal and cultural aspirations were, he also needed someone who'd tell him he was being an arse and to eat some chips every now and then. She toyed with sending Caius another message but then bottled it. She messaged Matt instead. They'd had many theories over the last week about what was going on.

Matt C
23.13
Oh this is a new development!!!
I'll get to the bottom of it
Enjoy your day off

You
23.13
I can't watch him eat another whole cake like that

SATURDAY

3

The Police Station

Caius had purchased a cafetière for two for his desk in the incident room a few weeks ago. The station only provided 'coffee' from one of those old-fashioned machines that dispensed scalding-hot, weak and yet simultaneously over-brewed brown slop, so he'd had to take things into his own hands. He locked it in the drawer when he wasn't at his desk. Some of his less civilised colleagues were wolves when it came to quality caffeine, amongst other bad habits. He was waiting for the kettle to boil in the break room and trying to stretch his glutes in a way that wouldn't raise the eyebrows of a casual passer-by who didn't know that he'd taken up running a couple of months ago as a means of gaining some control over his life. The kettle boiled. Caius filled the cafetière and took it back to his desk. It was a shame they didn't have a hob in the break room. Then he could crack out his Bialetti Moka pot. Caius looked down at his mug and asked himself when he had become such a wanker. Then he wondered what he could do about it. It was too late now. He liked the coffee.

'Which brew is it?' Matt asked.

'Just the Italian one again from that deli in Soho.'

'What do you mean "just"? *Bellissima,*' Matt said as Caius poured him a cup. His desk phone rang and he answered it.

Caius had already checked for missing people resembling their John Doe. There were more Alzheimer's sufferers who had wandered off in their pyjamas from their nursing homes than he cared to think about for too long. Besides, John Doe was wearing a panama hat, not flannels. Then he had spread John

39

Doe's files across an empty desk again. He picked up an article about Eliza's mystery boyfriend and then another where her parents complained about police incompetence during the initial investigation – they didn't think the girls in her year had been questioned thoroughly enough. Then he picked up an article on the death of Mrs Iona Chadwell, who had been headmistress of the school when Eliza was there and had been found to have been negligent by a civil court. There had been a copy of the fourth-form girls' class photo from the year Eliza went missing in the folder too. It had a cream-coloured card frame with the St Ursula's School for Young Ladies crest embossed on the top and the names of the girls written underneath. There was Eliza on the end: a freckled, slight girl. Caius read the names. One of the other girls looked vaguely familiar, but he couldn't remember where he'd seen her.

Matt hung up the phone. 'That was a DI down in St Ursula. She said it sounds like he may be a rather infamous local.'

'What's his name?' Caius asked.

'Unsurprisingly it's Martin Hartley. He's a retired optician turned amateur sleuth, apparently. He's approached the local police in St Ursula multiple times about various theories to do with the Eliza Chapel case. She thought Martin had an over-active imagination and had told him several times to join an art class at the community centre. Apparently, he had an associate, but she died two months ago.'

'Was it a natural death?'

'She had a bad fall and declined rapidly.'

Caius looked up Martin Hartley on the DVLA database. That was him all right. 'See if St Ursula know who his next of kin is, and I'll speak to Barry and see where we are in the body backlog.'

* ★ ★

'You forgot to make lunch!' Matt said, aghast. This was bad. Caius never forgot his lunch. His latest great joy was telling Matt about the history of a particular pasta shape. Matt thought about the sad ham and tomato sandwich in his desk drawer. 'That Vietnamese place has finally opened on the high street. We could go get bánh mì. You love bánh mì. You said it was a god-tier sandwich.'

'Will they give me extra chilli and pickled carrot if I ask?' Caius said.

'I'm sure they will, buddy.'

★ ★ ★

Matt and Caius were sat in the park near the station eating their sandwiches. Caius had of course been given extra chilli and pickled carrots by the owner who had taken pity on him and his crestfallen appearance.

'So?' Matt took a bite from his sandwich. 'Are you going to tell me what's going on, or is Amy going to text the woman from the theatre for you?'

'Would she do that for me?' Caius asked. He half meant it.

'Of course not. She has principles.'

'Héloise cheated on me, again. Different guy this time though. Mixing it up.'

'Ah, mate.' This had been Matt's leading theory.

'She's gone back to Paris again. For good.' Caius put his sandwich down on the bench but had to pick it up again as a flock of pigeons eyed it up and began inching closer and closer.

'I'm sorry. I was rooting for you guys.' Matt tore off a chunk of bread and chucked it along the path; the flock of pigeons cooed after it and left them momentarily in peace.

'It's for the best.' Caius laughed to himself, or rather at himself. 'I caught her last week on my day off. I was having such a good day too. I'd finally run all the way to the top of Parliament Hill in the morning. I was pottering about.'

'You love a potter.'

'I do! I stopped off at the farmer's market and bought a kabocha pumpkin to make a risotto with. I picked up a copy of *Ivanhoe* with a derpy dragon and moon-faced maidens on the front from the local bookshop.'

'Derpy dragons?' Matt had no idea what he was talking about.

'Yeah, derpy ones that people create medieval meme accounts about.'

'Right.'

'Then I went to one of those wanky barbers that pretends it's from the good ol' days when people routinely died from diphtheria and bought some beard shampoo and a tiny bottle of oil. I won't let those white guys cut my hair, but I'll absolutely buy mineral-enriched grooming products from them. It was a bloody good day. Well, until . . .'

'Until . . .' Matt patted him on the shoulder. 'Your beard looks great by the way.'

'I know, right.'

'What exactly happened with Héloise then?' Matt asked. As delightful as the rest of Caius's Saturday had sounded, he needed to get to the point.

'I came home, went to the sink and saw two glasses. One had lipstick on the rim and the other had the lip prints of the man I could hear fucking her in my bedroom.'

'Christ on a bike.' Matt grimaced.

'I went in and said: "Excuse me, mate, could you just get out of my girlfriend long enough for me to break up with her?"'

'Wow.' Matt put his sandwich down in shock.

'I thought this time maybe it would be different, but nope. I think I wanted it – us – I wanted us to work so much that I was willing to ignore all evidence to the fact that we were a terrible couple. If I'm truly being honest with myself, and when am I really, I chucked myself into it because I couldn't pursue . . . It wasn't right.'

'Meeting the right person at the wrong time still makes them the wrong person.'

'*Only Connect*, right.' Caius pulled out a string of pickled carrot and ate it. The crisp vinegar hit his tongue. Caius watched a pigeon-chasing toddler fall over and get comforted by their dungaree-clad mother. 'I was supposed to be on a date at the theatre. A woman I matched with on Tinder. She got stuck on a bus so didn't make it.'

'Are you going to try and see her again?'

'No. I don't think I will. She seemed nice enough, but I just wanted to get back on the horse more than anything. I don't think I should rush into a new relationship. That being said, I don't want to go home to an empty flat any more.'

'You're not a cat person either.'

'Nope. They make me sneeze.' Caius took a swig of the Coke Zero he'd bought with his bánh mì. 'How are things with you? Sorry, I've been a bit blinkered lately.'

Matt paused for a moment as he recalled the previous evening. 'Freja just announced she wants to have a baby in the next two years.'

'Do you want to have a baby?'

'I don't know. The world's an awful place. Do I want to make another person suffer through it?' Caius looked at Matt and Matt looked at Caius. They both knew what Matt's answer was. 'Let's pop to Sainsbury's before we go back. I'll browse the premium biscuits while you buy fruit that you make me and Amy eat because you're worried we'll develop scurvy. You *love* haranguing me about potential vitamin deficiencies,' Matt said.

'Matt, I harangue because I care.'

4

The Police Station

The Chief Superintendent appeared in the incident room. Caius had strong feelings about the Chief Superintendent, or 'call me Keith', as he had said to Caius multiple times in the pub the other week for the retirement do of one of the desk sergeants. Matt had convinced him to show his face. 'Call me Keith' had practically cornered Caius for a good hour – he'd clearly decided to get pally with him. Caius didn't play golf. It had been a tough old time.

'Good afternoon, sir,' Caius said. He did his best to sound perky and willing and compliant.

'Caius, Matthew. How are we getting on with the fellow from the theatre?'

'Martin Hartley, a retired optician, from St Ursula in Cornwall. Barry thinks it was natural causes but we're waiting on the post-mortem. There's a backlog. Matt's liaising with the local constabulary in St Ursula.'

'Excellent. You have capacity then,' the Chief Superintendent said.

'Yeah, we can take another case,' Caius said. Looking up at the Chief Superintendent from his chair, he could see that he'd bought a new nasal hair trimmer recently.

'There was a drowning in Richmond last week that they've not been able to look into properly. They're severely understaffed at the moment. They asked for you specifically.'

'Me?' Caius asked. He'd had nothing to do with Richmond. He'd not been anywhere near that part of London in ages. He wondered how they even knew his name.

'Oh yes. It's quite a thing, quite an honour to have a reputation like that, you know.'

'I see, well, anything to help out my fellow officers.' Caius smiled. He didn't mean it.

'Good man,' the Chief Superintendent said, before leaving. He had looked like he wanted to say something else, to joke around with them, but changed his mind.

'You know why Richmond are short, don't you?' Caius said to Matt once the Chief Superintendent had ceased to grace them with his presence.

'No, why?'

Caius leaned in and spoke low. 'They had a whole group of officers caught taking bribes from a gang of sex traffickers.'

'No!'

'Yeah, the Met are sitting on the press release because public trust is already so low. They're being prosecuted but it's all very under the radar at the moment. You know my mate Errol, he worked on it.'

'Fucking hell.'

Caius saw an email with a link to the post-mortem for Richmond's Jane Doe arrive in his inbox. He scrolled through it quickly, stopping only briefly to look upon her mottled and swollen face. Her grey hair was matted from her time in the water. 'This poor woman has been dead for over a week, and they've still got her in a drawer.'

'That's just awful.'

'That's the state of modern policing for you.' Caius drummed his fingers on his desk before snapping into action. They needed to hand the theatre case over. 'Right, Matt. Martin Hartley. Call back that DI at St Ursula and see if she has someone who can come and confirm it's him if they haven't found his next of kin.

Once we've got the post-mortem, we can arrange for St Ursula to deal with the rest of it.' Matt nodded as Caius continued talking for his own benefit. 'I'll start on Jane Doe. It says here that the estimated time of death was between 8 p.m. Friday 29 and 6 a.m. Saturday 30 August. I'll ask uniform in Richmond to check with every nursing home and community centre within five miles of the river to see if they recognise Jane Doe.' Caius knew how this investigation would end. Vulnerable, excluded people were the ones who lay unclaimed in metal drawers. If a person was close to their family, had many friends, or even just colleagues, then someone would notice their disappearance, someone would report them gone.

'And then what are you going to do?'

'Go home, watch a superhero movie and cry in my underpants.'

'No, you're going to text the pretty milliner.'

'How did you know she was a milliner?'

'Amy told me. She seems cool. She makes videos about German hat blocks on her Instagram.'

'Don't tell me you're following her?'

'Nah, mate. Her hat business is public though.'

Caius was itching to look. 'German hat blocks. That's pretty niche.'

'It's extremely niche, but we like niche. Niche means passion. I know you said you were thinking of taking things at a slower pace, but sometimes life chucks a really stunning lemon at you.'

'Lemons? Mate, melons.'

'Just ask her out to dinner, for God's sake, man.'

5

Calliope Foster Millinery

Callie's business comprised her and two rooms: a small show-room at the front and an even smaller workroom at the back. Callie rented the space for a song from Harriet's father, in fact, who had bought the odd bit of West London property over the years. It was at the back of a funny little building that had a bakery specialising in pastel-coloured meringues downstairs and a poky little flat above it. It wasn't quite a mews and it wasn't quite a broom cupboard, but it worked perfectly well for her. It always smelled like hot sugar outside. The showroom – where Callie saw clients by appointment only – was painted a gentle olive green with squishy pink velvet seats, polished brass fittings and a select few pieces of Victoriana that let you know you were in an establishment that understood the history of its trade. There was a little lacquered Japanese table where clients could pop their glass of champagne down while they tried to decide in the large replica (or rather convincingly fake) Chippendale mirror which shade of her signature 100 per cent British wool block beret would go best with the Aston Martin. Black or bur-gundy? Only for the client to inevitably decide: sod it, and buy both. They had two Aston Martins, after all.

Over the last six years, Callie had managed to build up a select clientele of women who liked to wear big hats when they drank their bubbles at the races, polo, society weddings, garden parties at the palace, poolside in St Tropez or on the yacht – you name it. Since she'd graduated from UAL she'd sent Harriet out every year to Ascot in the most beautiful hat she could muster. Good old Harriet dutifully did the rounds of the Royal Enclosure. 'My hat? Yes, it's gorgeous, isn't it. It's Calliope Foster. *Bespoke.* I am so lucky that we were at school together otherwise I wouldn't get a look in. She's booked up years in advance. Oh yes, I'm sure I could put a good word in for you.' One year Harriet started a rumour that Callie was so in demand that even the more attractive members of the royal household were on waiting lists. Harriet was good like that. She was good like that – good for hype if not consistency. Callie wondered whether that was because it made Harriet look like she was in the know. She was doubting everything about their friendship.

Callie had had a quiet morning but busy enough to distract her from the memory of being sat next to a corpse covered in sick. She had ordered some antique hat blocks from German eBay which had finally arrived. They were from the 1920s and 1930s – peak Sally Bowles. Round, little cloches that would be perfect for next autumn's ready-to-wear capsule collection. She'd sketched a few ideas, mused over a couple of shades she could dye felt hoods and the ribbons that would accompany them, before making herself a cup of Earl Grey.

Callie considered for a while whether or not to do an unboxing video for her socials but then realised her hair was a mess, and she was wearing an old Vampire Weekend T-shirt she had bought at Latitude years ago that was covered in white paint splodges from when she redid the workroom last year. That was definitely not 'on brand'. Or was it? She made the video and put in the description that she was having 'a low-key day focusing on her craft'. Callie hated herself. This wasn't why she had spent years at fashion school, this wasn't why she made art that people could wear, and yet here she was posting obnoxious videos on social media. A torrent of likes appeared, and she no longer cared.

Or at least that's what she told herself. It paid the mortgage on her shoebox flat on the wrong side of Ealing Common.

Harriet had been texting her all morning. For someone who didn't want Callie to be her maid of honour she would not stop sending over venue ideas – mostly Italian castles, but a very picturesque (*expensive*) beach resort in Kefalonia had also made it into the mix. This was despite her parents buying some pile somewhere that would've done – Harriet thought the ballroom was 'poky' and couldn't bear the idea of a marquee. She had started sending through the usual grand London hotels as well now. What was Callie's opinion of the decor at the blah blah blah? Which would have better food? Which would look the prettiest in the pictures? Which one would be the easiest to fly to Mauritius for their honeymoon from? Then there was the WhatsApp group she had been added to the week before with the other bridesmaids, all of whom were tepid friends of Harriet's from Bath uni, and of course Cousin Emily. Callie had already muted the group. She felt odd about it, and by odd she meant deeply uncomfortable. She knew she had been shunted and that there was no family tradition, yet here was all this expectation. If anything, she was really fucking annoyed, but Callie was alone enough in the world to need to cling to the familiar even if the familiar wasn't always that kind. Callie was sure Harriet's mother was actually behind it somehow. Mrs Simpson-Bamber didn't like her. She was always the model of courtesy around her, always asked the right questions, never said a rude word and yet Callie couldn't shake her dislike for her. The odd off-guard look she wasn't meant to catch, the odd flared nostril.

Callie pushed the thought to the back of her head, played a podcast about the history of underwear through her laptop, took out her sketch pad and started on the first designs for Harriet's headpiece or her 'modern tiara without the nuisance of dia-monds', as she had called it. Callie thought she'd knock out three quick designs that would keep Harriet happy for now. Her phone vibrated and she opened it, wanting it to be a message asking her out, but it was just Harriet wanting her opinion on whether gloves would make a comeback for brides. All Harriet did was want, want, want. What Callie wanted was the earnest-looking policeman who had offered a dead man a tissue to call her, but never mind. That was a weird night and an even weirder way to meet a chap. More than weird – to another person it was the sort of night that could have a profound effect – but she had decided to underplay it. It would make a good story in ten years when the shock of the man's death was just an untroubling little fact and not a terrible existential one. She was not a morbid person. She was a romantic. She was a milliner. If that wasn't the most romantic trade, then she did not know what was. Never mind Harriet. Never mind Caius. Never mind. Never mind. She downloaded Bumble. She deleted Bumble.

★ ★ ★

Callie banged the door knocker. It was shaped like the green man. She traced the oak leaves that made up his face while she waited for Dotty to appear. She'd had to grip his chin very hard to get any noise. Callie could hear the barbecue thrumming and doubted she'd been heard. She banged on the door with her fist, giving the green man respite. The house could not have been more urban if it tried and yet here were the trappings of country life. Roses in the tiny front garden climbing up, striving as hard as they could, above the decorative cast-iron porch that would not keep the rain from your head.

'Callie, darling!' yelled Dotty, her friend from fashion school, as she opened the front door. 'You made it. Isn't the weather gorgeous! It's not going to end for weeks. Don't you look divine! A negroni? A negroni for Callie, dearest Georgie,' she called to her husband, whose head popped out of the kitchen as he gave the briefest cheerful hello.

Dotty practically dragged Callie into the house – a bijou three-bedroom workers' cottage with delightful orchard-green tiling in the kitchen that was now worth a healthy seven figures – that she lived in with her husband, dearest Georgie. The view out of their bedroom window was of high-rise tower blocks that Dotty said gave the area that bit of integrity, a bit of spice, a bit of colour. They were incredibly wealthy, and although Callie had known her for well over ten years, she couldn't for the life of her tell you where their money came from. Callie had often suspected that the house had been bought for them by family and they were too embarrassed to talk about it in case it made them look less like bohemians and more like tiresome members of the landed gentry. Their wedding reception had been in the upstairs of a nearby pub. Callie had chatted to Georgie's relations for quite some time that day and they had been pretty mystified as to why the couple chose to hold the reception there and not the Dorchester if they really didn't want it at Dotty's father's house. Georgie, who was wont to drop his t's at the end of words and throw in the odd affected glottal stop, was a painter who never appeared to paint a thing and Dotty created a limited (extortionate) collection of silk cravats that she handprinted herself and sold in batches on her online shop for around twelve days of the year. The rest of the time they seemed to be on holiday. Callie wasn't going to ask questions now, what was the point, she was just going to consume all the negronis and any chorizo nibbles that came her way.

Callie said hello to the room, kissed a few cheeks of old friends from her days at the student bar, settled into Dotty's slouchy sofa with her first negroni and explained the Harriet drama to her in hushed tones.

'Wallpaper Harriet?' Dotty raised an eyebrow. She found Harriet, who she had met a few times, a little gauche when she talked about her latest Land Rover. 'I've got to say, darling, I know you went to school with her or whatever, but I'm not that fond of Harriet or how she talks to you.'

'What do you mean?' Callie knew what she meant but she wanted it spelled out to her.

'Well,' Dotty began. She'd been meaning to have this conversation with Callie for a couple of months and hadn't known how to broach it, but that evening she'd had enough negronis to be bold. 'At your birthday drinks she made that horrid comment about your weight, and you are just gorgeous. Georgie came away cursing her. He'd marry you in a heartbeat, you know. Asks me all the time if I want a sister wife. But I've told him that if anything were to happen then it would be us two running away together.'

'She probably didn't mean much by it.' Callie had heard the comment at the time but had decided not to be upset by it. 'Harriet's part of the furniture of my life now.'

'Darling, chuck her on the street with a sign that says "free" and someone will gladly take her, even if the handle keeps falling off the drawer.'

Callie rubbed her ear. She had a little scar behind it that itched every now and then from when Harriet had cut her hair and slipped when they were teenagers away at school. Well, that's what Harriet's mother had insisted had happened and had now been accepted as canon. It wasn't exactly how Callie remembered it.

'Really?'

'No, probably not. Just back away. Don't respond too quickly to her messages. Be busy. If you're lucky she'll have a baby next year, then she'll get other mummy friends and leave you well alone.'

'The problem there is that I am not lucky,' Callie said, watching as someone told someone else a joke in one corner of the living room and in the other corner a scandal was being whispered. 'Lovely party, Dotty.'

'I try.' Dotty passed her a second negroni. Georgie had appeared and told Callie she looked ravishing. Dotty called him an 'old flirt' and rolled her eyes and shooed him out to flip burgers bought from Ginger Pig.

'How's the love life?' Dotty asked, scanning the room quickly for unattached men.

Callie shrugged. 'I shall be single forever. It doesn't bother me. I'll just bounce around my little flat, go on nice little day trips to the seaside every now and then and eat whatever I want, when I want.'

'That sounds like bliss,' Dotty said, taking a sip of her drink. 'I only ask because Georgie's friend Casper keeps giving you the eye. He's also a sculptor. Arte Povera style. He's getting very fashionable. Did an amazing piece about dead turtles and plastic pollution earlier this year during a residency. Very moving. Plus, he's absolutely gorgeous and his family are basically the entire economy of Scandinavia. Does have an intense on-off thing that's been going on for yonks with a very pretty girl called Nell though.'

'That sounds very complicated, and I don't like complicated. I almost thought I'd met someone this week actually.' Callie explained everything that had happened at the Wankered Wilde production including the poor dead man.

'What a story. Poor git!'

'I know.' Callie polished off the last of her negroni. 'Caius, the policeman, just took charge of all this chaos. It was really hot. "Yes, officer, I'll come quietly."'

'And he hasn't texted you yet?'

Callie checked her phone. 'Nope. And I gave his colleague my card, so it's his move.' She turned it to vibrate. It vibrated almost immediately. It was Harriet. She'd penned an essay on her napkin preferences. She'd sent it straight to Callie and not the group. They hadn't even set a date yet. This was getting exhausting.

'He's playing it cool. I like the idea of a policeman. Must know his way around a pair of handcuffs. Oh, Casper alert.'

Callie watched him come over.

'Cas, Callie. Callie, Cas.' Dotty stood up, introduced them, winked and walked away in search of another negroni and a line.

'So, you're a sculptor?' Callie said.

'I am. And you're a milliner?'

'I am.'

'Are you *the* Calliope Foster?'

'Yes, why?' Most people didn't know or care who she was, but occasionally the odd person did and it made her feel unclean. There was something dirty in being known by name to all and sundry.

'My mother is obsessed with the hat you made for Lady Frodsham for Ascot last year. She was livid that you made her look so elegant. They were debs together and my mother is spectacular at holding a grudge. Your assistant told her that you didn't have room for any more clients this year.'

'Can I let you in on a secret? I don't have an assistant. I just sign off all my admin emails as "Amelia". The business is just me, so I can't take on many full-scale commissions. Amelia takes the flack so I can just get on with it.'

'Can I use that as leverage so I can become the favoured child?'

'That sounds healthy.' Callie smiled – she wasn't one to talk. 'I am sure I can do a better job for your mother than I did for Lady Frodsham. What's her name? I'll look out for her email.'

'Penny de la Croix.'

Callie's phone buzzed as she went to make a note of Casper's mother's name. Not that she needed to. Penny de la Croix was a boon. She had been a sloaney It Girl in the eighties (fluffy hair, pie-crust collars, granny's pearls) and had now become a society grande dame. Any hat she wore to Ascot was guaranteed to make it into *Tatler*, even *Vogue*. She was annoyed that she'd nearly missed out on that commission. 'Excuse me, I'm so sorry. I just need to deal with an email.'

'Not at all,' Casper said, relaxing into the sofa. He watched Callie walk away, before taking his phone out and texting his ex-girlfriend/girlfriend.

Callie found Dotty drinking gin in her bathtub. It was a deep clawfoot tub of the kind that certain people fantasise about. Whole Pinterest boards were devoted to its ilk. 'I thought it would be a funny shot for my stories, but now I can't get out. Hip hippo hooray?' Dotty held out a little baggie of purple pills with a hippo logo stamped on it that she took from her bra and offered one up to Callie.

'No, thanks. I'm working tomorrow.'

'Why?'

'Because I work for myself.'

'Exactly.'

'He messaged me.' Callie pulled the loo seat down and sat on it. That many negronis in such a short space of time meant she needed supervising when responding.

'Who, the policeman? Your little bit of rough?' Dotty leaned over the bathtub. 'Show me his profile pic? Oh, is he mixed race? I love mixed-race guys. I often wonder how I ended up with that pale entity downstairs. Whatever you do, say yes. You're going to be married within a year. I can feel it in my waters. Now help get me out of the damn thing; I need to pee.'

SUNDAY

6

The Police Station

'*Kalimera*,' Matt said as he came into the incident room, flexing his muscles for a day of paperwork.

'*Ohayou gozaimasu*,' Caius said. He was at his desk and had already sent Amy out to Richmond to follow up on a lead that had come in overnight. 'I brought you a green juice: spinach, celery and apple. Blended it myself.'

'Thanks,' Matt said. The rising pitch of his reply suggested he wasn't actually that thankful, but he'd drink a sip or two of Caius's cold soup to be polite. Caius was back to his old ways, so Matt assumed he'd actually texted the milliner.

'The DI from St Ursula came back to us. She said that one of their lot is actually up here on holiday and was happy to pop in and confirm that Martin is Martin. They're struggling to find his kin apparently. He was well known to everyone in the station it would seem, so we are off to the morgue later.'

'Woo, I love the morgue,' Matt said, swizzling around on his chair.

'I'm heading out west after that so if you could get the paperwork sorted to transfer Martin's body that would be helpful.' Caius had taken out Martin's St Ursula files and spread them across an empty table again. 'I still don't understand why he was at that play. It can't be anything to do with the Eliza Chapel case, can it?'

'Maybe he just fancied the look of it? Oscar Wilde is probably really popular among that age range. Quick-witted, nice costumes, comedy of manners et cetera.'

'Would this version have been his thing? I suppose he could have thought it was a straight performance.' Caius picked up one of the newspaper articles that Martin had in his dossier from the time of Eliza's disappearance and read through it. He skimmed through another article and then looked at the photo of Eliza's year. One of the girls still felt very familiar.

★ ★ ★

Darren Trelawny, the DS from St Ursula, confirmed that Martin was Martin and Barry, having just finished the post-mortem, had established that the cause of death was indeed a stroke. Caius and Matt were showing Darren out.

'So you're on holiday then?' Matt asked the Cornishman.

'Yeah, we thought we'd come up for a bit of culture. We're going to the theatre tonight.'

'Oh yeah, I don't go to the theatre enough,' Caius said, although after *The Importance of Beering Earnest* he did wonder if it wasn't for him. 'Are you off to the National? They've got an all-female cast Chekhov on. The one with the gun. You know. If a writer introduces a gun then they have to use it. *The Seagull*, that's it.' Caius had seen the posters on the tube with the female lead who'd briefly been the hot young thing a couple of years back and was making a return to 'serious' acting.

'We're off to see *Mamma Mia!*'

'Nice, I took my mum for her birthday the other year.' It hadn't been Caius's idea of a good evening but then he'd realised he liked ABBA more than he'd thought and relaxed into it. His mum had loved it, which was the important thing.

They got to the security door opening onto the reception area and Matt buzzed them out.

'Such a shame about Martin. He was a nice bloke actually. Him and Ruth got a bit caught up in the Eliza Chapel case though.'

'You've got to have a hobby, I guess. Ruth's dead, right?' Matt asked.

'Yeah, bad fall. Nice woman as well. She worked at St Ursula's actually.'

'Oh yeah, doing what?' Caius asked.

'She was a games mistress. Retired the year before Eliza went missing. I think she was dismissed actually. The general opinion around the station is that after Eliza disappeared, she got a bee in her bonnet about it and thought there was something worse going on than there was, but truth be told, all the cleaning staff, cooks et cetera lived local and no one would have ever sent their daughters there. They're turning the building into a luxury hotel and spa actually. The whole town is pretty excited about it. We're hoping it will bring people down in the off season. It'll be a lot of jobs when it's up and running, and a lot of jobs in the renovation too. My cousin is working on the site actually.'

'St Ursula's School for Young Ladies.' Caius stared at a spot on the wall for a moment as he gathered his thoughts. 'People don't just disappear like that though, do they? Especially teenagers.'

'There have been a lot of theories over the years. The prevailing one in the end was that she just walked into the sea.'

'Was there any evidence for that? Clothes on the beach? A note saying: "Gone swimming"?' Matt asked.

'None at all, but that's just the sort of thing a sad teenaged girl who had been abandoned at a boarding school would do, wouldn't she? Well, that's the line they went with. I'm not convinced myself, but the higher-ups are unwilling to reopen the case. Martin and Ruth tried.'

'Sounds about right,' Caius said, before they all shook hands. 'In any event enjoy *Mamma Mia!* You'll have a great time.'

7

Teddington

Amy knocked on the vicarage door. Local uniform had already been in contact with all the nearby nursing homes and community-based charities in pursuit of Jane Doe and the vicar from St Thomas de Cantilupe's had been in touch. They were missing a parishioner who also relied on their food bank.

'Hello, you must be the detective,' the vicar's husband said as he opened the door. 'Catherine is waiting for you in the study.' He showed Amy through the body of the house. It was a Victorian building. Poorly insulated, judging by the number of draught excluders scattered around the place. 'It's just down there,' he said, gesturing to the room at the bottom of a corridor dotted with family photos on the wall.

Amy thanked him and then went to knock on the door when it swung open and the vicar, a pixyish woman in her mid-forties with quick but weary eyes, appeared and mouthed an apology with her phone partially tucked up under her cheek as she did so.

'I'm sorry, your grace, but the police are here and I . . .'

The voice on the other line continued.

'Yes, of course. If you put it in an email, I'd be delighted . . . I have to go now. I'm sorry . . . I need to speak to the police about a missing parishioner. Goodbye.' She put the phone in her pocket. 'Sorry about that. I hate to hang up on the Archdeacon, but he keeps going on about roof tiles.'

'Roof tiles?' Amy asked, nodding as she thought about decaying roofs before remembering why she was there. 'You told my colleagues that you have a missing parishioner?'

'Yes, Lynne Rodgers. I popped round yesterday morning, and no one answered. She was supposed to be helping with the harvest festival the evening before, but she didn't come to the meeting. That's very unlike her, she's very involved. Nice woman. She'd had a hard life, I think. Lives on her own in a flat a few roads over.'

'Would you mind looking at a photograph of the deceased to confirm whether or not it is Lynne? It may not be pleasant.'

'Of course.'

Amy took out the photo of Jane Doe's face from the post-mortem. Apologising that her features might be distorted.

The vicar slowly nodded. 'That's Lynne. Definitely. Would you like me to formally identify her?'

'If you wouldn't mind. Not your first?' Amy asked sympathetically.

'No, not by a long shot.' She smiled weakly. 'Do you know how she died yet?'

'She drowned in the Thames.'

'How dreadful. Poor Lynne.'

'Does she have a partner that you know of?'

'No, I don't think she'd ever been married.'

'How well did you know her?'

'Quite well. She used the food bank here nearly every week and she usually came to the Sunday service. I think she lived abroad for a while but then had to come back. She was a little coy about her past but every now and then she'd say something like how she missed fresh coconut water. She'd had an admin job somewhere local for quite a few years, but she'd developed bad arthritis in her hands so she couldn't type any more and had to quit.'

'Did she have any close friends?' Amy didn't think the death sounded suspicious. She wanted to know that Lynne had friends though. That she would be missed by someone.

'She never mentioned anyone. She helped here quite a bit, but I don't think she was especially friendly with any of the parishioners beyond the usual pleasantries. She mentioned something about meeting her landlord recently, but I doubt that was a social call. I think her parents are both dead and she didn't have siblings. I should say that Lynne had had problems with alcohol in the past. She was open about it, and she was doing really well. Lynne's been sober since I've known her, but I got the firm impression from the odd thing that she'd said that she'd alienated people in the past.'

'Right,' Amy said, making a note that alcohol had marred another life.

'It's tough out there at the moment.' The vicar stared out of the window at a passing bird. 'Some parishioners come to church on Sunday because they can't afford to turn the heating on. You know who they are because they come in January but not in July. All I can do is try to keep both the body and the soul warm.'

★   ★   ★

Caius thought he'd explore the scene of Lynne Rodgers's last moments. He'd just interviewed a jogger who lived near Twickenham station. They'd come forward and said they'd seen her stumbling along the towpath at around 8 p.m. on her own near Ham House. After checking the tides that day, Caius thought it was likely she entered the water further up the Thames than Ham House. The river was no longer tidal beyond Teddington, so it narrowed down considerably the place where she entered the water. There was also a high amount of alcohol in the woman's blood, so it wasn't inconceivable that she fell in after having one too many, and there were quite a few pubs on or close to the river that were within a fifteen-minute walk.

Caius arrived at Teddington Lock and stared down at the Thames. He felt sorry for the river. Its tide cut off abruptly like that. It felt unnatural, but it also felt like 'progress' of some indescribable industrial sort. He wasn't sure why it had been done, but there it was: a neutered river. It was sunny and people walking their dogs chased after them and their shit with little black bags, and parents of small children with bare knees chased after them also, scooping them up before they fell into the failings of less responsible dog owners. Both the dogs and the small children wielded sticks larger than themselves.

As Caius walked down the path towards Ham, he thought that despite its current popularity, it would be isolated at night. The only artificial light would be coming from across the river in Twickenham. The post-mortem said that the woman's body hadn't been in the river that long – between twelve and twenty-four hours when she was found that Saturday afternoon – so she probably went in in the dark. It would be easy enough to stumble in, and easier still for someone to shove you and get away with it.

He carried on as the river curved and Eel Pie Island came into sight. A crew of eight young women, all lean and determined, rowed past him as he stopped in front of the gates of Ham House. It was coming up to lunch and Caius thought he might as well spend his hour walking around the mansion. He was aggrieved to pay the entry fee of £13 but somehow Valerie, a perky volunteer in a cosy fleece in warm weather who was selling tickets, managed to convince him to sign up for a yearly membership of the National Trust for £78.60. She was gifted. He ticked a box for Gift Aid. Caius knew he'd use his membership, but he didn't want to admit it to himself, so he filled the forms in with a playful air of performative resentment. It felt too old, too middle class. But then he supposed he probably was middle class now. He walked around the extravagant seventeenth-century house, asking himself how he managed to spend £80 like that. He learned about the courtiers who lived in mansions along the river because travelling by boat was safer than by road. He stared at portraits of boss-eyed women, and men with huge wigs who wore a lot of lace. He exited via the gift shop and bought himself an introduction to the Restoration era and a packet of fudge.

After waving goodbye to the wily Valerie, Caius walked back towards the river and followed it to Richmond where he stood for a moment at the spot where the body was found. People were merrily drinking outside the pub. He walked back through the centre of Richmond to meet Amy, crossing the road to avoid a group of neo-fascists with placards.

8

Calliope Foster Millinery

Harriet had walked into Callie's showroom more excited than when the *Financial Times*'s 'How To Spend It' supplement called her 'the most promising upcoming British wallpaper designer'.

'What's up? Is there a surprise Le Chameau sample sale?' Callie asked, half in jest and half in seriousness. Harriet was normally only this happy after a dopamine hit from shopping.

'Oh lordy, I wish. No, I have quit.'

'What did you quit?'

'My job.'

'Are you finally going it alone?' A few times a year Harriet would go on a rant about how much she hated the interior design firm she worked at. How they didn't value her talent. How she was going to set up her own company like the sexy reincarnation of William Morris (minus the socialism) that she knew she was. Harriet would then send Callie a business plan, which she'd look over and then make encouraging noises about only for nothing to happen.

'God no. I don't want to work any more. I don't need to. This way I can plan the wedding properly.'

'Congratulations.' Callie opened the little fridge she had for champagne for clients and opened a bottle. She claimed her monthly order from the wine merchants down the road as a business expense, so she didn't mind too much that it was a Sunday lunchtime and her business was technically closed, although she didn't get a day off.

Harriet picked up a reel of mossy-green grosgrain ribbon and twiddled with the end. Placing it under her nose like a moustache. 'Daddy asked that I mention the prospect of a blind date to you. Some friend's son, nephew or something. His name is Rupert, he didn't give many details, but he seemed very keen that you go. It sounded like you'd be helping him out, to be honest. I think he's got himself into a little trouble at work. Bless him, he likes to think he's a smooth political operator, but he always ends up looking like a bit of a tit.'

'He's trying to set me up with someone?'

'Yes, but the guy in question is probably rich, or at least well connected.' Harriet raised her eyebrows. No one called Rupert was broke.

'Just one date?' Callie had never known her father, and Harriet's had been the closest she'd ever had to anything like that. Not that they were even close or especially fond of each other. He was just the only man of that age who'd ever taken the vaguest interest in how she was getting on. Peter had been the one who'd pick them up from house parties in the summer holidays when they were seventeen and never complained when Callie threw up in her handbag in the back seat. He'd bring them bacon sandwiches in the morning and promise never to tell his wife about what had really happened to her peonies as the girls had drunkenly stumbled up the drive.

'Daddy said that if you're interested then to give him a call on his mobile.'

'I've actually got a date with a guy this week.'

'Oh, do tell! Do I know him?'

'I doubt it, he's a policeman.'

'I definitely don't know anyone as ordinary as that.'

Callie wondered whether Harriet knew anyone who didn't 'fit'. Everyone had gone to a fee-paying school, everyone had a battered Barbour jacket in the back of the Land Rover that they preferred to the Burberry trench coats they wore in town, and everyone had money even if they were being coy about it. Lots of money. Callie realised that she was actually the exception to the rule. She had been to private school but on a partial art scholarship with her grandparents picking up the rest of the bill. She had no money of her own. Only good luck, and the subsequent connections that she'd made along the way. She looked at Harriet chucking champagne down her throat as she faffed around with the paraphernalia of her trade and truly realised just how right Dotty was.

'He seems really lovely,' Callie said.

'If you say so. Always best to play the field though, darling. Always have another option lined up. A girl without choices is a sad thing. Now do you want to bunk off and get smashed at lunch? We could go get facials afterwards?'

'Sorry, I've got a consultation at 3 p.m.,' she lied. 'Was your mum interested in getting a hat from me for the wedding? If so I'll need to block time in for her.' Callie hoped to high heaven that Jane Simpson-Bamber was intending to go elsewhere.

'Oh, I don't know. I haven't spoken to her about it.' Harriet shrugged and did a little fake giggle. Callie knew she was lying. 'I'm off then, lunch to celebrate my freedom from serfdom beckons.'

'Tell your old man that I don't have the time to go on dates with this chinless wonder.'

'Your loss,' Harriet said.

'I've got a couple of sketches for you actually,' Callie said, handing Harriet the initial ideas she had for her bridal headpiece.

Harriet squealed, took the designs and spun out of the shop and towards the King's Road, relishing the idea of being snotty with the waiters at the Bluebird Café as she wrote Callie detailed feedback.

9

Lynne Rodgers's flat

The wallpaper in Lynne's living room was peeling in the corner from the damp. The smell of black mould permeated the whole flat. The stink clung to all the soft furnishings that had turned rancid from the humidity.

'The jogger who saw Lynne didn't really have much to say that we didn't know already. Anything in there?' Caius asked.

'There's nothing in the cupboards apart from half a jar of mixed herbs and a tenth of a bag of penne,' Amy said from the kitchen. 'The fridge is bare too.'

'There's nothing on the electricity meter either,' Caius said. He'd just checked the one under the stairs. He'd stopped in front of the mould that was growing above the living-room window as if it were a painting of the Madonna and he was moved by it. He studied it for greater meaning but only saw greed and moral rot. Caius felt a little hypocritical guilt push its way up like acid reflux. His father, a builder by trade, had purchased old houses and done them up. He sold some on but rented out others, amassing a small but not insignificant portfolio of properties in Archway. 'I'll find out who the landlord is and get the council to take a look at the rest of their properties. There was quite a bit of alcohol in her blood. Was there anything in the kitchen?'

'Nope, no bottles or cans in here,' Amy called.

Caius walked into Lynne's bedroom. The bed was made. Her clothes were folded neatly away into drawers. He looked through them quickly in case there was a bottle of whisky hidden underneath a jumper but found nothing. There was no phone. Caius had to assume that she had it with her when she went in the river, and it had been carried away with the tide or else sunk to the bottom of the murky Thames for a mudlarker to find in a hundred years. They hadn't found a note, just black mould and bare cupboards.

★ ★ ★

'Are we saying then that she fell off the wagon and into the Thames?' Amy asked. They were standing outside Caius's car now. 'It feels hard to argue against that.'

'You said the vicar told you that Lynne was living hand to mouth?' Caius asked.

'Yeah. She'd had to quit her job for health reasons. The vicar was under the impression that her drinking had alienated people, and she also couldn't tell me who her friends were even though she was really involved with the church.'

'Richmond will want this wrapped up quickly. I'll get them to find her next of kin, although it sounds like she doesn't have any.' Caius looked out across the road. He could see the trees that followed the river in the distance. 'I just want to be sure though. We don't have a timeline for her death. Between us we shall canvas the neighbours just in case, then if you could pop into every pub between here and the river and ask the bar staff if they recognise her. Maybe she'd had an argument with another patron or something, and they followed her out of the pub. I don't know. I'm grasping here. Ring your vicar back and ask to speak to the other volunteers who knew Lynne. You never know, she might have said something about a vendetta against the neighbours over the bins.'

'Sure.'

Caius opened his car door and took out a lunchbox from the passenger seat. 'Have a flapjack.' Caius held the box open for Amy to take one. He hated cases like this. Cases where it felt like all that needed to be done to have saved a life was the tiniest amount of compassion from the system.

'Did you make these from scratch?'

'Yes. Peanut butter and raisin, and I put extra flaxseed in it for the Omega-3.'

'Good to see you more like your old self.' Amy took one to be polite and wondered if it would taste like straw.

MONDAY

10

Calliope Foster Millinery

Penny de la Croix was very late. Callie looked at the time on the clock on the showroom wall. She'd bought it when she visited her mother last year for an excruciating weekend. They'd gone around local antique shops for pretty much the whole trip so they wouldn't have to meaningfully talk to each other, just comment on all the tat. Another ten minutes and she'd ring to make sure she was still coming. Callie went back into the workroom and started pissing about with feathers. She was feeling in a rut creatively, bored even. She needed to find something, or someone. She needed to find a muse. The doorbell rang and Penny was on the doorstep. She was wearing sunglasses, a crisp white shirt and a pair of navy-blue wide-leg trousers.

'Calliope, sweetie.'

'Hello, Mrs de la Croix. I'm so delighted to meet you.'

'Yes.' Penny swanned past her and into the showroom. 'Where do you work? In here?' She pushed through the door to Callie's workroom. 'Yes. This is better. I don't give a shit about all that flummery.'

Callie shut the door to the showroom behind them. 'Straight to business then. Tell me about the hat you need.'

'Oh, you're good. The hat I need not the hat I want.' She looked Callie up and down. 'Are you fucking my son?'

'No.'

'Good. I'd hate to lose a decent milliner.'

'Quite.'

'Nice dress. Bespoke?'

'I had a friend bastardise a Dior that I saw in the V&A.'

'And if you wanted an evening dress, who would you bastardise?'

'Schiaparelli.'

'How kooky!'

'I don't do kooky for the sake of it.'

'Good, because I am not a gimmick.' She chucked her handbag down on a chair. It was a very discreet Bottega Veneta.

They sat down to discuss Penny's needs. Her daughter was getting married next summer to a man she considered a 'no-hoper' from affected investment banker stock. She wrinkled her nose at this. 'She loves him, apparently, so what can one do?' Penny wanted something elegant, but distinct. She was thinking pink, but not baby and definitely not magenta. 'I'm not a matron wearing a department store fascinator to the Grand National.' They looked at some swatches. Discussed some shapes. 'You're right. No one would expect me to wear a pillbox.' It was a productive morning. Penny left her with repeated warnings that she fully hoped that Casper would get back together with his on-off girlfriend, and promises that if this hat was a success, then Penny would be back for all her millinery needs and she'd tell Stephen Jones to fuck right off. She purchased an off-the-rack wide-brimmed straw hat for an upcoming holiday – 'Just lounging in Mykonos with the old gang I knocked around with when I was young, and the children hadn't spoilt my figure. One of them just filed for divorce so we're going on a jolly.' Then she left, and the studio felt empty.

11

The Police Station

While Matt finalised the paperwork to close Martin's case, Caius was looking over his Eliza Chapel dossier one last time. He was boxing the papers up to be sent to St Ursula and eventually passed on to Martin's next of kin. Caius put the newspaper articles back into the folder he had found stuffed behind the bedside table in the hotel. Then he came to the photograph of the fourth form again. If Darren, the officer from St Ursula, was right then Ruth wasn't the games mistress the year this photo was taken, so why would she and Martin have a copy? They'd gone out of their way to acquire it. He wrote down the names of the ten girls in the photo in his notebook (a Moleskine he'd found reduced in the Covent Garden TK Maxx).

1. Beatrice Parker-Thompson
2. Annabel Hartnell
3. Sophy Oddfellow
4. Arabella Spatterley
5. Poppy Boswell
6. Sophia Patel-Jones
7. Claudia Pinkerton
9. Juno Smith
9. Mollie Gilbert
10. Eliza Chapel

He began googling the former pupils and found success with his first search. Beatrice Parker-Thompson, who called herself

Beatrice Parker, was currently gracing the London stage as Gwendoline in a version of *The Importance of Being Earnest* that put members of the audience at risk of being thrown up on.

★ ★ ★

There was a knock at the theatre manager's door. It was a cluttered room filled with rolled-up posters for old shows and boxes of loo roll, with one small window looking onto the back of Chinatown. The theatre manager had reluctantly vacated it when Caius had asked for a private place to speak to Beatrice.

'Come in,' Caius said. He'd never had an office per se, and he enjoyed the opportunity to say that. He swivelled about on the desk chair and then he realised that was how the Chief Superintendent probably started out. Enjoy having an office and it would inevitably escalate to a high level of middle-management pomposity.

'Back again, detective? Was the acting that criminal?'

Caius wasn't sure what to say to that.

'Don't worry, the show is a terrible idea. I know that. Just a comedy role for the old Spotlight CV. Comedy is my thing. I'm taking a one-woman stand-up show to Edinburgh next year actually.'

'Beatrice Parker-Thompson is your full legal name, isn't it?' Caius asked, trying to steer clear of a lecture on the vagaries of the acting profession.

'Yes, that's me.' She plonked herself down on the battered sofa opposite the desk.

'Do you recognise this man?' he asked, showing her a picture of Martin Hartley.

'No, should I?'

'It's Martin Hartley, the man who died during the Friday night performance. Does that name mean anything to you?'

'That was Martin Hartley who died?' Beatrice froze and her cheeks grew pinker. 'Gosh, yes. I knew of him. He'd sent a few messages through the "contact me" section of my website, and he'd called up my agent too.'

'Asking what?'

'He wanted to ask me questions about my schooling.'

'Your schooling?'

'I went to a girls' school in Cornwall called St Ursula's for a couple of years.'

'And what was it like there?'

'We all used to call it St Cursula's. It was rainy and none of the windows kept the cold out or let the sun in. The cracked pane above my bed in the dorm used to whistle when it was windy.'

'I think Martin was here so he could try and interview you about a girl from your year that went missing.'

'Why? I mean yes, Eliza disappeared but it was a long time ago. I don't really want to think about it.'

'I think Martin thought that you girls knew something about what happened that never came out at the time.'

'Do you think that's true?' Beatrice asked Caius.

'Perhaps.' Caius was intrigued. He was normally the one asking the questions. 'Did you know Eliza well?'

'No, I mean, I wasn't pally with Eliza. She would say anything for effect, and we all knew she was lying. No one wanted to be friends with a girl like that. Eliza spent a whole term telling us that her mum had taken her on a private jet to New York for the day. She hadn't been to the US. More likely Newquay than New York. It was common knowledge that her parents were the sort who scrimped and saved to send her to the school in the first place.'

'What about the claim that she had a boyfriend in the town?'

'Totally fabricated. We never saw any proof.'

'Any other things she said that you all thought were lies?'

'So many: the Duchess of York was her godmother, her father was buying her a pair of diamond studs for her birthday, that the prefects ran a secret society that killed a local once a year. That one was quite funny actually. We all ripped the piss out of her for that for a week. She must have got it from a book or a film or something, but to be fair the prefects were arseholes and intimidated the girls in the lower forms. Horsey girls, you know.'

'Yeah.' He didn't know, but the way she had said it made him think they were sadists.

'I feel really bad for Eliza. I do. I can't imagine what she's going through.' Beatrice bit a nail. 'There are so many crazies out there.'

'What do you mean?'

'A maniac with a St Trinian's fantasy who's kept her in their cellar this whole time.'

'I'm sorry, what?' Caius didn't think it was an impossibility but now all he could picture were those black-and-white comedy films with beautiful twenty-something actresses playing overly sexualised seventeen-year-olds brewing bathtub gin and getting into scrapes with the police. Tinky-tonky piano music, short skirts and class satire.

'Oh, nothing.' Beatrice looked ashamed of herself. 'I just . . . never mind. I'm being silly.'

'I take it you didn't like St Ursula's?' Caius asked. He wondered whether flippancy was a coping mechanism of hers.

'God no, I hated it. My parents finally pulled me out after Eliza went missing. A lot of parents did, and the school closed.

My parents didn't believe me before that, that it was quite as awful as it was.'

'Why was that?'

'The school painted a picture of a country idyll where we were being taught to be young ladies. Extracurriculars like flower-arranging, deportment, elocution, how to make a raspberry coulis to impress your husband's boss when he came for dinner. Proper 1950s bullshit, but enough parents were swayed by nostalgia it seemed. In reality the roof leaked, the food was appalling – I was on the verge of getting scurvy – and we slept in our coats in January.'

'There was a games mistress who left the year before Eliza disappeared?'

'Miss Miller? Yes, she was a good one. She used to bring us biscuits and bananas on the sly. I'm not sure what happened, but she probably kicked off one too many times about the conditions for the headmistress's liking. She used to complain to the old trout all the time.'

'What about the headmistress?'

'Horrid woman. Dead now, I'm sure. I think I saw something in the papers dredging up the whole debacle when she died. Mrs Chadwell was practically a fascist dictator. Half the staff were scared of her and were suffering Stockholm syndrome or something, and the other half had been schooled in the same manner and had an "it didn't do me any harm" attitude while drinking a bottle of whisky to get them to sleep every night.'

'Were you there the night Eliza went missing?'

'I was, but not in the dorms.' Beatrice closed her eyes as she remembered that night. 'We were in two smaller rooms of six girls anyway and I wasn't in Eliza's. Actually, there were only four girls in that room because two girls had been abruptly pulled out right at the end of the previous year. I'd been hit over the head in Lacrosse that afternoon, so I was kept in the sickbay all night for observation by the nurse. She wanted to send me to hospital, but the headmistress said that was too dramatic. The sickbay was the other side of the building. I thought I heard some kind of commotion on the lawn, but the nurse reassured me the next morning that I just had a bad concussion and had imagined it. I mentioned it to the police at the time.'

'What sort of commotion?'

'I'm not sure. It was so long ago now. A noise. I honestly don't think I can remember properly, and I did have a thwacking great lump on my head. Poppy Boswell had a great swing on her.'

'Are you in touch with any of the others from that year?'

'Not really. I've bumped into Sophy Oddfellow and Sophia Patel-Jones before she moved to New Zealand a few times over the years at parties, and Lippy pops up every now and then but she left the school the year before. Bellie Hartnell, now I bump into her all the time. She worked at the same law firm as my brother. Bellie was one of the four in Eliza's dorm room actually. I can't remember who else. Are you reopening the case?'

'No, no. Nothing like that. I've just been trying to work out why Martin was at the performance.'

'Why were you at the performance?' She was curious. She couldn't think of a worse way to spend an evening.

'I felt like a little culture.'

'There's little culture here.' Beatrice smiled at Caius who thanked her for her time and then she went back downstairs to warm up before her performance. Caius could hear a raft of tongue-twisters echoing up the stairs as she went. She meant to do some stretches but instead she went and sat in the dressing room on her own for a moment. Just a moment.

86

12

The Police Station

'What happened? You went off quite suddenly,' Matt asked. Caius had practically knocked over his mug of green tea as he'd dashed off.

'Martin had been trying to get in touch with one of the actors who was in Eliza's year at school.'

'That fits with the whole amateur sleuth thing. Did she say anything?'

'Perhaps. She said Eliza was a fantasist and a show-off who made stories up to impress the other girls who were all from wealthier families than her. Beatrice also said she heard a commotion on the lawn the night she disappeared, but she had a concussion, so no one took her seriously.'

'Are you going to ask for the case to be re-opened?'

'I don't know. I don't want to chuck my career away going after cold cases when there are more pressing ones to be worked on. There was another set of stabbings in Stoke Newington last night with no obvious culprit.' Caius was trying to talk himself out of being interested in Eliza Chapel's disappearance. They barely had the resources to look into burglaries going on around the corner let alone old cold cases.

'What is it?' Matt looked at Caius. He didn't believe a word he was saying.

'I just have this feeling I can't shake. Martin hid the papers. He was worried that someone was onto him.'

'Darren from St Ursula did say that Ruth Miller had worked at the school but was dismissed the year before.'

'Actually, Beatrice said Ruth Miller was always kind to the girls who were basically neglected. If she was fired for raising concerns . . . If Ruth was just a member of the public, then yeah, I would probably dismiss her interest too, but she knew these people, these girls intimately. Schools like that are kingdoms unto themselves. They have laws and customs, codes of honour. Lady of the Flies.'

The Chief Superintendent came in. 'Richmond was an accidental drowning then?'

'We haven't found anything to the contrary. Amy is out there now closing down the last leads to be thorough,' Caius said.

'Right. And the chap in the theatre?'

'Martin Hartley has been positively identified by a DS from St Ursula. Cause of death was a stroke. He was up in London researching the Eliza Chapel disappearance.'

'Both of your ongoing investigations are wrapped up then.' He looked relieved. 'We've had a rather busy year in this station, and we haven't been as quite up to scratch as we should be with completing our required personnel training modules.'

'Right,' Caius said. He had been hoping to be put onto the Stoke Newington case and didn't like where this was heading.

'There's a training day tomorrow on harassment in the workplace. All three of you are to attend.'

'No problem,' Caius said.

'Of course,' Matt said.

After the Chief Superintendent left, Caius turned to Matt. 'I bet they forgot to invite anyone, and we're the only ones free.'

'Timing's great though. Nothing like a sexual harassment seminar right before a first date.'

TUESDAY

13

The Police Station

'Did you notice how the course leader keeps trying to not look at you and Matt whenever she talks about anything racial?' Amy asked Caius. They had just sat through two hours of a presentation while being generally aware that not everyone in the room was taking it seriously. That it didn't apply to them. That they were above it, above the law.

'She also keeps singling you out for eye contact every time she mentions sexual harassment,' Caius said. Amy was the only woman in the room.

'There were some very flippant reactions to that section.'

They'd 'broken out' for twenty minutes and the three of them had stepped outside to stretch their legs. Each of them was relieved they worked together and not with anyone else in the room. Matt had popped into Sainsbury's for some paracetamol for a headache that might have just been outraged common decency banging around his head. Caius and Amy were waiting outside.

'Is it obvious to women which men are misogynists when they first meet them?' Caius asked.

'Not always, I suppose.'

'We catch men like that for a living and as a man I feel like I can spot them a mile off, but perhaps they act differently around women.'

'They may relax in front of you. You do look like a bit of a lad.'

'I'm a himbo at best.' Caius shook his head as he watched a woman flip the bird at a man who honked his car horn at her as he drove past. 'I suppose sometimes arrogance and entitlement can be attractive, right?'

'How do you mean?'

'Well, if you don't know the person well enough to be sure whether their arrogance is or isn't unfounded, then you may just mistake it for normal confidence. The guy with the "I know better than you attitude" may actually know better. Plus, confidence is attractive. Confident people get what they want. If they're good-looking too they can get more and more of what they want before anyone may question it.'

'It makes me really mad too,' Amy said, patting Caius on the arm.

'Did you hear someone stifle a laugh when the course convener started talking about sending pictures without consent on encrypted messaging services?' Caius asked Amy.

'I did notice that.'

Matt came back out of the shop with a packet of paracetamol, a bottle of water and a copy of *GQ*.

'What have you got there?' Caius asked.

Matt handed him the magazine and opened the water, taking a gulp to swallow the paracetamol. 'Rupert's modelling Burberry now.'

Caius bit the inside of his cheek as he looked over the advert. Sir Rupert Beauchamp – no relation – was one of the worst human beings Caius had ever had the displeasure of meeting. He had had concrete proof of it too, and yet here Rupert was swishing about in a trench coat on the back of a glossy magazine. It made Caius fucking furious.

★ ★ ★

Caius put his hand up.

'Yes,' said the course convener.

'Sorry, I had a question about encrypted messaging services.'

'Of course, ask away. It's why I'm here.'

'So am I right in understanding that these messages, although they cannot be accessed externally, if they contain content that is of an inappropriate sexual nature or derogatory towards those with protected characteristics, then that would be a sackable offence?' The whole room was looking at him.

'Potentially. The Met would definitely investigate these messages and then a decision would be made.'

'Hypothetically if there were police who had a private WhatsApp group called something stupid like "Thots and Robbers" where they made inappropriate comments, shared pictures or the personal details of individuals that they had come across in their day-to-day duties, then they could get sacked. Even for just being members of the group?'

'Yes, that's a dereliction of duty.' She looked at Caius. 'Do you want to lodge a specific complaint?'

'Oh no, as I said that was all totally hypothetical.'

The course convener nodded but looked concerned.

Matt leaned in. 'Is that true?'

'No idea. None of the clots in this building would be daft enough to add me to a group like that.' He could see a few fellow officers shifting around on their seats uncomfortably. 'Not beyond the realm of possibility though, is it?'

'You're going to get a shit present for Secret Santa again this year.'

14

The Police Station

Caius had just received a stern talking-to by Janet on the front desk. He had to take it on the chin. He knew the rules as well as anyone else: no personal post was to be sent to the station. Caius swore on his mother's life that he hadn't ordered anything and yet there was a delivery waiting for him after the training session finished. In the end Matt had to rescue him by placating Janet with some banana bread someone had left in the break room on their floor. She never bothered going that far up so their snacks were always a welcome novelty.

'What have you been buying now?' Matt asked, as the lift door closed with them inside. Matt had to press the button for their floor as the box Caius was carrying was that large. 'The Selfridges sale is over.'

'I haven't bought anything since I was so disappointed with the Ralph Lauren sample sale three weekends ago. I swear. I really haven't.'

'Why was it disappointing?'

'It was just crappy polos, and I emerged from the chrysalis of my polo phase last year.'

The lift doors opened, and they walked out and into the corridor leading to the break room.

'Not even a button-down collar shirt or two?' Matt asked as he held the door open for him. Amy was the only other person in there.

'Nope.' Caius dumped the box on the table as Amy took out the teabags from the three mugs of Earl Grey steeping on the side and added the milk. They didn't have any slices of lemon, so Matt had his black.

'Animals,' Matt said, sitting down at the table and taking his tea from Amy. 'Cheers.'

She put Caius's tea next to his box. As a rule Amy tried to avoid being the tea maker. She didn't want to be a trolley dolly, she wanted to be taken seriously, but Matt had observed that she hadn't made a cup of tea in three weeks, so she begrudgingly agreed 'just this once'.

'What have you bought this time?' Amy asked.

'Nothing! Jeez. I don't have a shopping addiction.'

'Open her up then,' Matt said.

Caius took the tape off the box and opened it. There was a letter on the top addressed to 'Detective Inspector Caius Beauchamp'. The envelope was made of a heavy, cream-coloured paper. Not the sort of thing usually found in the office stationery cupboard. He opened the handwritten letter and read it out loud to Matt and Amy.

Dear Caius,

My sincerest apologies for contacting you in such an impersonal manner. I would be delighted if you could join me at my club for dinner at 7.30 p.m. tonight as we have much to discuss. Address attached. I took the liberty of sending you the enclosed. It's a rather old-fashioned place with archaic dress rules but good for this sort of thing.

Yours sincerely,

Arthur Hampton

Who the hell was Arthur Hampton? Caius had no idea who he was. There was a card for a club in St James's called The Herakleion included in the envelope. He had heard of Boodle's and White's, he'd seen them referred to in novels, but he'd never heard of this club. He looked up the address that had been supplied on Google Maps – it was off a side street backing onto Green Park, but it wasn't coming up as The Herakleion, just a random business. Matt took the letter from him and read it as Caius looked through the box. He pulled out a shoebox containing a pair of Lobb's black Oxfords, a black bow tie and cummerbund from New & Lingwood, a double-cuffed dress shirt with marcella fabric on the front from Budd's and last and by no means least a suit bag from Gieves & Hawkes. Caius opened the suit bag to find a double-breasted evening jacket and a pair of matching pleated trousers. He checked the label: wool and mohair. 'This is a few thousand pounds' worth of clothes just for dinner with a man I have never met.'

'Are the sizes correct?' Amy asked.

'They're perfect. If I were a woman, I'd be terrified. This is serial killer stuff.' Caius said, opening the shoebox and looking at the Oxfords again. He'd never seen such a perfect pair of shoes, or such a perfect shirt, or such a perfect bow tie. It felt like either bribery – or an insult. 'Do I need to declare all this or something?'

'Who's Arthur Hampton?' Matt asked.

'That's a very good question,' Amy said, getting her phone and googling him.

'Should I be offended that I've been invited somewhere that he feels obliged to supply my clothes for? He obviously thinks I'm not posh enough to get in the door, let alone fit in. I know I won't fit in already, but why go to that effort? Why not come here? He's got the station address.' Caius looked at the shirt and realised his initials had been monogrammed onto the cuff, with a little crown logo above them. 'It must be somewhere he thinks he can discuss whatever he wants to discuss without the risk of being overheard.'

'His writing paper has an embossed coat of arms at the top,' Matt said, peering at it.

'There's an Arthur Hampton who's the MP for South Rutland. He's the Paymaster General, whatever that means,' Amy said.

'It means he gets to go to cabinet meetings without being responsible for anything in particular,' Caius said. 'It's an archaic role that's more of an honour than anything else.'

'I forgot you have a politics degree,' Matt said.

'Me too, mate. It was that long ago. Amy, does he hold any other positions?'

'Nope,' Amy said, showing him her phone. 'Is that weird?'

'It's unusual.' Caius gave her phone back. 'I have no idea who this guy is. He's a cabinet member but you never hear about him. How many people can name more than three cabinet members though? Not many. Unless there's been another scandal.'

'Peleus Arthur Hampton, he goes by his middle name for good reason, is the younger brother of a duke. I've got up his family's Wikipedia page. The coat of arms matches the one on the letter. It says here his brother never married so he's the heir presumptive. Arthur Hampton was a practising criminal barrister for ten years before being parachuted into a safe seat. He's married to a chartered surveyor called Jeremy,' Matt said.

'His family has a Wikipedia page? What am I walking into?'

'Are you going to go?' Amy asked.

'I'm far too curious not to.' Caius did have misgivings though. His jokes about bribery weren't unwarranted.

97

'You're going to have to get your skates on,' Matt said, checking the time on his watch. 'It's 5 p.m.'

'Bugger.'

'I've found a video of an interview with him on some obscure think tank's website from a couple of years ago,' Amy said, sending Caius a link to it.

'Cheers, I'll listen to it as I get ready. I haven't got time to go home.'

★ ★ ★

Caius was getting dressed in the disabled loo on their floor and had the interview playing in the background.

```
Interviewer:
How would you describe your politics?


Hampton:
I'm essentially an old-fashioned patrician Tory.
Although, if I were alive a hundred years ago I
would've been a Liberal, and two hundred years ago
I would've been a Whig. Five hundred years ago I
would naturally have been a feudal lord like my
ancestors.


Interviewer:
How curious. What do you mean by all of that?


Hampton:
Well, I believe simultaneously in the dignity of
the working man and that government should have
```

a light touch. People should be allowed to get on with the daily business of simple living. I'm positively feudal.

Caius laughed. Romantic libertarian drivel pretending to show an awareness of history. He was excited. That worried him. After the events of the summer, he'd been waiting for something like this to happen. He'd been bracing himself for a collision for the last two months and was relieved it was finally happening. Who was he going to meet? This pompous-sounding prick or something darker?

Interviewer:
And what do you consider to be the greatest challenge faced by today's 'working man'?

Hampton:
Climate breakdown.

The interviewer noticeably paused. That was clearly not the answer he was expecting. Caius was also caught by surprise, stopping for a moment to consider a man like Arthur Hampton who he assumed was chummy with oil company executives and keen to maintain the status quo, saying something like that so frankly. He checked the time and quickly dashed into the break room to down a pint of milk to line his stomach, taking his phone with him. Caius didn't want to drink more than he meant to and lose his wits.

Interviewer:
Really? And what do you think the solution is?

Hampton:

We in the West need to dramatically reduce our consumption of nearly everything. No more fossil fuels, no more polyester clothes that get dumped in the global south after one wear, no more steaks or salmon fillets but a diet based around pulses, and no more cars for personal usage. Renewable energy. Proper recycling. Sustainable agricultural practices. Better insulation while also accounting for hotter summers and extreme weather more generally. Rewilding areas that are not arable. And I don't mean just planting dead zones of homogenous trees but fencing land in and letting nature get on with it. Chuck a few beavers and the odd lynx at the countryside. Even wolves. All of these things would be great. They won't happen though.

Interviewer:
And why not?

Hampton:

We are inherently selfish and stupid creatures. We only think about our own immediate personal comfort. Currently, we do not have the political will to change and most personal changes, unless done en masse, do not have a big enough effect. The system needs to be changed. More than the odd tweak, the odd tax cut here and there, the odd bit of subsidised bus travel. Things need to fundamentally change. We need to utterly reorganise society along more traditional lines.

Caius quickly googled how to fix a bow tie as he leaned against the sink in the break room.

Interviewer:
And what happens if we don't radically change society?

Hampton:
Billions are going to die.

Interviewer:
Oh.

Hampton:
Not here. We are an island in a temperate zone with arable land and a history of manufacturing. We'll either become a densely populated haven or a fortress state.

Caius thought this interview was extraordinary. He had never heard a politician talk like that, especially one of Arthur Hampton's persuasion. It was all 'targets' and bluster usually. Caius dashed back to his desk where Matt and Amy were waiting for the fashion show. Matt had an old pair of silk knots in his drawer which he gave to Caius who normally wore button cuffs because he couldn't be bothered with the faff of cufflinks. He regretted not having his only pair with him. They had been a twenty-first-birthday present from his paternal grandfather whom he had been named after and were the only family heirloom he had. He put Matt's silk knots in and then tied the laces on his new Oxfords. They fitted perfectly.

'Well, if they ever let James Bond be mixed race . . .' Matt said. At first he'd found this all rather amusing, but now it was disconcerting. He gave Caius a look and Caius gave it him back. 'Don't be dazzled by any pigeon Latin.'

'I'll try.'

'I've got to get myself a tux,' Amy said.

'You'd look great,' Caius said as he put the jacket on and picked up his phone, wallet – not that he thought he'd be expected to pay but he didn't want to be caught short – and keys.

'Be careful,' Amy called after him as he got in the lift.

Keith the Chief got in on the third floor. Caius could feel himself going up in his estimation as he made small talk.

'Gosh, you look smart,' said the Chief Superintendent.

'Thanks, sir.'

'Where are you off to?'

'Just a charity thing.' The lie stung as it left his tongue, but he wasn't going to say that he was going to dinner in a St James's club in clothes bought especially for him by some unknown eccentric posh man with an unknown agenda and unknown political power.

15

The Herakleion Club, St James's

Caius had expected to be let in by a doorman in a green cap and matching coat, or something else nauseatingly deferential, but the place he turned up at just looked like a regular town house, albeit a large two-hundred-year-old one. The lights were off. He checked the card that had come with the letter again. Caius was at the right address. He rang the discreet brass doorbell and was buzzed in. He entered an empty hallway that had been painted a sunny yellow colour and a pretty young woman was waiting for him. This caught him off guard a little. She was wearing a smart black shift dress with a matching jacket, and a pair of very high stilettoes. Caius smiled at her, wider than he meant to.

'Mr Beauchamp?' She pronounced it 'Beecham', unlike Caius whose family pronounced it in a phonetic French manner. He was used to this, of course, but it still sounded wrong to his ear, like an unexpected flat note in a well-sung song.

'Yes.'

'Please, follow me.' She led Caius to the back of the house and into a sitting room. 'If you'd like to wait here for a moment, sir,' she said, gesturing to one of the large armchairs scattered about. Caius smiled at her again and took a seat. It felt like a doctor's waiting room, although these were not NHS squeaky plastic chairs but magnificent comfy things with backs like thrones. He looked around him at the few pieces of art on the walls. They were mostly small landscapes of the English countryside. Fat fluffy sheep grazing on hillsides. A heifer wandering by a stream.

A smartly dressed young man appeared through the door he'd just come through and put a glass of whisky on a small table beside Caius.

'Thank you,' Caius said. He didn't know much about whisky – he'd avoided it ever since getting horribly drunk on cheap bourbon at seventeen. The smell usually made him dry heave, but he took a sip of it anyway out of politeness. He didn't hate it and managed to drink half the glass. He was left to his own devices for ten minutes, wondering what the hell he was doing loitering in the backrooms of a random town house in St James's. Was this how he'd die? Lured into some gentlemen's club with a pair of fancy shoes and then dismembered?

'Mr Beauchamp. Follow me, please,' the young woman said, having reappeared silently. She looked too friendly to be an axe murderer's accomplice.

Caius followed her through a different door from the one she had led him through earlier. She walked down a burgundy-coloured corridor and stopped at a door at the end, holding it open for him. It led down into the cellar. There was nothing there. It hadn't even been plastered. As the son of a builder, he noticed such things. All he could see was a single light bulb dangling from the ceiling. 'Follow the passage at the bottom of the stairs all the way through, sir.'

'Thank you,' Caius said. He was glad he'd told Matt where he was so he knew where to start the investigation if Caius disappeared. He walked down the wooden stairs and into the cellar. He turned to his left and saw the passage. It was better lit than he had first assumed. Caius followed the short tunnel – the faintest hint of damp in the air – and came out in another cellar.

'Good evening, Mr Beauchamp,' came a voice from the top of this next flight of stairs.

'Good evening,' he said, before climbing up. Another young woman, dressed identically to the last one, smiled at him as she greeted him. It felt uncanny. These 'servants' were indistinguishable from each other.

'Lord Arthur is waiting for you in the red dining room. It's up the main staircase and on the right.'

'Thank you.'

'I am afraid that I must ask you to deposit any mobile phones, smart watches and any device capable of recording sound.'

'Of course,' Caius said as he fished out his phone from his pocket and gave it to her. He felt some separation anxiety. He looked around at this new building. It was much grander than the last one. He walked down the corridor leading from the cellar and into an elaborately decorated and foreboding atrium. The walls were covered in a deep blue damask wallpaper with a grand staircase in the middle. Caius had never seen this much gold. It was a bit blingy for his taste. He paused to look at the art on the walls. There were no more English pastorals; the paintings were all women with goodly thighs and men with lightning bolts and tridents in their hands. There were statues in the atrium. Caius stopped. He thought he recognised one from a list of stolen antiquities that Interpol had circulated in the summer. He walked up the stairs, turned right and entered a small dining room. There was one long table that could seat eight but was set up for dinner for two.

'Detective Inspector Beauchamp,' said Arthur Hampton, standing up and shaking his hand. Hampton pronounced his name the same way he did. Hampton had researched him. He then sat back down in his seat and gestured at Caius to do the same. 'The Chablis isn't terrible.'

A wine waiter appeared at his elbow and poured Caius a glass.

'I imagine this must present a puzzle to you. I also imagine that you like solving puzzles.'

'I have an idea of who you are and what you've been up to.' Caius looked around the room. There were more pictures on the wall. Caius recognised that the largest picture was of the birth of Aphrodite. It looked just like the famous Botticelli one, but he thought that was in a museum somewhere. 'What a beautiful building.'

'Yes, we do have a good collection here,' Hampton said, noticing that Caius had spotted the Botticelli.

'Which auction house do you use? Farleigh's?'

Hampton glanced over the menu. 'I wasn't sure whether you had the correct attire. There was once a time when all young gentlemen would have such things at the back of their wardrobes. But times change, and women wear elasticated athletic wear everywhere they go. I hope you don't mind me being so presumptuous. I'm glad we got the sizing right.'

'I'm a young gentleman, am I?' Caius hadn't expected to be spoken to like that, but he wasn't sure what exactly he was expecting. He was, however, surprised to be treated as an equal.

'Yes, of course you are.' Hampton put his menu down. 'I can recommend the crab.'

'Why am I here?'

'The ultimate question.'

'I don't mean philosophically.' Caius wasn't in the mood for facetiousness. 'I mean, why am I here right now with you, dressed up like this and having dinner?'

'All very good questions. We're having dinner because that was all my schedule would allow, it's civilised, and I wished to make your acquaintance properly.'

A waiter arrived.

Arthur Hampton did not look up at the waiter as he placed his order. 'The smoked salmon and celeriac remoulade, followed by the lamb shank. For pudding I'll just have some berries.' He looked at Caius. 'I'm giving up sugar.'

The waiter turned to Caius who did make eye contact and then smiled awkwardly.

'Um, the heritage beetroot and goat's cheese stack, then the pea and mint tortellini, please,' Caius said, trying to copy how Hampton ordered but failing as it felt rude. 'I won't have pudding.'

The waiter left wordlessly.

'No pudding? I doubt you're pre-diabetic like me, although abstemiousness isn't the worst quality for a man to have. The food here has improved a lot in recent years. It used to primarily be chops – lamb chops, pork chops, chops, chops, chops. The mere thought is giving me heartburn.' Hampton took a sip from his wine. 'Your grandfather is still alive, correct?'

'My father's father is, yes. Why?'

'Oh, nothing.' Hampton looked at him as he nodded slowly. 'Does he still have all his mental faculties?'

'Why do you ask?' Caius bristled at this line of questioning. Why was this man interested in his family?

'Just making conversation,' Hampton said a little too brightly.

Caius stared out of the window. He could just about see the trees in Green Park. He realised that the building he was in was behind the one he had entered, and the tunnel must have been dug underneath the two properties' small adjoining gardens. 'What's with the cloak and dagger stuff? Or rather, dinner jacket and dagger.'

'This is my favourite club. It's also the most discreet. It feels very sneaky, doesn't it, entering through a vacant building on another street? It's not public knowledge, you see. Not just anyone can join, and we like it like that. To the outside world this building is the offices of a family-owned chartered surveyors.'

'Old school ties?'

'God no. Anyone who can afford the fees can go to the right school. No. This is reserved for particular families who founded the club.' Hampton took his napkin off the table and placed it on his lap in anticipation. 'I thought it best to meet in person. To make sure you fully comprehend your new brief.'

'What brief?'

The waiter returned with their starters.

Caius had googled cutlery etiquette in the taxi and was confident that all he had to do was work his way inwards.

'There's a case you closed this week that I am sure was murder,' Hampton said, picking up his knife and fork and digging in.

'Martin Hartley! I knew it. It's that girls' school. I knew he and Ruth Miller had found something out, but the local police didn't take them seriously.'

'I'm sorry, I know nothing of that case.' Hampton took a bite of his salmon. 'No, I'm talking about Lynne Rodgers.'

'The Richmond accidental drowning?'

'It was murder. I had hoped you would have discovered this on your own. No matter. We're here now and the food isn't terrible.'

'Lynne was a desperate woman living in entrenched poverty who couldn't take it any more. There are no witnesses to suggest anything to the contrary. No members of the public saw anything suspicious. Her alcoholism had resurfaced. She couldn't cope with how hard her life had become, drank a bottle and fell in. It's awful, but it's not unheard of in this day and age.'

'Was she really so impoverished?'

'According to the vicar at the food bank she was. Lynne had

lived abroad, ran out of money and had to come home. She can't have had much in the way of savings. Then she developed bad arthritis and couldn't work any more.'

'She lived in Brazil.'

'Is that important?'

'Our current extradition treaty with Brazil was only signed in 1997. Lynne started working as a secretary at Symington & Chase Textile Manufacturers Limited in 1987. Two years later the chief executive, Robert Symington, raided the pension fund by moving it through various limited companies in various off-shore tax havens in order to run off with his secretary to Brazil.'

'What?'

'That, at least, is the official story.'

'Did that not happen?' Caius wondered why none of this had come up on their systems when they first identified Lynne.

'Not quite. Lynne did indeed board a plane to Brazil with a small wodge of cash, however not a pension fund's worth. I need you to find out what really happened at Symington & Chase.'

'You had my team put on the case in the first place, didn't you? Not because Richmond was understaffed.'

'I did, although I believe they are actually understaffed.'

'So you've been what, watching Lynne?' Caius realised that Hampton must have known who Lynne was before they did. Richmond hadn't got round to identifying her after all.

'Not closely enough, it would seem. She was extradited to the UK in 1998 and interviewed under caution. She failed to give up any useful information and there wasn't enough evidence that she had colluded with her lover in the theft at all. Consequently, she was released.' Hampton finished his remoulade and set his cutlery down on his plate. 'Robert Symington did not get on the plane from Heathrow with Lynne. The seat booked for him was empty. The pension fund has never been recovered and no one has seen Robert since that day. It was suspected that he either used another passport or took a different route to Brazil entirely. Perhaps Lynne was lying before. I need to know the full truth and I need it done discreetly.'

'Why are you asking me?' Caius stared at Hampton.

'I have faith in you.' Hampton shrugged.

'Why on earth do you have that? How do you even know who I am?'

'You have form in looking into cases and then "falling silent" on them when needed.'

'I don't know what you're talking about.' Caius had signed away his right to talk about the events of the summer. He couldn't talk about Clemmie's death, or Help for Hippos, or Hereward or Yannis, or even Nell. He couldn't talk about the fact that he was sure a lot of the art in this building had been looted from archaeological sites all over the Mediterranean. He'd signed away his conscience.

'I'm a government minister and Clemmie O'Hara's murder happened during silly season.' Hampton picked up his glass and took a sip, wincing slightly. He obviously didn't think the wine was up to it. Not that Caius could tell it wasn't good. It just tasted like white wine. 'Lynne was murdered. That is all. She did not end up in the Thames of her own accord. Now you know that, you will do anything you can to solve it. You are motivated by duty. You chose to become a policeman after your sister's murder because your sense of responsibility towards others impelled you to do so. A very practical act of *noblesse oblige*. You are my very own knight errant.' The waiter came and cleared their plates, and a wine waiter poured them a glass each of Beaujolais.

Caius couldn't help but look cynical as he tried to get his head around how Hampton was speaking to him as if he were his superior officer. Since when did a random MP get to tell him what to investigate? But he did have to wonder if this was an opportunity if he held out a little longer.

'All right,' Hampton said, acquiescing to his new squire. 'If you look into Lynne's murder, then you can have carte blanche to investigate this girls' school you were talking about too.'

'Am I making a deal with the devil?' Caius was trying to weigh up whether pursuing a cold case with very little physical evidence was worth being indebted to this man, as gracious as he might well have appeared. Although, thanks to Martin Hartley, the Eliza Chapel case might have a new lead and he couldn't really pass that up. Could he pass up a 'damsel' like Eliza?

'The devil does not exist and, if he did, he'd be a damn sight more attractive than I.'

'Are you embarrassed?' Caius couldn't help himself. He didn't get to sit in front of men like this. He didn't get to tell them what he thought. In truth, Caius needed to have a little dig, a poke. A small attempt at clawing back some of his dignity.

'About what?'

'The fact that Lynne was dependent on charity; the fact that food banks exist.'

'Oh yes, deeply.'

'Then why aren't you doing something about it?'

'I am. That's precisely why you're here.' Hampton had spoken with a finality that let Caius know that that was the end of his questions. Caius didn't understand totally what was going on. All he knew was that Lynne might have been murdered after all and that Hampton had been right about him: that he would not stop till he got to the truth. He was worried that Hampton was some sort of aristocratic eccentric, but worse than creating a weird rockery on his estate he had an undefined mysterious government position with influence and appeared to know everything about Caius down to his collar size. 'All of the original case files from the Symington & Chase case will be sent to you immediately.'

They ate the rest of their meal. It was an odd dinner. They talked about veganism, gardening, his grandfather's war record, the general state of the world. They talked about what they were reading: Caius regurgitated a line from the introduction of his recently read edition of *Howards End*. He said with some confidence that it was really a novel about which section of the middle class inherits England, which seemed to delight Hampton no end. Hampton then talked at length about *A Room with a View*, which Caius sheepishly admitted he hadn't read yet. 'Ah, but the yet is important. It means you intend to read it, which is half the battle.' Dinner over, Caius toddled a little drunk back through the tunnel and into the night air where Hampton had a car waiting to drive him home. It was late, the roads were quiet, his head felt light and his morals weighed heavily upon him.

WEDNESDAY

16

The Police Station

Caius, Matt and Amy had been moved to an incident room on a different floor, one even higher up in the building than usual. The ninth floor was vacant, now that officer numbers had decreased so much. Most of the space was taken up with boxes of posters and leaflets for whichever trendy policing tactic was popular and bits of spare riot gear.

'Discretion is everything,' the Chief Superintendent said as he looked around their new incident room. 'We've put you all the way up here to make that easier for you.'

'Thank you,' Caius said as he tried not to look at the water mark above his head.

'I am very proud that it is my officers who have been singled out for this special cold case initiative.'

'Yes,' Caius said. He tried to find a golf analogy or something but failed to find anything and settled for a vaguely relevant slogan from a WWII poster. 'Loose lips sink ships.'

'Exactly that: discretion.' The Chief Superintendent left them to it eventually as officers from the front desk carried in the promised boxes of records from the previous investigation.

'Let me get this straight. You didn't have pudding?' Matt asked once the three of them had finally been left in peace.

'No,' Caius said, leaning back in his chair. 'I don't know why. I panicked. He ordered berries and I didn't want to look weak for asking for extra custard. There was sticky toffee pudding on the menu.'

'Sticky toffee? Sticky toffee! I don't care what kale thing

you've brought with you today, we're getting pizza for lunch to compensate,' Matt said.

'Can you explain this whole thing again?' Amy was opening one of the boxes of old files. A plume of dust flew up in the air when she took out the first file. 'I think I'm missing something.'

'Hampton is adamant that Lynne was murdered because of her involvement thirty-odd years ago in the theft of a pension scheme.'

'Sure,' Amy said, nodding. 'But why does he care?'

'I don't know, but it feels super fucking dodgy,' Caius said. He'd come away from dinner last night with a clear impression that Hampton had tried to bamboozle him. Hampton hadn't given him any proof whatsoever that Lynne had been murdered, after all. Caius was clearly supposed to accept his word for it. He wondered how he'd come to be a puppet for the literal establishment.

'I think we should say no to the case,' Amy said.

'Me too, but I don't think that's an option.' A sense of foreboding had fallen over Caius. The Chief Superintendent had merrily gone along with whatever scheme this was being passed off as so there was no one to protest to.

'Why us? There are whole units that specialise in cold cases,' Matt asked. A guy he'd trained with worked in one.

'He said he knows that we'll do a good job and not talk about it,' Caius said, wincing as he got up from his chair and picking up a case file. He flicked through it for a moment before putting it down again, having found the words for what was bothering him. 'And now we find ourselves in a morally dubious position where we are investigating a real crime with real victims but at the benefit of a very powerful man with an unknown agenda and no apparent accountability. I can't work out his politics even after that think tank interview. I said that we would look into the pension's theft in exchange for us being able to dig a bit more on the Eliza Chapel case. There's something there, even if Martin Hartley did just have a regular old stroke.'

'What's the plan then?' Amy asked.

'I will split across both cases. Matt, you're on Lynne Rodgers and Amy, you're on Eliza Chapel. Lynne and the pension theft will be my main focus for now.'

'Oh.'

'Everything OK, Amy?'

'Yeah, fine.' Amy wasn't fine, not really. She didn't like being put on the side case. She wasn't going to get promoted if she was faffing around with no-hopers like this.

'All right then,' Matt said. He put up Lynne's photograph on the whiteboard again and rewrote everything that had been on the board two days before when they had initially closed the case. He then started writing up the timeline of events based on the old case files.

Timeline:

12 July 1989
– Lynne Rodgers purchases two one-way tickets to Brazil on the company credit card.

16 July 1989
– The pension fund (approx. £10.3m) is transferred to S&C Pensions Growth Ltd.
– S&C Pensions Growth Ltd which is registered to Robert Symington is dissolved. The cash has been transferred to an account in the British Virgin Islands. Cannot be traced.

17 July 1989

– Lynne boards a plane at Heathrow. Take-off at 11.34. Robert doesn't arrive.
– Cassandra Symington (wife) says he went to work as normal that morning – claims to have had no prior knowledge of the Brazilian 'research trip'.
– Tricia Jones (accounts assistant) and Peter Simpson (finance director) claim Robert did not go to the office in the morning before the flight. Pat White (accounts) away visiting family so not interviewed.
– Harold Stephenson (shop foreman) also interviewed in case manual workers saw anything, but nothing is reported. Harold at the hospital with his mother that morning (appointment confirmed with hospital staff).

21 July 1989

– Pete Simpson (FD) tries to get a report on the pension fund ahead of a meeting the coming week. Raises the alarm.
– Brazilian authorities refuse to assist investigations.
– Cassandra Symington claims that she has not heard from her husband since 17 July.

'I feel like a bit of an idiot that we thought it was an accident,' Caius said, reading over Matt's timeline.

'I thought you said Hampton didn't give you any direct proof that it wasn't an accident?' Matt asked.

'Well, no.'

'We may still be proved right then. If Hampton is as dodgy as we think he is, then he may be using Lynne's death as an excuse to get us to poke around.'

'Yes, but poke around what – and to what end?'

17

Calliope Foster Millinery

Callie's phone buzzed. She ignored it. She carried on sewing a band onto a panama. It buzzed again. This time she decided to check it (Harriet was usually in Pilates at this time of the day). She put the hat down and unlocked her phone. It was Jim. They never really messaged each other. They bumped into each other at parties, had a drink and a laugh in the corner only to then repeat six months later at another party. Nothing more, nothing less.

Jim
10.02
Hello!!!! Remember that MP?
Charming chap at the party who chatted with us for a bit

You
10.02
In the gorgeous slouchy Italian jacket?

Jim
10.02
Probably???? Not much of a jacket expert . . .

You
10.02
Arthur something?

Jim
10.03
Yesss! He's just invited me to a dinner party on Friday night

You
10.03
You must have made quite an impression. Good for the old career!

Jim
10.03
'Tis not I who made the impression. He's asked that you come too

You
10.04
Lordy

Jim
10.04
Are you free?
I bet he has very good wine

You
10.04
I don't think I'd know what to say. I really don't follow politics that closely

Jim
10.05
Talking shop is usually taboo with guys like Hampton!
They're more interested in either art or horse racing. You
sit perfectly between those two things

You
10.05
I suppose I do

Jim
10.05
It's just dinner and you are always a charming guest

You
10.06
You old flatterer

Jim
10.06
Honestly, it would really help me out! I'd owe you one!
I'm stuck in backbencher hell atm. These fuckers just care
about rare bird sanctuaries or not building on green belt or
whatever their little singular obsession is

You
10.07
Go on then

Jim
10.07
You superstar!

You
10.07
Let me know when and where

Jim
10.07
More deets to follow
How's the wedding stuff going?
Harriet making you hunt for the perfect napkin? Inigo's calling her Ring Kong . . .

You
10.08
Shhh but I've muted the wedding planning group. I have set a reminder to check it at the end of the day or face the wrath of Harriet

Jim
10.08
Rather you than me
I've said yes for both of us
7 for 7.30
Don't worry about bringing anything

You
10.09
I hope you realise I really don't pay much attention to
politics

Jim
10.09
Me neither

18

The Police Station

Matt had a piece of pepperoni pizza with vegan cheese in one hand. He'd finally succumbed to the unfortunate reality that he was probably lactose intolerant. In the other hand he had the original senior investigating officer's final report on the disappearance of Robert Symington.

'The leading theory was that Robert Symington stole the money and planned to run away with his secretary to Brazil. She booked the plane tickets for the pair of them, but then he got cold feet and left the country another way. They thought he might have driven to mainland Europe and flown to Brazil from there. The original investigation found a receipt for French, Spanish and Portuguese road maps in the drawer of his work desk and his car was missing,' Matt said, taking a bite of pizza before the toppings slid off. 'Another theory, although totally unsubstantiated, was that Robert left the country and went elsewhere. South Africa maybe.'

'Right, but then why would he still send his mistress on that original flight?' Caius asked. He'd ordered the 'vegetarian' with extra artichoke hearts and was peeling them off the pizza and eating them with his fingers.

'That's where the theory falls apart for me too. He might have wanted her out of the way so he could make off with the money on his own?'

'Is that SIO still around?' Caius asked, dipping a pizza crust in garlic sauce.

'Nope, I've already checked. Unfortunately, he died a couple of years ago.'

'Right. To start with we need to re-interview everyone who worked at the company at the time. And then his wife.'

'Everyone? The first investigation didn't interview any of the women who worked on the shop floor. Only the staff in the back office.'

'Of course they didn't.'

'I'll compile a list and start tracking them down. It wasn't a huge company, it won't take long.'

'Amy, are you sure I can't offer you a piece of pizza?' Caius asked her.

'Nope, I don't want your overhyped cheese on toast,' she said, waving around her chicken and couscous salad. 'I brought salad today so you'd leave me alone about my fibre intake, and then you go and let Matt talk you into *pizza*.'

'I'm so proud of you.' Caius handed her a sheet of paper. He had made a drawing of two different boxes. 'I've got my notes here too from when I spoke to Beatrice the actress.'

'Actor. Actress is a gendered term.'

'Noted for next time I go and see my doctrix.'

'So Beatrice?' Amy asked. The git had read one jokey book on Latin and here he was making bad puns about noun endings.

'Yes, she said the girls were split into different dorm rooms.' He pointed at the two boxes he had drawn. One was labelled 'Eliza's room' and the second box 'Others'. 'Beatrice wasn't in Eliza's dorm and in Eliza's room there were only actually four girls. Two had been pulled out the year before. She mentioned there were a couple of girls from her year that were there at the time that she still bumped into in London – Sophy Oddfellow and Bellie Hartnell.'

'Bellie?'

'That's what I wrote down. She may have just said Bella

in a really posh way that I misheard.' Caius drew four circles in one box and six in the other. Then he wrote B. Parker and S. Oddfellow above two of the circles in the room marked 'Others', and B. Hartnell and E. Chapel above a circle each in the box marked 'Eliza's room', leaving two remaining girls to be identified in that room. 'Anyway, apparently Ms Hartnell was in the room of four with Eliza. If Eliza had a secret would she be more likely to tell the girls who shared her room than the others? I didn't get the impression from Beatrice that she was popular, so perhaps proximity became more important when it came to her confidences, even if accidental. Beatrice heard a commotion that night. Someone knows more than they said they did fifteen years ago.'

'Who are the other two girls in the room?'

'I don't know. I wrote a list on the back of all the girls from that year. Read through all the documents from the original investigation, which feel a little on the light side considering the case – it'll only take you all afternoon – and get in touch with Bella Hartnell and go from there.'

'Sure, right after I finish my delicious leafy salad.'

'I'm so very proud of you,' Caius said.

'This pizza is delicious,' Matt piped up. Amy stuck her tongue out at him and Matt blew her a kiss.

Caius went back to peeling the artichokes off his pizza and reading through the seemingly endless financial documents from Symington & Chase.

★   ★   ★

Amy had found Annabel Hartnell's LinkedIn account after she had finished reading the reports from the initial investigation into Eliza's disappearance. Caius's notes were right, she had worked at one of the Magic Circle law firms. It had a gym in the basement and a doctor and a dentist on site so that you never had to leave the building. She had graduated from Cambridge with a degree in law and following solicitor training had worked at the firm for six years in their property team. She had left six months ago to work for Hartnell Estates, her family's company. Amy googled Hartnell Estates. There was a lot of corporate speak around 'heritage', 'tradition' and 'solid British values' on their website, but what she gleaned was that they just owned properties in London and Bath. She then found Annabel Hartnell's Instagram page, but it was set to private. She had a Twitter account, but she hadn't posted on there since 2017 and even then there was nothing useful, only legal geek stuff.

'Hi there, could I speak to Annabel Hartnell, please? When's she back? No, it's all right. I'll call then.' Amy put the phone down. 'Annabel is on annual leave,' she called to Caius, who was pacing up and down the office, trying to get to grips with Robert Symington.

'All right, Amy. That's a good start. Best call it a day for now,' Caius said while reading a financial statement and looking confused.

She looked at him pointedly and coughed.

'What?' he asked.

'You've been very coy this week,' she said.

'You have actually,' Matt added as he put down the transcript of Symington's wife's interview. 'I'm desperate for details. Normally you're very obvious about things like this.'

'Like what?' Caius asked.

'Your date with the gorgeous milliner who was not put off you by a sick-covered corpse. That's the pinnacle, mate,' Amy said as she started putting her phone away in her bag.

'Right.'

'Look, I know you and Héloise had this intense on-and-off thing, and don't get me wrong – when I met her that one time I liked her – but I don't think you were right for each other,' Amy said.

'Real blunt today, Amy,' Caius said. He shrugged. He knew she was right, but he was trying to play it cool in case tonight didn't go anywhere. 'Charming, so charming. Keep it up.'

'What I'm really trying to say is: wear a good shirt and go somewhere expensive. But not billionaire despot expensive. Just a little spenny, you know,' Amy said, before heading for the lift. 'But don't be flash.'

'So . . .' Matt said, nodding at the documents Caius was poring over. 'Those financial statements look a bit complicated.'

'Yep,' Caius said.

'I think we need to look at them again tomorrow with fresh eyes. Maybe we should call it a day now too?'

'Yeah.' Caius looked at his watch. It was 5.30 p.m., bang on. 'What are you up to tonight?'

'Not much.' Caius looked at Matt. Matt looked at Caius. Matt shrugged. 'Give me all the details right now. Where are you going? What are you going to wear? Where does this milliner live? You can't go to a restaurant too near to either of your flats because it's presumptuous.'

'Are you OK?' Caius asked, interrupting Matt before he spiralled any further.

'Nope.'

Caius gave Matt a manly supportive pat on the arm. 'I've booked a table at an Italian restaurant for 8 p.m. It's on the quieter end of the King's Road, so it's not too far from her work. She lives in Ealing so it's not too too close to there either.'

'Nice. Italian is a sexy cuisine, but don't order anything with lots of tomato sauce because you will get it all over you. And remember to both eat garlic.'

'I've already checked the menu. They do Venetian small plates.'

'Yes good, you can share things, but don't be funny about who has how much of what.'

'I promise I won't. If that goes well then there's a wine bar a few doors down.'

'I like it. I like it. And what are you wearing?' Matt wiggled his eyebrows as he made gentle fun of Caius and his fastidiousness.

'I will send you options.'

'You know damn straight you will.' Matt laughed.

'Mate, are you all right?' Caius asked.

'Are you suggesting that my obvious attempt at living vicariously through you is a cry for help?'

Caius had the impulse to hug Matt, but he only really hugged his mother any more. Instead, he gave him another pat on the arm and resolved to find him another pack of odd-flavoured biscuits.

19

The King's Road

Caius was early. He'd gone straight back to his flat and changed from his work clothes into a pale blue linen shirt, a pair of chino-type trousers and brown loafers – he was going out for dinner in West London, after all. He took a picture to placate Matt's burgeoning despair but told him that that was the only option he was willing to consider and walked briskly to the tube. He'd downloaded the menu onto his phone and was salivating over burrata, wild mushroom and ricotta crostini, and cacio e pepe arancini on his way out west. He checked the time on his phone. No message from Callie, so he texted saying that he was outside at the exact moment she texted him to say that she was outside too. He looked around for her. She wasn't there. He called her. She'd gone to the Veneziano in Covent Garden, not on the King's Road. She apologised profusely as she rushed towards the tube. He tried to sweet-talk the hostess round to moving their booking back, but she basically told him to fuck off, so he slunk off to the wine bar.

Caius ordered a Rioja that he thought he might have been ripped off on and Callie arrived just as he spilled a dribble down the front of his shirt. He should have chosen a white wine, much safer. The tables outside the bar were practically on top of each other and he was sat far closer to two very bored-looking women than he liked, but he had got to watch the locals as they went about the evening. He stood up to greet Callie, blushing a little and knocking the small table, causing the wine list to fall onto the floor. Callie stooped to pick it up.

'You look lovely,' Caius said, rolling onto his heels. Callie was wearing a midi dress made out of a bold red-and-white block print that looked outrageous compared to the greige the rest of the bar's clientele were wearing. It fitted her perfectly. He had been a little annoyed that she was almost an hour late, but now he no longer cared.

'Thank you,' she said, kissing him on the cheek. 'I am so sorry. I'm such a cock. You said the King's Road, but I've been to the Covent Garden one before and I just went there on autopilot.' She didn't hate what he was wearing. Very safe, but she could work with that.

'Well, you're here now.' He'd forgotten to down a pint of milk before he left and now felt a little wobbly. He hadn't realised he was this much of a lightweight.

'I am, and I'm very very very very sorry.' The Parisian cafe set-up meant they had to sit next to each other rubbing shoulders.

'I can see that you're very very very very sorry.' Caius started laughing, the Rioja had gone to his head. Callie started laughing louder because the only way not to be embarrassed was to be the loudest. The two chic women next to them who kept taking staged photos of each other 'having fun' wrinkled their noses and raised their eyebrows, confused at the sight of people actually spontaneously enjoying themselves. 'Can I get you a drink?'

'I'll drink anything,' Callie said.

He went to the bar and ordered a bottle of Picpoul (safer for his shirt which he was now dabbing with a napkin, hoping desperately that she hadn't noticed) and a few bar snacks.

'I hate to put a downer on this evening, but how did the poor guy from the theatre die?' Callie asked Caius when he returned.

'Oh, it was natural.'

'Poor, poor man. I just keep thinking about how awful the smell was.'

'Yeah, it wasn't the most dignified way to exit this world.' He'd smelled worse, but that wasn't a first date conversation.

'My hat got splashed.'

'Oh no. I did wonder. It was a lovely hat.'

'It's all right. I just got rid of the ribbon. It's seen worse at Henley.'

'As in the regatta? Rowing and boats and stuff.'

'Yeah. Silly coloured blazers and grown men urinating on people's front lawns.'

'You're a bit posh, aren't you?'

'Is that a problem?'

'It would be classist of me if it was.'

'I'm not really posh. Single mum, little cottage in the arse-end of nowhere. My grandparents were a bit and gave my mum money to send me to private school, but I don't have tuppence myself. I've got some friends from uni who are on the fancy side, who occasionally invite me to things like Henley.'

'What did you study?'

'Fashion, can you not tell?' Callie laughed in mock outrage and ate a couple of habas fritas that Caius had brought back from the bar with him. 'What about you?'

'I studied politics and French at Sheffield.'

'Nice. Year abroad?'

'Yeah, I studied at the Sorbonne, but mostly I went clubbing. My memories are of hangovers, eating lots of wonderful bread and zoning out at the back of lecture halls.'

'That is the life.' Callie leaned back in her chair, took a sip of wine and sized him up. 'We should probably get all the awkward first date questions out of the way before we get down to the serious business of having fun.'

'All right, I'll start. Last relationship,' Caius said. This was the one he wanted to get out of the way first.

'I was dumped a month before our wedding last year, you?' Callie wanted to be upfront about it but was also quick to turn it back round to Caius.

'Found her cheating on me, for the second time.' He felt compelled to leave the timings out.

They looked at each other and both comically shrugged before returning to their wine. 'What are your three favourite things to do?' Callie asked.

'Reading. Running. Cooking or maybe pottering around farmer's markets. I'm turning into a terrible food snob. You?'

'Drawing, going to galleries and eating. I am also a food snob. Do you want to get married and have children?'

'Yes and yes. Two, maybe an accidental third,' Caius said.

'I say one and see how terrible it was. I was eight weeks premature and my mother claims that the trauma put her off having any more,' Callie said, rolling her eyes at her own mention of her mother.

'Tell me about your family,' Caius said.

'My dad pissed off before I was born. My mum never really got over it and shuffles about her little cottage like an ancient hedge witch holding grudges, even though she's recently remarried to quite a kind man. He's henpecked and she's horrible and I avoid her at all costs. You?'

He tried to think of a way to describe them both: his father had an almost metallic quality and his mother was all air, but that sounded a bit mad – the wine had definitely started to get to him – so he stuck with the most obvious facts. 'My dad's family are Jamaican and my mum's are Irish.'

'You must have brilliant family parties.'

'Oh yes, we like to have a good time. My dad is a builder – he used to buy and renovate old houses – and my mum was a teaching assistant. They've retired to France now though. My dad's doing up their place out there.' He wasn't going to mention that his parents had recently sold their impeccably renovated farmhouse and bought a dilapidated chateau for the price of a studio flat in zone 4 just yet.

'Siblings?'

'I had an older sister, but she died.'

'Oh God, I'm so very sorry.' Callie touched his hand.

'Yeah. She was amazing. It's why I became a police officer actually. Her case didn't really get the attention it deserved.'

'Oh God.' Callie thought that was such an awful thing to hear. He was a kitten with a limp.

'So now I hang around theatres waiting for disappointed actors in the grip of existential crises to throw up on already dead audience members.'

'That poor man. I felt really weird about having been so close to a dead body.'

'You're English. My family in Ireland had my great-auntie Orlagh in an open coffin in the front room. It's really soothing, I guess, to be able to properly say goodbye before they move on.'

'That sounds much more joyful.' Callie nodded and finished her wine but found the idea fairly odd. Caius poured them each another glass. 'OK. As a policeman you must come across some dodgy chaps. What are the actual red flags? Not the "he wears cheap shoes" kind of stuff, more like the "that one's a serial killer". Just so I know, of course.'

'I would avoid anyone with a history of stalking,' Caius began, wondering if she would class his shoes as cheap. 'That's not always going to be known to you though. OK, I would be wary of anyone who "love-bombs".'

'What's that?'

'It's when the other person showers you with over-the-top affection, attention or gifts. It's usually the first sign that they're highly manipulative.'

'So you won't be sending me flowers tomorrow then?'

'Would they be well received?'

'That depends on how the rest of the night goes.'

The two women next to them turned to face Caius. 'I am so sorry, I couldn't help but overhear,' the one next to Callie said in the broadest Essex accent. She'd come out west to take pictures for the 'gram. 'Love-bombing?'

'Yeah, big no-no,' Caius said.

'So if I go on a date with a guy and he sends me a Gucci handbag and three dozen red roses the next day you're saying he's dodgy?'

'There's a fair chance.'

'I told her I didn't like the look of him,' the second woman said to Caius. 'He sent you like twenty texts the next day and got shirty when you didn't respond straight away.'

'Trust your gut,' Caius said.

'Also,' the second woman began, 'where can I get pepper spray?'

'You see it all the time on US TV shows so it's been sort of normalised, but it's actually illegal over here.'

'You don't say.'

Callie leaned back in her seat. Their legs were pressing against each other. 'I'm hungry.'

'Me too,' Caius said, getting up quickly. 'Enjoy your night,' he said to the two women.

It was a warm evening and the bus fumes from passing 4×4s mingled with the balmy breeze that blew through Chelsea.

'What do you fancy?' Caius asked Callie. He looked around at the restaurants near them as she slid her arm into the crook of his. 'The Lebanese place is still open.'

'I fancy Morley's.'

'I've not had their chicken in so long. I can't believe there's a Morley's here though.'

'There isn't, but there's one near my flat . . . and then for afters, I fancy you.'

THURSDAY

20

The Police Station

Matt and Amy looked at each other over the tops of their computer screens. Amy mouthed at Matt. Matt mouthed back at her. They'd both noticed that Caius was wearing his chinos and brown loafers, which he would never do to the office, and Matt was sure that he was wearing the back-up shirt he kept at the station – it had a crease across the middle from where it had been folded. Amy was also positive that she'd caught a whiff of 'feminine' deodorant when she'd come in that morning. They were texting each other their theories, hoping Caius wouldn't notice that Amy picked her phone up as soon as Matt put his down.

'The date went well,' Caius said, without taking his eyes off the original interview transcript of Symington & Chase's shop foreman Harold Stephenson. 'Thank you for asking.'

'I've found Tricia, the accounts assistant,' Matt said, raising an eyebrow at Amy. 'She lives up in Nottingham now. I've got a call with her later on today. Harold the shop foreman is still alive, well into his eighties and conveniently lives in Barnet, which is helpful as we have no details for any of the machinists and he might remember at least a couple of names. Here's the biggy though. The finance director at the time was one Peter Simpson-Bamber, or just Peter Simpson as he was known then.'

'Who is he?' Amy asked; the name sounded familiar.

'The fashion mogul?' Caius asked, his ears pricking up.

'Yep. He's a backbencher now,' Matt said, putting the report down.

'We'll interview him last,' Caius said, wondering if Simpson-Bamber had much of a professional relationship with Hampton. Caius stood, picking up his phone and car keys. 'Let's start with Harold. Amy, before you try and track down the rest of the girls from Eliza's year, could you please do a quick look into Simpson-Bamber? See if he's got any form.'

'No problem,' she said to Caius, who was already halfway to the lift. She was pleased that she'd get a chance to prove her worth, again. Amy wanted to get promoted in the next year or two and that wasn't going to happen if she was being sidelined with less important cases.

★ ★ ★

Harold Stephenson lived in an immaculate 1930s semi-detached. A home for a hero. There were hanging baskets either side of the front door with fuchsias tumbling down from them. Purple ballerinas swinging in the dry breeze. The grass out front was trimmed to within an inch of its life. It was also still bright green, while all of Harold's neighbours' lawns had withered. Harold was clearly ignoring the lingering hosepipe ban that had been enforced all summer.

Caius knocked on the front door. 'Detective Inspector Caius Beauchamp. Can I speak to Mr Harold Stephenson?'

'I am him. If this is about my lawn, then Terry at number forty-three can get stuffed. I have water butts out back. I was collecting water all winter.'

'No, we're not here about your lawn. I would like to ask you some questions about Robert Symington,' Caius said. He watched Harold frown slightly at the name before recovering his composure.

'Oh, it's been quite some time since I heard any mention of that man. You'd better come in,' Harold said, making way for Caius and Matt to enter.

'Tea?' Harold asked.

'No thanks,' Caius said as he and Matt sat down on a brown velvet sofa with patches of woven flowers.

'So you've reopened the case then?' Harold asked.

'Yes,' Caius said, taking in the room. It hadn't been decorated in years. He was a man who lived in the past. It was immaculate though. Not even a speck of dust on the television screen.

'Robert Symington's father was a nice man. Big hulking giant. Lived for rugby. He was evacuated at Dunkirk, you know. Proper spirit, that man,' Harold said.

'And what about Robert?' Caius asked.

'He was, well, he was a bit of a . . . You know. He wouldn't have got the job if it weren't the family firm.'

'Was he incompetent? Prone to mismanaging other aspects of the business?' Matt asked. He wondered whether Robert had run up any debts that weren't on the company's official finances.

'You mean, did he try and nick more than the pension fund? I don't think so. He wasn't incompetent as such; he just didn't have a flair for the business, you know. Took the job out of duty to his family's history. I got the impression that he felt trapped actually. You could see that he was holding his breath a lot of the time.'

'Were you surprised that Lynne was involved?' Caius asked. There was something in Harold's demeanour, like he had an itch that scratched back, that Caius couldn't work out.

'I know men in those positions often have flings with their secretaries.' He paused for a moment and swallowed. 'She was a nice girl. Quiet. Sang in a church choir.'

141

'Are you still upset with Robert and Lynne?' Caius asked. Harold had looked like he was remembering something deep and wounding, something that had festered and yet his tone was light and breezy. Everything he had said about Lynne was short and factual.

'I was very angry for quite a while, but I don't think it helped. I never quite trusted the management – my parents were Marxists – so I squirrelled away some personal savings. It hasn't been too tough on me, but some of the girls have really suffered. Worked there for twenty, thirty years and puff. Most of the girls were in their fifties when it happened so didn't have a chance to save anything up. Puff. Gone. I was only there for three years before the theft and then the company folded straight after. The board of directors dismantled the company and sold it off piece by piece to cover the debt. I started three months before Robert did actually. His father had packed him off to do some fancy business course and once he'd finished studying the old man handed the factory over to him.'

'Have you been in contact with Lynne since?' Matt asked.

'Lynne?' Harold made a face that Caius couldn't quite place. Confusion perhaps. Caius wondered what exactly it was that was making Harold uncomfortable, perhaps he was just getting on and despite appearances was struggling to remember everything perfectly. The theft had been thirty-ish years ago, after all.

'I'm sorry to inform you that Lynne Rodgers died last week. She'd returned to the UK and had been here for some time,' Caius said.

'Oh.' He seemed taken aback by the news. 'May I ask how it happened?'

'She drowned in the Thames,' Matt said.

'Right.' Harold nodded.

'Do you keep in touch with many of your former colleagues?' Matt asked.

'Only a couple of the girls. A lot of them are dead now. Cheryl. Nice girl. Lives down the road. Pops in still for a drink at Christmas. Used to do the fiddly bits with the zips and there's Julie. She did the linings.'

'If you wouldn't mind giving my colleague their details,' Caius said.

'Of course,' Harold said, getting up and walking over to the drawers under a fish tank. 'I've got my address book around here somewhere.'

Caius watched a goldfish swim around a sunken castle. 'Did you ever meet Robert's wife?'

'Cassandra. Yes, very pretty girl. Hard to think Robert would leave her, but then you don't know what goes on inside someone else's home.' Harold held open his address book for Matt who took a picture of Cheryl's and Julie's details. 'Beautiful girl. Nice family. I think she'd been to finishing school in Switzerland. Robert used to get her to pick the final designs because she was classy.'

'What do you mean?' Caius asked.

'Well, one thing that Robert learned on his fancy business course was that he didn't need to pay a person full-time to design the coats. It used to be a very charming young man called Richard, but I called him Dickie. He had the most beautiful suits. Very talented. What Robert started doing was paying designers per design. They didn't have permanent contracts you see, and it was just the one invoice. So out went Dickie with his proper pay and his pension and matching pocket squares, and in came all these kids with mad haircuts. They were all young, just graduated from fashion school or wherever Robert found them. They didn't know how much they were worth – I heard Robert boasting to Pete about the money saved once in the canteen when they thought they couldn't be heard. I think Dickie got a nice job on Savile Row after that.'

'What did you think of Pete?' Caius asked.

'Slippery fish, that one. Oiled his hair back onto his head so he looked like Dracula. It was the eighties, but he wandered about the factory in a pinstripe suit and red braces, dropping stories about going to Ascot. He was a yuppie idiot. All pretend though; I know a barrow boy when I see one. Done all right for himself though, didn't he?'

'Yes, he has,' Caius said as he stared at the wallpaper border on the wall opposite for a moment, trying to imagine whether this transformed barrow boy was more involved in the theft than had initially been supposed. 'If Robert hadn't disappeared, what do you think would have happened to the company?'

'I know what would have happened. Robert gave us all a big speech on his first day – he was going to make the company more upmarket. Cashmere, pure wool. Like Burberry or Belstaff, you know. One of those proper British establishments. He wanted to open a shop on Regent Street rather than sell to lower-end department stores like his dad had done. The best of the best. He'd been over to Italy and Paris on trips to see how their ateliers did it. That's why no one batted an eyelid when he started talking about a research trip.'

★ ★ ★

'What did you think of Harold?' Caius said to Matt on the drive back to the station.

'Neat as a pin,' Matt said, staring out of the window as they drove through North Finchley. 'He didn't know that Lynne was dead.'

'Yeah.' Caius nodded in agreement. 'If you could try and get hold of Cheryl and Julie when we get back. That's two new potential witnesses who weren't interviewed the last time round.'

'Sure.'

Caius drifted away for a moment. 'Are roses tacky? I think they may be tacky.'

'Half a dozen red ones are probably a cliché, but what do I know? I'd just ring the closest florist to where you want to send them and ask for a bouquet to be delivered.'

'Yeah. Best not to overthink it.'

'I can literally see you overthinking it.'

21

The Police Station

Amy had assembled a dossier for Caius on Peter Simpson-Bamber and his empire. The press had fawned over him at various times in his career as a retail god so it wasn't hard to chart his career. He was a self-made man, a millionaire many times over. His time working at Symington & Chase was a mere footnote. Following the company's collapse he went it alone, opening a womenswear factory in East London where he made tights and stockings before quickly branching out into woollens and then pretty much everything else: first a shop called Fulham Girl, then a national chain. He shifted production to Asia and made even more money, before selling it to a private equity firm and going into silk scarves, which again he sold off.

Amy found a few of the silk scarves on eBay; they still sold for significant money second-hand. Rarer designs were going for a few hundred pounds. They were mostly kitschy: flowers, horses, ropes and anchors, but after reading a fashion blog she discovered there was a rare memento mori design that was surprisingly morbid that people went crazy for. It was a collector's item that rarely came up for sale any more. Peter Simpson-Bamber then created a handful of boutiques called Janey's that dealt only in luxury accessories: handbags, sunglasses, not-that-precious jewels. They only existed in upper middle-class havens: Bath, Cheltenham, Edinburgh, Oxford, Cambridge, Chelsea. He still owned these, or rather his wife Jane now did. Amy wondered whether that was a hobby for her. Something to keep her busy. Or was it a tax dodge?

Amy had also found that along the way Simpson-Bamber had amassed an impressive property portfolio, buying a mixture of commercial and residential buildings. Amy looked at his property company – it was called West London Estate Holdings, not the most imaginative name – and again his wife was listed as the sole director. Then she pulled him up on the UK Parliament website and checked the Register of Interests tab but neither of these businesses were listed. Simpson-Bamber must have given legal and financial control solely to his wife. That felt dodgy to Amy. He clearly didn't want close scrutiny. She looked at his page on the UK Parliament website again. He only sat on one committee: the Joint Land Reform and Usage Subcommittee.

'Caius, what do you think of this committee?' Amy said. Caius and Matt had just returned from interviewing Harold. Matt sat down at his desk and called the numbers for Julie and Cheryl.

'Why the hell is a man like Simpson-Bamber interested in a committee like that?' Caius asked, pulling up his chair and sitting next to Amy at her computer.

'He owns property, but it's all in West London,' Amy said.

'Simpson-Bamber does have a rural constituency, but still it's not remotely within his interests. You'd expect him to be on committees about business development and international trade. It's where his expertise is.' Caius took over and clicked onto the details of the subcommittee. 'It's a legislative scrutiny committee so it focuses on introducing a potential bill. Ah, Hampton is on it too.'

'Has he got us to poke around Symington & Chase in the hope that we find something incriminating? Something he can use to remove a rival on a random parliamentary subcommittee?'

'That feels extremely petty,' Caius said. He couldn't help but feel there was more at stake here. 'What else have you found out?'

Amy explained what her 'dossier' consisted of. 'I've colour-coded it.'

'That's why they pay you the big bucks,' Caius said, reading over her research. 'Excellent highlighter work as always, Amy, and look at these tabs.'

'I do my very best.'

'And what about his family situation?'

'Appears to be happily married to Jane. They've been married since 1990. One daughter called Harriet born in 1990. The dates don't quite add up, if you catch my drift. Harriet's socials are all private. I found a couple of pictures of her and her fiancé in the posh people at parties section of magazines. She's a fan of a certain Calliope Foster's hats beeteedubs. She wears one to Ascot every year. They're very chic.' Amy knew that Fi would murder to get her hands on one of Callie's hats; they were a mixture of whimsy and classic Englishness. She hoped that Caius didn't bodge it, so she'd get a discount on Fi's birthday present.

'Really?' Caius said. He assumed that Callie must have lots of clients, she seemed successful. She had her own business cards. They'd been on one date and he didn't want to scare her off by cross-examining her about a random client. Besides, if he took that approach with every case he'd be on the phone to Calvin Klein every other week asking if he knew so-and-so who wore pants designed by him. He was sure Callie wouldn't know all of her clients personally.

'Harriet designs wallpaper for a very fancy interior design company,' Amy continued. She was surprised that Caius wasn't more interested in that little titbit. 'Her profile is on their website.' Amy changed tabs and showed him. 'They don't list the price of their wallpaper per roll.'

'Toto, we're not in B&Q any more.' Caius took a sip from his water bottle. It had a compartment for adding fruit so as to infuse the water. He'd chucked some frozen berries in that morning. It looked bloody. Amy and Matt were both concerned he was going to buy them these for Christmas.

'There was an engagement announcement in *The Times* for Harriet and Inigo Chetwynd. He sounds rather la-di-da. I found Inigo's LinkedIn. He's some sort of finance strategy genius. He doesn't really do socials much either, but I did find a couple of corporate blog posts he wrote for his company on investing in the BRIC economies.'

'That sounds riveting. What about Mrs Simpson-Bamber?'

'Jane writes blogs about styling on their boutique's website. Nothing out of the ordinary is jumping out at me about her. She did write a very interesting blog about scarf rings and now I'm going to buy one for Fi's Christmas stocking.'

Caius didn't know what a scarf ring was, but he nodded along anyway. 'Did you know who Simpson-Bamber was before you started researching him?'

'Nope. You?'

'Yes, he made a huge gaffe a couple of years ago. He used the word "coloured" on *Question Time* when asked about immigration. Got torn apart in the press for a few days and he's not been in the public eye much since then. He does occasionally make some fairly intense speeches in the Commons about "the profligate and work-shy" that are popular with a certain type. I can't quite get a grip on him: he's hugely inappropriate and puts his foot in it but we're also supposed to think he's a shrewd operator. That isn't the same guy. What do you think, Peter or Jane?'

'What do you mean?'

'One of them is the brains behind it all and the other is there for show. Their continuing business interests are in her name, aren't they?' Caius leaned back in his chair.

'Yes, I wasn't sure if it was a tax thing maybe?'

'There was a girl on my course at uni actually – did she work for him? I feel like I saw her share something at the time of the gaffe. She was a proper politics nerd, but she told a good joke too. Abigail. God, what was her surname? Begins with a B.'

'Do you mean Abigail Bootle?' Amy asked.

'Yes!' Caius straightened and opened up Facebook and saw that they were still friends.

'She has a politics podcast that's really popular. Fi listens to it all the time.'

'Ah, man. She was nice as well.'

'Everyone's at it now. My nan is thinking of doing one.'

'You know, what I don't get about people like Peter Simpson-Bamber is that if I were as rich as he is I wouldn't bother going into politics. I would just be on holiday all year. Read books, eat good food, take up a niche hobby.'

'I'd love to make pots,' Amy said.

'I can picture you with your own kiln. I think I'd enjoy woodwork.'

'Do you want me to take an even closer look at Jane and Harriet Simpson-Bamber? I can do a proper deep dive,' Amy said expectantly.

'No, it's all right. Matt can do that. You can go back to looking into the girls from St Ursula's.'

'Sure,' Amy said. She tried to think of the picture of Eliza that was in the papers when she disappeared rather than her own ambition.

Matt put his phone down. 'I've got hold of Cheryl and Julie. They're both coming in later today and I've got a call with Tricia from accounts in fifteen minutes.'

'Great,' Caius said, leaning back in his chair. 'Elevenses?'

'What have you got for me?' Matt asked, rising in his seat.

Caius opened his drawer, pulled out a packet of lavender shortbread and chucked it at Matt. 'I stopped off at a Waitrose this morning and saw these.' He wasn't going to tell them it was the one by Callie's place, and he'd only stopped there so he could buy a toothbrush. He turned to Amy, offered her an orange and said, 'When you develop odd obsessions with weird biscuit flavours, I'll indulge you every now and then too.'

'I like this milliner,' Matt said. It sounded more wistful than he had meant it to.

'Anyone fancy watching videos of this old duffer with me?' Caius said, searching for Simpson-Bamber on YouTube.

Video title: 'MP says what we're all thinking about benefits cuts (2015)'

Peter Simpson-Bamber:
What my honourable friend here fails to mention, yet again, is the significant number of benefits claimants who just don't want to work. And I say to that, make them. Make them work. This country did not get where it is by being work-shy. We were not the workshop of the world because of our bone idleness. We were the workshop of the world because we got out of bed in the mornings, put on a tie and went to work. And we would work. We would work hard.

'Yikes,' said Matt as he opened the packet of lavender shortbread.

'What did that even mean?' Amy asked.

'Very little,' Caius said.

The next clip began to play.

Video title: 'Peter Simpson-Bamber (Fulham Girl) denies indirectly causing fourteen deaths (2007)'

Interviewer:
Fulham Girl was the main client of the Bangladeshi factory where fourteen women perished in a fire last week.

Peter Simpson-Bamber:
Yes, what a terrible, unavoidable tragedy.

Interviewer:
Unavoidable? The factories work on such small margins.

Peter Simpson-Bamber:
[Interjecting] Yes, well, that's the way it's done.

Interviewer:
They can't afford to pay their workers properly, let alone maintain their premises. This tragedy is the direct result of your company's cost-cutting policies.

```
Peter Simpson-Bamber:
Don't be ridiculous, you stupid girl. Business is
business. Just that, nothing moral about it.
```

'Is he that much of a heartless bastard?' Caius asked. He was pretty sure that everything was moral, nothing was ethically neutral and even if some things were neutral, then business would definitely not be.

'Or just dim?' Matt asked.

'I think he's both,' Amy said.

```
Video title: 'Fast Fashion. Environmental degrada-
tion? (2014)'
```

```
Interviewer:
Mr Simpson-Bamber, you've been credited with
creating fast fashion as we know it. Can you
describe how you revolutionised the high street?
```

```
Peter Simpson-Bamber:
It was quite simple really. I removed the season.
In the past you could walk into a shop, see a coat
and it would still be there in two months' time.
What I did was to sell fewer items of an individual
design but have more designs overall. Every time
you walk into one of my shops it's different. You
have to buy it when you see it.
```

'This one sounds business savvy,' Caius said. He thought this interview sounded coached. It was too polished compared to his other efforts.

'Give him time,' Amy said.

Interviewer:
This change has been credited with a huge increase in the size of the average wardrobe. Is this a good thing?

Peter Simpson-Bamber:
Of course it is. Consumers want choice, right?

Interviewer:
What about the charges of environmental waste that this causes?

Peter Simpson-Bamber:
Bollocks!

[Peter Simpson-Bamber storms off - the words 'set-up' can be heard off screen.]

[Cut to footage of polluted rivers.]

Interviewer:
Most fast fashion is poor quality and can't be worn for long - often made from plastics AKA fossil fuels. Charity shops are inundated with cheap, gimmicky party dresses that no one wants.

'And there we go,' Matt said, taking a bite of another biscuit. The next video autoplayed.

Video title: 'Peter Simpson-Bamber on what's wrong with modern women (2010)'

Interviewer:
What's changed in the fashion business since you started carving out your empire?

Peter Simpson-Bamber:
Women have changed. They're just not interested in looking nice any more. We sell a lot of grungy boots. No nice stilettoes to go with pretty dresses. Yes, women have changed. They're not as attractive, are they? Do you find them attractive? I don't. We've had to expand our range of sizes because the girls just don't care to restrict themselves like they did in my day. I was in Central London this week and it's just all these fat lesbians walking about.

'That went from dodgy uncle to hate crime really fast,' Amy said.

Video title: 'Bumbling MP trips'

[Peter Simpson-Bamber gets on stage at a business symposium in the City. His gait is noticeably wobbly and his cheeks pink. He trips and lands flat on his face. The audience is uproarious.]

'And we're back full circle to embarrassing uncle,' Caius said. He was trying not to laugh. 'Who the fuck is this man?'

'Can you tell me about your time at Symington & Chase, Tricia?' Matt asked over the phone. Caius brought him a cup of tea. It was a herbal one. Matt was disappointed.

'I was an assistant in the accounts department. My cousin was a pattern cutter, she got me the job. I did well at my maths O Level, you see.'

'And what did you do on a day-to-day basis?'

'I dealt with the invoices. I reported to Pete who reported directly to Robert. I didn't go anywhere near the pension scheme.'

'Sure. Did you know about Robert's trip beforehand then? Did you see receipts for their plane tickets?'

'Yes and no. I knew Robert was going on a research trip and taking his assistant with him, but I hadn't been told where to. No one had said – in hindsight that was dodgy but at the time it was fine, you know, whatever. The secretary said she'd bought the plane tickets on Robert's company credit card, and she was going to sort the receipts out when she got back. There was no online banking then, so I took her at her word.'

'I see, and what did you think of Robert?'

'I don't believe what they said about him in the papers at the time. I just don't think he was capable. He was, well, a weak man. A bit wet.'

'In my experience, the weaker the man the worse the crime.'

'By weak, I suppose I mean he wouldn't think of doing anything like that. I don't think he was smart enough and I don't think he was desperate either.'

'How do you mean desperate?' Matt had been wondering how desperate Robert would've been. Divorces weren't that difficult to obtain, and neither was it hard to sell a company.

'Well, he had a nice life. Running the family firm, pretty young wife, nice house.'

'And a mistress?'

'Now that is what bothered me so much about the reports in the papers. He loved Cassandra. He really did. Doted on her. I remember him walking through the office on Valentine's Day with the biggest bunch of roses. He let us all go home early that day too. That would make him a romantic, wouldn't it? I refuse to believe Robert ran away to Brazil with his secretary. I can't even remember her name. She was a nondescript woman. A background person, you know.'

22

Calliope Foster Millinery

The doorbell to the showroom rang. Callie wasn't expecting anyone. She left her work – an intricate piece of embroidery to go on a bespoke beret – on the workbench and went to answer it. Max, her former fiancé, was standing on the doorstep, as was a courier holding a bunch of flowers. She opened the door, took the flowers from the bewildered courier, and told Max to fuck off. The doorbell rang again. Max hadn't fucked off.

'What do you want?' Callie asked him as she opened the door again. Her arms were outstretched across the door frame, physically blocking him from her space in case he was under any illusion that he'd be welcomed in for a cup of tea and a cosy chat.

'I . . .' he began, but then tailed off as the power of her glare knocked the bravado out of him.

'What?' Callie asked. The contempt she felt for him had begun to subside into something closer to pity, but she still didn't want anything to do with him.

'Those flowers aren't from me.'

'I know they're not.'

'Who are they from?'

'I beg your pardon. What business is it of yours?'

'Of course it's my business.'

'Why are you here?'

'I miss you. I'm sorry. I was confused. I didn't know what I wanted, but what I needed, need, is you.'

'I want you to leave and never come back.'

'No. I now know what I want, and what I want is to apologise

158

properly. I know you've blocked me on everything. You haven't responded to any of the letters I sent you, so I think you probably binned them before you even read them,' he said. Callie interrupted him before he could get any further.

'What you really want is for me to say that it didn't hurt. That it didn't hurt that you broke up with me just before our wedding, that it didn't hurt that you'd been shagging around your office, that it didn't hurt that my entire idea of my future, which was supposed to be our future, was destroyed by whatever childish fuckwittery you want to blame it on. Oh your parents weren't great, neither were mine. I never had a father. Doesn't make me an arsehole though, does it? I don't give a flying fuck what you want, but I'll tell you what I want. I want a man who gives me flowers and not chlamydia.'

Callie shut the door on him again and went back into her studio. She was too angry to pick up her needle. She had her phone grasped tight in her hand. Callie ignored Max when he rang the doorbell another dozen times. She considered calling the police. Not that she thought they'd do much about it. Max would say sorry, he'd walk away. She'd feel bad about wasting their time. She thought about ringing one particular policeman who would probably try and do something, but he was on the other side of London. In her anger Callie had forgotten all about the flowers that she had been sent. She looked at them now, the flowers she had almost screamed that she wanted, the flowers that they'd negotiated the night before. White roses so fresh they were almost green, rangy delphiniums and eucalyptus. She read the card.

Are you free on Saturday? I'd love to see you again.
Caius

Callie took out her phone to send him a message – something flirty but not too keen. He'd seen her naked, but he didn't need to know she liked him that much. Besides, Callie felt something close to vulnerable, raw, after Max's little visit. A wound that she thought had scabbed over had split open and started seeping. She didn't want it to become infected, to contaminate whatever might come with poison and pus. Callie decided to message Caius later when she was less wound up and had had a cup of tea. She quickly checked her emails as she waited for the kettle to boil and found one from Harriet.

Darling,
I've agonised over this for days. I truly have and I don't know how else to say this but the designs you did for me aren't very good. I'd go as far as to say that they were a bit shit. Can you send me better ones – by tomorrow perhaps?
Hx

The audacity of that kiss. Callie screenshotted it and sent it to Dotty and then replied to Harriet.

Darling,
Are you for real? Harriet, fuck off. I am an award-winning professional with a waiting list longer than a sheet of your overwrought wallpaper and I will not be spoken to like that any more. I've had enough of all your little digs. I don't want to associate with you. I will not be your bridesmaid. I am removing myself from all of your annoying group chats. Do not contact me.
Cx

23

The Police Station

'If you could state your name for the tape, please,' Caius said, setting the recording up and relaxing into his seat. Cheryl looked like she could be one of his mum's friends.

'Cheryl Townsend. Oh, this is very weird,' she said gleefully.

'Weird?' Caius asked. He wasn't expecting her to say that. He understood that being in a police station was odd for most civilians who thankfully had nothing to do with the police most of the time, but she was different, excited almost. 'What do you mean?'

'My psychic told me that I would find myself in a situation this year where I'd help a tall dark stranger with an unsolved mystery.'

'Right,' Caius said. It was going to be a long afternoon. 'Cheryl, you worked at Symington & Chase, is that correct?'

'Yes, I was a machinist. I used to do the zips, and the buttons. All the fiddly fastenings really.'

'I see.' Caius was relieved to get a straight answer out of her. 'Did you know Lynne Rodgers?'

'The mousy secretary? Yeah, I knew her. Wouldn't say boo to a swan. I didn't believe she could have an affair with a married man when I heard. You want to know about the stolen pensions, don't you?'

'What can you tell me about what happened?'

'He did it, you know. He really did.'

'Who?'

'Robert Symington. I know the girls all thought he was a

softie because he remembered everyone's birthday and bought them a box of Milk Tray, but I think he did it.'

'Why do you think he did it? Did you hear or see anything?'

'Yeah. I saw something.'

'What was it?'

'His aura was dark.'

Caius nodded. Auras were clearly nonsense but Cheryl's gut reaction to Robert Symington might not have been. 'Anything else?'

'A brand-new bright red Jaguar convertible.'

'A Jag?'

'Oh yes. Sometimes I stayed later than the other girls. My bit was always the second to last thing to do on a coat. Harold would stay to make sure you clocked out correctly so you'd get your overtime and little Linda – bless her, she got ran over by a car a couple of years ago – would be the very last one sewing on the labels. She was only seventeen and Harold didn't like us walking about at night on our own – he's a proper gent – so I'd clock out and sit in the canteen and read a magazine or a book or something, and once she was done Harold would drop us both off home. Anyway, it was the day before Robert Symington disappeared and I was up there reading my book with a cup of cocoa waiting for little Linda to finish up. I happened to look out of the window and I saw Robert getting into a bright red Jaguar convertible for a few minutes and then getting back out again. He looked peeved. It was parked under a streetlamp, so I saw him clearly.'

'Did you see who was in the car?'

'No, but there was something going on there. I could tell. I thought it was very odd – that's why I can remember it. Robert got in happy and left absolutely miserable. I don't know if it was his dealer, but that was a very nice car.'

'Robert was a drug user?'

'I never saw anything, but he had money. That being said, it could've been a chum of his, or even a girl. I never saw them clearly. I'd seen the Jag a couple of times actually. Usually parked a few streets over from the factory. Someone trying to be discreet, I'd say. Why else would they be meeting up like that when everyone else had gone home.'

Caius made a note to himself about the car. 'What did you think of Peter Simpson, the finance director?'

'He looked flash, but I always thought he was hardworking. I'm surprised the pension heist got past him. He was clever.'

★ ★ ★

'Thanks for coming in today, Julie,' Matt said, smiling at the pleasant-looking woman in front of him. Her perfume was quite strong though, very floral.

'Oh no, not a problem, detective.'

'Julie, what did you think of Robert Symington?'

'Slimington?'

'He was slimy?'

'Oh yeah. Never tried anything on with anyone, or at least not that I heard, but he liked to look. I don't know why, his wife was gorgeous. Nicely spoken too. I only met her once when she came to the Christmas party the year before it all went tits up, but she was lovely.'

'Were you surprised by the theft of the pension fund?'

'Yeah, it was a family firm. It's been there since the reign of Edward VII. Old Mr Symington used to say that all the time. He'd have been so mortified about what happened. Thank God he was already dead by then, or it would have finished him off.'

'Did you ever see anything suspicious?'

'Not that I can recall. It was so long ago now, but I have to say I never liked Pete.'

'Peter Simpson?'

'Yeah, he had a chip on his shoulder bigger than anything you'd serve up with battered cod. What was the phrase? "Upwardly mobile" – that was him. Didn't like you to know that he was just a lad from Hackney.'

24

Clapham

Amy had been searching for St Ursula's fourth form all afternoon. She wrote all their names on the whiteboard. Caius had already spoken to Beatrice and Annabel was on holiday until Monday. She was working her way down the list.

1. ~~Beatrice Parker-Thompson~~
2. Annabel Hartnell in Tuscany till Monday
3. Sophy Oddfellow – Clapham

She'd found an address for Sophy Oddfellow in Clapham North (almost Brixton really – it probably made this former boarder feel edgy) and had discovered that she worked in business development for a vintner's down that way.

In the wine shop a small, brown-haired woman in a striped Breton top and red lipstick stood behind a till. Amy wondered if she was unconsciously trying to dress like a stereotypical Frenchwoman, so you'd think she instinctively knew that actually a Chablis was a type of Chardonnay. She looked nervous as Amy came over.

'Are you Sophy Oddfellow?' Amy asked.

'Yes,' she said. Amy saw her take a sharp breath in.

'DC Amy Noakes. Is there somewhere we can talk in private?'

A young man with pinched cheeks and strawberry-blond hair took over from Sophy as the two women went to the stockroom to talk. He had tried to catch Sophy's attention, but she was too relieved to not be on the shop floor to notice.

'Nice place,' Amy said.

'Yeah, it's my fiancé's new business. I'm helping out while he gets set up. I don't have much of a flair for the wine trade, I'm afraid.'

Amy nodded and then got straight to it in her usual fashion. 'I'm investigating Eliza Chapel's disappearance and I understand that you were in her year at school.'

'I was,' she said, fiddling with her hair and staring at the floor. She hadn't heard anyone say Eliza's name in a very long time. She still dreamed about her though – as a floating rotting head that laughed at her. It was how she imagined what had happened to Eliza. Sophy didn't think of it as a nightmare, just a probable fact. She was surprised that anyone else was still thinking of Eliza, let alone the police. Eliza had just become a spooky foot-note to her life. 'Gosh, that was a long time ago.'

'What can you remember of the night that Eliza went missing?'

'Um, let's see. Well, Bea had a great whack from Bossy so she was in the infirmary. We were all so gutted.'

'Because of her concussion?'

'Well, it meant that she got out of the prefect Halloween ritual.'

'What's that?'

Sophy stared for a moment at a wooden wine box behind Amy's head on the shelf. 'We weren't supposed to tell anyone that it happened. No one would have believed us, well apart from Miller the games mistress who'd caught wind of it. She asked me about it once actually.'

'And what did happen?' Amy asked.

'There were a few prefects and the head girl who held a witch trial. They said it was their "duty". This had been happening there forever, but the head girl that year was especially into it. They said they were the "Daughters of Hecate". You'd have to hold your hand over a flame for twenty seconds. If you could you were a witch too and you joined the "Hecate Club".'

'What do you mean, the "Hecate Club"?'

'I don't really know. The only person from our form who had been tried left suddenly at the end of the previous year. Pretty girl. I can't remember her name. I've blanked bits of that place out. We were all so jealous because she passed. They barely chose anyone to be tried as a witch. We teased her for it. There was a bit of an incident actually because one of the other girls got so jealous. I think that's why she left the school. It was both an honour and a curse to be chosen.'

'What would happen if you failed the trial?'

'You'd get dunked in the pond as revenge for all the witches drowned. A girl in the year above got chucked in the year before. Then you were shunned. No one could talk to you. Those girls often left. It was pretty horrible. It's a closed environment so you would've been truly alone.'

'And the night that Eliza went missing was one of these trial nights?'

'It was supposed to be, but then they never showed up and we all went to bed disappointed. We all thought it was because Bea was supposed to be next, so they never bothered. They picked the prettiest girls. That's why no one ever mentioned it to the police. It was supposed to be a bit of fun, but it could have very real consequences. You know what girls are like. But at the time it felt a little more menacing than that, and now I'm wondering . . .'

'Wondering what?'

'Whether they went to the other dorm and took Eliza instead

of Bea from ours. I always wondered whether she failed the test, and something went wrong.'

'What, like a hazing that went too far?'

'Yeah. A lot of the girls were well connected. Their families could have hushed it up or something.'

Amy nodded. It wasn't beyond the realms of possibility. 'Who was in the other dorm other than Eliza?'

'Bellie was, definitely. She complained constantly that Eliza farted in her sleep.'

'Bellie as in Annabel Hartnell?'

'Yes.'

'Why do you call her Bellie?'

'Because she was as thin as a willow, and we were all so jealous.'

Amy opened her eyes wide – she was glad she wasn't a teenager any more. 'Who else? I've got a list of names I can reel off.'

'Let me think.' She twiddled her hair. 'The squat one shaped like a barrel. Mollie, that was her name. I heard she moved to LA and works in film now.'

'And the other girl?'

'Oh, that was Claudia. Masses of hair. She died a few years ago. Breast cancer. Had one of those funny genes that means it's almost certain. They didn't catch it in time.'

'Are you in touch with Mollie at all?'

'No. I do see Juno out and about though. She married very young and looks very tired all the time. They keep having girls.'

'Do you think Eliza was the sort of girl who the "Daughters of Hecate" would have chosen?' Amy had seen the class picture; Beatrice and Eliza, she hated to think this, were not in the same class looks-wise.

'Eliza? Well, no. Not pretty enough, but who knows. As much as I can remember she was a bit annoying. Used to lie through her teeth about stuff that no one cared about. She told me once that George Michael was her godfather and that he took her to London Zoo to pet tigers for her birthday. Definitely not "Daughters of Hecate" material.'

'Can you remember any of the names of the prefects, or the head girl?'

'The head girl? Oh yeah. I remember that psycho's name. It's plastered everywhere you go. I can't get on a tube without Lavinia's stupid grinning face trying to hawk some naff clothing line.'

25

Caius's flat, Tufnell Park

Caius thought he'd try and bake a loaf of bread. He found himself walking past the new artisinal bakery that had opened at the bottom of his road on his way home from work – the area was getting even fancier, something he didn't think was possible once a fintech founder who only seemed to wear grey T-shirts moved into the house at the end – and was disappointed they'd already closed for the day. He'd popped into the supermarket to buy yeast, sunflower seeds and strong bread flour and then went home, where he could knead the hell out of a lump of dough. The thoroughly pummelled dough was now rising next to a warming oven as Caius lay on the floor, trying to stretch out his hamstrings before he did his daily squats.

He had found a recording from fifteen years ago of an interview with Arthur Hampton talking about wanting to revive Saffron Walden's eponymous medieval crocus-growing culture. It sounded like a joke, but he wasn't sure. Caius didn't get the guy. He couldn't work out his personal philosophy. Was he a silly Little Englander? Or was he something else? Chronically nostalgic perhaps. Or was the rarefied aristocratic oddity act just that, an act? Was waffling on about saffron just a cover?

Hamstrings stretched, Caius sat up and checked his phone. He'd had an acknowledgement through to his email saying that Callie's flowers had been delivered, but she hadn't said anything. Caius didn't think he could've been any clearer about his intentions, so he would just let the invitation hang in the air. The oven was warm enough now and he separated the dough into two smaller balls and tried to shape them like he'd seen on the online tutorial. He set a timer and then put on a playlist of energised dance music and did his squats. Caius then picked up *Ivanhoe*, read a page describing the state of vassalage of the franklins of England and put it down again. Héloise's departure had rather unsettled his literary habits. He wondered if there was a movie version he could watch instead. If not, he'd settle for whatever version of *Robin Hood* was available. Something about Arthur Hampton made him want to hide in the imagined past. His phone buzzed; he'd had a reply to a message he'd sent on Facebook earlier.

Today, 14.23
You
Abi, I know this is out of the blue, but I have a work matter that I need your help with. My number is +4479XXX if you could call me that would be great!

Now, 19.52
Abi Louise
Caius, it's been so long! How are you doing? My work rates are available here on my website: www.abigailbootle.co.uk

You
Abi, I'm so sorry I wasn't clearer about what I do. I'm a DI in the Met. Are you free to chat tomorrow? I'm working on a case and I think you may have background info on some of the individuals involved

Abi Louise
Is there a way I can check that?

You
Of course, you can call 101. Here's my collar number:
CNXXX

Abi Louise
OK, you're legit. Sorry, there's so many creeps out there

You
Don't worry, I'm not offended. Always best to check

Abi Louise
I can meet you tomorrow morning?

You
Perfect

The timer on the oven went off. He took his loaves of bread out then sent a picture to his mother to prove that he wasn't starving, and one to Matt because they were already getting excited about this year's *GBBO*. He settled down in front of his TV, undecided over whether to play a round of FIFA or give *Ivanhoe* one last go. His phone buzzed again; he had a WhatsApp message.

Callie
20.09
Hello handsome
The flowers are beautiful. Thank you
Saturday would be lovely. I forewarn you I may be hungover though

You
20.09
I accidentally joined the National Trust last weekend so I thought I'd make the most of my membership. Fancy driving out to a house and getting lunch in a gastropub somewhere? Sound too onerous for your future hangover?

Callie
20.10
As long as you let me sleep in the car on the way there . . .

You
20.10
No problem
You can come round to mine on Saturday morning and we'll go from there

FRIDAY

26

Hackney Wick

Caius was running late. The overground line had been having signalling problems all morning, and a young woman's skirt had ripped half off as she walked up the steps to the platform, so he'd lent her the jacket he'd been carrying – the forecast had predicted a short burst of rain that morning ending the drought – to cover her modesty while she waited for her mum to pick her up. She'd cursed the cheap online 'boutique' she'd bought the flimsy thing from. Apparently, the skirt was part of the line of some reality TV star. She regretted risking it for £15. He'd left Abi a message on her phone saying he was running half an hour late, but he wasn't sure that she'd picked it up as she hadn't responded. He finished the latest episode of her podcast as he rounded the corner to the cafe and saw her at a table engrossed in a copy of *The Cutter*, the satirical political magazine, as she waited for him.

'Abi,' he said, stopping at the table. He made his apologies; she said it was fine. They kissed each other on the cheek. This was something that nineteen-year-old Caius had never dreamed would come true. He'd had a bit of a thing for Abi all the way through uni but had been far too terrified to talk to her beyond general pleasantries in seminars. 'You look exactly the same.'

'Caius, you old flatterer. I look older despite all the retinol. You, however, look very well. You've really grown into your-self.' He thought that was a compliment and he decided to take it as such. In fact, she might have even been flirting with him.

'Can I get you anything?' he asked; it was only courteous, after all.

'I'm good, thanks.'

He went into the cafe. He knew this bit of Hackney. The cafe (and co-working space, naturally) had once been a laundrette that Caius had walked past on the way to his mum's cousin's house. The new owners had tried to stay in touch with the building's utilitarian past: they'd put vintage washing powder adverts on the walls, their logo was a suds-covered bar of pink soap, and they'd suspended hundreds of clear plastic balls in a net on the ceiling as unconvincing bubbles. He ordered a cup of tea and a vegetarian roll (a small omelette made from two free-range eggs with sautéed spinach, a thick slice of Gruyère in a soft white roll baked on the premises and a generous dollop of sriracha) and then went back out to Abi.

'How've you been since uni?' Caius asked.

'All right, yeah. Doing a bit of everything at the moment. I've got a podcast now.'

'Yes, I've been listening.'

'We're really popular among a core demographic of "apathetic millennials" and "despairing gen xers",' she said as Caius nodded along. 'And I do the odd talking head and opinion piece, you know "meidja spiel". Bits of consultancy here and there. So you're a policeman now?'

'I am indeed.'

'Nice to know there are a couple of good ones out there.'

'Well . . .' Caius tailed off as a waitress brought his tea and roll over. He took a sip of his Earl Grey. It tasted too perfumed, like laundry detergent.

'I looked you up,' Abi said.

'Not a good idea.' Caius took a bite of his roll. It was delicious and he hated that. He wanted to hate the fake laundrette, but he couldn't when they made food this good.

178

'You've worked on some harrowing cases. Ever think you'd want to talk about it on a podcast?'

'I thought your podcast was about politics, not true crime.'

'All crime is political, you know that.' Abi raised her eyebrows and gave him a knowing smile. She was just as he remembered, but even more confident now than she had been in the student bar. 'What happened on the Clemmie O'Hara case? I read the coroner's report but there's clearly more there, right?'

'No comment,' Caius said, before pointedly and yet playfully taking a sip of his soapy tea.

'Fair enough. I've got to try,' Abi said. She took a sip of her coconut milk latte. 'What did you want to ask me?'

'Before I say anything, I want to clearly state that this is an active investigation and any public comments by you could pervert the course of justice.'

'Yes, yes, I know the drill.'

'OK. You worked for Peter Simpson-Bamber, didn't you?'

'Three years as his parliamentary assistant. He had me and a guy called Jim working for him. Jim's a nice bloke. He's moved on now too.'

'What did you think of Simpson-Bamber?'

'Tried to swing his balls around, but his wife had them in her handbag.'

'How do you mean?'

'Peter – and now don't get me wrong, he's right to – treats it all too seriously when everyone else is treating it like a game. Westminster is a huge chess match for hubristic public school boys. Peter's really ambitious and very blunt about it but in the wrong way. He was always after a ministerial position, but ultimately he wanted the top job. Unfortunately for him he just wasn't, isn't, good enough for that. He makes gaffes, says the wrong thing. Doesn't stop Peter from taking silly little pot shots at the real contenders every now and then though.'

'Like who?' He quickly listed off a couple of cabinet ministers that came to the top of his head before saying, 'Arthur Hampton?'

'Exactly like Arthur Hampton, who he used to blame for his never getting off the backbenches. Although Hampton's a man who doesn't want to be PM. Hampton likes things how they are. I'll tell you now, he does not get nearly as much scrutiny as he should. Don't get me wrong, I like the man. He's hard not to like. Exceedingly charming. I've never met anyone who could command a room like that. Terrifying stuff, charisma.'

And Caius knew it too. The confidence that Hampton had was practically hypnotic. 'What did you mean about Simpson-Bamber's wife's handbag?'

'He wouldn't have got anywhere near as far in politics if it wasn't for his wife. Peter is a cockney lad done good, but he just doesn't have the smoothness to mask it, or the charm to pull off a wideboy act. He's not patrician. He's not Oxbridge, not boarding school, not Sandhurst. He doesn't have the rhetoric. He uses the wrong fork and misjudges his colleagues. His wife, however, is one of those women whose tea parties were basically the Yalta Conference with dainty cucumber sandwiches and fondant fancies. If she *had* been at Yalta, Stalin wouldn't have dared annexe Poland. They were delicious. She smoothed out more than an IKEA bedding-section worth of wrinkles for him over the years with tea and cake diplomacy. Jim and I used to call her the Lady MacBaked Goods.'

'Do you know much about his career before politics?'

'Fashion retail. Basically invented trend-led fast fashion. Obscenely rich. It's funny when you meet him: you don't get the impression that he's as shrewd as he must be in business matters. But then, if he was just hammering down garment quality and labour costs in India to swell his profit margins, then his success isn't surprising.'

'Anything dodgy there?'

'Potential human rights and environmental abuse but find me a high street shop that's more ethical. I think he was at Symington & Chase when that all went tits up. But you already know that, don't you?'

'Abi,' Caius said, raising his eyebrows. 'No comment.'

Abi shrugged and smiled at him. 'He didn't like to talk about it. Jim warned me off ever mentioning it on my first day, although of course it did come up eventually. It was odd actually; I think he was rather hurt by the experience.'

'Hurt? How do you mean?'

'I don't know, but you got the sense that there was some betrayal, and he was the victim.'

'And did he ever talk about it explicitly to you? Any theories he had about what happened to Robert Symington and the money?'

'No. God no.'

Caius took another bite of his roll as they watched a couple of teenagers blasting music walk past. 'Are you aware of an agricultural committee that Simpson-Bamber and Hampton are both on?'

'I'm not. That's definitely not Peter's thing. He bought a place out in the sticks for Jane to decorate and where he plays the country squire a couple of times a year, but he's a city boy really. Send me the name of that committee and I'll have a dig.'

'Thanks.' Caius wondered if he had unwittingly given her the next episode of her podcast.

'I'll see if anyone I know has more info. There are some odd bills going through Parliament at the moment. I don't know if you've noticed?'

'There was one on changes to the inheritance of aristocratic titles recently. Who cares about that? It's not important. It'd affect like two hundred people tops. My local Boots has a hygiene bank bin where you can drop off shampoo because people can't afford to wash.'

Abi nodded and took a final sip of her coconut latte. 'It's probably just the poshos covering their backs as per. I can ask around about it though if you think it's important. You never know, I might be able to eke a think-piece out for the *Guardian* opinion page.'

27

The Police Station

'A homegrown pagan cult with a fire ritual that went wrong?' Caius asked Amy. He was sceptical but then it did actually sound plausible for an isolated girls' boarding school.

'It's the best theory I have at the moment,' Amy said, spinning around on her swivel chair, staring at a brown patch on the ceiling. The roof must leak in the winter. She'd move to a different desk by then. 'They only picked the prettiest girls to join their cult, apparently.'

'Boarding schools are weird places.'

'Yep.' She had updated the whiteboard with the information she had received from Sophy Oddfellow. 'According to Sophy, Annabel and Mollie were in Eliza's room, so I'm going to focus on them for now. I've left a message with Mollie Gilbert's assistant and I'm just waiting for Eliza's parents to call me back. They said they'd ring at 11 a.m. . . . . It's 11.30 now.'

'They're probably building up to the call,' Caius said as he dunked his tea strainer in and out of his mug and looked at the list of names on the board.

1. ~~Beatrice Parker-Thompson~~
2. Annabel Hartnell – on holiday until Monday – in EC's room
3. ~~Sophy Oddfellow~~
4. Arabella Spatterley
5. Poppy Boswell – hit Beatrice on the head the day before
6. Sophia Patel-Jones

Amy's desk phone rang. She put it on speakerphone. Caius and Amy then introduced themselves.

'I just feel so guilty,' said Mrs Chapel. The line was a little crackly, but they could hear the pain in her voice. 'Eliza told all these stories about that place, but we couldn't believe that any one of them was real. She was blessed with an incredible imagination.'

'What sort of things did she say?' Amy asked.

'Oh, you know. The usual moaning. But then they started to get more and more fanciful. We thought they were funny stories to make us laugh. The food was awful. The roof leaked. They slept in their coats in the winter. A girl got scurvy. Another girl had been pinned down and had all of her hair cut off because she was too beautiful, and the other girl was jealous. The head girl was carrying out demonic rituals, killed a local and the teachers had colluded to hide the body or something. The poor girl was obviously bored. We should've sent her to a more academic institution. We were just taken in by the prospectus. All the "soft talents" they'd bestow. My husband had an old golf buddy whose daughter had been, and he kept raving about it. He said that his daughter had all these opportunities now. I wish I'd sent her to the local comp. Better to befriend Darrens and Chantelles than suffer like that.'

'Was she scared of anyone? Staff members maybe? Other pupils?' Caius asked, as he tried to reason paying for the privilege of neglecting your child.

'The head girl. Lavinia, I think her name was. She would not stop talking about her. Petrified.'

'Right.' Caius thought it was unlikely it had much bearing on the case but people kept mentioning the head girl as well as the two girls fighting. 'And the girl who was pinned down? Do you know anything more about her?'

'Only that the girl whose hair was cut and the girl who cut her hair off both left at the end of the previous year. Eliza would not stop talking about it over the summer break.'

'I see.'

'Was there a strong culture of bullying at the school?' Amy asked.

'Apparently so.' Mrs Chapel began to cry. They did their best to console her from across the Channel without promising anything.

The call over, Caius turned to Amy. 'Do you know who the head girl was? Lavinia?'

'To my shame unfortunately, yes. She was a contestant on last year's *Love Is Deaf.*'

'Is that a reality show?'

'Yeah. The one where the contestants pair up in an isolated Ibizan villa, but no one is allowed to speak. They have to complete tasks silently to win date night privileges where they can finally talk to their love match.'

'I'm glad I don't know what that is.' Caius opened up YouTube and searched for a clip of Lavinia on the show.

Narrator:
Lavinia already has a warning for calling Chloë a 'cheap little Geordie whore' during last night's silent council.

[Cut across to footage from yesterday. Swimwear-clad and tanned young men and women sit silently around in a circle looking furtively at each other. Dan, a young man with an immaculately groomed goatee wearing a pair of tight aquamarine shorts, looks incredibly sheepish as he tries to avoid looking directly at Chloë, a young woman wearing a neon-pink bikini. Cut across to Lavinia who is wearing a fluorescent-green bikini.]

'They're all so attractive and yet absolutely terrifying,' Caius said. He'd never seen this many people with hyper-white veneers. 'These people are all just teeth.'

'People can watch what they want, but I personally consider this brain rot,' Amy said, shaking her head.

Lavinia:
You cheap little Geordie whore.

[Lavinia storms off and Dan goes after her.]

Narrator:
Tonight the group decide whether love really is deaf, whether Lavinia's behaviour has gotten her eliminated from the chalet and whether Chloë really is a 'cheap little Geordie whore'.

[Sponsored by Miss Applied – see the look, live the look, be the look.]

Caius paused the clip of St Ursula's former head girl practising the school's so-called 'soft talents' of grace and decorum. 'I wondered who she was. She looked famous but also not famous, and I had no idea why I kept seeing her face everywhere. There have been adverts for her Miss Applied mini skirt and bralette combos all over the tube for the last couple of months and I couldn't work out what was going on there.' He only knew what a bralette was because it was written in bright pink on the ads. Caius got the brand's website up on screen to see if they had a bio of Lavinia – which they did, but it didn't say much at all – and had a quick look through the corporate governance section too. 'Jane Simpson-Bamber has a minor but significant stake in Miss Applied. She sits on the advisory board. Are these cases linked?'

'That's one hell of a coincidence,' Amy said.

'It would be, but the Simpson-Bambers are rich and presumably very well connected in the fashion industry, so I'd expect them to have interests here and there. Especially as he made his money in fashion.'

Amy nodded. 'Is Jane acting as Peter's representative or is she the real brains behind the outfit, so to speak?'

'That's the question that is bugging me about them, Amy.' Caius had been wondering this too. If Jane was the brains, then it would explain why he'd gone into politics and not on holiday. Peter Simpson-Bamber needed to prove himself.

Amy had more questions, and many more concerns about the ethics of their escalating investigation. 'Peter Simpson-Bamber looks like a bit of a twat who has got in over his head but is there more going on there? I mean with Hampton.'

'Almost definitely, but at the moment I haven't got a clue what. Hampton is out to get him though, that's clear enough.' Caius blew air from his cheeks and closed his eyes. 'It makes strategic sense to speak to him last, he's the most "powerful player" on the board and we want to speak to those on the periphery to get a better idea of the context of the case, but I don't want to interview him. I'm worried that we're being set up.'

'How do you mean?'

'Hampton became aware of Lynne Rodgers's death before we'd even identified her. I think he's using her murder as an excuse to get us to poke around the past of a rival. The embarrassment caused by Symington & Chase being brought up again could be too much for Simpson-Bamber's reputation maybe? Or it undermines him in some way perhaps? Removes him as a contender for a leadership bid? Or stops him from getting a promotion? What if we find something else out, something personal, and that gets used as leverage?'

'Like what?'

'Well, Simpson-Bamber's previous ownership – and his wife's continued involvement which may very well be the same thing – of all these fashion brands, for a start. There's no way they can sell a dress for £2 and it be ethical. The cost of the fabric, transportation, the labour involved – someone somewhere is being taken advantage of.'

'All that stuff is pretty common knowledge. I don't think people care,' Amy said, rubbing the sleeve of her shirt as she tried to remember where she'd bought it from and how evil they were.

'There's something odd going on. Hampton getting us to take the case from Richmond in the first place is calculated. He knows about the summer – he told me so himself – and if he knows that then he knows we've been silenced once before and that he can do it again. That we'll just melt away and not see the investigation through.'

'And his little dinner with you. What was that about?'

'Hello, chaps, and welcome to the literal establishment. We used to be served too many lamb chops with our port. I bought the clothes you're sitting here in because you're too low born to understand what is required of a gentleman. What did he think I'd do, waltz in there, jump on the table and start singing "Knees Up Mother Brown"? I don't get it. I don't get why he invited me there and made small talk about gardens.'

'What are you going to do with the clothes?' Amy asked. She knew he liked looking good and he wouldn't want to part with the shoes, but they also seemed grubby.

'For the moment I'm going to keep them, I doubt this is the last we'll see of Arthur Hampton,' Caius said, sitting back in his chair. He felt like he'd been bought. For all his jokes about bribery, he found himself in a position that he didn't think he'd ever be in. Compromised by a beautifully tailored dinner jacket. He intended to request an itemised bill for the things Hampton had sent once this investigation was over and pay for them himself, but for now he needed to focus on solving Lynne's case – the consequences of which were the only way he'd be able to make sense of it all – and he needed to play along and play the game, at least for now. 'Track down Lavinia and see if there's anything to the whole witch trial thing. It could just be bored, isolated girls stuck in a leaky school, neglected by the staff, letting their imaginations get the better of them.'

'I'm pretty sure that's why they weren't interviewed in depth the first time round.'

'Fair point.'

28

The Police Station

Caius's personal mobile phone rang. The number was unknown to him. It was probably a scam, but he answered it anyway.

'Caius, how are we getting on?' asked Hampton.

'Oh, um, hello,' Caius said. He didn't think he'd given Hampton his number.

'Sorry, no time for pleasantries today.'

Caius was alarmed to realise he was disappointed by that. 'We've tracked down a few of the machinists from the factory who all have contradictory opinions, but nothing concrete yet.'

'I see.'

'It takes time. Especially when a case has been cold since the 1980s.'

'Yes, yes. I've had someone on my end have a look into the circumstances of Symington's wife. She had him declared legally dead, remarried and changed her name. Have you got a pen?'

'Sure,' Caius said, reaching for one of his beloved Muji fineliners that Matt and Amy were banned from using.

'She goes by Cassandra Hunstanton now. H-U-N-S-T-A-N-T-O-N. Call me as soon as you have anything "concrete". An apt phrase for a builder's son.'

'OK.' Caius felt like he'd been put back in his place, again – a place devoid of formal evening attire but rich in glottal stops.

Hampton hung up. Caius wondered why, if Hampton had the resources and the desire to investigate Cassandra Symington – let alone get hold of his bloody personal number from God knows where – then why did he bother involving him and his team in the first place. He took a deep breath and watched a pigeon walk along the window ledge before googling Cassandra Hunstanton as she was now called. She was a wildlife artist living on the Norfolk coast who specialised in depicting birds. He looked at her portfolio online. Her chunky monochrome woodblock prints were charming, the sort of thing you'd buy for an active aunt who enjoyed the odd hike up a coastal path. He rang the number on her website.

'Hello. May I please speak to Cassandra Hunstanton?'

'Speaking.'

'Hi, my name is Detective Inspector Caius Beauchamp from the Metropolitan Police. May I ask you a few questions?'

She hung up.

'Hello, can I please speak to—' he began again.

'No thank you. No scammers. Take me off whatever database I'm on.'

'Madam, I am genuine. Please call 101 to verify that or alternatively please call the station.' Caius gave her the switchboard number. 'I'm looking into the Symington & Chase case.'

Five minutes later she rang him back.

'I'm so sorry. I get so many dodgy calls these days. The odd journalist or some pod-person asking rather personal questions,' she said. Cassandra sounded brittle. Not just her accent, which was cut glass, but there was something detached and disdainful but also stiff, bored or even mocking. Caius thought that if she were in front of him, she would've been rolling her eyes and lolling about.

'It's quite all right. I understand. You can't be too careful. Mrs Hunstanton, may I please ask you some questions about your former husband Robert Symington?'

'If you must,' Cassandra said, dragging out the 'must' with all her breath.

'When was the last time you saw or spoke to Robert?'

'The day he disappeared. He woke up rather early even for him. He was usually up at the crack of dawn, but he said he needed to pop into the office before going on his trip. I had no idea that anything was wrong.'

'No idea whatsoever?'

'I had the smallest inkling that there may have been a flirtation or something at work with some woman. He'd make sure to dress up a little more on some days. You know, wear a nicer tie, an extra spritz of cologne. But I wasn't certain. It could quite easily have been all in my head, but then they said they thought he was having an affair with his secretary of all people.'

'What do you mean?'

'Well, it's a cliché, isn't it? So terribly boring. Besides, she wasn't much of a looker. She was a nice girl, from what I saw at the Christmas party the year before, but rather timid. Not his usual type. Robert was one of those men who needed to be bossed about. He had to make too many decisions at work, so he liked strong women. The girl before me was a dreadnought in human form.'

'I see. Were you bothered by the idea of an affair?' Caius wondered if the breeziness in her voice was just distance, or was it an actual lack of feeling.

'No, I don't know that I was. Probably because I thought ultimately that he wouldn't dare do it – a little flirting here and there is one thing but leaving me for some other woman is completely different.'

'Did Robert have a drug problem?'

'No. He liked a drink a little too much, but that's not the same thing. He wasn't an alcoholic either, before you ask. Just fond of a tipple.'

'What did you think of Peter Simpson-Bamber?'

'He was just a plain old Simpson then. Peter is a good sort, deep down, if a bit of a snob. Double-barrelling a name like that is so affected. I'm sure that was his wife's idea.'

'Are you still in touch?'

'Oh no.' Caius heard a tension creep into Cassandra's voice but then she seemed to quash it with drollness. He almost heard her eyeballs roll over the telephone. 'I've bumped into him over the years at the big social events, you know. Glyndebourne, Cowes, Chelsea Flower Show and so on. I can't resist going to Chelsea every year on the last day to buy plants cheap.' She paused for a moment. 'Have you had another sighting of Robert? Every few years a tourist in Rio de Janeiro claims to have seen him on a beach.'

'No, no. Have you had any contact with Lynne?'

'She's never called me. I imagine she'd be too embarrassed. I did get a weird letter in the post that claimed to be from her just recently. Is that why you're calling? Is there someone out there sending iffy letters?'

'I regret to inform you that Lynne has died.'

'Ah, right.'

'What did the letter say?'

'It was an odd mix of begging for money and outlandish claims that Robert never made it to Brazil. I can't remember now. I only skimmed it. It was quite upsetting. My husband did something with it.'

'If you've still got it, could you bring it in? You can drop it off at your local station and tell them to contact me.'

'I'll ask Bill what he did with it. I think he binned it though.'

'Thank you for checking.'

'You know, I always thought . . . oh I don't know.' She paused for a moment before recovering herself. 'I've always thought that Robert didn't have it in him to just leave like that. He'd have left a note or something. I think he's probably dead. Couldn't live with the shame of what he'd done and killed himself. That makes sense, doesn't it? He'd have called from Brazil to tell me it was over; I think he would have done me that courtesy at least, but perhaps he never got there.'

Caius didn't doubt the validity of the idea but he did doubt that Robert Symington had been known for his courtesy. 'Thank you for your time, Mrs Hunstanton.'

Caius got up from his chair and walked around the room for a few moments as he took in what she had said.

'Was she helpful?' Amy asked.

'Yes, I think we've missed an angle here. We went with the assumptions from the first case, that even though there was no proof Robert Symington caught that flight to Brazil that he got there another way. That he drove to Portugal and caught a boat over or something, but what if he did take a drastic way out? And if he is dead, then where's the body? And what bearing would any of that have on Lynne's murder? Lynne ran out of money and came home, so she obviously didn't have the pension pot. What happened to all that money? Why did he steal the pension pot in the first place? He owned a functioning business. If he wanted money, he could've just sold it.'

'There could be a lot of shame in selling the family firm?'

'More than stealing from your workers?'

'No, that's worse.'

Caius stared at Amy. He still had the Miss Applied website open. 'Where have you got with Lavinia?'

'According to her Instagram stories she's living it up in Sardinia until tonight.'

'Let's get a hold of her tomorrow then.'

29

Holland Park

Jim had waited for Callie at a nearby pub before Arthur Hampton's dinner party. They'd had a quick gin and tonic to take the edge off. They both felt oddly nervous. Callie showed Jim the email from Harriet, and her reply as they finished up their drinks.

Jim patted her on the shoulder as they left the pub. 'It's probably a good thing you've set "boundaries" with Harriet even if the boundary is made of barbed wire and patrolled by rabid Alsatians.'

'Do you know who else is going to be there tonight?' Callie asked, changing the subject. She was beginning to regret having worded the email so strongly. You couldn't go back from that.

'No, sorry. It could be Westminster bods, but it could be anyone. Hampton's known to enjoy collecting "interesting people" and for chucking oddball bohemians at mothball-riddled aristos.' Jim quickly checked the time on his watch and stood up, anxious that they arrive at the sweet spot between on time and fashionably late that showed he was serious but not too much of a keeno. 'It's probably a good idea to steer clear of politics talk altogether, Cal, and definitely not to mention the Simpson-Bambers.'

'Why?' Callie asked, not that she cared to mention her ex-friend's family in polite company.

'Peter is in the doghouse, again. He thinks he has a duty to kick hornets' nests. I wouldn't be surprised if Hampton asks you a few questions about him on the sly though. To see if he can get a little inside gossip,' Jim said, stopping abruptly as Google Maps told him he had reached his destination.

'He's a funny old fish, Peter,' Callie said, leaning against one of Hampton's neighbours' garden walls to change out of her flats and into a pair of satin, blushing-pink heels. She was wearing a long chartreuse skirt made from handwoven Irish linen from an acquaintance's slow fashion line and a crisp white shirt. 'I always get the feeling he wants to be my friend or something. It's odd. Nothing creepy, of course, nothing inappropriate. He was really concerned when Max and I hit the rocks. He rang me up and everything and then met me for a coffee. He said it was a rent review but it clearly wasn't.'

'Peter can be quite decent really,' Jim said, double-checking his emails to be sure that he had in fact got the right house number. 'He's not a bad guy. I just don't think he's cut out for politics. He should go back to selling mini skirts. Yeah, it's definitely this one.'

They looked up at a large white stuccoed town house set back from the road with a small garden out front. They were deep into hedge fund and oligarch territory, although this house had been inherited and not purchased, but like their neighbours, Hampton and his husband had installed a gate with cameras. Jim rang the bell, and they were buzzed in.

'I'm rather nervous,' Jim said, looking Callie in the eye. 'These are the big boys.'

'Jimmy, you too are a big boy now,' Callie said, patting him reassuringly on the arm. 'You're wearing your big boy pants.'

★   ★   ★

'I really don't want to be stuck next to some idiot with bad breath and a snaggletooth all evening. Can you not put me on the end and next to Tabs?' asked the tall, broad-shouldered perfect form of a rakish Englishman. Sir Rupert Beauchamp, who had recently been voted England's most eligible bachelor in a poll for *Tatler*, was sulking as he leaned against the door frame to Hampton's study. The dinner guests had all started arriving, but Hampton needed to dash a couple of emails out.

'No, this girl is very pretty. Her name is Calliope and she's a milliner.'

'Millinery used to be a front for prostitution during the Georgian era, you know.'

'Yes, we all read *Fanny Hill* at school. Look, nothing needs to happen, you're not getting engaged to the girl, but you do need to get back out there. You're getting older. You need to settle down. Have a family. If anything, she's not a suitable match, but Callie will just be a nice diversion. A pretty, clever young woman you can chat to civilly for a couple of hours. That is all. You need to learn to build rapport with women, treat them as equals.'

'I don't want her. I want—' Rupert was cut off before he could continue his longings.

'We've been through this.' Hampton sighed. He turned away from his laptop and looked at Rupert. 'Even your psychiatrist thought it was a good idea. I ran it by him the other week.'

'Well, if that is the case then I may as well leave now.' Rupert's eyes narrowed. It pissed him off that Dr Beddowes had had a little chat with Uncle Arthur.

'Rupert, stop being so childish.'

'What's her name again?'

'Calliope Foster.'

Rupert took his phone out from his pocket and found her website. He scrolled through her photos. 'She's not bad-looking actually.'

'I told you; I have excellent taste in women. It's just wasted on me now.'

197

The alarm system buzzed, letting him know that more guests had arrived, and Hampton let Jim and Callie in through the gate.

'Now go down there and be affable, and don't drink too much. You've just got off coke, we don't need you switching to booze.'

Rupert rolled his eyes. He couldn't wait for his month in rehab to be an amusing anecdote rather than a stick to beat him with. Not that Arthur and Jeremy usually beat him with anything more than the lightest of comedic touches; they had always been almost kind towards him as his late mother's oldest friends. It had been rather a shit year for Rupert though. And yes, that might sort of possibly partially have been down to his own slightly careless actions in the loosest way, but still – they were the closest thing to family he had and all he really wanted was unconditional compassion.

★ ★ ★

A gregarious man wearing a wonderfully tailored pair of dark green trousers and subtle Gucci loafers showed Callie and Jim in. He was holding a bottle of champagne in one hand and two empty flutes in the other.

'Hello, you must be Jim and Callie. I'm Jeremy, Arthur's husband. Lovely to meet you both. No shop talk, Jim, all right? Have a drink.' He gave them each a flute and poured them a generous glug of Pol Roger. They exchanged clunky contemporary English how-do-you-dos and assorted pleasantries about the weather, and Callie handed him a box of chocolates that she had hurriedly picked up that afternoon from the tiny, bejewelled Prestat shop in an arcade between Piccadilly and Jermyn Street. She knew full well that 'don't bring anything' actually meant 'do bring something tasteful'. 'Oh Prestat, my favourite. You can come again,' he said to Callie, winking at her.

Hampton appeared. 'Jim, nice to see you,' he said, shaking his hand. 'Apparently, we're not allowed to talk shop this evening, so I've run out of conversation already.'

'Me too. I practically live under my desk,' Jim said, nervously taking a sip of his champagne.

'Well, rents in this city have got rather mad. You must be saving a lot of money that way,' Jeremy said. He ushered all of them through to a cosy and yet spacious sitting room cluttered with inherited Victoriana and solid wooden furniture. Velvet and William Morris. Pastoral scenes of the English countryside in gold frames. There was a piano by the window with silver photo frames of family members and what Callie assumed were godchildren on top. Jeremy turned and introduced Jim to an older couple stood near the piano. She couldn't help but notice that lingering by the marble fireplace with an empty glass was an extremely handsome man. He was staring directly at her. Callie met his gaze, only briefly, and tried to remember where she had seen him before. He was the sort of man that ten years ago, maybe even five, she would've been desperate for. But in her post-Max era, she was slightly sceptical, even if he did exude so much physical charm that her heart skipped that silly proverbial beat. By the time Callie looked up again he was ignoring a blonde girl who was talking rather animatedly. She got the impression that she just needed to talk and didn't care whether anyone was actually listening. Callie thought that was sad. No one must have listened to her as a child. Callie did, however, recognise her from a previous frantic google ahead of Penny de la Croix's recent consultation as her recently engaged daughter Tabitha.

'Rupert, Tabitha, this is Calliope. Calliope, these are Jeremy's dreadful godchildren. Calliope is a milliner,' Hampton said, appearing at her elbow before Jeremy called him into the kitchen to help him strain the gravy.

'You're not *the* Calliope Foster, are you?' Tabitha asked.

'Guilty.'

'My god, Mummy is obsessed with you. You're her new favourite creature.'

'I'm making her hat for your wedding actually.'

'Sorry, darling, it's been called off.' Tabitha started to tear up, but she marched herself out of the room before causing a scene.

'I'm so sorry, I didn't know,' Callie called after her. Her next thought was why had she not been told that the hat was no longer needed.

Rupert wasn't strictly laughing at Tabitha, but his eyes had crinkled up half in ennui and half in a knowing mocking of general female hysteria. 'I wouldn't worry, that's the third time she's cried since she got here, and that was only forty-five minutes ago. We could probably start keeping time by her mania.'

'I take it the relationship ended badly?' Callie couldn't understand why he found the situation amusing.

'Yes. She found out he'd been visiting a dominatrix twice a week who spanked him and called him "a rotten little toad" for outrageous sums.'

'Oh.' Callie could see why that might be troubling.

'Tabs is upset that he kept it a secret. She would've been happy to have done it herself rather than send him out of the house for such specialities.' Rupert looked at her. He was confused by her confusion – it was very clear-cut to him. 'If you knew them both like I do then I can assure you, you'd find it funny. They'll be back together by the end of the week and having exhibitionist sex in every public toilet you can find west of Hyde Park Corner.'

'I should probably go and apologise.'

'If you feel you must.'

Callie followed the sound of gentle sobbing upstairs to a bathroom. She knocked on the door. 'Tabitha, it's Callie. I'm so sorry. I didn't know. Are you all right?'

'I'm sorry. I've made you feel most unwelcome.' Tabitha swung the door to the bathroom open and let her in before closing the door behind her. 'It's just a little raw and I've had a glass of champagne and it all just keeps bubbling out.'

'It's a really shitty thing to go through.' Callie smiled at her. When she'd found out that Max had been cheating on her with practically every woman he'd come across, she'd ugly cried on the tube and had been comforted by a very sweet group of American tourists who gave her a lovely pep talk. They were sorority sisters on their summer break. 'I was supposed to get married last summer but my fiancé Max shagged his way around his office. I only found out because one of his colleagues took me aside at his work's summer party and told me that was why so many people there couldn't look me in the eye.'

'Oh my god, what a howling shitbag.'

'Oh yeah.' Max was, still is, a howling shitbag, Callie said to herself. 'It gets easier. That pit at the bottom of your stomach closes and then you'll go on a date with someone else and they may not be the one, but you'll enjoy it and you'll keep going on dates. I have every faith that you'll find someone who'll make you even forget that your howling shitbag ever existed.'

'Oh, you are lovely, aren't you?' Tabitha glanced up at Callie and fell just a tiny bit in love with her.

'Not really. My first thought was that I'd just put the order in for the silk for your mum's hat with my French supplier and they can be real gits about changes to orders.'

'She'll wear it to something else. She's been coveting you for a while. She used a fake name to try and get an appointment because she thought you wouldn't want to work with someone so fusty and old-school, and it didn't work.' Tabitha took out a concealer from her bag and touched up her undereye make-up, and then gave herself a slick of lipstick. 'My dear fucking half-brother Casper is quite the favoured child this week. Don't worry. He'll mess it up soon and I shall be back on top.'

'Did he get back with his ex-girlfriend in the end?'

'Oh, shush. Mummy and her mouth. We don't talk about her. Rupert has a thing for Nell too. Best to pretend she's dead. That's what I do. I had brunch with a corpse last week.'

'I actually went to the theatre last week and the guy next to me had a stroke, died, and then an actor threw up on him. It was dreadful.' Caius flashed through her mind – she suppressed the thought, not wanting to associate him with the smell of sick.

'Oh my god! How awful.'

There was a knock at the door. Callie opened it. It was Rupert.

'Grub's up, girlies,' he said, holding the door open for them. Tabitha marched out of the bathroom and trotted down the stairs to the dining room and Callie followed her out of the bathroom. Rupert, who was still holding the door open, watched her as she went.

'I didn't make a good first impression, did I?' Rupert asked, following her down the stairs.

'Not the worst.' Callie had met men like him before, more than met a few times. He was all charm and no trousers. Rupert would treat her like the centre of the world while he was next to her, regaling her with stories of nights out gone wrong or the odd bit of gossip from the inevitable people they knew in common – London was small after all if you came from a particular background – but then nothing. They'd leave the party and disappear into the night only to weakly smile at each other across the bar at some old school friend's wedding reception in three years' time. She reminded herself to lie back and think of Jim's career.

'Are you going to tell me off for my "lack of empathy"?' Rupert asked, with a roguish glint in his eye. He relished a good verbal skirmish with a pretty woman.

'Would it make a difference?' Callie countered. God, he had very blue eyes that were full of mischief.

'Of course not.' Rupert smiled.

'I shan't bother haranguing you then if there is nothing to be gained from it. I'd much rather talk about something else.' Callie stopped in front of the door to the dining room and waited for Rupert to open that door for her too. He did. She couldn't fault his manners in that sense – he'd clearly been raised in a particular gentlemanly way. She was unsurprised that they had been placed next to each other. She had Jim on one side – he was also next to Tabitha – and Rupert on the other. Rupert held Callie's chair out for her as she sat down.

'Touché,' he said.

'We don't stand on ceremony here,' Jeremy said, before waving his arms around at the piles of food on the table.

Rupert leaned into Callie and almost whispered, 'Pass the potatoes.' His leg pressed against hers as he reached over to take them from her.

'That's not a sexy thing to say,' she said, before passing them to him anyway. Oh dear, now she was flirting back. She helped herself to lemony garlic roast chicken, a small potato or two, some of the sautéed green beans and the leafy salad.

Callie could hear Tabitha asking Jim how long they had

been together and Jim batting it away with an 'oh no, we're just old friends' and a small sigh. 'I used to work for her best friend's father.'

Callie could also feel that Rupert was paying attention to that conversation too. She thought the others around the table were a mixture of politicos (you could tell because they wore the most inoffensive colours) and a couple of arty types wearing bold spectacles and chunky perspex jewellery. Gallerists or antique dealers. They were talking about the National Theatre that, Tate Britain this. Oh! Serota, dear Nick! What a darling he is!

Remembering that she was a guest after all and it was important to be well behaved for the sake of Jim's career, Callie turned to Rupert who was delighted that she wasn't ignoring him any more, although he tried to hide it. 'What do you do?' she asked, finally looking at him. That was a safe subject. Rupert could stare at her all he liked with those beautiful eyes, but she was determined to stay resolute in her ultimate rejection of him.

'I suppose I'm a restaurateur, although I'm thinking of packing it in. It was fun for a while, but I'm bored by it now.'

'And what are you "packing it in" for?' Callie was surprised he was involved in anything so corporeal as food.

'I write, and I mean to do so seriously.'

Callie thought Rupert looked earnest in this and was surprised he had an artistic bone when she had assumed that he probably worked in finance. This was a relief to her, and she relaxed. The evening wouldn't drag too much, she was on familiar ground now and he wasn't terrible to look at. Most of her acquaintances were creatives with probable Coutts accounts.

'I've got a meeting on Monday with an agent about my novel,' Rupert continued. 'But we shall have to see how it goes. I somehow managed to lose a chunk of it so I had to rewrite the ending. This new one is much better though. Much more painful.'

'What's it about?'

'It's a sweeping family saga, I suppose. Tonally, somewhere between *The Edwardians*, *The Forsyte Saga* and *Cakes and Ale*, and yet devastating. There's reluctance and obsession. Grief and desire. Sex and misery. You look like you read?'

'Not nearly enough.' Callie couldn't remember the last time she met a man who seemed enthusiastic about reading, but then she remembered that she had and that she quite liked him. She stared down at her plate and felt guilty. It wasn't that Caius was forgettable, quite far from it, but Rupert had some sort of preternatural appeal. 'I'm not fussy though. I'll just about read anything.'

'Good.'

'What do you mean, "good"?' Callie asked, taking a sip of wine.

'Well, if you said "no I don't read" then you are a lost cause, and the evening will drag. If you said "I only read bodice rippers, or things with vampires" then likewise. "Not fussy" means that you'll give anything a try once. Someone who says they don't read "nearly enough" knows the value of a good book but has a busy life. You have your own business and a woman like you undoubtedly has plenty of her own friends.'

'Right.'

'What I mean to say, is that you have balance.'

'Has anyone ever told you that you overthink things?'

'I hear that all the time, but I've yet to find either a way or a woman to stop me from doing so.'

'No woman can solve that for you.'

'Could one not?'

'No, definitely not.' Callie took a sip from her wine, still feeling guilty that she had momentarily forgotten about poor sweet Caius who she had such hopes for.

'You are wicked, Calliope Foster. Positively wicked.' Rupert poured himself a glass of wine and shot Uncle Arthur a look down the other end of the table. 'For the record, I think "pass the potatoes" is one of the sexiest phrases in the English language.'

★　★　★

Dinner was over. Pudding, a delicious passion fruit and mango meringue, had been practically licked from the bowls. More booze was consumed. The volume of the room got louder and louder. Jim's cheeks were flushed in a way that could only be caused by claret and Callie had drunk more than she had meant to. She had given up the lingering traces of sarcastic resistance to Rupert and was now treating him with pure sincerity which she could tell he enjoyed.

'Did you always want to be a milliner?' Rupert asked.

'No, I sort of fell into it. I was good at art and textiles so I studied fashion. My mother was desperate for me to study something else, anything else, but that only made me more determined. Then I got to design school and I just didn't like working on clothes so much. I ended up doing a module in millinery and then stuck at it.' She could see him lapping up the details of her life and for a moment she worried that she'd be caricatured in whatever he wrote next. 'Did you always want to be a writer?'

'Yes. It's in my blood. Byron was my great-grandfather, however many times over.'

'Ah, that's what that is.'

'I was scared to write for a while. Well, no, I wrote but I couldn't quite bring myself to share it with the world. It was too private.'

'Why?'

'I was in love with someone, but too much had happened and hadn't happened at the same time. It all came to a head recently. No one was spared.'

'That sounds awful.'

'It was, for all of us. I'm in therapy.'

'Good for you.' Callie smiled at him as Tabitha got up from the table and gestured for Callie to follow her, joking about 'girls weeing together et cetera, et cetera'. Tabitha went up the stairs and into the bathroom again, beckoning Callie to come in too.

'Don't shag him,' Tabitha said, grabbing Callie by the hand. 'I know he's charming and that face, but you're far too lovely. He'll only fuck you up.'

★　★　★

Jim kissed her on each cheek, called her 'darling' many times over and fell into the back of a black cab that might or might not take him the long way round. Rupert offered to walk Callie to the overground station, but she politely declined. He tried to insist, saying that there were all sorts wandering around at night, but she insisted even more firmly that she was fine. Callie knew that if he walked her to the station then he would somehow end up back at hers even though that wasn't where she was intending to sleep that night. His air of privilege was familiar, but this time she felt like his privilege unduly included her.

'Why do I feel like you want to eat me whole like the big bad wolf?' she asked Rupert, who had capitulated to just escorting her to the door.

'I don't know what you mean, Little Red Riding Hood.'

'Why do you look so familiar?'

'Well . . .' he began.

She tilted her head at him. 'Burberry?'

'Yes, I modelled for their most recent campaign. I'm never doing it again.'

'*Brava!*' Callie used that bit of pilfered Italian to power herself to the tube alone. She left Rupert leaning against a stone pillar on Arthur Hampton's porch, watching her wiggle away in a pair of shoes that had clearly got the better of her. He lingered as she leaned against a lamppost to slip into more comfortable shoes. It was a shame; he'd enjoyed watching her struggle.

★ ★ ★

'I like her very much,' Rupert said as he leaned back against the armchair he was lolling about on.

'I told you you would,' Hampton said. He poured them both a glass of port. Rupert's was smaller.

'No, don't. I want her.' Tabitha was sprawled across the sofa.

'Tabitha, darling, remember when we had the talk about there being multiple sexualities?' Jeremy said, peering over his glasses at his favourite goddaughter.

'What do you mean?' she asked.

'Well, do you think you'd like to just hang out with her or hang out and kiss her?' Jeremy asked.

'Is there much of a difference?' Her phone pinged. Joly had left her another voice note that she played to the room.

'Daaarling, it's me. I miss you. You can spank me and call me a "rotten little toad" if you really want to . . .' Joly sounded drunk.

'What Uncle Jeremy is trying to say is: do you want to spend your life with that "rotten little toad", and I say that as one of his best friends, or do you want to kiss girls with soft lips and better hygiene instead?' Rupert asked. He took out his phone and watched a video of Callie talking about vintage German hat blocks.

'I'm not sure,' Tabitha said, floundering for an explanation of how she felt.

'Well, perhaps you should take the time to explore now that you're unattached,' Hampton said, smiling at her. 'A person's sexuality can change over time, you know.'

'What did you mean before about Callie not being quite suitable, Uncle Arthur?' Rupert asked.

'Her mother's family are fine. Grandfather was a banker. Good Yorkshire farming stock. Catholics, but who cares about that these days. Her father, on the other hand. We shan't go there.'

'How do you mean?'

'A bit rogue, shall we say, but I shan't go into it. I didn't know when I met her; she has her mother's maiden name. I'm glad you had a fun evening. From my end of the table you seemed to be having a lovely conversation.'

'We like rogues,' Tabitha said, scrolling through her Instagram and following Callie. 'Don't we?'

'No, we just like Rupert, for some unfathomable reason,' Hampton said.

30

Kentish Town West Station

'Hello, spur of the moment thing happening here. I might have had a few. Where do you live again? I just got off at Hampstead Heath overground. I hope you're not already busy, because you're about to be. Byeeee.' Callie had let the wine get the better of her and had gone to Caius's on a whim. Or rather closeish to where he lived – she wasn't exactly sure, but she knew he lived close to the Heath because he'd said he liked to run around there.

★   ★   ★

'I'm sorry, I didn't even check to see if you had plans before barrelling in. I just got on the overground,' Callie said from the front seat of Caius's car, a slightly battered Volvo that he affectionately referred to as Sven. The wine buzz had dissipated, and she was a little embarrassed of herself, but she tried to fill her words with an undercurrent of sexual tension. She'd waited outside the overground for ten minutes, hoping he'd call while also checking the route back to hers just in case. She had been just about ready to turn around, tail between her legs, when he called and said he'd come and get her. She could feel a sheepishness creeping up on her. Normally she'd try to pretend to be chill for at least a month after meeting someone, but it had been a year since she'd experienced anything close to intimacy. She'd missed it. Max turning up had pulled that need into focus.

'It's all right,' Caius said, stopping at a red light. He gave her a quick smile. 'I was just doing a face mask when you left that charming voicemail.'

'Were you really?' Callie asked, giggling a bit. She had definitely drunk more than she had intended to.

'No, although I keep thinking I should get a proper skincare routine going.' The lights changed. 'How was your dinner party?'

'Oh, it was all right. My friend Jim was the one invited really, and I went to even up the numbers.'

'Was it fun?'

'Good food, excellent wine.'

'Sounds like a perfect evening.'

They skirted the outside of the Heath, then Tufnell Park before turning up Dartmouth Park Hill and into Caius's road. He pulled over and parked his car.

'Swish area,' Callie said, getting out.

'I'm only a police officer. Don't get excited. I'm not paid much,' he said, holding the garden gate open for her and then the front door. 'My Irish grandfather bought the house years and years ago when it only cost whatever was in your pocket at the time. They'd let you have a mortgage for a shilling and a button. My neighbours must have had to promise Satan the soul of their firstborn to afford theirs. My mum inherited it and then Dad converted it into flats. I'm supposed to be saving up to buy my own place while I live here.'

'And are you?'

'Not really.' Caius pulled a face. 'Ish . . .'

'Give me the grand tour then,' Callie said, throwing herself down on the sofa and taking off her trainers. Her toes were still sore from the heels she'd been wearing.

'Well, there's not much to see. This is the kitchen/diner/

general living space. We walked past the bathroom on the way in and the bedroom is just over there. Do you want a cup of tea?'

'Just water.'

'Anything to soak up the wine? Toast?'

'Um.'

'Would it sway you if I told you that I baked the bread myself?'

'Did you make your own butter?'

'No, that's made by Mr Lurpak.'

'Get you, buying premium brand butter. That's why you can't afford to buy your own place.'

They ate toast on the sofa. Callie then had a shower and nabbed one of Caius's T-shirts to sleep in. Then they sat up talking about silly things, and trivial things, and existential things, the ones that have a propensity to blindside you on a random day.

SATURDAY

31

The Police Station

Matt was eating a slice of Caius's bread at his desk as he finished a call with Tricia from accounts' cousin, the pattern cutter. She hadn't said anything new. Caius had left half a loaf for him yesterday when he was on his day off. Matt had been in a rush that morning and didn't have time to have breakfast at home. He was trying to think of a way to tell Caius that the crumb wasn't quite right, although it was more than edible, while also trawling through Fulham Girl's old financial reports. Caius had asked him to find out as much as he could about where the original seed money had come from for Simpson-Bamber's first business after the collapse of Symington & Chase, but he was having no luck finding anything out of the ordinary in their accounts. Matt then found an interview with Simpson-Bamber in the *Financial Times* from over a decade ago, when he had just sold Fulham Girl to a private equity firm.

'The inspiration for Fulham Girl came from my wife. Jane is a meticulously dressed woman. She always likes to make sure that she's well put together. Elegant but also original, with a real eye for colour, pattern and texture, and I think there were a great many women who aspired to dress like that, still do, in fact. Fulham Girl is as British an institution as afternoon tea and a day at the races. It has a slight cheekiness to it, a sense of whimsy, but ultimately it knows its heritage and is quite straightforward.' Simpson-Bamber then goes on to say that in many ways without his wife Jane, Fulham Girl might not have existed at all as her father gave him a loan to open their first store in Fulham Broadway. 'Without that support we wouldn't have been able to launch a rubber duck in the bath, let alone a ground-breaking multi-million-pound business.' Jane now designs scarves for Simpson-Bamber's latest venture Forthwright, which he describes as more of a hobby for a restless businessman than anything else.

Matt started searching for more information on Jane Simpson-Bamber but hadn't found much beyond numerous glowing interviews in fashion ('the eternally divine Jane Simpson-Bamber was the best-dressed woman at last month's Breast Cancer Boob Ball at The Connaught') and house design magazines ('Jane Simpson-Bamber has sympathetically ren-ovated her Palladian wreck into one of the most beautiful houses in Leicestershire'). He assumed that her name before marriage was just plain old Jane Bamber, but he wasn't finding any records for her. Eventually he found an interview with Jane talking about her boutiques.

'I wanted to do something a little different this time. With Janey's I have collected all of my favourite pieces and put them in one easy place. Purposeful curation is so important. All of the pieces are beautiful but also usable and useful. And I also wanted the shops themselves to be an experience. I want you to enjoy being there. I even had a specific scent commissioned for the boutiques – it's very green: geranium root, pear and freesias – because I want you to know exactly where you are.' Jane then professed her love for perfume, claiming to have a reputation amongst her friends as a bit of a connoisseur. 'I'm trying to convince Peter to go into fragrance, but he just loves Westminster so much.'

32

A nail salon in Earl's Court

Amy had gone to Lavinia's apartment building early that morning. It was a large plate-glass modern block with sad little balconies overlooking the tube line in Earl's Court, but she wasn't there. The building manager had said he'd seen her leave an hour earlier wearing her gym kit. He seemed to have enjoyed that. Amy, who had been a sixer in the Brownies and had her orienteering badge, found Lavinia on Instagram and saw that she'd posted a picture of herself doing squats with her trainer half an hour ago. She'd tagged the location in her post; it wasn't too far so Amy set off for the gym on foot. She was going to use Lavinia's Instagram stories to a map of her location.

The gym was an underground lair of fitness freaks next to a Nando's. Amy assumed that was so they could come out after a session and eat a whole chicken. She presented her warrant card at the reception desk to be told that Lavinia had left ten minutes ago. Amy checked Lavinia's Instagram again and she'd since posted a picture of herself getting a green goddess protein smoothie from a juice bar further down the high street. Lavinia was gone by the time Amy got there. The cashier said she'd been talking very loudly about getting her nails done on the phone to someone. Lavinia hadn't taken a photo of which salon she was going to, so Amy checked Google Maps for the closest ones, popping her head in, waving her badge and asking if Lavinia was there. She finally hit lucky on nail salon number four. Amy felt like she deserved a badge. Lavinia was obliging, although the manicurist had only started on one hand. The staff were all nervous of Amy being there. She wondered whether it was because they feared she was immigration, and if the Vietnamese women working there were trafficked. Although it could have been Amy's general demeanour – she just wasn't into this sort of preening.

'Is there anywhere private we can talk?' Amy asked.

'You can use the waxing room, it's free for another thirty minutes,' said the beautician in charge.

'Great, thank you,' Amy said.

They left the main salon and went into a side room that smelled pleasantly synthetic. Lavinia popped herself on top of the salon bed, annoyed that she had precisely one nail painted. This was going to throw off her schedule for the whole day. 'What's it about this time?'

'This time?'

'Possession or whatever.'

'Um, no. My team are reviewing cold cases. I'm here to ask you a few questions about Eliza Chapel.'

'Oh God, not all this again. I didn't sleep properly for two years.'

'Why did you not sleep properly?'

'I was terrified there was an axe murderer around every corner. Full-on paranoia, panic attacks, PTSD, the total works. I had to go to a lot of therapy. Daddy was not pleased – not the family way, apparently.'

'I'm sorry to hear it was so difficult for you. It's understandable that you found it traumatising. Do you mind if I ask you about it?' Amy was treading carefully – Lavinia was what her dad would call 'highly strung'. Amy hated that phrase. She thought it really just meant distressed. Yes, Amy could see that behind the attitude Lavinia was distressed.

'It's fine.' Lavinia swallowed.

'I understand that you were head girl at the time?'

'I was. I had a special tie and a pin shaped like a shield that said: "Head Girl".'

'Would you mind telling me what happened that night?'

'Sure, but I don't know how useful I'll be. I didn't know anything was amiss until the next morning when there was all that commotion. My dorm was on the floor above so none of us heard or saw a thing.'

'Did you notice anything unusual earlier that night? What about earlier that day?'

'I don't think so.'

'Was there anyone hanging around the school that shouldn't have been?'

'Oh no, that place was a fortress. The OG St Ursula was supposed to have had a retinue of a thousand virgins, you know, and that was definitely us.'

Amy nodded. 'What can you remember about Eliza?'

'Not much. I don't think she was especially memorable, other than she used to tell great thwacking lies to me and the prefects. Funny ones too. Always had us in stitches afterwards. Not that you could let on to her face. We didn't want to give her ideas.'

'I see. Someone we've spoken to mentioned something about a ritual that you were involved in?'

'Oh that, the "Daughters of Hecate". That was just a bit of fun that year's head girl did every Halloween. It had gone on every year for yonks, and the rumours got more and more ridiculous as each year passed.'

'What was it exactly?'

'Well, the prettiest girl in each form was chosen to "perform the ritual". Really all we did was go down to the kitchen, make everyone cocoa and tell them to make up a lie about what happened. There was a girl the year before who started telling the others the truth, so the previous head girl chucked her into the pond. It was a ridiculous little game.'

'And that year?'

'Let me think.' Lavinia stared down at her black workout trainers for a moment. 'The girl who we chose from Eliza's form had left the school the year before. We were going to pick another girl in her place, but she was away or something. So we decided not to pick anyone from that form. The headmistress kept that school on lockdown, especially at night. She knew about our little witchy game, but she allowed it for morale reasons. To be honest, I think the old bat was a sadist and she thought that anything that might scare the girls into behaving was a good thing.'

'Right.'

'Look, this girl Eliza – she made stuff up for attention. Right? It was a spooky night. She probably got out of bed to wander around the corridors looking for a ghost and something bad happened to her.'

'How could "something bad" happen to a girl in the grounds of a school that you've just described as a fortress?'

'I mean, between the more feral girls and some of the staff, then yes, it's possible something went wrong and then was covered up.' Lavinia started giggling nervously, but Amy could see terror begin to creep across her features.

'That's the crux of it, isn't it – how can something so bad happen to a child somewhere that they're supposed to be incredibly safe?'

'I don't know.' Lavinia stared at Amy, her eyes widening as her mind seemed to drift. 'You know, deep down I've never believed the idea that Eliza wandered off or had a boyfriend in town. My therapist said that's why I used to hyperventilate until I was twenty-two. I was petrified of bloody axe murderers lurking round corners.' Lavinia leaned back onto the salon bed; the chemical floral smell of hot wax floating through the air smelled comfortingly familiar to her. She thought about the alarm system in her flat and whether it was good enough. Whether someone could just waltz into her building and hide in her wardrobe and wait for her to come back home.

'Thanks, Lavinia.' Amy paused for a moment and wondered how best to say what had been bothering her about Lavinia all morning. 'If I could give you a piece of advice as a police officer.'

'Sure?' Lavinia sat up and looked at Amy and wondered whether Amy wanted advice in return about her eyebrows, but said nothing.

'I would only post pictures detailing your daily routine once you're long gone from that place and nothing that you do religiously at the same time and location every week. I basically tracked you down using your stories. Most of the stuff you post that isn't an ad is in one small neighbourhood. It's not the best idea to broadcast your every movement in real time to however many followers you have.'

'Oh.' Lavinia nodded. That made sense. Lavinia lay back down on the bed, and couldn't decide whether to call her therapist first or get a new security system fitted. She started doing her breathing exercises and naming the things around her.

'Are you going to be all right?' Amy asked.

'Yeah, I'm fine. I'm always fine.'

33

Crawley Bottom House

'I'm too hungover for this much gilt,' Callie said, reacting badly to the house's blinding golden plasterwork. There was a lot of it, and it was a sunny day. Plus she was still miffed that a volunteer had taken away her coffee cup on entry to this part of the house. She'd stolen another one of Caius's T-shirts and was wearing it with the skirt she'd been wearing last night and her comfy trainers. She didn't have any sunglasses though and that was awful. She took a sniff of Caius's T-shirt because it smelled like him and it made something inside her flip.

'Three more rooms, and then you can take your coffee back from the mean man,' Caius said, looking at a painting on the wall of a nicely chubby woman holding a bundle of wheat. He'd caught Callie sniffing the T-shirt he'd lent her out of the corner of his eye and now he was worried that it hadn't actually been clean. She didn't pull an 'ick' face; he hoped it was OK. He opened up his guidebook that as a member of the National Trust he received for free: 'The art in the house reflects the source of income of the landowning Bertran family who had held these lands since the Norman conquest.' It then had another paragraph on how they had enclosed Crawley Common. The Bertrans eventually ran out of men and the last Bertran, a homely-looking woman – they had just walked past her portrait – had married a merchant who had worked for the East India Company. Her descendants were fabulously rich before the last of them bought it at the Somme and the dynasty finally ended.

'I should take some pictures. I feel like I'm in a bit of a creative rut at the moment,' Callie said, staring at the wheat-wielding goddess in front of them.

'How do you mean?'

'Well, I suppose I'm bored.'

'We need to find you a new muse.'

'Yes, but I am a muse myself. I should be enough,' Callie said, taking out her phone and going to photograph a picture of some classical woman with a boob out and a big urn under her arm when a volunteer came up to her.

'No photography,' she said, pointing to a cardboard sign sat on a marble-topped armoire adorned by naked little cupids.

'Terribly sorry,' Callie said.

'Come on, let's get you some postcards from the gift shop,' Caius said, taking Callie's hand and leading her out of the room and away from the still tutting volunteer. They glanced quickly at the remaining couple of rooms as they walked through them, then went to the gift shop where Caius realised that the postcards were £1.50 each whereas a book on Gainsborough was £12, so he bought Callie that instead. He hoped it was a romantic gesture. Once Callie was reunited with her coffee, they exited the house and another volunteer shooed them away from the gardens.

'I'm afraid the gardens are closed for a wedding,' said the volunteer. This one seemed apologetic at least. 'We're a very popular venue.'

They set off back towards the large village the house was on the outskirts of, and more importantly the pub on the high street.

'My mother, who is rather grand for her station in life, thinks that getting married in the grounds of a country house that the family does not own is in "exceedingly poor taste".'

'Really? Well, what are us normies supposed to do?' Caius realised once the words had left his mouth that actually his parents did technically own a chateau even if half the roof was coming off and it was only worth £300K.

'Stick to church halls and hotels where they belong,' Callie said as she took a deep swig from her now cold coffee. She needed the caffeine. 'My ex-best friend is getting married next year. She was getting a bit excessive with the planning and was being far ruder about it all than I could bear. Our friendship reached its natural conclusion.'

'Does that make you sad? Sounds like something you might need to grieve over the loss of.'

'Grieve? I suppose I should,' Callie said, wondering whether to go into much detail about what had happened with Harriet or whether it would be boring to him. It bored her, after all.

'Friends can be so important, can't they? Close ones are the family we choose, and when that changes it can be devastating.'

'Gosh you sound wise.' Callie knew he was right, but she didn't want to dwell on it. Not yet. It felt too raw. 'This village is so sweet. When I grow up, I want to live somewhere like this.'

'You look pretty grown up to me,' Caius said, taking Callie's hand in his. They stopped in front of the village green. Although the grass was dead and yellow, and the rain promised for yesterday hadn't appeared. They looked up at the solid, boxy Norman church behind it. There was a row of workers' cottages made of red brick and charm then a post office, a bakery and a greengrocer along one side of the triangular green and on the other, larger cottages and a Victorian house with a 'For Sale' sign. He couldn't imagine a place more like England. That was until the cricket began. The scene was a vernacular living history, the old ways persevering. The village green. He was overwhelmed by a nostalgia he didn't think he was capable of feeling. They walked over to the parish noticeboard. There was a sign on top saying it was maintained by the Village Green Preservation Society. Callie leaned her head on his chest as they surveyed it. There were posters for the choral society's coming performance of Handel's *Messiah*, film night at the church hall, wassailing. 'What's wassailing?'

'You sing to the apple trees so you have a good harvest.'

'They're going to need more than song if this weather keeps up.' Caius raised his eyebrow. 'You said that like it was a totally normal thing to do.'

'What? What? Is it that weird? I grew up in the country, that doesn't sound weird to me. The nearest village has an annual contest where they lift sheep and whoever lifts the heaviest sheep above their head is known as King Ram for the following year,' Callie said, before turning back to a notice about the village's history. She gave Caius a coquettish look and he put his arm around her shoulder. 'Apparently, the woods on the edge of the village are supposed to be sacred to the fairies. Lots of funny sightings over the years and the graveyard is supposed to be haunted by a white lady.'

'That explains the ghouls who work at the house.' Caius furrowed his brow at all this childish whimsy. He wasn't one for ghost stories, but then in his line of work he came across real monsters every day. 'It does feel a little magical round here,' he said, acquiescing to her supernatural explanation for the village's allure.

They held hands as they carried on their way, turning down the side of the green with the house for sale. The village's war memorial came into view and they stopped to look at it, Caius skimming the names of the 'glorious dead' underneath 'Lest We Forget'.

'"I, too, saw God through mud".'

'What's that?' Callie asked.

'A poem I read once.'

They turned down the road to the pub. The Moon Under the Water was a wooden-framed structure and Caius had to dodge low-flying beams to get to the bar.

'May I please have the all-day breakfast and a large glass of orange juice,' Callie said.

'Are you an overgrown hobbit? This is your second breakfast of the day.'

Callie checked her wrist for a watch that wasn't there. 'It's already 1 p.m. so I've missed elevenses and lunch, so I've got a lot of catching up to do.'

'I'll have the roast beef, please,' Caius said, handing the menu back to the barman.

'And to drink?' asked the barman.

'Tap water's fine,' he said, but then he saw the barman raise an eyebrow – things were hard enough for pubs these days. 'Actually, I'll have a lemonade.'

'Sure,' the surly barman said. 'I'll bring it over.'

'Thanks, we'll be out back,' Caius said as they went out into the walled garden. They sat down at a wooden table with a Pimm's parasol and watched bees buzz around the flowers. The roses and lavender that the bees laboured over were struggling like the grass on the green had been.

Callie's phone, which she had put on the table, vibrated. She picked it up to check who it was and then put it down again. 'This guy I was next to at dinner last night added me on Instagram and keeps messaging me. It's weird, he has like no photos on there and doesn't use his real name; it's definitely him though.'

'I see,' Caius said. He tried not to be funny about it. It wasn't like they were a 'couple couple', even if they had done the deed. But then he worried that he'd come across as too nonchalant.

'I don't mean . . .' Callie began. 'I mean, I don't like him. He's just pretty persistent. I've not responded to any of his messages, and he's sent like five already today.'

'Well, if you're not interested you can tell him that. Most people will be fine about it and then disappear back into the ether.'

'But what if he's not fine about it?' Rupert had been charming, very charming. She could see how easy it would be to fall under his spell and she could also see that that charm came from a certain type of intensity that if it was turned onto you could burn you up. He was a man who'd persevere. The firmest 'no' would never deter him.

'Is that why you came over last night? Because you were worried about him?'

'No. I was just horny.'

'Well, just tell him it was a pleasant evening and you enjoyed chatting to him, but you've met someone, and they've completed extensive firearms training.'

'Have you?' Callie said, typing a firm but polite response.

'I'm only joking. I'm not going to go round and threaten anyone – but yeah. I never use it though, and it was nowhere near as fun as the advanced driving course.'

'He's the type to think what I just sent him is a challenge and not a gentle let-down, but I'm sure he'll get the hint when I ignore him.' The barman came over with their drinks. 'I can't believe how much that wine affected me. I'm no longer twenty-two.'

'I know, I feel old too. I'm thirty-four and I feel like I'm a sprightly ninety-four.'

'This is such a delightful little village. Only forty minutes into King's Cross on the train,' Callie said as their drinks arrived. 'I keep fantasising about moving to the countryside and dyeing my own wool with flowers and herbs I foraged, but then I realise that makes me sound too much like my mother and so I hunker down into my little flat for another winter of London smog.'

'Do you really not get on?' Caius had assumed that her description of her mother on their first date had been hyperbolic.

'No, God no. There's whatever went down with my biological dad which she subconsciously holds me accountable for. Plus, she has this stupid hang-up about my weight. I'm not built to be a size eight but she just cannot help herself. It's not a healthy relationship. She's one of those women who'll survive on a handful of almonds a day. Whereas I'm clearly made to be able to plough a field.'

'All the best women can work the land. But in all serious-ness, you're unbelievably beautiful.' Caius took a sip of his drink as his compliment floated in the air between them and they both blushed.

'Thank you. You're not hideous yourself.' They peered through their eyelashes at each other.

'That's a really difficult dynamic to have grown up with.' Before he could ask her any more questions their food came out. Callie became too engrossed in her bacon and sausage to spill her guts and Caius was distracted by a Yorkshire pudding as big as his head.

★ ★ ★

Caius picked up a navy-blue jumper and searched it for holes. They'd stopped at a charity shop on their way back to Caius's car.

He already had a copy of *A Connecticut Yankee in King Arthur's Court* under his arm. It sounded silly and he liked the cover. He'd never read any Twain so why not start there?

'Oh no, that looks synthetic,' Callie said, feeling the sleeve and then finding the label. 'Yeah, that's acrylic.'

'Is that bad?' Caius knew he was supposed to be avoiding plastics, but he'd never considered that even clothing counted. He supposed that everything was made of polyester these days.

'Well, every time you wash it, it will release microfibres.' Her attention wandered over to the bric-a-brac section. A 1960s coffee pot with matching cups caught her eye, but she didn't have room for it in her flat. She was going to buy it anyway.

'Oh, I see,' Caius said, overwhelmed by another thing to think about when considering his appearance. He was already concerned with cut and colour but now here came a whole other layer of guilt-based environmental complexity.

'The best thing you can do is wear the clothes you have until they fall apart or sell them on. And when you buy new stuff buy it second-hand,' she said, picking up a hideous teapot shaped like a wonky thatched cottage. She loved it. She'd keep her sketching pencils in it.

'I see.'

'Sorry. I'm being preachy. With what I do I consider myself to be "slow fashion", you know. I actually buy all my stuff second-hand pretty much unless it's from a mate's company. I've got a few friends who have small ateliers that make three types of dress and do bespoke measurements. Heaven forbid I have to get my sewing machine out. You can get real second-hand bargains online.'

'Show me how this witchcraft works.'

★ ★ ★

'I was going to make a roasted vegetable and green lentil lasagne, but now I'm bidding on Dunhill ties on eBay instead,' Caius said from his sofa.

'Oh, but that sounds yummy.'

Caius didn't look up at her. 'You're making a little wounded animal face, aren't you?'

'Yes, I'm a puppy with a broken leg and the only thing that will help is lasagne.'

'I could just order a lasagne from the Italian down the road, and . . .'

'Sex and pasta. Perfect Saturday. And tomorrow we're not getting out of bed.'

MONDAY

34

The Police Station

'*Buongiorno*, what did you think of my bread?' Caius asked Matt as he sat down at his desk after a delightful weekend off. Caius had brewed them both a cup of green tea as he left Cassandra Hunstanton a voicemail asking whether she'd found the letter from Lynne. He then tried to discreetly restock his drawer with a clean shirt from home in case he stayed for another impromptu sleepover at Callie's, but he knew that Matt had seen.

'*Buenos días*. The crumb was a little tight, but I won't turn down the next loaf you bake, buddy,' Matt said, turning his computer on.

'Yeah. I think I was taking something out on the dough.'

'You don't say? Oh come on, tell me. How was your date on Saturday?'

'Me and Callie went around a country house and had lunch in a pub.'

'Yes, you live your best grandpa life, old man.'

'Nice weekend? How is the sprog situation?'

'Currently writing a pros and cons list.'

'I have no advice to give, I'm afraid, other than if you don't want them, don't have them.'

'Sage, that,' Matt said, going to take a sip of tea but stopping as it was too hot. 'Where's Amy this fine morning?'

'She's at the dentist's, back in later. This morning we are going to finally speak to Peter Simpson-Bamber. Thanks for the notes, by the way.'

'No problem. We should speak to his wife after as well.'

'That's a good idea. Actually, you tackle her, and I'll interview him at the same time. That way if there's anything to collude over, they can't.' Caius leaned back in his chair and watched a crow fly past the window.

'What's bugging you?' Matt asked.

'I'm just thinking over a theory that maybe Simpson-Bamber was in cahoots with Symington to steal the pension fund, but double-crossed and then killed him to cover it up, finally using the funds to start up his first business. Lynne Rodgers would've been the last loose thread. Robert doesn't turn up at the airport, Lynne knows something has happened and goes to Brazil because she's scared. Simpson-Bamber thinks she's out of the way, but then she is extradited back. She keeps quiet for a bit but then things get worse. She's living in desperate circum-stances. You should have smelled the damp, Matt. It was like a cave in there. It was horrendous. People shouldn't be living like that. Proper Dickensian shit. A person in those conditions might try and blackmail the multi-millionaire who she knows got his start by theft and murder. She sends a letter. Cassandra Hunstanton said she may have received one from her recently, so Lynne might have been contacting people related to the crime. Simpson-Bamber meets up with her for a discreet stroll down the Thames. She has a couple of drinks as Dutch courage, but she lets her guard down and he pushes her in the river while they're walking along it, discussing her terms.'

'It's plausible, but that jogger said they'd seen her on her own on the towpath?'

'True, but we're not certain of the exact time or location that she went into the Thames. We've narrowed it down but there's no CCTV and no witnesses to the act itself.'

'There's something else bugging you?' Matt asked. He could tell that Caius's mind was working harder than it usually had to.

'I've got a side theory. The second interview you found with Jane Simpson-Bamber was telling. She talked about the boutique as purely hers.'

'Yeah, but they've put her name on it, to be fair. Is it just a hobby though?'

'I don't think so. She gave the clear impression that this was not her first business.' Caius found the interview again and read a line out loud. '"I wanted to do something a little different this time" and then she says she wants to open a perfumery but her husband isn't interested. Why the disconnect?'

'So you're saying, what?'

'Jane is the brains. She's the one on the Miss Applied advisory board. I thought she might be a puppet for Peter, but I think she's the puppeteer. We've seen the videos of Peter acting like a total prat. The whole Fulham Girl thing – he gave her credit twice for that, twice. Her dad gave him the money and then he claims she was the 'inspiration' for the brand. Jane is the one coming up with the ideas, but he spouts them and becomes the face of it all. The eighties were still rough for women.'

'What bearing would any of that have though?'

'Simpson-Bamber's reputation is based on him being a very successful businessman but if it gets out that he just takes credit for his wife's achievements, then game over for his political career.' Caius finished his cup of tea. 'Oh, don't let me forget that I need to report Lynne's landlord to the local council for not doing essential repairs.'

35

Portcullis House, Westminster

Caius was waiting in a small room that smelled of stale coffee. Peter Simpson-Bamber was in a meeting and Caius had been directed to his office to wait for him. It wasn't a particularly impressive office. Pokier and less grand than you'd imagine. There were no wooden panels or decanters of whisky – just three utilitarian desks, a sad-looking potted lily and a simultaneously bored and yet overworked assistant. This grad, a young woman called Florence who'd received a hard-earned first from Durham, was typing away at her computer, every now and then tutting out loud. Caius didn't think she was aware she was doing it.

'Is it someone's boundary fences?' Caius asked.

'Sorry?' she asked.

'You keep tutting, so I assumed it was a constituent complaining. Neighbours fighting over fences: a tale as old as time.'

'Not this time,' she said, smiling at him. She wasn't used to being around someone else. Peter and Tom, his researcher, were usually off skulking around Parliament, or having lunches with journalists, or dinners with think tanks, or generally scheming over ways to make him prominent enough to become a cabinet minister, whereas she was left to deal with petty emails from irate constituents as the institutions they relied on collapsed around them. 'GP waiting times.'

'I bet you get all the fun tasks.'

'You'd be in the money.' She checked her phone and rolled her eyes. 'Peter's coming back now. His little agriculture committee meeting just finished.'

'What's the committee for?'

'Oh, um. Well, it's odd. I'm not sure anything actually gets done there.'

'I see. Do they just talk about rural stuff?'

'Recently there was a lot of debate about orchards and how we have the perfect conditions for growing apples, but we're still importing crazy amounts. They're thinking of subsidising farmers and putting in legislation to stop the import of things like that. Peter is very against it. He thinks it's a rejection of the markets. Goes on little rants about autarky.'

'I see,' Caius said, thinking about it for a minute. 'I thought it was more about reforms around land ownership?'

'You'd think, but it's actually a committee made up of mostly landowners . . .' she began, but then Peter Simpson-Bamber opened the door. He was on the phone.

'Tom, I don't care. Just fucking look into it.' He hung up and shoved the phone into his pocket. 'You must be Detective Inspector Beauchamp. Any relation to the late Sir Edgar Beauchamp?'

'No,' Caius said, very firmly.

Peter looked at Caius and then at Florence. 'Flo, go and get yourself a coffee and I'll see you in an hour,' he said, giving her a paternal smile.

'Sure,' Florence said, almost jumping out of her seat with glee. She picked up her bag and shot out the door. She hated being called Flo, but not quite as much as she low-key despised Peter.

'She'll be gone within a year, too bright for the job,' Peter said, sitting down at his desk once Florence had gone. He looked at Caius, sizing him up. 'How can I help you?'

'I'm looking into an old cold case – the Symington & Chase pension theft.' Caius hadn't meant to be so blunt but something

239

in how Simpson-Bamber looked at him made him feel like directness would be the only way to get anything out of him.

'I was the finance director, what more do you want me to say?' Peter leaned forward and met Caius's gaze, holding it there. The unresolved Symington & Chase scandal had hung around him like an ill-borne miasma.

'Lynne Rodgers died recently. She drowned in the Thames.'

'She's back in the UK?' Peter looked surprised.

'Yes, has been for a few years.'

'Why didn't your lot prosecute her then?'

'The officers who questioned her at the time deemed that there was not enough evidence to suggest that she was involved in the theft.'

'Really?' Simpson-Bamber shook his head, laughed to himself and then looked at Caius who he expected to show the same amount of scepticism.

Caius shifted around in his seat. He wasn't sure what to say to that. Caius's accent had got broader since the beginning of this conversation, and Simpson-Bamber was starting to drop his affected RP in response. Despite the mild air of belligerence he had when they began the interview, Simpson-Bamber seemed to be warming to Caius as he suspected he was like him: a working-class lad on the up. 'To your mind, what happened at Symington & Chase?'

'Theft pure and simple. That greedy git saw an opportunity and took a chance. It happened all in one night, you know. Robert, as the chief exec of a family firm, had access to all the bank accounts and funds that I did. Things weren't as secure as they are now. I was actually off that afternoon. I've always thought that was a calculated move on his part. I'd been to the dentist for a root canal. Dreadful pain I was in.'

'Yes, you mentioned that in your interview the first time round. Who knew that you'd be out?'

'Robert. I told him over lunch the previous week that I wouldn't be back in that afternoon after my appointment. And Tricia and Pat in accounts obviously. Pat's dead now. I went to his funeral about ten years ago.'

'Did you have any inkling that the theft was about to take place?'

'Perhaps in hindsight I might have seen that something was going on.'

'How do you mean?'

'Well, I thought that Robert was just having an affair. God knows why. Cass was something else.' Simpson-Bamber sat up straight and seemed a little embarrassed of his recollection of his former boss's wife.

'Who with?' Caius pressed. There was something there. Caius wondered if he knew more about Robert's affairs than he had previously admitted to.

'I don't know.' Simpson-Bamber stared at the pen pot on his desk for a moment. 'But not Lynne his secretary, to be sure. I know that's the idea the police went with then, but I couldn't see it myself. She wasn't that sort of woman. I think her parents were quite religious. Grew up sheltered. She was literally buttoned up to the neck with those flouncy blouses that everyone wore back then.'

'So you don't think they were having an affair and what, Lynne just did her job and booked the tickets to Brazil without questioning him?' Caius still wasn't clear on the dynamic of Lynne and Robert's relationship.

'Seems like the most likely scenario to me. Like I said, she was clearly sheltered and naively did whatever she was told to.'

Caius considered it for a moment. Peter's theory didn't explain Lynne remaining in Brazil though. 'Did Robert have a drug habit?' Caius asked. He wanted to test Cheryl's drug dealer theory.

'I don't think so. I never saw him act like he had.'

'I see. The business trip that was scheduled for Brazil. Did you know about that?'

'I wasn't aware of where they were going. I assumed it was Portugal. There are a lot of quality manufacturers there and he'd mentioned it a few times. Lynne was going to sort the expenses when she got back. I trusted him, both of them actually.'

'Why?'

'I was younger then. Naive. Bought into all the guff.' Simpson-Bamber played with a paperweight on his desk for a moment. 'Robert had been to university and then got an MBA. Ultimately it was his family's firm. I just took him at his word, and to be honest, I'd just met my wife and was a little distracted. You wouldn't know it to see her now, but she could be quite the tempest back then. I think Robert chose his moment perfectly. I was preoccupied generally and then out for the afternoon at the dentist when the theft occurred.'

'Do you know of anyone then who drove a red Jaguar convertible?'

'A Jaguar?' Simpson-Bamber leaned forward. 'Why do you ask?'

'Robert was seen getting into one on a couple of occasions just before the theft.' Caius could see that the Jaguar meant something to him.

'No, sorry.'

'Are you sure? One of his drinking buddies had one maybe?'

'Sorry, I don't know. We didn't go down the pub together.'

'That's all right. I didn't expect you to remember a detail like that.' He was sure Simpson-Bamber had remembered something. 'It was so long ago.'

'Yes, it was.' Peter Simpson-Bamber stared down at the paperweight on his desk as he spoke and seemingly forgot that he wasn't alone. He remembered himself and looked Caius in the eye, giving him a wide smile that was almost a grimace.

'Did you ever hear from Robert or Lynne after the theft and flight to Brazil?'

'No. I had thought Robert would do the decent thing and at least call his wife, but I don't think that ever happened.'

'Were you friendly with Cassandra Symington then?' That had after all been pretty much what she had said too.

'Yes, we were friendly, I suppose. As friendly as you can be with your boss's wife. Nice woman,' Simpson-Bamber said, straightening his tie. 'Didn't deserve to be treated like that.'

'You said you were in a relationship with your wife by then? Did she know the Symingtons? Did you socialise as couples at all?'

'No, we didn't socialise with them. I actually met Jane at work. She did a bit of freelance design work for the company.' Simpson-Bamber looked out of the window and into the courtyard below. Caius could tell he was thinking something important over.

'And the rest is history.'

'Ancient history.' Simpson-Bamber smiled weakly.

'I read an article where you said that you owe your business to your wife.'

'She was the first Fulham Girl. She did the design side of things initially and I dealt with logistics, money. You know, the boring stuff.'

'It was your wife who provided the initial investment, right?'

'Yes, a loan from her family. We couldn't have done without

it. Paid them back every penny.' Peter Simpson-Bamber stopped and gave Caius a wearily triumphant look. 'I know what you're really asking. People are always so desperate for me to be dodgy. There have been all sorts of ridiculous rumours over the years and not one of them has been true, but I have won my share of slander cases. I didn't steal the money to set up my own business. It was a legitimate loan. Everything I've ever done is above board and legal and I have the paper trail to prove it.'

'I'm sorry. I have got to ask,' Caius said, shrugging slightly theatrically to reassure him. For a man of his achievements and stature Caius felt like Simpson-Bamber needed reassurance. Caius had warmed to Simpson-Bamber in an odd way. Yes, he was bolshy and an old duffer with extremely questionable views, and he had probably committed some sort of crime against humanity somewhere in his business dealings, but Caius couldn't quite shake the feeling that he was a victim somehow, that their conversation had unlocked something deeply sad in him. 'I've got to tick the boxes.'

'Of course. I understand.'

Caius took out his card and gave it to Simpson-Bamber as he went to leave. 'In case you think of anything else.'

'Thank you,' he said, taking it from him.

'Oh, and congratulations on your daughter's engagement.'

'Yes, that. Thank you.'

'I'll show myself out.'

36

Eel Brook Common, Fulham

Matt knocked on the brass doorknocker of the red-brick four-storey house. It was shaped like an especially pompous lion. A small woman opened the door wearing a pair of spotless white linen trousers and a navy-blue and white Breton top, as if she were about to set sail on a yacht. She took one look at Matt and said, 'Sorry, I haven't ordered any sushi or whatever, it's not even 11 a.m.'

She closed the door on him so quickly he didn't have a chance to explain himself. He knocked again. She didn't answer. Matt rang one more time. Still no answer, so he propped open the letterbox and shouted through it. 'Mrs Simpson-Bamber, my name is DS Matthew Cheung. I'm an officer with the Metropolitan Police.'

She opened the door soon after that. Matt immediately flashed his warrant card.

'I'm so sorry. One can't be too careful.'

'I understand,' Matt said. He understood far too well. 'May I come in?'

'No one's dead, are they?'

'No, madam.'

'Good.'

She led Matt through to a room at the back that he knew wasn't the main living room. She probably didn't want him sitting on her sofa.

'Now how can I help you?'

'My team is investigating an old cold case. I understand that your husband was the finance director of Symington & Chase when the pension theft occurred.'

'He was, yes. Not that Peter had anything to do with it. He doesn't have a bad bone in his body. He had dental work done that day on a rotten tooth and I picked him up after. He was drooling out of one half of his face.'

'Right.' Matt's phone buzzed. He quickly read a message from Caius. 'I understand that you were a freelance designer there.'

'One of many actually.' She shifted around in the bright white armchair she was perched on. 'They had sacked the bitter queen who they had full-time for a whole host of young up-and-coming designers. We were paid on a design-by-design basis. Much cheaper than hiring someone full-time. I didn't go there much though. I'd knock off a handful of designs every three months, turn up and show them to Robert, talk about the specific stitches needed to make them work, suggested the odd fabric et cetera, and then I would leave half an hour later.'

'But you were there enough to meet your husband?'

'Peter is a go-getter. He sees something he wants, and he goes after it. I was no different. He's dogged. It's a quality that has got him very far in life.' She leaned back in her chair, as if asking him to look around at the room, the house. The millions of pounds' worth of bricks and mortar she swanned about in between yoga classes and facials.

'What did you think of Robert Symington?'

'I was greatly surprised by what happened.'

Matt noted that she hadn't answered the question. She clearly didn't want to talk about Robert as a person, only as a criminal. 'Did you know his secretary, Lynne?'

'She rang me four times a year to book my next design meeting with Robert, but that was it. I couldn't have picked her out in a crowd.' Matt looked at her for a moment and tried to place the feeling she clearly had for Lynne. He thought it was somewhere between disgust and pity. He wondered exactly where that came from.

'Did you ever hear from either of them after the theft?'

'No, of course not.'

'Why "of course not"?'

'I barely knew either of them. They didn't owe me a call.'

'Lynne Rodgers died the other week.'

'Oh really.' Something like righteousness crept into her voice. 'Happens to us all.'

Matt looked at her and the small flash of unconscious cruelty disappeared from her face. 'Do you design much any more?'

'Oh no, I chucked all that in a long time ago, when my daughter was little.' And became a lady that lunches, Matt added silently.

'What about Janey's?'

'Oh that, I just pick a few things out of our stockists' brochures a few times a year. It's a lark.'

'I see. I read an article actually where Mr Simpson-Bamber credits you with being the inspiration for Fulham Girl.'

'Peter is such a romantic. I helped out a bit with the designs in the first couple of years but that was all.'

'And the loan from your family?'

'Yes, Daddy was very sweet about that. Couldn't have done it without him.' Jane Simpson-Bamber stood up. She was finished with entertaining Matt's questions, and she wanted him gone. 'Was there anything else, detective?'

'No, that was all. Sorry to bother you.'

'Not at all. Happy to be of help.'

37

Caius's police car

Caius made calls as he snaked his way through the congestion to meet Amy at the offices of Hartnell Estates. First he called Arthur Hampton who unsurprisingly was busy and left him a voicemail.

'Hello, it's me. I don't have anything *concrete*, but we do have a new theory. Call me back when you have a chance.'

Caius then rang Matt. 'It's impossible to check Simpson-Bamber's alibi,' Caius said, shoving an almond protein ball that he'd batch-blended into his mouth. He wished it were a Snickers. 'No dentist would keep records going that far back. We're taking his and his wife's word for it that he was incapacitated at the time. The original investigation team confirmed he'd had an appointment that afternoon for dental work but who's to say that stopped him?'

'Jane Simpson-Bamber picked him up afterwards and apparently he was drooling,' Matt said. He'd stopped off for sushi on his way back from Fulham. 'There's something off with her. She looked almost smug when I said Lynne had died.'

'There's something off with him too. I think there are three distinct possibilities: firstly, Simpson-Bamber was genuinely incapacitated by the dental work and couldn't have stolen the money; secondly, he was drooling but not too badly and still managed to do it; and thirdly, he was drooling and woozy in bed but instructed his girlfriend on how to move the funds. It's a great alibi for the two options where he made off with a pension fund.'

'What did you think of Peter?' Matt asked, picking up a California roll with his chopsticks.

'He seemed unafraid to speak to me, although I'm pretty sure he lied towards the end, but I can't pinpoint what exactly it was he lied about. The car that Cheryl mentioned seemed to unsettle him, but he claimed to know nothing about it.'

'Politicians . . .'

'Was it a lie he believed himself?' Caius had often observed people lying to themselves first and foremost, and then casually lying to him about the untruth that was now keeping their grip on existence steady. 'Abi, my old uni acquaintance, said that she thought there was some hurt for Simpson-Bamber around the Symington & Chase case. She said he acted like he'd been a victim and I agree with that.'

'Do you want to get both the Simpson-Bambers in formally?'

'Not yet. We don't have proof of anything.'

'So what do you suggest?'

'If they were involved our visit will have spooked them. Especially when they realise that we spoke to them both at the same time. It's a watch and wait situation. They'll incriminate themselves eventually – we just need to be there when they do. In the meantime, I've got a few calls to make, loose threads to pull on. I'm going to meet Amy now so we can speak to the elusive Bellie Hartnell together.'

'Oh, Jane Simpson-Bamber mentioned the designer who was sacked in favour of all the freelancers,' Matt said as he put a piece of pickled ginger on his avocado maki.

'The same one Harold mentioned?'

'Yes. Called him a "bitter queen".'

'Delightful.'

'Casual homophobia and racism all within five minutes. I thought it might be worth tracking him down.'

'Good idea,' Caius said as he stopped at a pelican crossing for a group of primary-school children on an outing. They all wore matching yellow safety jackets and marched in twos, holding pudgy hands.

'All right then. *Arrivederci.*' Matt hung up and vindictively finished his sushi.

★   ★   ★

'Hello, is that Mr Harold Stephenson?'

'It is, yes.'

'Hello, Mr Stephenson, this is DS Matthew Cheung. We met a few days ago.'

'Yes, I remember you.' His breathing sounded fast.

'I was wondering whether you remembered anything else about the designer you mentioned? You said his name was Richard or Dickie. Do you know how to get in touch with him?'

'No.'

'Do you remember his surname at all?'

'No, sorry.' Harold hung up. Matt wondered whether he'd upset the old man somehow. It couldn't be pleasant dragging all this up again.

38

Calliope Foster Millinery

Callie was searching through a drawer for her personalised notecards. She ordered them direct from a printer with her name on. She felt that Arthur and Jeremy were the sort who expected thanks to come on paper, landing on their doormat with a gentle thud and not in a text message with a ping. Jim had just texted her the address and another thank you for coming and being charming. She finally discovered the notecards under some stray feathers. Then Callie found her favourite fountain pen and wrote a polite but brief missive thanking Arthur and Jeremy profusely for such a lovely evening. She was procrastinating over blocking her trial cloches using the antique German blocks. She'd dyed the hoods already and the ribbon was cut and waiting to go but she just couldn't get herself into gear that morning. The phone rang.

'Calliope Foster Millinery, Amelia speaking. How can I help?' Callie put on a higher-pitched voice when she pretended she had an assistant.

'Hi there, this is Hayley Cook. I'm a producer for the BBC coverage of the RHS Chelsea Flower Show. We are already thinking ahead to next May. We were wondering whether there would be a chance that Calliope would come on for a segment about women's straw hats – you know, something about how to snazz up an old one with a little posy in the band? We know she uses silk flowers in her work, but we thought it could be a fun little thing to do if she came on and did it with real flowers.'

'Calliope is unavailable at the moment but if you could email over the information about fees et cetera then I can pass it on to her and get back to you.'

'The fee is the standard BBC one for outside experts in light entertainment shows, so not much, but it's something and the exposure will be huge. Streamed into millions of homes. We're happy to do a quick edit of all the footage for her social media and ours too.'

'Calliope doesn't really have a need for exposure, but I will see what she thinks and get back to you.' Callie/Amelia took down Hayley's phone number and said someone would be in touch. Callie wasn't sure if she needed more publicity or even whether she needed her business to be any bigger than it already was. It was just her and she was already working weekends. She didn't want to hire anyone else. She liked the little niche she had found herself in – forty or so bespoke hats a year, and four off-the-rack collections. It paid the bills. Callie lived how she wanted. What was the point in endless growth? She also didn't want to be a household name. She wanted to be a little secret. Perhaps that was why she was feeling so off – perhaps she had too much success and what she really wanted was to go back to just creating hats for the sake of it. Callie used to make weird little pillboxes that were more art than fashion when she first started out. That was until she got a mortgage and had to start making more commercially pretty hats to pay it every month. Before that she'd rented a room in Dalston with friends and made whatever she felt like.

The doorbell rang. A courier was waiting outside. Callie opened the door and signed for a package. It was from Hermès. She checked the label, and it definitely had her name and studio address on it. She opened the package and found a beautiful silk scarf the colour of a clementine with yellow chrysanthemums and white daisies arranged in a diagonal pattern. There was no note attached. Callie took out her phone.

'Hi, it's me,' she said.

'Hello, you,' Caius replied.

'You didn't buy me a silk scarf from Hermès, did you?'

'No,' Caius said. He started to panic but tried hard to hide it. 'Should I have?'

'No, not at all. I would not expect you to spend £300 on a whim like this.'

'I mean, I do like you a lot. I just haven't bought you any silk scarves.'

'Don't worry, I'm not saying you don't like me or trying to make you buy me things.'

'Are you OK?'

'Yeah.'

'Are you sure?'

'Yeah, yeah. I've felt a bit off all morning. I'm probably just hungry. It's most likely a gift from a grateful client. I end up spending quite a lot of time with some of my regulars and they don't always have friends. I get amazing Christmas presents from them. What are you doing tonight?'

'Either YouTube yoga in my living room or going for a run.'

'Could you do that round mine? In fact, I can probably find a better workout for you.'

'Can I come round to your studio after I leave here? Is that all right? I'm curious about where you work.'

'Yeah, let's do that.'

'No Morley's this time though. It gave me heartburn – I'm getting old.'

39

Caius's police car

'Hi there, DI Caius Beauchamp, can you help me? Is it possible to check the cars taxed by an individual? No, not their current car. I'm looking for one they may have owned about thirty years ago.'

* * *

'Abi, it's Caius. Just wondering whether you'd managed to dig anything up your end. Catch you later, mate.'

* * *

'Yes, I would like to lodge a formal complaint against a landlord in your area who has been letting tenants live in a property that wasn't fit for human habitation.'

* * *

'I'm looking for a birth certificate for a Jane Bamber. I'm afraid I don't have any more details for you other than she's in her mid-to-late fifties. Or a marriage certificate. Jane Bamber married Peter Simpson in 1990, that I do know.'

* * *

'Hey, Caius, I've done some digging around,' Abi said.
    'Thanks, mate. What have you found?' Caius asked.

'I've got bugger all about this land reform committee you mentioned other than most of the people on it are connected with large landowners. They're all big beasts though, no wonder Peter was keen to muscle in. Nearly everyone I know who vaguely moves in that circle clammed up when I asked about it, but I did hear that they are low-key widening the scope of their focus to broader economic policy. There's something dodgy there. This committee sounds like it's actually a broader forum for a group of old boys with vested interests.'

'Right.' Caius thought that sounded about right. Hampton was going to try and get legislation through with his weird committee acting as a second cabinet.

'I do, however, know a guy who knows a guy who said that Hampton's brother is ill.'

'How ill?'

'Terminal.'

'So the bill about inheriting titles is what?'

'It's family drama.'

★   ★   ★

'What's your new theory then, Beauchamp?' Hampton asked. He pronounced it 'Beecham' this time. He'd called Caius just as a van cut him up at a roundabout. Caius was trying to smooth out the road rage from his voice.

'Lynne goes out there to Brazil as planned and waits for Robert. He never arrives and is too scared to come home. Years later things get even worse back here and she begins blackmailing the people she knows stole the money.'

'So you think "the people" who stole the money killed Lynne to keep her quiet?'

'Exactly.'

'What proof do you have?'

'It's just a theory that needs testing.'

'And you think it's people, plural, and not a person.'

'The Simpson-Bambers are our prime suspects. Jane worked there as a freelancer too. She was never interviewed the first time round, but we're sure they're both hiding something. We also have some doubts about Peter's alibi and are wondering whether he used some of the stolen funds to start his fashion empire.'

'Do you need anything from me?' There was a satisfied tone to Hampton's voice.

Caius took a deep breath. He couldn't believe he was doing something so unethical, and plain lazy, but he just wanted this case over so he'd never have to speak to Hampton again. 'I want them both tailed. They might give something up. I wouldn't get that approved normally without substantial proof, and my Chief Superintendent will be very reluctant to use our scant resources on such an old case. Can you handle that at your end?' Caius knew this was wrong. So wrong. If anyone from the Met found out he'd asked to have anyone followed like this, let alone an MP, without the explicit permission of his superior officer then he'd be hauled in front of a tribunal. But he was desperate to get the case over with. It was the only thing he could think of to artificially push this murky investigation along and be done with Arthur Hampton.

'I'm sure I can. Hopefully it'll lead to something *concrete*.'

40

Hartnell Estates, Mayfair

Caius pulled up in front of Hartnell Estates. He'd spent the drive over thinking about what it must be like to go to boarding school. He'd have to ask Callie, although he didn't want to sully their relationship with questions for his work. She'd vaguely mentioned that she'd boarded but hadn't gone into much detail other than that she'd hated it and wouldn't subject her own children to that. Amy was waiting for him. Caius gestured for her to come over and she climbed into the passenger seat.

'How was your weekend, the dentist and Lavinia?' Caius asked.

'Relaxing, not as bad as I feared and surprisingly helpful actually. She said the "Daughters of Hecate" was just a school-sanctioned game they played every year on Halloween. She also corroborated Beatrice Parker's and Sophy Oddfellow's accounts that Beatrice wasn't in the dorm and that no girl from the class was selected for the ritual. "The witches" didn't go to the fourth form that Halloween because Beatrice was the one chosen that year as the previous girl had left. Lavinia had years of panic attacks because of that night. In her words the school was "like a fortress". The bad actor most likely had to have been there amongst them the whole time.'

'Yeah, that'll give you PTSD all right. Where does that leave us?'

'It depends on what Bellie has to say, but to my mind the two options are: it was either the girls in her dorm or a staff member who escaped closer scrutiny at the time. Did Beatrice seem like she was lying to you?'

'No, she just wanted me to take an interest in her one-woman Edinburgh show,' Caius said, offering Amy a protein ball which she gracefully declined.

'I don't think either Sophy or Lavinia were lying either,' Amy said. 'What do you think ultimately happened to Eliza?'

'It wasn't a kidnapping. There was never a note and Beatrice thought the family didn't have money in the first place. Why would a kidnapper target one of the least well-off girls when there were bound to be others whose families were very well-to-do. The original investigation didn't find any signs of a struggle, no blood, nothing. So either they just didn't find the spot where she was killed, or she didn't die in the school. Beatrice heard a noise on the lawn so maybe the latter.'

'That's why they gave so much credence to the idea that she ran away with a boy,' Amy said, imagining a pimply-faced youth.

'A boy that not one of her peers thinks is real.' Caius thought the boyfriend hypothesis was nonsense – just old men project-ing onto teenaged girls. It was a fairly remote all-girls' school for starters; which boys would they have met?

'According to the original investigation no one in the town of St Ursula had ever seen her with a boy either.'

'We'll need to go down there eventually,' Caius said. He'd never actually been to Cornwall. His parents were more 'package holiday to Spain' types. It was a shame it was going to be in a professional capacity. 'But first, Bellie Hartnell.'

'What a mean nickname.'

★　★　★

Caius and Amy were offered tea, but both refused it. Annabel Hartnell's office was a fairly large room on the ground floor of a converted Mayfair house. There were black-and-white pictures on the wall of buildings in London and Bath. Each column-clad stone building was a Hartnell family asset.

'Ms Hartnell,' Amy began.

'Call me Bellie. Everyone does.'

'Bellie, we are investigating Eliza Chapel's disappearance,' Amy said, before being interrupted again.

'Have you finally found a body?' Bellie asked.

'You think she's definitely dead?' Caius asked.

'I can't see how she isn't after all this time. Honestly, that school. It wouldn't be allowed now that they have all these safe-guarding measures. A girl in the second form was hospitalised with tetanus. Caught her arm on a loose nail in the "gym".'

Caius couldn't fault Bellie's logic. 'We understand that you were in Eliza's dorm room.'

'Yes, I was.'

'Can you tell us what happened the evening she disappeared?'

Bellie relaxed into her chair as she began the story that she'd clearly perfected over many years of cosy dinner parties. 'It was Halloween, so everyone was borderline hysterical about the silly witch trial thing, but it didn't happen. We told a few ghost stories, scared ourselves stupid, ate some sweets that we'd snuck in from weekend trips into the town, and went to bed.'

'When did you realise that Eliza was missing?'

'In the morning, but I did wake up when she went to the loo in the night. She was a bit clompy when she walked. I heard her get up and leave the room. It was so cold, I couldn't get back off. I stayed up for a bit. Read under the covers with a flashlight, drifted off eventually but I didn't see or hear Eliza come back.'

'Any idea of the times of any of that?' Caius asked.

'No sorry, but I must have been reading for at least twenty minutes.'

'And you didn't see or hear anything amiss?'

'No, but it was an old building and the walls were pretty thick, I should think.'

'The other girls in your room, Mollie and Claudia, did they not see or hear anything?' Amy asked.

'Not that they told me. Claudie's dead now, poor love. Mollie lives in the States. I hear from her every now and then.'

'Was anything untoward going on at the school?' Caius asked.

'Beyond its mere existence?'

'Yes,' Caius said.

'I wouldn't be surprised. We'd heard that the Upper Sixth had hidden bottles of vodka under the floorboards in their dorms. Wouldn't shock me if they hid the odd boy in there too. Half the staff were dodgy. We had a geography teacher called Parsons who'd been chucked out of another school the year before for drinking on the job. My cousin boarded there, and she told me.'

'Did Eliza have a boyfriend?'

'No. Poor Eliza liked telling stories. She told us that she had a boyfriend, that he was six foot tall, with sandy blond hair, wore Jack Wills gilets and drove an Audi sports car. I mean, c'mon, you must have seen pictures of her. She just had a crush on Henry, the headmistress's adult son. That's who I've just described. He drove an Audi. He was quite spoilt. The headmistress doted on him. She was divorced, I think. She definitely didn't have a husband. We might have been spared some of her worst excesses if she did. Henry wasn't there often. He was on a grad scheme or something in London; the headmistress used to boast about it. He only appeared a couple of days of the year towards the extremes of term, or if it was the headmistress's birthday or whatever. Special events. It was a girls' school and he was the only vaguely attractive young man we would see for months on end. He kept himself to himself. Don't blame him. He was very highly thought of in some quarters, shall we say. Beatlemania sort of nonsense. Henry wasn't anything special, he was just there.'

'Was he there the day Eliza went missing?' Amy asked.

'I can't remember.'

'There were two other girls who left abruptly at the end of the previous term. Was there anything "off" there?' Caius asked.

'Hat the Brat and Lovely Lippy?' Bellie asked in turn.

'Is that what you called them?' Amy didn't think those could possibly be legal names.

'Yeah, Hattie was a spoilt little thing, and Lippy was a legend. They were best friends but one day Hat the Brat snapped and pinned Lippy down and hacked away at her hair. Poor thing. I never quite understood why they were as thick as thieves. Their parents removed them both after that. Not sure what happened to either of them. I'm sure Lippy's hair must have grown back by now. Lippy was a hoot. I'll have to look out for her. Oh God, what were their surnames.'

'Can you let me know when you remember?' Amy asked, handing Bellie her card.

'Sure.'

'Did you all get on? Did any of the girls have it in for Eliza?' Caius asked.

'She was a bit annoying but generally there was a bit of a "we're all in this together" mentality. We were already suffering by being there, there was no need to make it worse.'

'Thanks, Bellie,' Caius said. 'If you could give us the personal details you have for Mollie that would be really helpful.'

'Did the original report mention the headmistress's son?' Caius asked as he paced up and down next to his desk back at the station. He didn't remember reading about him in any of the original case notes. He was so obviously a person of interest that it seemed impossible for him not to have been interviewed unless he was abroad at the time of Eliza's disappearance.

'No, he wasn't recorded as being there at the school. Given his age, if he was he would've been a prime suspect,' Amy said, watching Caius rub holes into the soles of his shoes.

'Put him on the to-do list, Amy.'

'So how's it going with Callie?'

'It's going well, I think. I'm going to hers tonight.' Caius stopped still. 'Although some mystery person is sending her Hermès.'

'Aw, I'll start picking out an outfit for your wedding.'

'Calm down.'

'No I won't. You've got the heart of a romantic lesbian, Caius. You see a pretty girl, talk to her once and then she moves in by the end of next week.'

'Amy! Is that homophobic?'

'No, I don't think so. Just a stereotype that I'm misapplying to you and your little lesbian heart.'

'All right, all right.' Caius changed the topic. 'What's going on with you then? Something grown up, I bet.'

'Well, my lovely cottagecore-obsessive girlfriend has redecorated the living room in the flat, again. She keeps buying floral tat and creepy cross stitch from vintage shops. Fi's leaning into this tradwife aesthetic. She looks so unbelievably cute in her little pinnies, but she also keeps getting hit on by very questionable men on public transport who think she's a submissive straight woman.'

'Cool.' There were a few internet buzzwords there that Caius was going to have to google later.

'She's also sending me profiles of really fugly rescue cats. Oh and I'm thinking about taking up krav maga.'

'I'll come with you. I've been mistaken for an Israeli person before. I may as well learn to fight like a Mossad agent.'

Amy shuffled about uncomfortably, which Caius noticed immediately. Amy wasn't one for shuffling, more for coming straight out with it. 'Caius, I want to get promoted in a year or two.'

Caius nodded. He'd guessed as much. 'You're definitely competent enough to get promoted. Do you want to sit the exam soon?' Didn't mean he wouldn't miss her though. He'd felt like the three of them had got into a good rhythm.

'Yes.'

'Let's arrange that then. You're a bloody good officer, Amy. I'll be sad to see you go but glad to know you're out there doing your thing.'

'Thank you, Caius.' She knew that Caius couldn't have two detective sergeants, but she felt a pang at the idea of leaving. She checked her phone for the time. 'See you tomorrow, guvnor.'

'Have a nice evening rescuing your new fugly furbaby.'

Caius quickly checked his emails and then grabbed his spare shirt and toothbrush from his drawer, shoving them into his backpack with his running gear. He had been planning on running home from work. Matt came into the incident room.

'Cheryl passed on that we're looking into Symington & Chase again and I had another machinist call, but they had no clue the theft was coming. Harold Stephenson wasn't helpful, and I've been ringing round tailors on Savile Row and so far no one called Richard of about the right age works there. I've left a few voicemails.'

'Keep at it. I've asked for the Simpson-Bambers to be tailed.'

'The Chief Superintendent approved that?'

'Of course he bloody didn't, but we have friends in high places now.'

'Arthur Hampton is not our friend.'

'If it makes this case go quicker,' Caius said, looking at Matt for the briefest moment and then at the floor, searching for his misplaced integrity. 'Are you OK?'

'Yeah, yeah.'

'Oh come on, it's me.'

'Baby stuff still.'

'I'm sorry, man.'

'It's tough. I love Freja, but I don't want kids and that means we should break up, which is what I'm going to go and do tonight.'

'Oh, *muchacho*, I'm sorry.'

'Me too, mate. Me too.'

41

Calliope Foster Millinery

'So this is the infamous scarf?' Caius asked as he stared at the orange box on Callie's workbench. He didn't like this scarf business – no one sends a £300 scarf to someone for no reason. He was worried he had a rival. Caius thought he'd have to up his game. Dinner next week somewhere Amy would call 'spenny' maybe. He wondered whether it was too early on to suggest going away somewhere for the weekend.

'It is. I still haven't worked out who it was from. They'll call me when I don't call to thank them.'

'Ring Hermès. Someone on their end left out the note that was supposed to go with it.'

'That's far too active,' she said, putting her handbag on a stool and gathering her detritus. 'So, what do you think of my little hovel? It's cute, isn't it?'

'Adorable, like stepping back in time, but you should get a doorbell with a camera for extra security.' Earlier in his career Caius had worked a lot of burglaries and had also developed a habit of making sure he always knew where the emergency exit was. Mr Safety, but he had caught himself feeling a little jealous over this scarf and wanted her to know that he was dependable. He was wondering if it was Callie's ex. Caius thought you'd have to be insane to walk away from her and would probably try anything including a £300 scarf to get her back. 'You can vet people before you open the door then. I can get you a fake security camera for the alleyway round the back which will act as a deterrent, and legally your back door should be a fire door with a push bar to exit. Email your landlord about that immediately. They're violating workplace health and safety legislation.' Caius looked up and saw Callie's bemused face. 'Sorry, work mode.'

'You don't really talk about your work much.'

'Trust me, you don't want to hear about it.'

'No, I do. What are you working on right now?' Caius theatrically zipped his lips. 'All right, fine. What if I googled you?'

'Please don't.'

'It can't be that bad,' she said as she typed his name into Google and opened the first result.

'The first link you'd find is a statement that I made to the press after a six-year-old was murdered by her stepfather.' He didn't say that her stepfather had dismembered her in the bathtub, smashed her face in so the police would struggle to identify her and then put her body into a suitcase which he abandoned in a wood fifty miles from their house.

'Fuck,' she said, scanning the article.

'I told you.'

'Yeah, you did tell me.' Callie had taken his security assessment of her workrooms as a bit of a joke before, but now her skin was crawling, and she felt unsafe.

'Show me what you're working on. You said something about cloches?' He wasn't exactly sure what a cloche looked like other than it was clearly going to be bell-shaped.

'You can see my cloches anytime.' Callie took him over to the two completed hats that were resting on display heads. She'd found the energy to block them eventually. 'I give all my hats names like Sophie in *Howl's Moving Castle*. This is Petunia and this is Margot. I only got round to finishing off two today. Had to do the banking.'

'What's that from again?'

'What do you mean, what's that from? *Howl's Moving Castle* was my favourite book growing up. No sex for you, we're watching a Studio Ghibli film instead. Fine, we can do it after.' Callie picked her keys up, ushering Caius out of her workroom, and switched off the lights. 'Fuck, that poor little girl. My god. How awful. How do people do such awful things?'

'I didn't sleep well for months after that case.'

★   ★   ★

'Miyazaki added the war bit in. It's not in the book,' Callie said, looking at Caius who tacitly agreed that movies were never better than the books they're based on.

'I still liked it though. It's sweet,' Caius said.

They were curled up on Callie's sofa. She kept insisting her flat was in Ealing Common, but it was really in Acton and Caius kept teasing her about it.

'Do I say yes to the BBC and do the Chelsea Flower Show thingy?' Callie played with a split end. She probably should start putting a little effort in, now she was sort of seeing someone.

'Do it. It's better to be in demand and turning down work than not have enough.'

'You just want to point out your girlfriend on the telly to your mates.'

'Yeah, I do.' Ha, girlfriend, Caius thought. He wasn't going to tell Amy that though.

'Typical man.' Callie picked up her phone and quickly bashed out an email to Peter about the fire door. 'Putting silk flowers on my straw hats is one of my signatures, so it does make sense for me to be at the Chelsea Flower Show.'

'There was a little bunch on the hat you wore to the theatre.'

'Yes, that was monkshood. It means "knight errant". I was going through a bit of a forlorn romantic phase when I made it. I have to make some of the silk flowers from scratch because they're too obscure. I took a special evening class for six months to learn how.'

'Hang on. Monkshood means what?'

'"Knight errant". You know, like King Arthur and shit.' Callie jumped up from the sofa and grabbed a slim volume from her bookshelf. She showed him the cover of *Language of Flowers* by Kate Greenaway and started flicking through it.

'Can't you just have a message put on the little card the florist sends over?'

'Well, yeah, of course, if you want to be obvious about your feelings,' Callie said, laughing. 'This was my great-grandmother's. I had a bit of a Victoriana obsession when I was a teenager. I spent all my pocket money in Past Times.'

'So each flower has a different romantic meaning?' Caius asked, looking over her shoulder at the book.

'Yes.' She flicked through it. 'Pick one and I'll look it up.'

'Roses.'

Callie got to 'R'. 'Depends on the type. Deep red roses mean "shame" whereas white roses mean "I'm worthy of your love".'

'What about foxgloves?'

She flicked back to 'F'. '"Insincerity".'

'That makes sense.' He paused for a moment. 'Did you crack that out and go over the bouquet I sent you?'

'No. God no. I'm intense, but I'm not *that* intense.'

TUESDAY

42

The Police Station

Caius got into work early. He'd stopped off at Waitrose, bought Matt five packs of lavender shortbread and left them on his desk ready for him. His mobile rang.

'The wife stayed in last night, but the husband dined out with the daughter alone,' said Hampton.

'Right.'

'Gets odd even for him though. He gets the daughter to swab her cheek in the bogs. He's overheard saying that a cousin of his has died recently from breast cancer and he wants her to check if she has a mutated gene.'

'Is it possible to see a report on their movements last night?'

'No. We don't write things like this down, do we? I'll let you know if anything further transpires.'

Hampton hung up and Caius took a deep breath. He knew he'd crossed the Rubicon by asking to have the Simpson-Bambers tailed, that he was more compromised now than he needed to be. Caius regretted his poor judgement, but he still thought it was the only way he was going to speed this case up. Symington & Chase was thirty years ago – a good handful of potential witnesses were already dead – and he knew that if the Simpson-Bambers were involved then he and Matt would've spooked them. He hoped they were spooked enough to give something away. Caius took out his phone and found Callie's personal account on Instagram and requested to follow her. He felt like they'd reached that step, that they could be mutuals. He resisted the urge to scroll down and see if there were any pictures of her ex still up. He got up to make himself a lemon and ginger infusion when Matt's desk phone rang. Caius picked it up.

'Hello, is that DS Cheung?' came the voice from the other end.

'He's away from his desk at the moment, but may I help? I'm DI Caius Beauchamp, his superior officer.'

'Yes, I'm just responding to his inquiry yesterday. Could you let him know that Ritchie Gaskell, our head cutter, did used to work at Symington & Chase in his twenties. He would come to the phone but he's busy this morning measuring clients.'

Caius took down the name of the tailor and then checked his emails. Not one of his outstanding inquiries had come back to him yet. He sent a few chasers, and left another voicemail asking Cassandra Hunstanton whether she'd found the letter from Lynne.

Matt and Amy came in. They'd been in the same lift. Amy gave Caius a quick 'heads up, something's wrong with Matt' nod and sat down at her computer.

'You found the coat designer,' Caius said, handing him the Post-it note with the name of the tailor written down. 'He's busy this morning, apparently.'

'Great,' Matt said. He noticed the biscuits, picked up the packet and smiled.

'Mollie, our fourth-form boarder, has come back to me finally,' Amy said, scrolling through her email from the LA producer. 'She'll ring at 5 p.m. our time.'

'Brilliant. In the meantime, could you start tracking down the teachers? Let's see if time has given them a bit of clarity.'

'Sure. I'll check whether any of them have acquired a record since too.'

Amy had written the names of all of the teachers (and one former who had demanded that she be interviewed) of St Ursula's who'd been interviewed the first time round on the whiteboard. Then she crossed two off – the two who they knew were dead – the headmistress and Miss Miller the former PE teacher and amateur sleuth. Caius stood next to Amy as she did it, taking in the information in front of him. Two facts felt like the core of the case, but Caius couldn't see how they fitted together. Firstly, all the girls from Eliza's year they'd interviewed had said Eliza made things up for attention. And secondly, the 'Daughters of Hecate' was just a prank the headmistress knew about and ignored.

'Did no one interview the staff?' Caius asked, looking at the board.

'The staff?' Amy asked, confused. She had the transcripts of the teachers' interviews from the first investigation in front of her. 'What do you mean?'

'I've seen pictures of the school. A place as big as that must have had a groundsman. What about cooks, cleaners, even an odd-jobs guy who tried to patch the holes in the roof up. You know, the people who actually make things work.'

'There's no record of anyone like that being interviewed. Presumably because it happened at night.'

'Yeah, but what happened had a root cause from before that night.' Caius thought it was mad that no one had interviewed any of the support staff at the school. The original senior investigating officer must have been a snob as well as a misogynist. 'They'd be locals, wouldn't they?'

'Most likely. People can't afford to travel for those sorts of poorly paid jobs.'

Caius called the St Ursula station to speak to his new friend Darren. After a little chat about *Mamma Mia!* and Angus Steakhouse, Caius told Darren that they were looking at the Eliza Chapel case as part of a routine check on cold cases and asked whether he knew of any locals who had worked at the school. As a matter of fact, Darren did know some of the staff because his mum had been a cook there briefly. Darren agreed to get as many of the staff as he could find together at the St Ursula police station for Caius and Amy to interview the next day.

'Road trip!' Amy said, immediately googling local B&Bs.

'Let's try and get as complete a picture as we can before we go. Amy, start with the staff who live in and around London. A couple of the teachers might. Most private schools are in the South East. Oh, and look up the headmistress's son, if you haven't already. Henry. Let's just check that he wasn't actually there.'

'Sure.'

'Tea, anyone?' Caius asked. Amy declined. Matt looked up at him.

'Builder's, two sugars.'

'Of course, buddy.'

43

Calliope Foster Millinery

'Morning, Peter. I wasn't expecting you today, was I?' Callie said, opening the door to her ex–best friend's father and her landlord. An uneasy description of her relationship with him. She braced herself for whatever he was about to say. He might be there to chuck her out for telling Harriet to fuck off. She'd been in her workroom looking up smart doorbell systems. Caius had already ordered the fake camera and promised to come round with a drill on his next day off. The thought made her feel a bit squishy inside. Callie wasn't going to let him know that she was capable of using power tools herself.

'No, I was on my way in to the old nine to five and saw your email. Do you want to show me the door?'

'Yes, sure. Come this way.' She took him through to the workroom. Perhaps Harriet had realised she was out of line and hadn't said anything. Callie didn't want to move studios. She didn't think she could afford to rent anywhere else in this part of town.

'You're right, that should be a proper fire door. I'll get one installed ASAP.'

'Thank you, I didn't realise. A friend of mine pointed it out. He thinks I should get a doorbell with a camera too for extra security.'

'A friend?'

'An almost boyfriend.'

'Is he nicer than the last one?'

'Infinitely.'

'What does he do? Something boring in the City or is he creative like you?'

'Neither, I suppose. He's public-spirited.'

'So he's what, a lawyer? Does lots of pro bono work for blind,
homosexual refugees.'

'He's a policeman.' Callie never used to be sure what Peter
really meant when he said things like that. As Harriet's father
she'd always given him the benefit of the doubt and assumed he
was making a joke, even if it was one that was tonally a little off,
but after Jim had mentioned the animosity between Peter and
Arthur Hampton she'd googled him. She didn't like his politics,
and she wasn't sure they were jokes now. Callie always voted
Green because she cared about the environment. Reading the
news made her sad so she avoided it; she now felt the same way
about the middle-aged man in front of her.

'Well, that is a surprise. Out of you and Hat I always thought
you'd be the one to make the grand marriage. You're the pretty
one.'

'Sod grand, I just want to be happy.' Callie laughed. She didn't
think that was an appropriate comment.

'Wise, very wise. I was worried for a moment you were going
to say that you were dating Arthur Hampton's little gremlin.'

'Oh, did Jim tell you we went to that dinner party?'

'Jim? No. I've not spoken to him since the engagement do.'

'I'm confused.'

'Sir Rupert Beauchamp. Hampton wanted me to set you up
with him after he met you at Hat's party. She said she mentioned it. I'm glad you declined.'

'But I was invited by Arthur Hampton to a dinner party last
week. I was sat next to Rupert.'

'Steer clear, m'dear.' Peter had recently made it his business to try and get to the bottom of this latent scandal that might be to his advantage after the engagement party, but he'd only heard reluctant snatches of gossip thus far. 'Lord knows how Hampton managed it, but he's kept the boy clean in the press. Managed to spin the sordid affair so it makes him look like some sort of lovelorn romantic hero but there are a lot of terrible rumours flying about.'

'All right.' Not that she especially valued Peter as a judge of character, but it wouldn't be too hard to 'steer clear'. She had left the dinner party with a wine buzz and a deep feeling that Rupert was far too intense to be anything more than a glancing acquaintance or quick fuck, and she wasn't in the market for that these days.

'What are you doing for lunch today?' Peter asked.

'Oh, I don't know. Wander over to the Co-op and buy my weight in hummus.'

'Why don't you come to Parliament and join me? You've never been before.'

'Sure, why not?' She didn't have any clients in and all she had planned was sewing ribbons on the remaining cloches now that Penny de la Croix's order was in jeopardy. Callie had left her a voicemail to confirm whether she still wanted the hat, but she hadn't heard back.

'Lovely. Go to Portcullis House for 12.30 p.m. and ask for my assistant Flo. She'll make sure you get to the right place.' Peter Simpson-Bamber stared at the door again. 'I'll get someone to come and look at the door pronto.'

'Am I in trouble?'

'I don't know. Are you?' Peter looked at her quizzically.

'If you want to chuck me out for telling Harriet to fuck off then you don't need to do it over lunch.'

'You told her to fuck off?'

'I did. And I don't regret it. She can't send rude emails like that and there be no consequences. Sorry, you're her father but she was out of order.'

'So you stood up to her finally. 12.30 p.m. See you there.'

Callie started googling Rupert. She came across the Burberry pictures first and then found a profile on 'Britain's most eligible bachelor' in *GQ* before going to the fount of all society gossip, Dotty.

> *You*
> *09.33*
> *Dot! Do you know Rupert Beauchamp by any chance?*
> *I live under a rock but you know literally everyone in London*
>
> *Dotty*
> *09.37*
> *Super hot but AVOID!!! Absolute player. Apparently he's good at it but still. Casper hates him*
> *Negronis soon?*
>
> *You*
> *09.37*
> *Yes! Yes! Yes! When are you free?*
>
> *Dotty*
> *09.40*
> *On our way to Crete for a week. I'll call when we're back*
> *How's it going with your new beau?*

You
09.40
He's so nice

Dotty
09.40
Too nice?

You
09.41
Maybe . . .
I don't know

Dotty
09.41
Oh Cal. Bad boys break hearts and leave you in pieces. Nice ones make you cups of tea in bed when you have cramps What about the sex????

You
09.41
😈

Callie went back to the search results and scrolled past the Burberry pictures and read an article in a gossip section of a tabloid about how Rupert's scandalous ex-girlfriend had died, with a huge number of details of how awful she'd been to him. Manipulative. Shallow. No one said the words 'gold digger' but that was the subtext of nearly every piece, or rather hit job. Callie read another article about the coroner's verdict of misadventure and a couple of interviews with Rupert talking about how very sad he was to have lost such an old friend. He spoke about her as if they hadn't been living together until accordingly quite recently before she died. The next paragraph showed pictures of his estate and a brief history of his esteemed family. This second type of article was accompanied by even more shots showing just how gorgeous he was. He reminded Callie of a statue of Apollo: beautiful, chiselled and cold. Thank goodness she wasn't single. She didn't need to deal with a man with that much past or that much cheekbone.

44

Westminster

Callie was having her bag searched when she heard a familiar voice behind her. Vowels round and every 't' a sharpened dagger. 'Well, if it isn't the most celebrated milliner in England,' came the voice, clear and clipped.

Callie was embarrassed that her heart skipped the smallest beat as she walked through the metal detector, which beeped loudly. 'I broke my wrist when I was a child. There are some pins in it.' A security officer took out a portable metal scanner and started waving it over Callie's body. Callie was then given a temporary security pass and waved through. She scanned the area for someone conceivably called Flo. Rupert appeared beside her. 'Good afternoon, Rupert.'

'Good afternoon, Calliope,' he said, discreetly looking her up and down. He liked her dress. It was simultaneously modest and indecent. A midi length with long sleeves in emerald green that made her eyes shine. The neckline had a touch of wench about it. 'About dinner?'

'Look, I'm seeing someone. I'm very flattered that you would ask me out, but I have to decline.' She had an epiphany. 'Thank you for the scarf, but you really shouldn't have. That was you, wasn't it? There was no note.'

'I shall have words with my man at Hermès. I crafted a perfect little missive to go with it.'

'Enjoy your afternoon, Rupert.' Callie scanned the foyer for Flo and tried not to think of a certain set of photographs of him that she'd seen online.

'Dinner tonight?'

'I told you, I'm seeing someone.'

'And it's not me?'

A 'no' was a 'no'. Callie had no desire to tell him any more about her personal life.

'Excuse me, are you Callie?' asked a young woman in a Hobbs suit that looked far too serious for the light hiding behind her eyes.

'Yes. You must be Flo. Nice to meet you,' Callie said, going towards Peter's assistant, relieved to see her.

'Peter asked me to walk you over to the Strangers' Dining Room. He'll meet you there.'

'No need, I'm on my way there too. I shall escort her.'

'Brillo pads,' Florence said, turning to leave before Callie could object.

Callie could see there was no wriggling out of this. 'How are you allowed to just walk around here?'

'Oh, I'm doing a bit of research work for Uncle Arthur. It's only temporary, you understand.' Rupert held out his arm, which she didn't take, as he led her towards the underpass that connected the modern building to the Palace of Westminster. 'He likes to make sure I'm gainfully employed every now and then. I get into trouble when I'm not. The bastard pays me minimum wage though. He says that I don't need the money. What are you doing here?'

'I'm going to hide in a broom cupboard to make a political point.' Rupert looked down his nose at Callie, squashing any suffragette spirit she had until she told him the truth. 'I'm meeting a family friend.'

Callie felt awkward. She didn't want to ask him questions about himself, encouraging the idea that she was interested in him, but she knew he'd only ask her more questions if she didn't. She pressed him on the state of his literary endeavours. He told her how it was progressing at great length as she pretended to be mildly interested all the way to the Strangers' Dining Room, which was clad in wooden panels and cherry-red flock wallpaper. Callie and Rupert waited in a short line to be seated. Callie looked up at the ceiling's intricate woodwork for a moment, remembered herself and stopped gawping. The Thames flowed past the window. The hostess asked them both who they were meeting. She took Callie over to a table set for two but then came back and asked her to follow her to Rupert's table instead.

'I thought we may as well all have lunch together,' he said.

'Well, I'm not so sure . . .' Callie began, but she capitulated, feeling crushed by the weight of expected decorum. She was after all a guest in the middle of a bustling dining room full of some of the most notable people in the country. She did not want to cause a scene, be an embarrassment. Callie sat down on the chair that Rupert held out for her.

'Rupert, and young Calliope – what a pleasant surprise,' said Arthur Hampton, appearing suddenly. 'Don't you look lovely.'

'I'm meeting Peter,' she said, standing up. 'Rupert insisted that I wait with him.'

'Did he now? How courteous of him.' Hampton smiled at Callie, ready to send her off to what he was sure would be a dreary lunch with Simpson-Bamber. Hampton could tell she didn't want to be there, but also that Rupert was trying very hard to not look at her in a way that suggested he wanted to eat her alive. Hampton remembered when he used to be like that – he had hoped that Rupert was going to grow out of it after his intervention in the summer, but apparently not. Hampton worried he'd been too hasty in holding his dinner party experiment.

'Thank you so much again for dinner, Arthur. Did my card arrive? Of course, it didn't. I didn't post it – I ran out of stamps and it's still here in my handbag.' Callie took out the envelope and handed it over to Hampton who took it with a smile.

'I'd be delighted to save you the trouble. Stamps cost a fortune nowadays,' Hampton said.

'Someone in government should do something about that,' Rupert piped up.

'Oh hush, you,' Hampton said to Rupert. He tried to hide behind a certain playfulness, but Callie felt the cold steel beneath it. 'It was delightful to see you.'

'It was so lovely to see you too,' Callie said, clutching her bag as she spied Peter entering the room. She smiled at Hampton, and then went back to the table she had been at originally. Callie could see the poor hostess watching everything unfold with curiosity as she once again rearranged the seating plan at the whims of these people.

'There you are,' Peter said, sitting down at the table. He was slightly brusquer than he usually was. 'What was that I just saw?'

'Nothing.' She was still unsure why she was there. 'Thank you for inviting me today.'

'You're very welcome.' Peter poured them both a glass of water from the carafe on the table. 'Is this still the Margaret whatsherface look?'

'Pretty much,' Callie said, smoothing out her dress across her lap. 'It feels quite odd to be inside the building that tourists take pictures of. Looking out of the window in this room is some sort of Alice in Wonderland flipped world.'

'Yes. We're on the inside looking out, as it were.' Peter picked up the menu and started browsing. 'Busy morning?'

'Yes and no. I did none of the work I was supposed to do, but I did get yet another call from an influencer who wants a hat for free for a wedding so I can get "exposure".'

'You've got to admire the cheek.'

'Haven't you just?' Callie half smiled and looked out of the window again.

'What's wrong? You seem a little sad and that's not like you.'

'Oh, nothing really.' She wasn't sure that he knew what she was like. They saw each other twice a year maximum and, except for Max-gate, they barely made it past small talk each time. 'No, just a little ennui. I'm sorry. Hardly the right attitude for lunch. I'll give us all indigestion.'

'What are you discontent with? Your new chap?'

'He's far too new for me to be discontent with. No, I just can't quite place my finger on it. I think I might have fallen out of love with my work. I've worked hard to get to this point and here I am, having achieved everything I set out to, and yet it feels a little hollow. I work for myself. I create beautiful hats that people delight in, but it's just not quite enough any more. It's not serious work, is it? Does it have any real value? Do people need it? Am I doing something worthwhile?'

'It sounds like you've just grown older, and you need a new challenge.'

'Yes, you're probably right.'

The hostess came over and they ordered. Peter had the soup of the day, followed by pan-fried cod with vadouvan-spiced butter, fennel and potato rösti, samphire and runner beans. He skipped dessert. Callie ordered miso-roasted squash with cashew nut 'feta', sesame tahini purée, parsnip crisps and sesame dukkah and then the sticky braised beef cheek with charred hispi cabbage, beef fat–roasted onion, creamed potato and gremolata.

She skipped pudding too. They were both happy with tap water. All of the food was, of course, subsidised by the taxpayer.

'You must be wondering why I asked you here today.'

'A little. I'm assuming it's wedding related. No?' She'd been asking herself this very question all morning, but she didn't feel like Peter was going to give her a genuine answer. Something about him said he wasn't at ease, that he wasn't going to be forthcoming. Perhaps it was just their location. He was surrounded by his peers (and actual peers).

'Oh God, that fucking wedding. I want her to have whatever she wants but I don't need to hear about it constantly,' Peter said, before wondering why Callie looked so confused.

'Look, if Harriet has sent you as some sort of peace envoy, then respectfully I decline. I'm calling time on our friendship. I know you're her father and forgive me if this is rude, but I don't want to be friends with her any more.' Callie caught sight of Rupert across the room.

Peter took a sip of his water. 'No, I asked you here because I need to know what your mother has told you about your father.'

'My father.' Callie was taken aback. She couldn't fathom why that interested Peter, and why mention him now? He'd known her since she was eight years old. 'Barely anything. That he was a bastard who wanted nothing to do with me, and that she wishes she'd never met him. Honestly, she's one more gin in the early afternoon away from calling me up to say she should have got an abortion.'

'Oh.' Peter's phone pinged and he excused himself to check it. Judging by his expression Callie thought it was something bad. He continued to scroll through something, ignoring her entirely as the colour drained from his cheeks. Callie politely stared out of the window for a minute while he read whatever it was. He put his phone down and then tried to pretend everything was fine.

'Are you all right, Peter? You look like you've had a shock.'

'I rather have. Sorry, what were you saying?'

'Just that my mother is a charming woman.'

'I tell you what, let's finish up here and then we'll go for a walk along the river. It's not autumn yet, and I'll tell you a story about a company I worked for when I was your age.'

'All right,' Callie said as their starters arrived.

★　★　★

'Calliope, what a name. It has to be a sign. She said she's seeing someone. I think she's lying,' Rupert said, ever the classicist.

'If someone lies like that, it means they don't think you can take a simple no,' Uncle Arthur said.

'Are you sure? Sounds like an invitation to try harder to me.'

'Yes.' Arthur Hampton took a sip of his Bordeaux. 'I am very sure.'

'Very sure? I used to do three girls a night in second year and now I can't even get this one bloody girl to message me back. My form hasn't declined that much.'

'Rupert.' Hampton stared at him. 'Don't talk like that. You can't make jokes like that any more. Not after what you did.'

'I told you. It was nothing. Just a lot of fuss over a one-night stand and a detective who's got it in for me.' Rupert had repeated these words often enough to himself and to Uncle Arthur, but deep down he knew. He knew what he'd done. He knew what he was. Callie was chatting away to the sack of ham she was dining with. 'It's true, I swear it is. You believe me, don't you? I'm not a monster. I was just in love. Painfully in

287

love. And I had to do something about it finally – I just perhaps went a little too far.'

Hampton changed the subject. This wasn't the place to get into it, again. At least he was saying 'too far' now – that was an improvement. 'How do you like being a parliamentary researcher?'

'Far more than I expected, but uppers are my wheelhouse. Thank the gods I'm not researching hedgerows again.'

'Land management is important to people like us.'

'Like us? You mean the ones who own all the land?'

'Yes, we own it but more importantly we manage it, and we do so well. It's part of the reason we're still here. We Hamptons aren't Normans, you know, we are Saxons. We held on by the skin of our teeth and made good marriages with William the Conqueror's family.'

'This talk again. I'm not actually related to you, you know that. I don't care about your ancestors.' Rupert took a bite of his food, knowing that his lot were Norman baronets who got lucky plundering India. 'Talking about good marriages, I think Callie would yell at me if I stepped out of line. Really let me have it. I need that. That's what Nell . . .' He trailed off. 'Callie has good hips. That's a woman who will have sons. I bet she could really take a railing.' Rupert was trying to wind Hampton up now.

Hampton looked sternly at Rupert. 'Calliope, as pretty and clever and diverting as she is, was merely an exercise for you. A practice in behaving like you should. This cad about town thing you do ages very quickly after thirty-five. You need to grow up.'

'Why do you care so much? I mean, beyond our personal history. Our only connection is that your husband was my late mother's best friend. And she's been dead for twenty-five years. Why do you get to lecture me on decorum? Is it a bad thing for me to be gadding about, enjoying my only shot at existence?

Does it matter if I don't have a legacy and just spend my days in epicurean bliss? Does it matter if I never marry? Does it matter if I never have children? Does it matter if I'm the last Beauchamp?' Rupert took a sip of his sparkling water; he'd wanted a glass of wine but been denied it and glanced up at Callie who still seemed deep in conversation with the old fuddy duddy. He couldn't be the one she was seeing. He was old enough to be her father, but not in a sexy sugar daddy kind of way. 'I really need to get laid. I'm very stressed right now.'

'I've given all the bouncers in every nightclub both east and west of Mahiki your picture and they know not to let you in. Even the ones in Shoreditch.' Hampton looked across at Rupert. 'We need to get you a new hobby that isn't between a woman's legs.'

'I've always fancied stamp collecting.' Rupert rolled his eyes.

'You are a very sad little boy, and that's mostly my fault.' Hampton, in a rare moment of physical affection, patted Rupert on the arm.

Rupert pulled away. 'Don't you dare take credit for this.'

'I should have packed you off to rehab years ago.'

'All my failures are mine and mine alone, and I shall bear them, with neither honour, nor dignity. All my victories are and forever will be pyrrhic. These are the stars that I was born under. It has nothing to do with you.' Rupert was getting het up, and struggled to contain himself.

'You can't be a martyr to your own character, Rupert. Believe me, I tried that once. You can't self-destruct like that. I won't let you.' This time Hampton put his hand on Rupert's arm, and Rupert let him.

45

Savile Row

Caius and Matt were in a large basement room of a prominent Savile Row tailor frequented by actors in search of tuxedos for premieres and businessmen looking for a suit, for anything really, that distracted people from how they had made their money. It smelled pleasantly musty with a hint of ancient masculinity. Caius could see tourist trainers and well-heeled feet walking past on the street above. Matt was busy texting. Caius assumed he was talking to Freja by the quiet air of heartbreak that hung around him and left him to it. He picked up a swatch book of Harris Tweed that had been left on the workbench in front of them and flicked through it, thumbing a couple of warm brown twills and thought that if he ever had the money he would get a suit made with a matching waistcoat. Caius shuffled uncomfortably on the stool he was perched on. Why did success look like the trappings of the landed gentry even now? Why did he aspire to look like a squire? He thought of the window displays that they'd walked past on Savile Row. Union Jacks and bull dogs. Velvet smoking jackets and penny farthings. Bowler hats and paisley-patterned ties. All of them selling the idea of an England, and thus a Britain, from a hundred years ago – because that was the peak, he supposed. The last time an Englishman truly felt that it was his destiny to rule the world and go out there and take, steal and plunder exactly what he wanted. And yet the world whom England has not so graciously ruled was here buying it up. Still taking visible cues of wealth from the old imperialist. Heritage as industry. That's all the English had to sell now the factories were gone, just a sanitised visual distortion of their history. Caius needed to get his Irish passport sorted. Matt sighed loudly, killing Caius's ambling daydream of moving to Dublin.

'You all right, mate?' Caius asked Matt.

'Not really. I will be though.'

The door opened and in walked Richard Gaskell. 'Gentlemen, sorry for keeping you waiting. I've had some exacting fellows from overseas in this morning – they're going on their first grouse shoot later this year.'

'That's quite all right, Mr Gaskell,' Caius said, getting up from the stool. 'We are investigating an old cold case that we think you might know something about.'

'Symington & Chase?' Richard asked, almost gleefully.

'You've been expecting us?' Matt asked.

'I've been waiting for this character assassination for thirty years.'

'What do you mean?' Caius asked.

'Jane fucking Bamber is what I mean.'

'The finance director Peter Simpson-Bamber's wife?'

'Stupid man. Never marry a harpy, boys. She got me fired so that nepotistic MBA baby could hire her as a "freelancer". He sacked me to hire his bit on the side.'

'Robert Symington was having an affair with Jane Bamber? Are you sure?' Caius asked as Matt gave him a quick side glance.

'My best mate was running a chichi little Italian restaurant in Pimlico at the time. I'd eat there every week because he never charged me properly. Anyway, I saw them canoodling in a booth a month before I was sacked. I didn't say anything to anyone at the time because it wasn't my business, until it bloody was. Robert fired me to hire her. My work was good, look where I've ended up, and I don't believe he was saving money. More like him bunging a wad over to his bit extra.' Ritchie made a gesture with his hands as if he were serving them something with a flourish.

Caius clapped his hands together at the discovery. 'But wasn't Peter dating her?'

Ritchie leaned in conspiratorially. 'Petey was being strung along by the little strumpet. Probably waiting to see if Robert actually would leave his wife for her. I doubt he would have. Cassandra was a very elegant woman. Her family were very well-to-do too. Not like Jane. She settled for Peter Simpson when Robert disappeared on her.'

'Did you bring this to the attention of the police when Robert first went missing?' Matt asked.

'I tried, but let's say the observations of a person like myself were not heeded. They thought I was just a disgruntled former employee. Besides, I think Pete had been formally questioned and said she was with him during the theft. She'd picked him up from somewhere at pretty much the same time the money went missing.'

'Did anyone else know about Robert and Jane?' Caius asked.

'Not that anyone said to me. If one of the girls on the shop floor knew then everyone in London would have known. Peter wouldn't have kept dating her if he knew. You could see that he was a proud man. I couldn't say for Pat in accounts. He kept himself to himself and barely looked beyond the end of his nose. Did his job and went home again. Tricia who did the invoicing was a nice girl who'd come and have a chat with me on breaks and she would've said something. Harold wouldn't have stood for it if he knew. He would've kicked up a big fuss about the morals of a family firm. He was an upright member of the community sort.

Righteous fury, you know. He thought I still lived at home with my mother. Kept telling me to meet a nice girl and settle down. Easier not to correct him.'

'Other than spotting them out to dinner once, do you have any more proof?' Caius asked. He wanted something physical that he could use to justify having the Simpson-Bambers followed.

'Oh, you bet I do. That snooty little cow couldn't help herself, could she?' Ritchie said, opening a drawer in his workbench and taking out a small pale blue cardboard box. 'I've been carrying this around with me for years waiting for you two to come.'

Matt and Caius peered into the box as Ritchie took out the obscure 'memento mori' scarf that Amy's dossier had mentioned.

'For my money, having seen them both in the flesh, the female cameo looks enough like Jane Bamber and the male one like Robert Symington to suggest that Jane was missing her former lover. It's subtle though. Old Petey would've lost it if he'd realised.'

46

St Albans

Amy had so far only found one former staff member of St Ursula's who lived close to London: the bursar. Most of the older ones had retired to the south coast or the South of France and the younger staff members – if they were still teaching at all – were working abroad in places like Dubai and Shanghai. She'd found a former history teacher and a former French teacher who had done just that and had omitted their early careers at St Ursula's from their LinkedIn profiles. The English teacher ran a wool shop in Gloucester and the chemistry teacher ran a cattery just outside Glasgow. She'd get in touch with all of them in due course. The bursar, however, lived in a terrace near St Albans cathedral. She called in advance, and he was happy to see her. Amy knocked on the door, a small red one, that even she would have to crouch under to get inside. A neat-looking man in a yellow-and-blue-checked shirt opened the door.

'You must be the detective I spoke to,' he said, shaking her hand. 'Leonard Post, nice to meet you. Come in, come in. Tea?'

'No, thank you,' Amy said, coming into the house. She showed him her warrant card and he offered her an armchair, which she took. 'I'm DC Amy Noakes. As I said on the phone I am part of a team looking into cold cases, including the disappearance of Eliza Chapel.'

'Nasty business that.'

'Do you remember Eliza?'

'I remember the hullabaloo but no, not her personally, sorry. The girls were all just a blur of mustard jumpers, I'm afraid.'

'Right,' Amy said. She was wondering why she'd bothered to drive out here. 'Fine. Tell me about St Ursula's.'

'Well, it had been the site of an abbey but that had been torn down after the disillusionment of the monasteries. The land was given to a favourite of Henry VII's who tore it down and put up a new house. That burnt down in the Gregorian era, and the current building was then put up in the Cretan style.'

'OK, and what was it like to work there?' Amy wasn't much of a history buff but even she knew that most of what he had said was nonsense.

'Awful. I just needed the money. I don't mind telling you because it was so long ago now, but I was unceremoniously let go from my previous school because I'd forgotten to collect the fees from the fifth form for three entire years. The parents had realised but just didn't say anything, hoping they'd get away without paying. Old Chadwell didn't ask too many questions when she hired me.'

'Do you mean the headmistress, Mrs Iona Chadwell?'

'Yes, her. Dreadful woman. Ran the place on a shoestring, barely fed anyone anything, all while her snivelling brat of a child drove around in a sports car.'

'You think there was financial mismanagement?'

'Oh, definitely. I wasn't sure how she was getting away with it and I oversaw the books, but I would not be surprised.'

'You never saw any evidence of theft or fraud?'

'None, I'm afraid.'

'What were the other staff like?'

'Petrified. Or they were sadists willing to be beaten by her. All of 'em a sad bunch, sat in a sad house in a sad corner of Cornwall wishing their lives had turned out differently.'

'Did any of the staff members appear to be at all predatory around the girls?'

'Not that I recall. She was careful not to employ young men. There's always a risk of a twenty-one-year-old PE teacher who has their eye on the eighteen-year-old netball captain and that's the sort of scandal that would close a school like that down. Well, other than disappearing students, that is.'

'Can you remember anything particular happening to that year of girls? Like a school trip gone wrong? An offhand comment by a colleague that didn't chime right? Any colour really.'

'Oh, well, there was that kerfuffle with the two sisters.'

'You mean when one of them pinned the other down and cut her hair out of jealousy?' Amy had heard this story repeated so many times now, but no one else had said they were sisters.

'Yes, those two girls. I remember there being a big to-do over the skirmish, but the real scandal was that staff members had started to twig over the little arrangement the girls' father had with Chadwell. The girl who "wasn't" his daughter looked more like him than the one with his surname. There were a few rumours going round the staffroom. I think the father caught wind of it at parents' day at the end of the year and pulled them out. You see, it was between the headmistress, me and the father: he was paying the fees for both girls, but no one had told them or even his wife that they were half-sisters. Less than a month between them too.'

'So that's why the girls left the school. Did any of the girls in their form know?'

'I doubt it.' Leonard leaned back in his chair. 'Teenagers are too self-absorbed. I see him in the papers every now and then. Terribly rich – I don't know what people do with all that money – and now he's in Parliament. Harriet and Calliope. That was them. Simpson-Bamber is the chap. I've got a terrific memory for names.'

'Hi, Bellie, this is DC Amy Noakes. We spoke yesterday,' Amy said as she sat in her car. She needed to be sure. She was dreading the bursar being correct.

'Hello, detective. Any more news on Eliza?'

'Well, actually, I was hoping you could confirm the names of the two girls who left the school the year before Eliza went missing?'

'Hat the Brat and Lippy.'

'Yes. Harriet Simpson-Bamber and Calliope Foster?'

'Bingo. Gosh you're good at your job.'

47

Victoria Embankment Gardens

Callie sat on a bench watching people play ping pong on the permanent tables in the park. Callie had texted Caius a short, vague message saying that 'everything had gone to shit'. He'd asked for more details, but she withheld them. Then he asked where she was, which wasn't too far from where he and Matt were stuck in traffic, so he decided to take his lunch break then and there. He was concerned, of course, but he was at heart a gallant man and hoped his appearance (albeit not on a white horse) might be of some comfort to her. Callie saw him walk through the wrought-iron gate as she got off the phone with her mother. Theirs had not been a cordial conversation. Callie had told her that she'd had lunch with Peter, and he'd told her that he was her father. Her mother, in a spirited effort to pre-empt some of that afternoon's burgeoning chaos, had decided to catch a train to London, effectively adding to it. Cassandra was getting in to King's Cross in just over an hour and Callie wasn't going to open her front door to anyone for the next week just in case it was her.

'What happened?' Caius asked. He'd left Matt in the car. Freja had called him when they were interviewing Richard Gaskell. 'Something gone wrong at work?'

'I don't know that I can explain it at the moment because I don't really understand exactly what's happened.' Callie's phone buzzed and she checked it. 'And now my former best friend is having some sort of breakdown and won't stop calling me. I feel terrible because I told her to fuck off. I was so mean. It's all a mess. I don't fucking know what's going on.'

'It'll be all right, I promise.' Caius gave her a hug and stroked her hair as she sank into his chest. His phone vibrated; Amy was calling him. He ignored her. 'Have you eaten?'

'Yeah.' Callie couldn't begin to describe lunch.

'I'm afraid I don't have long so I'm going to go to the Pret and grab something. Do you want to come?'

'I'm just going to stay here; I fought hard for this bench. I stole it from some tourists.'

'Do you want anything? Are you thirsty? What about a nice cup of tea?'

'No, I'm fine.'

Caius bought himself a chicken and avocado sandwich – the protein pots were calling out to him, but he didn't think that gnawing on either a hard-boiled egg or a chunk of smoked salmon was necessarily a good idea this early on with someone new. He bought Callie a bottle of water and a tiny hazelnut truffle to cheer her up. He walked back to the bench to find a family of Canadians picnicking. His phone buzzed.

Callie
14.49
Sorry, I need a bit of alone time. Thanks for rushing over though. You're a sweetie. I'll call you soon x

Caius wondered if this was a brush-off but decided to take her at her word. He drafted and redrafted his response a couple of times before being annoyed with himself and sending something simple.

He sat down on the grass, turned his phone off so he wouldn't keep checking for a reply, and ate his sandwich. He was wishing that he'd got the protein pots after all, or even the macaroni cheese and a chocolate muffin, as he tried to keep at bay the idea that he might have just been given a gentle goodbye. It was still exceptionally warm for September. People were walking about in light cotton dresses and shorts – although he knew that short-wearing was not a reliable indicator of the weather in Britain. Matt appeared beside him.

'There you are. Your new bestie has been trying to call you but you're on silent or something so he rang me. I don't know how the hell he got my number. There's been a "fracas".'

'A fracas?'

'At the Simpson-Bambers' house. Uniform are over there now, but we should head over too.'

Caius got up from the ground, dusted the grass off the back of his suit jacket, and picked up his rubbish. 'We better get down there.'

'Where's Callie? I want to meet her.'

'She had to go.'

48

Eel Brook Common

Caius and Matt pulled up to the Simpson-Bambers' house in Fulham. Caius spotted a couple of cashmere-clad yoga bunnies at their windows, trying not to be seen peering out on their neighbours' misfortune. A panda car was parked on the grass verge opposite the house, and they could already hear screaming coming from inside the house. Amy called before they got out and Caius picked up this time.

'How was St Albans?' Caius asked.

'Very picturesque,' Amy said. Caius could hear something was off with her.

'Was the bursar helpful?'

'Yes, he was.'

'And?' Caius asked. It wasn't like Amy to not come straight out with it. 'Amy, what is it?'

'The two girls who left St Ursula's the year before Eliza disappeared are Harriet Simpson-Bamber and Calliope Foster.'

'Shit,' Matt said.

'The bursar thought that the reason they both left the school wasn't because of the big fight they'd had but to avoid a scandal. The staff had begun to realise that the girls had the same father.'

'Double shit,' Matt said.

'Thanks, Amy. Good work,' Caius said, before hanging up and turning to Matt. 'I'm such a fucking eejit. Callie said she was there to see an old friend in the play and I just didn't ask who. Shit. Shit. She's Simpson-Bamber's daughter. That's it. That's what Hampton was after. He wanted us to poke around to find a scandal to get rid of Simpson-Bamber. MP's secret love child is always a classic. Shit.'

'What are you going to do?' Matt asked.

'The only thing I can do,' Caius said, tapping his head on the top of the steering wheel. Just when he met someone, someone who had a perfect mix of sarcasm and joy pouring from them, it turned out they were connected to this mess. And not just that, Callie was connected to two very big, jumbled-up, chaotic cases that he might have already blown his career over. He didn't know what Callie would say when he told her that he was investigating her father or the school she went to. Would she not care? Would she take him at his word that it was all just a coincidence? He doubted it because he wouldn't.

They both got out of the car and walked up to the wide-open front gate. Shattering glass was added to the cacophony of sound coming from the house as they reached the front steps. Caius felt someone watching him and he turned around. Callie was leaning against the garden wall. She had been hidden from view from the street.

'What are you doing here?' Callie asked.

'Work, I'm afraid.' He gave her a weak smile.

'Hat called me again when I was on the District line home. I stupidly picked up and she was a mess. Apologising for the email, crying that her dad had lost his mind, her mum was throwing the good dinner sets at him, and begged me to come over and help.'

'Right,' Caius said, kicking himself for not realising sooner that Harriet wasn't just a fan of her work. 'Your friend in the play was Beatrice, wasn't it?'

'Yeah, Bea and I went to school together for a bit. Why do you ask?' She didn't understand why Caius was asking that now of all times.

He wanted to leave the doorstep and go to her, but Matt gave him a quick elbow in the ribs. 'Don't go anywhere. We need to talk. You can wait in the car if you want? It'll be calmer in there.'

'I need some air,' she said, but she moved away from the house all the same and stood under a tree on the green. Caius and Matt walked in. Peter Simpson-Bamber was on the stairs dripping blood on the sand-coloured carpet. When he'd described his wife as being a bit of a 'tempest' what he really meant was that she had a mean left hook. His nose looked out of joint. One of the uniformed officers was trying to get what had happened out of him but he just kept laughing.

'I think he's in shock,' the officer said to Matt who called again for medical support, before he searched the rest of the house to see if there was anyone else there. Caius walked into the living room to find Jane Simpson-Bamber simultaneously throwing breakables at the other uniformed officer who was trying to calm her down and hurling expletives in her husband's direction.

'Mrs Simpson-Bamber,' Caius said with a boom that he only used for the worst social disorder. 'Stop, now.'

She stopped, taken aback, and then went to pick up a vase to chuck at him. In that moment, the uniformed officer took her chance, deftly tackled her to the ground, handcuffed her, read her her rights, and arrested her for aggravated assault. Jane Simpson-Bamber was then escorted out of the house. She saw Callie as she went and called her 'the daughter of a whore' before the officer told her that enough was enough and shut her up in the back of their police car. A photographer, who had conveniently arrived at just the right time, got a picture of that moment for tomorrow's front page. It was one of the best photos they'd ever taken: the composition, the angle, the fury, the ambulance in the

303

background, the car door held ajar as Jane got in, the stance of the officer tense with action. It was an accidental Renaissance masterpiece.

Caius looked around at the carnage in the living room and then went back out to Peter Simpson-Bamber on the stairs. A medic had since arrived and was cleaning him up.

'He hit his head when he fell so we're going to take him to A&E just in case he's got a concussion,' the paramedic told Caius.

'I want him afterwards,' Caius said as he wondered where Matt had gone. He walked into the kitchen and saw him calming Harriet down.

'Daddy just said that I wasn't his child, and he was having me removed from his will. I don't understand. He got me to do a swab yesterday. Said it was to check for cancer genes, but he fucking lied to me.'

'That must be really tough. Have you got someone you can call? Your partner perhaps?'

'He's busy, but my best friend is waiting outside. My mother was yelling something about Callie, but I didn't get what she was saying.'

Caius and Matt looked at each other.

'Let me get someone to take you home, Ms Simpson-Bamber,' Matt said.

'Apparently, it's just Bamber now.'

'Would you like me to ring your fiancé?' Matt asked, giving Caius a nod to get Callie away from the scene. 'I think it might be a good idea to have him there to support you.'

'He's in fucking Zurich.'

Caius stepped out of the house and found Callie. She had wandered down the road and was perched on a neighbour's wall as she watched Jane be driven away.

'Jane just hurled a fantastic amount of abuse at me,' Callie said.

'I'm sorry. She's not shown the best judgement today,' Caius said, trying to gently usher Callie away.

'She's always hated me. Now I understand why. She must have had her suspicions.'

'Be prepared for Harriet to have strong feelings about your paternity.'

'I know all about Harriet and the strength of her feelings. She pinned me down and cut my hair off when we were fourteen. I don't know why I forgave her then. It was easier, I suppose, when we ended up at the same school again.' Callie looked up at him and realised that she hadn't told him that. 'Why are you here? You're based in north London, aren't you? You knew, didn't you? You already knew what Peter said to me at lunch.'

Caius took a deep breath. 'I've been investigating Peter and Jane Simpson-Bamber. They are both suspects in a case I'm working on.' He didn't know how to make that fact palatable. Nothing he could say to make it not stick in his throat or make it easy for her to swallow.

'Hang on.'

'I swear that I—' he began, but Callie cut him off.

'Did you know about my parentage, about all of this mess before we, um, we first met? Did you sleep with me so you could get information on whatever is actually going on here?'

'No! I didn't know about your connection to the cases I'm working on until ten minutes ago.'

'Cases?'

'Yes. One of them is the theft of a multi-million-pound pension scheme thirty years ago.'

'And you think the Simpson-Bambers did it?'

'I can't talk about it.' Caius stared at his shoes. He could see how furious she was with him. Until five minutes ago she had trusted him, but now she was looking at him with wounded eyes and growing fury.

'Fucking hell, Caius. You did know who I was, didn't you? Thought you'd worm your way in with me to get close to them. Did you follow me? Took your chance by sitting next to me in a theatre. Did that old guy even have a stroke? Was he an actor? God, I'm such a chump. I even gave you my card. I chased you.'

'That's not what happened. I promise.'

'Why don't I believe you?' Callie looked up at the door as Peter Simpson-Bamber was being led out by the medic. Callie couldn't look at him and he couldn't look at her. She watched Peter being put in the back of the ambulance. 'You said cases. My connection to your cases, plural.'

'My colleague needs to interview you in regard to the disappearance of Eliza Chapel from St Ursula's girls' school.'

Callie laughed. 'I knew you were too good to be true. All I need now is for Max to turn the corner.'

Matt coughed loudly as he came to the front door with Harriet.

'Do you want to wait in my car for a moment? While Matt sends Harriet on her way. She assaulted you when you were at school, right?'

'Yes.' Callie started walking further down the road so Harriet wouldn't see her and took out her phone to book an Uber to pick her up from around the corner. She couldn't bear to think about Caius right now. Too much was already racing through her mind as the small mysteries of her life began to make sense. 'I couldn't understand why Peter was charging me such a low rent on my workshop, but today he said he bought the building for me and my grandparents didn't pay my school fees, he did.'

Caius wanted to touch her, reassure her that as awful as it all felt it wouldn't be this bad tomorrow, but he knew she'd prickle like a cat if he tried. 'Look, I'll call you later when you've had a bit of time to take in everything that's happened today, and I'll try to explain things more clearly.'

'I won't answer, but I suppose I should turn up to be sodding interviewed. As long as you're not the one doing it.'

'Any time after 9 a.m. Ask for DS Matt Cheung.' Caius stared at his shoes. 'I swear that I—'

Callie waved him off and started walking down the road just as a squad car arrived to take Harriet home. The half-sisters passed each other without friendly acknowledgement. As Harriet began piecing together the things her mother had ranted about, she stared at Callie through the car window, and then started banging on it. Callie for once stared straight back at her and faced her wrath.

49

The Police Station

Jane Simpson-Bamber's solicitor was very expensive, Caius thought, judging by the cut of his suit. He was sitting away from the table with one leg crossed over the other so that Caius (who'd just entered the room) could see from the sole that the shoes were *italiano*. The room was quiet but for the noisy ticking of the solicitor's watch that he kept theatrically flashing as he checked the time, huffing as Caius started the recording.

'And what charges have you arrested my client on?' the solicitor asked.

'Two accounts of aggravated assault.'

'Against whom?'

'Two uniformed police officers who were responding to calls about a domestic disturbance at the property she shares with her husband. Mrs Simpson-Bamber threw an assortment of china, ornaments and glass vases at them.'

'And what proof do you have?'

'The officers were wearing body cams as part of a trial to improve community policing outcomes. I also witnessed this behaviour first hand. It may of course become two counts of aggravated assault and one of GBH depending on whether Mr Simpson-Bamber decides to press charges. He was found unconscious by the responding officers, after all.'

'Wimp,' she said.

'Don't comment.' The solicitor stood and picked up his briefcase. 'If that's all, it's best we go. We'll see you at Her Majesty's convenience.'

'Actually, there's another case I want to question you on, Mrs Simpson-Bamber.'

'And what's that?' the solicitor asked. Jane Simpson-Bamber wisely remained silent as per the solicitor's instructions.

'The theft of the Symington & Chase pension fund, and the murder two weeks ago of Lynne Rodgers, Robert Symington's secretary and lover, who drowned in the Thames.'

'That's preposterous,' Jane Simpson-Bamber said, laughing at the ridiculousness of what Caius said. 'She lives in the Copacabana.'

'Where were you on Friday 29 August?' Caius asked.

'I was at Nobu with Harriet, Harriet's fiancé Inigo and Peter. Their engagement party was the following day, but I wanted to do something just the four of us beforehand. After Nobu we came home, and Peter and I watched *Mad Men* until the small hours with a nice Pinot Noir.'

'May I have a moment with my client?' asked her solicitor.

'Of course,' Caius said, leaving the room.

★　★　★

'They're going to be a while,' Caius said to Matt, who was waiting in the corridor for him. 'I think he thought he could get her off on just a minor charge and then swan back to the office.'

'Why does he keep doing that thing with his watch? It's hardly intimidating.' Matt passed Caius a cup of tea and a folder full of documents that Caius had asked him to print out – the results of all his inquiries that had just flooded in – and a copy of a finance document from Symington & Chase that he saw in a quick glance confirmed his suspicions. 'Peter Simpson-Bamber is being escorted over from hospital. Mild concussion and they had to set his nose back,' Matt said. They grimaced at each other at the thought of the crunching sound Simpson-Bamber's nose would have made.

'Yikes. You all right to do him? Her solicitor is going to drag this out. He's clearly billing her by the hour if he wears shoes like that.'

'How did it go with Callie?'

'She thinks I slept with her for information.'

'Ah, mate.'

'Have you seen *Clash of the Titans*? The original one. There's a bit where the gods are toying with people's fates. I feel like a chess piece being battered about. "As flies to wanton boys" et cetera.'

'What are you going to do?'

'Not much I can do. I told her the truth. She'll either believe me, or she won't. Can you interview her tomorrow? I can't speak to her in an official capacity. I should resign from the case.'

'Do you think Hampton would let you?'

'Nope, but I will try after this.'

'What about Cornwall?' Matt asked.

'We'll have to see what happens with madame in there, but Amy might have to go on her own.'

'I just saw Amy in the break room. She said she's found Henry Chadwell. He's working in a private equity firm in Mayfair.'

'Tell her to get him in.'

★ ★ ★

'Mrs Simpson-Bamber, can you please describe where you were the day before Robert Symington's disappearance?' Caius asked.

'It was so long ago that I cannot possibly be expected to remember that,' Jane Simpson-Bamber said.

'Can you remember what you did the day he disappeared along with the pension fund?'

'Now that I do remember: I picked Peter up from the dentist. He'd had some work done and was woozy. I stayed with him to make sure he was all right.'

'Can you remember anything else about that day?'

'No.'

'Have you got anything further to ask my client? Because it seems like you're grasping at straws here,' said the solicitor.

'I don't need straws to grasp at when I've got government documents,' Caius said, patting the paper folder he'd had tucked under his arm when he'd come back into the room.

'What are those?' The solicitor was calm; he was going to enjoy this.

'All in due course. I know what you were doing the night before Robert Symington disappeared and it wasn't playing nurse. One of the machinists saw Robert get into a red Jaguar convertible outside the factory late that evening. That was your car. I wouldn't be surprised if Robert had actually purchased it for you.' Caius took out the DVLA record that he'd requested of all the cars Jane Simpson-Bamber had had registered for tax since she had passed her driving test. They'd sent over the record while he was at the Simpson-Bamber residence. It included a red Jaguar not unlike the one that Cheryl had described.

'That's circumstantial,' said the solicitor.

'Is it? When another employee claims to have seen you sharing an intimate dinner with Robert a few months before his disappearance?'

'Robert and I knew each other purely through business. We often would meet up to discuss work.'

'So he sacked Richard Gaskell for purely business reasons?'

'It was cheaper to hire freelancers.'

'You were the only freelancer he ever really used. We have their financial records. He only ever bought a handful of designs from others. Just enough to stop anyone from questioning him, I'd say. I don't need to get out my calculator to see that year he paid you much more than Richard's salary had been.'

'My work was better.'

'I think he fired Richard and hired you as a freelancer to keep you in a manner to which you wanted to become accustomed.'

'This is all supposition,' the solicitor said. He checked his watch again.

'Is it?' Caius leaned back in his chair. 'I spoke to your husband this week about the pension theft and something I said rattled him, but I wasn't entirely sure why. Now I know. I asked him whether he'd had a red Jag like the one Robert had been seen getting into. He knew straight away whose car it was. That's why he lied to your daughter and got her to take a DNA test. They normally take a little while to come back, but I suspect he paid more to have the results expedited. Harriet isn't his biological child. She's Robert's, isn't she?'

'No comment.'

'Here's what I think happened: you and Robert were having an affair; he wanted to leave his terribly suitable wife and his onerous inherited family firm behind. He planned on stealing the pension fund and then flying to Brazil where he couldn't be extradited. Something goes wrong. The pension disappears, but so does Robert. Were you supposed to fly out there too at some point, but you never heard from him? Or is it worse than that? He ditched you the night before for his secretary?'

'No comment.'

'How about this then: you realise you're pregnant, panic and

312

settle for Peter who you hope doesn't think too hard about the dates.' Caius pulled out the small box that Richard Gaskell had given him from the back of the folder and proceeded to take out the silk scarf. 'It's the "memento mori" design that you did for your husband's scarf company a couple of years after the disappearance. I take it you were having a rough time and were pining after your lost love. The big question here is, did you get to the pension fund first? And did you kill Robert to do so? Or maybe you killed him because you couldn't handle being rejected for a woman you clearly looked down on?'

Jane Simpson-Bamber looked appalled at this question. Her wounded pride long suppressed coming to the surface, full victim-hood ensued. 'Robert dumped me. The night before he left for his "research trip" he dumped me. I met him in my car, told him I was pregnant and then he ended it then and there. Told me to get it taken care of and then got out of the car. I never saw him again. I didn't know he was going to steal the money. I didn't know he was shagging that walking piece of lint. I knew something was up, but I thought it was just Robert preparing to petition for a divorce.'

'You really didn't know about the theft?'

'No, I didn't. All he told me was that he was splitting up with Cassandra and that he had a plan for the firm. I thought he was going to sell it. Why not sell it? It was a solid concern.'

Caius agreed with her that the obvious thing was to sell the company. 'And Lynne? Did you suspect they were a couple?'

'Like I said, I had no idea he was knocking around with her too.' Jane looked disgusted at the very concept.

Caius took out another piece of paper. Her birth certificate. 'You were born Jeannette Bamber in Merseyside. Your father was a docker and your mother a cleaner.'

'It's not a crime to reinvent yourself.'

'Of course not, but where does a docker get the money to set up a fashion company? Let alone one who'd been dead for ten years at this point.'

'No comment.'

'Did you steal the pension fund? You had time when Peter was knocked out and drowsy with his dental work. You were close to both of the men who had all the information you would have needed to do it. You're smart. You could've managed it.'

'I didn't steal it.'

'Where did the money come from to start up Fulham Girl then?'

'I sold my parents' house when my mother finally died. It was just before I started at Symington & Chase . . . I initially started freelancing there because I wanted to see what it took to have my own company.' Jane stared down at the table as she was consumed by embarrassment. 'I didn't want to admit to Peter where I grew up, so I lied to him and said that my mother had been dead for years and that my father was living in Spain. I said that the money from the house was a small business loan from my father. He then "died" soon after and was "buried" out there, so Peter never met him. I flew out to Spain for two days for the "funeral". Peter couldn't get out of work and Harriet was at nursery by then. I stayed in a hotel on the Costa del Sol for a night feeling like a fucking idiot and then I flew back. Being ashamed of where you come from is not a crime, detective. It's called myth-building.'

'Can you prove any of that?' Caius couldn't quite believe that anyone was that snobby they would fabricate a parental funeral rather than admit to being a Scouser to a Cockney.

'I've still got the paperwork from the sale in the attic. You'll find it's the exact amount that I gave to Peter to start Fulham

Girl. Peter paid "my father" back every penny. He put the money into an account of mine. It's still sat there. I've never touched it. I've just let it accrue compound interest for all these years.'

'Mrs Simpson-Bamber will be happy to provide those financial details,' said the solicitor, standing up. 'If that's everything, detective, then charge my client with aggravated assault and we'll see you in court, where she'll get a slap on the wrist and community service.'

'An officer will be round to collect that paperwork, Mrs Simpson-Bamber.' Caius noted the time as he ended the interview. The solicitor had waited until he could bill for the next hour before wrapping it up.

★ ★ ★

Caius was watching Matt interview Peter Simpson-Bamber, whose nose was swollen and whose eyes were turning black, from the other side of the glass. Peter hadn't yet said anything to contradict his wife's account. He had, however, said that he'd had an idea where the 'loan' had come from, but he just went along with it for the sake of his wife's pride.

'I had a fling with Cassandra Symington just before Robert disappeared. She'd come to me a few months before asking if I knew what was really going on with Robert. She felt that he was being distant with her and suspected he was having another affair. She wanted to know whether it was one of the girls in the factory. We became friendly and then one night we . . . I wasn't in a good place myself. Jane and I kept breaking up and then getting back together again and again. By the time Cassandra found out she was pregnant, so had Jane. I calculated that there was more of a chance that Jane's baby was mine than Cassandra's.' He shook his head at his abominable maths skills. 'I got it the wrong way round. Harriet is a clone of Jane, but Callie looks like the spit of my old mum. I wish things had gone differently. If I could do it all again, I wouldn't choose Jane over Cass. It felt easier, cleaner that way.'

'Did you know that Jane and Robert had had a relationship?' Matt asked.

'I suspected a flirtation, but I didn't think it was serious.' Simpson-Bamber shook his head again. 'Cass was married and besides, there was a small amount of suspicion at the time that either me or Cassandra was involved in Robert's disappearance. Can you imagine what everyone would've thought if she and I . . . That we stole the money and killed Robert. It wouldn't have been good for anyone to live under the threat of allegations like that.'

'The girls were both at St Ursula's, right? And you paid for both of them?'

'Yes, for a while.' Peter was curious about this switch in questioning but kept talking anyway. 'I thought Harriet was mine and it became apparent very quickly that Callie was also mine. I agreed that I would pay for some of Callie's upbringing and I had the two girls go to school together, hoping that if they didn't know they were sisters then they could at least be friends. Here we are though. They're not sisters after all.'

'And why did you pull the girls out of St Ursula's?'

'A few things – Harriet's tantrums had got worse for starters – but mostly because Cass didn't think the school was much cop. Having boarded herself she knew more about that sort of school than I did. She was insistent that I take Callie out.'

Matt ended the interview and left the room to get Peter a glass of water.

Caius's phone vibrated. It was Hampton.

'Was your theory correct?'

'It was not. However, Jane Simpson-Bamber has been charged with two incidences of aggravated assault against police officers, and I'm pretty sure they're going to have a very messy and public divorce mostly owing to the fact that most of their assets appear to be in her name and she was the driving force behind their businesses.'

Hampton didn't say anything.

'They hate each other right now, but they're sticking with a joint alibi for the night Lynne was murdered. They were at Nobu and then went home together.'

'Ah.'

'That's his parliamentary career over anyway. No one will take him seriously after that. He'll be on a reality TV show next year. Are you not pleased?'

'Do you think my motives are so base, so political?'

'Yes.'

'Good. I didn't think you were soft.'

'Look . . .' Caius began. Callie hadn't messaged him, and he was too scared to message her.

'What did you want to ask me?'

'No, no, um. Lord.' Caius took a deep breath. 'I shouldn't be on this case any more. It turns out that I sort of have a personal connection to both cases.'

'A personal connection?'

'I've just started seeing a woman.'

'Ah.'

'I'm not going to go into it but it's a conflict of interest. It

317

wouldn't be right for me to—' Caius said but Hampton cut him off before he could get to the end of his sentence.

'See the Symington case through to the end.'

'It's not ethical. Matt and Amy are perfectly cap—'

'I'm sure they are. Carry on your investigations, I can handle any potential questions around your involvement further down the line and I'm sure you can smooth things over with your young lady. I imagine it's nothing a bunch of flowers can't solve.'

'That's not how it works. The application of the law should be fair and free of bias.'

'That is exactly how it works. This is England, after all.' Hampton paused. 'How is your little folly going?'

'You mean the disappearance of a fourteen-year-old girl.'

'Such public spirit. It's a delightful quality. Exceedingly endearing. Don't lose it. Don't become an old cynic like me.'

*   ★   ★

'Mr Simpson-Bamber, may I ask you some questions off the record?' Caius asked as he set down the glass of water that Matt had fetched for Peter.

'It depends.'

'There's a colleague of yours, Arthur Hampton—' Caius didn't get to finish his sentence.

'Lord fucking Arthur.'

'Yes. I've had a good look over your parliamentary career,' Caius said. He remembered the conversation he'd had with Abi. 'And I can't help but wonder why a man with your obvious talents has been passed over for a ministership.'

'What do you think? I'm sure that fucker blocked my knighthood too, you know.'

'Why?' Caius wasn't sure whether this complaint was just Simpson-Bamber's ego at play or the crux of Caius's whole sordid business with Hampton.

It might have been the recent blow to his head or relief that his life's biggest secret was now out in the open, but Peter Simpson-Bamber was feeling very chatty. 'The man is insane. He has some personal philosophy that I can't work out, and somehow he has carte blanche to do what the hell he bloody wants. And what he wants is a total mystery. He has the PM under his thumb, they were at school together. The PM is an idiot who hasn't got a single idea on how to make this country better. He just sits there and does as he's told. Looks good on camera. Hampton disappears into the background and then reappears periodically with another weird policy that taken on its own doesn't look like much but I'm sure when you put them all together, they're building up to something.'

'How do you mean?' Caius asked.

'For one thing, he's changing the UK's drug policy without a single debate in Parliament. Hampton is running a covert "trial" in London where a company he's set up is selling small quantities of MDMA to members of the public through pubs. A man like Arthur Hampton doesn't get permission however, he asks for it after the fact.'

'Purple pills with a hippo stamped on them?'

'You're aware of it?'

'It's in my periphery. So, this "trial" was to see what?'

'Supposedly it was to ascertain whether recreational drugs can be sold in small quantities to the public in a "safe and regulated" way, but I know a monopoly when I see one. Who do you think will ultimately be in charge of handing out licences to sell these pills? He's going to make a fucking fortune. Wants to export as well.'

'I see, and the land reform committee that you're on with Hampton – what goes on there?'

'I joined out of curiosity because I couldn't work out what they were doing. Most of the committee is made up of members connected to large landowners. They just get angry about imported apples.'

Caius wondered why anyone cared that much about apples. Air miles or something environmental perhaps. He had begun to wonder whether the committee was functioning like a second shadow cabinet, but apparently not. 'Any other bills that Hampton is working on at the moment?'

'The last one was on the inheritance of aristocratic titles.'

'I saw that something went through, but I'm not sure of the particulars.' Family drama as Abi had called it.

'It's simple enough. Non-legitimate heirs can now inherit titles as long as the current titleholder (their biological parent) agrees, and a DNA test confirms their parentage.'

Caius wondered who would ultimately benefit from a law like that as he walked Simpson-Bamber to the back of the station to avoid any press that might be lurking. He wouldn't have been surprised if Hampton had set that in motion already. Caius asked him where he was staying.

'I'll call my daughter from the taxi,' Simpson-Bamber said as the car he'd booked turned up.

'Harriet?' Caius asked as Simpson-Bamber opened the car door and got in.

'No, my daughter's called Callie.'

'You have two daughters,' Caius said, shutting the door.

★ ★ ★

'I tried to quit the case, but Hampton won't let me,' Caius said as he looked through the financial records that Jane Simpson-Bamber had very quickly supplied, proving that she had indeed sold her parents' house and transferred the money over to her husband to start Fulham Girl.

'That's not surprising; you're his new favourite pet,' Matt said, looking over the notes he made from the interview. 'What did you think of the Simpson-Bambers?'

'I don't know,' Caius said, staring at his mobile. He'd not had any messages from Callie. 'This case is so woolly. I still don't feel like we've got to grips with Robert's movements the day he went missing. His wife said he left early to go to the office before his "trip", but no one saw him there so he must have been and gone before 8 a.m. at the latest. Someone would've seen him otherwise. Or he never went to the office, and it was just something he told his wife.'

'I can start again with the timeline if you want?' Matt asked, looking up at the whiteboard.

'No, it's all right. I don't think it would help. We're missing something though, aren't we? Go through the rest of the surviving staff and double-check their movements. One of them might have seen something that morning but didn't realise its significance at the time.'

'No problem. Harold, the factory foreman, was at the hospital with his mother, but I'll get onto everyone else.'

Caius stared up at the whiteboard. 'I'm still going to go with Amy to Cornwall. I'll drive there tonight and come back again tomorrow.'

'Are you sure? It's five hours away.'

'Yeah, I want to leave London for a few hours at least. See some open fields as I drive down the M5.'

'Caius,' Amy said, coming into the incident room. 'I can't get hold of Henry Chadwell. I spoke to his assistant, and she said he's in Frankfurt for meetings but he's back in the London office tomorrow.'

'He's the headmistress's son who Eliza had a crush on, right? I'll pick him up for you tomorrow,' Matt said. It would mean him staying late to look over Amy's notes, but he didn't have anywhere better to be. 'What's the headlines on him?'

'Works in client management for a finance company. Has done for the last six years. He was at an investment bank for ages before that,' Amy said, picking up her notes and summarising them. 'According to LinkedIn he has an English degree from Exeter, and he wrote his dissertation on the sexual politics of Samuel Richardson's works. He's president of the Samuel Richardson Society. Doesn't have much in the way of social media other than an Instagram but he's never posted anything on there.'

'OK. I'll read up on him tonight.'

'Cheers, Matt. I'll get you some fudge,' Caius said, before turning to Amy. 'How would you feel about driving down to Cornwall tonight?'

'I actually have krav maga tonight.'

'You're going without me?'

'I thought I'd scope it out first then tell you about it if it was any good. But yeah, tonight's fine. Are you mad at me? I'll buy the snacks for the drive down.'

'Damn right you are.'

50

Callie's flat, Acton

'Darling, I know you're in there. I can feel your malignance sliding out under the door. Are you binge eating a tub of ice cream? Is that why you won't open the door? You shouldn't eat your feelings. Come on, we need to talk. I'm sorry. All right. I'm sorry I didn't tell you that Pete was your father. Can you blame me? He may be rich now, but he is terribly gauche.' Cassandra Hunstanton, formerly Symington née Foster, was talking to her daughter through the letterbox of her bolted front door. 'I loved him at the time, if that makes it better.'

'Not telling me who my father is, is not the same as telling a child that their father was a bad man and by extension so were they,' Callie yelled, finally opening the door. 'He was a bad man because he chose Jane over you, right? Well, I'm choosing me over you so get the fuck out of my life. You malignant cancer of a woman.'

'Darling, I know you're upset, but you have to understand that my life was turned upside down and you were collateral. You were an accident. A pretty accident when you get yourself together, but an accident nonetheless. He comforted me when things were going poorly with my first husband, and one thing led to another. Callie, let me in. I'm your mother. I raised you. You owe me. I am your mother. You are so entitled.'

'I did not ask to be born. I do not owe you shit. You do not get a medal for providing the very basics of care. I'm done with this. I don't want to ever see you again. Don't ring me. Don't send your pathetic "poor me" grovelling letters. You are not the victim here. If you're not gone in five minutes, I'm calling the police to remove you.' Callie slammed the door shut.

Cassandra pissed off eventually and one particular policeman did happen to ring Callie, but she sent him to voicemail. She opened her Instagram and saw that a certain roguishly handsome baronet had slid into her DMs again, hoping to slide elsewhere.

RB
14.22
I'm so sorry if I was a little forward at lunch. I didn't mean to make you uncomfortable. I just haven't been able to stop thinking about you. I'll make it up to you over dinner tomorrow if you would like to join me?

You
17.45
That would be lovely

Callie got into bed and hid under the covers wondering whether it was possible for an adult to be smothered by a summer-weight duvet. Her phone started buzzing. She picked it up thinking it was probably Rupert asking for a picture of her boobs, but it was Harriet leaving her voice notes in between her 'father' calling. Callie ignored them both. Then Harriet started texting message after message. They started out nicely enough, claiming confusion and pleas of just wanting to talk, but then she started accusing Callie of trying to steal her life. Saying that Callie was jealous of her. Had always been. That she harboured feelings for Inigo. Callie blocked Harriet from her phone and not just WhatsApp. Then Inigo rang and Callie answered it. She'd always had a soft spot for Inigo and the way he usually managed to rein in Harriet's worst excesses. If anyone could get Harriet to leave her alone it was him.

'I'm going to need to move my 11 a.m. meeting, Lucinda,' Inigo said.

'Sorry, what?' Callie said. She should have hung up, but this pantomime had caught her by surprise.

'Hang on, just give me a moment,' he said in a quieter voice before performatively saying, 'I've got their details here some-where. I'm meeting their head of Legal. One second, Lucinda.'

Callie could hear Inigo moving around and then a door shutting.

'Sorry for the subterfuge,' Inigo said.

Callie wasn't sure what to say.

'Are you all right?' Inigo asked.

'Not really.'

'Harriet's gone absolutely nuts. She's literally rolling round the living room screaming because you won't answer the phone. I'm going to go stay at Jim's. I can't take it any more. I thought getting engaged would fix things, but it hasn't worked. She's been getting more and more het up about the wedding and now she's hysterical and I think she's still fucking that kid from Freddie's Flowers. Did you know about that?'

'No.'

'I didn't think so. You would've come straight to me if you had.' Inigo froze, then did a large sigh. 'The Eurostar? Tonight? Really? Lucinda, can you push back on that? You already have. I guess I'll have to go then.'

Callie heard a muffled exchange and a door slamming. She hung up.

51

The Police Station

Caius gave Matt a quick nod as he went home for the day after processing Jane Simpson-Bamber's charges and reading up on Henry Chadwell.

'You're on mute,' Amy said. The video was lagging.

'Oh, I'm on mute,' Mollie said. The slightest Californian twang had snuck into her voice. That low drawl at the back of her throat mixing with sharp English consonants.

'Hi there, Mollie, I'm DI Caius Beauchamp. You've been messaging with my colleague DC Amy Noakes. We're working on a cold case that you may be able to help us with.'

'Eliza?'

'Yes.'

'Bellie messaged me and said that you guys were legit and not scummy tabloid journalists.'

'What can you remember about Eliza?' Amy asked.

'I think she was lonely. Depressed even. It wasn't a warm place. I've talked about it a lot in therapy. We were basically a dorm room of teenagers parenting ourselves because our parents gave that responsibility to an institution that didn't love us, and didn't carry out the basic duties of care,' Mollie said.

'When you put it like that,' Caius said, nodding. 'A lot of the other girls we spoke to seemed to think that Eliza was a fantasist.'

'Of course she was. Your imagination is an easy place to escape to when you're trapped in a place like that.'

'Did you think any of the things she said were true?' Amy asked.

'It's hard to pull a single one out when they've been eclipsed by the outlandish. Have you heard that she said the Duchess of York was her godmother? She wasn't. I asked her.'

'Asked who?' Amy asked.

'Fergie. She's actually one of my mine.'

'Right,' Caius said, nodding away. 'Did you hear anything that night?'

'No, I'm quite sensitive to sound so I slept with earplugs in. Still do.'

'Did anything seem amiss when Eliza went missing? Did you notice anything out of place? Anyone acting different from usual.'

'Actually, yes. I only remember because the old thing was shot to buggery and I tripped over it every morning. God, I miss talking to other Brits – I said "bugger" to a colleague the other day and they didn't know what I meant. They googled it on a work computer and got a verbal warning. Very awkward.'

'OK. What did you notice?' Caius asked.

'Anyway, I told the policeman who came to interview us, but I don't think he even bothered to write it down. They didn't take any of us seriously, even Bea who swore blind she heard something on the lawn.'

'Right,' Caius said, hoping that a firm, encouraging noise might help Mollie along to the point of her story.

'Anyway, the next morning the rug that was on the landing near our dorm was gone. I only noticed because I used to trip over it all the time. It was on the way to the bogs and I'm not a morning person, at least I wasn't before I moved to California.'

'Uh-huh.'

'It was a tattered oriental-style one, curled up oddly in the one corner. Moth-eaten like the rest of the place. It wasn't huge but I swear it was there when I went to brush my teeth that night.'

'The rug disappeared?' Caius asked.

'Yes. I thought I was going mad. The policeman said that a cleaner had probably just moved it temporarily for a proper rinse and I was confused. That rug was so grim I don't think the cleaner could've moved it to shampoo. Too busy trying to fight the dust and the moths and the rot for anything as Byzantine as cleaning the rugs.'

'OK, thanks, Mollie. If you think of anything else. You've got our details.'

The video call ended.

'A rug is a fantastic way to dispose of a body if it was an impromptu killing. Who the hell investigated this case,' Amy said, making a note to poke around their reputation later.

'Someone who didn't want to imagine that a girl's body had been carried away in a rug.' Caius checked his watch. 'You head home, grab your stuff and I'll pick you up in two hours.'

52

Caius's police car

'What about a podcast on the climate crisis?' Amy asked, flicking through her podcast app.

'Is it hopeful that we can all collectively get our shit together, or is it doom and gloom?' Caius asked as he changed lanes.

'Ummm . . .'

'I'm going to say no to that one then.'

'There's a true crime podcast on Eliza's disappearance actually.'

'Hard pass,' Caius said as he turned off the M25 and onto the M4.

'I listened to the last episode out of curiosity.'

'And what did they conclude?'

'Sex trafficked from Cornwall to France via Guernsey and then to Morocco.'

'That's spectacularly bonkers, and probably racist. Abducted by a sheikh nonsense.'

'They're basing it on a sighting that some British tourists had in a market in Marrakech of a woman who they thought looked a bit like Eliza.'

'I've got an audiobook of Gemma Arterton reading *Zuleika Dobson*,' Caius said. He had been saving it for his next run.

'I like her.'

'Me too. She has a nice clarity to her voice. I'll put that on at the next services. I think there's a McDonald's coming up.' Caius hadn't been to one for months. He didn't think he could stomach it but what else was he to do when that was pretty much all the service station had to offer other than cold Ginsters pasties. 'We can stop off there.'

'Have you ever read any Samuel Richardson?'

'No, can't say that I have.'

'I only ask because Henry Chadwell is a member of a literary fan society.'

'Yeah, you said. We should give it a go. One of the pillars of English literature et cetera. There's bound to be a version on Audible.'

★   ★   ★

'Volume One of *Clarissa* is nearly thirty-four hours long,' Caius said as he downloaded the recording. He'd read the blurb; it sounded hard going. He wasn't sure he was in the mood for some sort of weird eighteenth-century melodrama about female virtue.

'How many volumes are there?' Amy asked.

'Three and they're all that long,' he said, taking a slurp of his strawberry milkshake.

'Cornwall isn't that far away.'

'Let's give it half an hour and then see how we feel.'

★   ★   ★

Ten minutes had passed and there was not a fry left in the parked car nor a willingness to continue listening to *Clarissa*.

'Fuck me,' Caius said, turning the recording off and putting Radio 1 on instead, before pulling out of the service station car park. 'I'm just going to read the synopsis on Wikipedia when we get to the B&B tonight.'

Caius, perched on the edge of the bed in the B&B, hung up. He'd called Callie for the second time, but she didn't answer. He left her alone. She would talk to him if she wanted, and he didn't want to press it in case she told him to fuck off. He thought about last Saturday and found the house on the village green on the estate agent's website. It was for sale for £900,000. He did the maths and if he convinced his dad to sell his flat and let him have the money – it would be his one day anyway – and if Callie sold hers then they could've bought it. Never mind. Never mind. Never mind about that house with sweet little Minton tiles in the hallway, a kitchen with an island, a garden with a pear tree and raised beds, a tiny primary school around the corner, and a greengrocer's opposite. Never mind. Never mind.

WEDNESDAY

53

Pirate's Cove Bed & Breakfast, St Ursula

'How would you like your eggs?' asked Maria, the B&B owner, placing a pot of tea in front of them. She fidgeted with her hair, trying to tuck it behind her ears and failing. The weatherman on the news had predicted the last week of September was going to be the hottest on record, and Maria hoped they'd be able to stay open for a week longer than they normally would. She wondered whether one extra review from these last-minute Londoners would make a difference. She doubted it, but it wasn't going to stop her from throwing everything she had at them.

'Scrambled, please,' said Amy. Maria smiled. Nice and easy.

'Poached for me, thank you,' Caius said. Maria nodded and wondered where the malt vinegar was. Everyone else recently had asked for fried or scrambled.

'Help yourselves to cereal and juice,' Maria said, gesturing to the table at the side set out with mini Kellogg's boxes and a jug of both apple and orange juice, before returning to the kitchen with their order.

'It's nice here. I wish I were here on holiday instead of work though.' Caius looked around the breakfast room. It was a sweet little place. The decor was coastal rather than nautical. There were no pictures of lighthouses in the loo or any fish-based paraphernalia, instead the walls were painted white with hints of grey and accents of sunny yellows. They helped themselves to cornflakes and orange juice.

'Darren has corralled all of the old staff that he could find at the station for 9 a.m., so we have an hour to kill before that. We should get the lie of the land, and scope out the town,' Caius said, eating a spoonful of cornflakes.

'From what I saw out of my window this morning it looks lovely.'

'I'm overlooking the car park.' Maria hadn't had any other rooms ready at short notice.

Maria came through the doors with their full English breakfasts. 'Sauces are just on the table in the corner.'

'Thanks,' Caius said. He had been looking forward to this – a plate of stodge to power him through the day.

'You must be the police come down from London then?'

'We are.' Caius hadn't ever lived in a small town and hadn't realised how quickly news could spread.

'My eldest sister used to clean up at the school. She hated it. Said she found mushrooms growing on the curtains. Not a nice place. You don't know how those people can bear to send their children away to schools like that when they should be tucked up warm at home. It's neglect, plain and simple.'

'Did you live here when Eliza disappeared?' Caius asked.

'No, I was living in Ilfracombe then, sorry.'

'Oh no, not at all. No need to apologise,' he said, smiling at her.

'Did you know Ruth Miller or Martin Hartley at all?' Amy asked.

'Oh yeah, I knew them. Good people. They both came to my sister's birthday party last year. It's that sort of place, we're in each other's pockets. I'm going to Martin's funeral later this week. Give him a good send-off.'

'What was he like?' Caius asked. That night at the theatre felt so long ago now.

'Martin looked at you for a little bit too long. It were as if he

336

was trying to see what you were thinking. It were as if he could see everything about you. You'd expect an optometrist to be like that though, watchful, I suppose. Perfect vision.'

'We heard that he and Ruth were very interested in Eliza's disappearance.'

'They had a bit of an Agatha Christie complex, looking for a puzzle to solve. They were bored, understandably. People retire out here but they're not from here. They don't have family. It's easy enough to make friends I guess, but the bungalows at the top of the hill are the last stop between either a care home or a coffin.'

'Right, yeah,' Caius said. He tried to work out the last time he'd taken his grandfather out for the day from his care home. Far too long ago. He should remedy that soon.

'Although they seem to have been right,' Maria said. Her earlier professional determination for at least four stars had dissolved and she was instead feeling chatty. 'You're here now because Martin died in front of you or something? Darren plays five-aside with my Carl.'

'What was Martin's theory on what happened?' Caius, after all that had happened since Lady Bracknell threw up over Martin's body, still didn't know exactly what Martin suspected.

'I don't know. I never asked. I think they were trying to be coy about it, but my sister used to clean for Ruth and knew her quite well. They were friendly by the end. Ask her. Darren's got her coming in for you.' Maria checked the time on her phone. 'Right, I've got to be going. I'm a teaching assistant in the off season. Carl will come and collect your plates.'

'Thank you so much for breakfast,' Amy said.

'Best poached eggs I've had in a very long time,' Caius said.

'You're very welcome.' Maria beamed. 'If you could leave us a nice review online, we'd really appreciate it.'

54

The Police Station

Matt stared down at his to-do list (in no particular order: Robert Symington's timeline; interview Callie; track down Henry Chadwell), then he stared out of the window and then finally he stared at his phone. He reread the last conversation he'd had with Freja, then he deleted their chat thread and her contact details. He'd collected his belongings from her place the night before and there was nothing left to say, so why bother keeping it all. Matt wasn't a 'drunk dial at 3 a.m. after a break-up' person, and he wasn't a 'let's go for a coffee in six months to catch up' sort of person either.

He did a quick google for Arthur Hampton using the news search function. It had become a ritual every morning. He was looking for that one piece that made Hampton and his fascination with Caius make sense. Yes, Caius was pretty good at his job but he still couldn't understand why he had been singled out by Hampton. The pit in his stomach grew every time he thought of it – something wasn't right. Matt still hadn't found that missing piece. He saw the time and went back to his to-do list.

'Hello, is that Tricia?' Matt asked.

'Yes, speaking,' she said.

Matt reminded her of who he was. 'Could you confirm the time that you got into the office the day of the supposed research trip?'

'Oh, my brother used to drop me off on his way to work, so close to 8.30 a.m., I'd say. It was at the same time Pete got in. I only remember because my brother nearly ran him over as he walked towards the factory from the car park that day. It was raining and the grip on his tyres wasn't great. My dad had been nagging him to change them for weeks but it was the summer so he kept putting it off. I kept apologising all morning, but Pete was nice about it. Raining in July, eh. That's English summers for you. Well, not any more, I guess.'

'Was there anyone there when you got there who wasn't normally in that early or vice versa?'

'Not that I noticed,' she said, pausing for a moment. 'Actually, you know what, Harold wasn't there, which was odd because he liked to be there before the girls all clocked in at 9 a.m. sharp and usually he made me a nice cuppa.'

Matt looked up at the timeline on the board. Harold was taking his mother to a doctor's appointment that morning and was late in. 'Thanks again, Tricia, bye.'

Matt ended the call just as Peter Simpson-Bamber arrived with a very officious-looking solicitor. He'd decided to press charges against his wife for GBH. Matt thought the solicitor had told him to as it would play well in their divorce proceedings: evidence of Jane Simpson-Bamber's domineering personality, so domineering in fact that she punched her husband unconscious when he finally challenged her on her historic infidelity and asked for a divorce.

55

St Ursula

It was eerily still. They had walked down a road of squat stone terraces towards the harbour; there were only four cars. Caius had peered into a couple of windows and hadn't seen much apart from greige walls and that IKEA sofa that every rental property had. He could see leaflets for weekly supermarket bargains beginning to pile up in the hallways.

'Half the town has been hollowed out by second-home owners.'

'I don't think there's much fishing going on either,' Amy said, pointing at the harbour. 'Most of those boats are for sailing.'

A few fishermen – far fewer than you'd expect – walked along the quay and away from the boats, while Caius and Amy meandered towards the police station. They walked past a gift shop that sold knickknacks made of rope, handmade soap and locally produced sea salt. The ice cream and fudge shops were boarded up. Caius checked the opening times and saw they were open only on the weekends between September and October, closing entirely over the winter before opening again in March. A clothing boutique selling luxury Breton tops, fisherman's caps, quilted gilets and novelty wellingtons for children had one bored shop assistant inside. They passed the church, named for the now infamous St Ursula who along with her entourage of eleven thousand virgins had been martyred in Cologne, or so Caius gleaned from an information board. They carried on up a cobbled street towards the police station.

★ ★ ★

'Everyone, these are the officers from London,' said DS Darren Trelawny to the room of assembled townsfolk. 'They're going to be interviewing each of you in turn.'

Caius introduced himself and Amy to a room of sceptical-looking people. 'Thank you for giving up your time today. One of you may have seen or heard something that may be useful to us. I'm sure Eliza's disappearance has hung over your community for all these years, and we just want to put an end to any speculation. Please refrain from discussing your recollections, as we don't want you to be influenced by each other.'

★   ★   ★

Caius, Amy and Darren were having a five-minute break before interviewing the last couple of people.

'Have you had any breakthroughs?' Darren asked.

'Most people seem to just remember how run-down the building was, the rude headmistress, and how distressed the girls and three-quarters of the staff were,' Caius said.

'I was a teenager myself when it happened. Me and my dad went out with the rest of the search party and combed through the woods between the school and the town. I think that was when I decided to join up actually.'

Caius nodded.

'What do you think of the original investigation?' Amy asked.

'I think it was lacking actually. Between us, I think my predecessors were unwilling to look too closely. Worried about the repercussions if they did. A lot of those girls were from quite important families who'd kick up a big fuss and get the school closed. It was a big part of the local economy.'

'Do you think there was a cover-up?' Caius asked.

'I've been thinking about it since I came to London, and there has to be. I don't like to speak ill of the dead, but my dad reckons that John Chenoweth, who was in charge, could've been on the take. He retired not long after, bought a big house and get this, it was in Devon.'

'Devon?' Caius said.

'Oh yes, Devon. Teenagers don't just disappear into thin air and Cornishmen don't move to Devon. I'm sure Eliza would've told someone if she had been feeling that depressed. That's what teenaged girls do. Unless the other girls were bullying her?'

'It seems to me that they were all bemused by her if any-thing,' Amy said, eating a digestive biscuit. 'Eliza liked making stories up.'

'What if one of her stories wasn't made up?' Caius asked. He sat down on an itchy hessian chair. 'What if one of the outlandish things she said was true. I doubt Sarah Ferguson would've had her done in for claiming to be her goddaughter but something else.' Caius explained to Darren what Mollie had told them about the disappearance of the rug on the way to the bathroom on the night Eliza disappeared. 'All this hangs on a rug.'

Amy checked the time on her phone. 'We should interview the last couple of people. Cathy Pascoe, one of the cleaners, or Jason Denzel, who was a gardener?'

'I'll take Cathy,' Caius said decisively, before turning to Darren. 'You couldn't have a quick look into John Chenoweth, could you? See if your old man was right about whether John fled in shame to Devon.'

'Only reason I can think to move there,' Darren said.

★ ★ ★

'Yes, I was Ruth Miller's cleaner. Nice lady,' Cathy said.

'Did she ever tell you what she thought had happened?' Caius asked.

'She was pretty coy, but I did overhear her and Martin once. They were talking about Halloween. They thought the fact that it happened on that specific day was really important.'

'Did they ever say why?'

'No, not to me.'

'Cathy, am I to understand that you were the one responsible for cleaning the dorm rooms?' Caius had already been informed at great length of the division of cleaning duties by a previous interviewee.

'I was, yes. Not that you could call it cleaning. I moved dust around from one side of the room to the other.'

'Did you ever find anything that in hindsight you'd consider worrying when going about your duties?'

'How do you mean? The girls' possessions or the school's?'

'Either. Anything that jumped out at you? Anything that shouldn't have been there?'

'More of them were on the pill than I cared to think about for an all-girls' school. Better safe than sorry though.'

'Was Eliza on the pill?'

'I don't think so. They were fairly young, what, fourteen or fifteen, but in that year there was one. The girl who was really quite pretty. I found it under her pillow one day. I just put it back. I didn't want to be responsible for something bad happening.'

'So this girl had a boyfriend?'

'Presumably. God knows who though. They were cloistered up there. That old witch kept that place like a medieval nunnery. A trip into the town on Saturday was as exciting as it got. They weren't allowed phones. They were like bricks then, no internet access like now, but if we found one we had to hand it in.'

'Were there any of the staff members who you might suspect of having a sexual interest in any of the girls?'

'No one is jumping out at me. The staff were either sad older women or bewildered younger women who never stayed around for long. I'm sure they were underpaid. Definitely underfed.'

'What about the bursar?'

'Nice bloke, really forgetful. Called me Mandy. I'd say it was Cathy and he'd say he'd try to remember then he'd forget. That or he just wanted to make me feel small. I think it was the former though.'

Caius took out his phone, did a quick google and showed Cathy Beatrice's headshot from her agent's website. 'Is this the girl you thought was on the pill?'

'Yeah, she's turned into a looker, hasn't she? Always was a pretty one.'

'And did you tell Ruth about this?'

'Of course I did. To be honest, I think that was why she hired me. Another person who had been there. Someone else who'd had a chance to stop something terrible from happening if they only had realised.'

'There was a rug between Eliza's room and the bathroom. Do you remember it?'

'Oh God, that ugly thing. I remember it because I tried to have it thrown out, but the headmistress insisted it stayed. Something about having rugs about the place kept the heating bill down. It was moth-eaten and an absolute nightmare to clean. Clumps would come away when you vacuumed it. Why?'

'Did you ever remove it to clean it?'

'No, far too much effort. It needed binning not cleaning. Did it get binned? You know, I'm not sure now. It might have done in the end. It was gone one day anyway.'

'Thanks, Cathy.'

'Not at all. Leave our Maria a nice review. She does a good breakfast.'

'She does indeed.'

★ ★ ★

'My cousin is the site manager up at the old place,' Darren said, once Caius and Amy were finished. 'He said they're going to start work next week, but I said actually you wanted to have a look round today. So he said all right – we can go straight after lunch.'

★ ★ ★

They were outside the two rooms that had served as the fourth-form dorms. Caius, Amy, Darren and Darren's cousin Sam were tiptoeing around the first floor, trying to avoid rotten floorboards. Sam had insisted that everyone wear hard hats and high visibility jackets. They stood peering into what had been Eliza's room. The flocked wallpaper had peeled off the walls in patches and tattered curtains clung to their fastenings. Metal-framed beds were still lined up against the walls with mouldering mattresses on top.

'Where's the bathroom from here?' Amy asked.

'It's down here,' Sam said, pointing towards a long thin hallway that had originally been a service corridor that ran between the two wings of the house. 'There are actually two bathrooms there. Three loos and three shower cubicles in each.'

Caius peered down the corridor, looking for the rug that wasn't there. 'Where does that door at the very end go to?'

'It was built as a staircase for servants, accessible from all floors. It goes right down to the ground floor. Next to what I believe was the infirmary. We found a couple of beds, thermometers and boxes of plasters down there when I was here for my last recce. The staircase has got a fire exit at the bottom onto the grounds,' Sam said.

'Is that important?' Darren asked.

'I don't know yet. Where did the headmistress live?' Caius asked.

'In the old gamekeeper's cottage just across from here. It's a shortish walk from the staircase if you go round the pond. It's all a bit overgrown now though. You'd need a machete to get through it. We're turning the cottage into a crèche for the guests. This place is going to be amazing when it's all done up. The Malaysian company that's bought it are sparing no expense. Spa, Michelin-starred restaurant, horse riding, swimming pools. They want to do conferences and weddings here. It's going to be huge for the town. People will be coming for breaks out of season.'

56

Mayfair

Matt was standing in the offensively neutral waiting area of a Mayfair private equity firm. Initially he had thought that all the art on the walls were Jackson Pollock knock-offs. The odd dribble of red or yellow revolted against the taupe misery of the place, until he realised they were real Pollocks and the security guards standing by the lift were for the art not the people who worked there. The receptionist, a polished woman who was tailored to within an inch of her life, had dumped him in a side room ten minutes ago. His phone rang.

'*Bon après-midi*, any luck with Henry Chadwell?' Caius asked.

'I'm at his office now,' Matt said.

'Take him back to the station and formally interview him. He wasn't interviewed the first time round as presumably he wasn't there the night Eliza went missing but I just want to be sure.'

Matt walked back out to the main reception area. He had a good look at the logo this time and realised that Henry worked at the same company as Harriet Simpson-Bamber's fiancé Inigo.

'Excuse me, I need to speak to Mr Chadwell. It's a matter of urgency,' Matt said.

'I'm so sorry,' she said, looking on edge. 'Mr Tatton, our CEO, wants to have a word with you.'

'Why?' Matt asked. He'd made it very clear when he arrived that he was here to speak to Henry Chadwell not the CEO. There was no need to bother him.

'I don't know, but he was very insistent.'

The lift pinged behind them.

'Detective . . . I'm sorry, I didn't catch your name. I'm Toby Tatton. Follow me,' said a lean, tanned man who, judging by the receptionist's reaction, was the firm's revered CEO. He practically scooped Matt into the lift and pressed the button to take them up to the building's penthouse.

The whole top floor was Tatton's office. His assistants – for he had two, one for diary management and one who remembered family birthdays – sat at desks facing the lift. They jumped into action as soon as the lift doors opened.

'Tea, coffee?' asked one.

'No, thank you,' Matt said.

'Suzanne is in there already,' said the second assistant.

Matt followed him into his office. The building was on the edge of Green Park, and they had a view of Buckingham Palace. Tatton sat down on a sofa next to a self-possessed woman and gestured for Matt to sit down opposite them in an empty armchair.

'This is Suzanne, our HR director,' said Tatton.

'I understand that you've asked to speak to Henry Chadwell,' she said.

'Yes,' said Matt.

'What about?' she asked.

'I can't tell you that.'

'Are you a financial investigator?' asked Tatton.

'No.'

'Oh.' He looked relieved.

'Do you think Henry has committed some sort of financial crime?'

'No,' Tatton said firmly.

'What's going on?' Matt asked.

'Henry resigned this morning. He has refused to work his

notice and is taking his remaining annual leave instead,' said Suzanne. She had been writing down everything that was said in shorthand. 'We have concerns about his mental state. He is usually quite a calculated, considered man and he sounded quite frenetic.'

'Where is Henry now?' Matt asked.

'We don't know. We're worried that he's had a breakdown of some sort. We're a very caring firm that takes our employees' mental health very seriously. We had thought that perhaps you had "news" for us?'

'No, I would just like to speak to him.'

'So would we,' said Suzanne. She looked at Matt and put her pen down.

'Henry worked in client management, right? I take it you're worried that in his distressed state he what, divulges something about a client that he's not supposed to?'

'As per company policy Mr Chadwell signed an NDA when he began working for us, and we hope he honours that,' said Tatton, standing up. He wanted Matt gone now he knew he wasn't attached to a specialist financial crimes unit.

'Right,' Matt said, wondering what use that NDA would be if Henry had had some sort of breakdown. 'Do you mind if I ask you a few questions about Henry, Suzanne?'

'Of course,' she said.

'Does he work closely with Inigo Chetwynd?'

'I'm sorry?' Suzanne said.

'Do they work closely together?'

'Inigo works closely with everyone due to the nature of his role,' Tatton said. He shifted his weight around.

'Interesting,' Matt said. He could see he'd clearly hit a nerve by asking about their wunderkind.

'I'm afraid Mr Chetwynd is away from the office today,' said Suzanne.

'Yes,' said Matt. Inigo was probably at home consoling Harriet. 'Thank you for your time.'

★ ★ ★

'Mate, I've asked for uniform to check out Henry Chadwell's place in Dulwich,' Matt said. He'd called Caius straight after he'd called the specialist task force that dealt with financial crimes to give them a heads up that something might be going down. He wasn't sure that anything dodgy was going on at the PE firm but Tatton's reaction to him asking questions about Henry and Inigo was odd.

Caius put Matt on speakerphone in the car for Amy to hear too. 'He's AWOL from his job and they think he's had some sort of breakdown.'

'Shit.' Amy regretted not having tried harder to speak to him before.

'We need to find him,' Caius said as an idiot in a stupidly large SUV tried to overtake him. 'Amy, have you got a signal? See if you can find anything on Henry. Matt, we're driving back now. Google Maps says we'll be back in four hours. We're coming up towards the M5. Let me know when you hear from uniform in Dulwich.'

'Sure,' Matt said, before tentatively changing the subject. 'Callie's not been in yet.'

'I didn't think she would,' Caius said.

'I'll call her if she doesn't appear soon,' Matt said, taking the responsibility – liability – away from Caius.

57

Calliope Foster Millinery

The first thing Callie had done that morning was install the new doorbell that Caius had recommended. He was right. It was bloody brilliant. She sat in the back of her workroom and watched on her newly downloaded app as nearly all the people she didn't want to talk to rang it, and she just pretended that she wasn't there. Her mother. Apparently, her father. Her former best friend who, having had further conversation with not-her-father-but-actually-Callie's, was currently banging her door down as she demanded to know why she'd been written out of his will. She was watching Harriet get more and more irate. It was exactly like when they were teenagers and Hat the Brat would just go ape-shit and tear down the curtains in their dorm room. Mrs Simpson-Bamber had spent a small fortune on child psychologists to work out that Harriet didn't want to go to boarding school. They carried on sending her anyway. The 'advantages' were just too good, too many.

The second thing Callie had done was to rearrange her client meetings for the day – including Penny de la Croix who still wanted the pillbox after all for another wedding. Callie didn't give her clients a reason why – she felt it made her more mysterious and just a little powerful. Any power she could grapple back from the fuckers she prostituted her art to was something to celebrate today. She watched Harriet finally give up and then, ten minutes later, a courier arrived. She signed for the package. Inside it were five more Hermès scarves – each one a different design.

You
10.40
You really didn't have to send me any more scarves

RB
10.40
I thought they were rather elegant

You
10.41
You're making an unnecessary dent in your bank balance

RB
10.41
Don't worry about that
7 p.m. tonight, The Court House Marylebone. Ask for me

You
10.41
What do you mean ask for you?

RB
10.42
I own it

Rupert had something of Max about him. That was the only reason she could think of for why she was still going to dinner with him. Max was charming, if only superficially, confident and eloquent, and so was Rupert. Max worked in an advertising agency and was prone to 'blue sky thinking', whatever that was, and she could tell that Rupert, despite his obvious earthly desires, was a man whose head would be in the clouds for eternity. Neither of them were practical men, but talkers and poseurs. They were both quite distressingly handsome in the classical sense, intense and all-consuming, and that was why she suspected people let them get away with things. Why she had let Max get away with everything for far too long.

Callie wondered if she was going to dinner to challenge herself. It was a test to see if she was as weak as she thought she was – whether she was capable of choosing something else for herself. When she and Max had broken up and his things had been left in boxes in her building's entrance, she berated herself for choosing him, for choosing to stay with him when he'd 'slipped up' previously, for buying a wedding dress when her gut told her not to.

For a moment Callie hovered over Caius on WhatsApp. He'd last been online half an hour ago. He'd called her once last night but nothing since. Caius had seemed so decent, so benevolent and so honest, but she had been fooled again. Callie laid her head on the workbench. Why couldn't she be allowed to be happy? Why was she denied it? Refused it.

Callie checked the time. She should do her civic duty before they sent a car after her.

★ ★ ★

Matt had Callie state her name for the tape – the first tape. She described to him what had happened yesterday.

'I asked for a fire door for my workroom from my landlord as an acquaintance said that it would be safer,' Callie said.

'Right,' Matt said, knowing full well that the acquaintance in question was a shared one who sometimes got a bee in his bonnet about health and safety as well as the fruit intake of those around him. 'What then?'

'My landlord, Peter Simpson-Bamber, came round that morning, agreed to fit a new door, and then invited me to lunch at his work.'

'Can you please clarify your relationship with your landlord?' Matt asked. He didn't want to cause Callie any pain, but he couldn't let her off either.

'At this point he was just my former friend's father.' Matt smiled at her sympathetically as she began to elaborate. 'I had lunch with him in Parliament. Afterwards, he asked me to go for a walk down the Embankment. He had something he needed to say. I thought it was going to be about Harriet's stupid wedding, but then he told me that he had instructed his solicitor to begin divorce proceedings. Apparently, my mother had been married to a man, a swindler, who had deserted her, and he'd been there in "her hour of need". He's the one who paid for my school fees and gives me an unbelievably cheap rent on my workshop. He gave my mother money for the deposit on my shitty little flat in Acton. Harriet on the other hand had been given outright a gorgeous pied-à-terre overlooking Clapham Common. That's my villain origin story in full. The secret spare who's now the only heir. I wonder how much I'm now worth.'

'What happened after that?' Matt asked. He had his hand hovering over the button to pause the interview. She looked like she might cry.

'I sat in the park at the back of Embankment station for a bit but then began heading home. After receiving a series of distressed voice notes from Harriet, I spoke to her on the phone and she asked me to come to her parents' house in Fulham as her mum had had some sort of breakdown, and I just went. I felt responsible maybe. Anyway, the front door was open, and I just sort of put my head through. Jane was throwing things – you could hear trinkets smashing periodically and her screaming at Peter – so I waited just outside for Harriet to come out. Jane has never liked me; she probably always suspected my paternity, and I didn't want to be in her line of sight. I heard Peter yelling about how he couldn't believe that she'd lied to him for all those years and that he'd already changed his will with neither of them getting a penny. Then there was silence for the briefest moment and then I heard Harriet becoming hysterical. I didn't see what happened though. Then your lot arrived.'

Matt ended this part of the interview and got Callie a cup of tea. He put a couple of the fancy lavender biscuits that Caius had bought for him on a little plate. She looked sad. She deserved a biscuit. He also thought he deserved a biscuit, although not as much as he'd needed one yesterday or the day before that. He brought them in and put them in front of her. 'I hope you don't think I'm interfering, but Caius is one of the best people I know, and he really likes you. He didn't have a clue you were connected to any of the cases until yesterday.'

'I read an article last night about undercover policemen fathering children with the women from the political groups they were embedded in,' Callie said.

Matt left her alone. After ten minutes Amy, who had just got back to the station, came into the interview room, and began interviewing Callie over her time at St Ursula's.

'Callie, I understand that you were in Eliza Chapel's dorm room the year before she went missing,' Amy said, for the second tape. Matt had told her about their off-the-record conversation and she was keen to stay as professional as possible.

'Yes. I can't remember much about my time there though.

That's probably a coping mechanism. I just know that I hated it. But I do remember that I liked Eliza. She used to say the most outlandish things. It was funny.'

'Do you remember anything about the "Daughters of Hecate"?'

'Oh, the Halloween witch thing. I had totally forgotten about that. I was the "chosen one" in our form.'

'What did it entail?'

'A lot of squealing and hysteria from the other girls in the dorm when they came to collect me wearing black capes made from old curtains, but then the "daughters" all went and drank hot chocolate in the kitchen. There was cake as well, which was weird because we basically lived on overboiled carrots and tinned potatoes the rest of the year, but then it was the old witch's birthday. She probably wanted to keep us all busy while she cracked open the sherry and actually sacrificed virgins. Harriet was so mad I was picked and not her. I think that was one of the reasons she ended up chopping a chunk of my hair off.' Callie rubbed her afflicted ear.

'Did you ever meet the headmistress's son?' Amy leaned in.

'Yeah, he was nice-ish. Half the school was in love with him, but I never really saw it myself. He gave me a chocolate bar once because he said I looked sad.'

'Do you think that he could have been dating Eliza?'

'Oh no. I don't think so. Eliza was . . . Well, if you expected any of the girls in our year to have had a boyfriend it would've been Bea. Besides, he was what, twenty-one, twenty-two and we were fourteen, fifteen. That's gross. He was a grown man.'

★ ★ ★

The door to the incident room opened. 'Sorry, Caius, we've got a woman here who says she has some evidence for you,' said Janet.

'Did she say who she was, Jan?' Caius asked. He'd been moping at his desk while Matt and Amy spoke to Callie.

'Cassandra Hunstanton.'

★　★　★

Cassandra Hunstanton, Callie's loathed mother, was waiting for him. Callie looked like her, but he was sure she wouldn't appreciate being told that. Cassandra handed Caius a manilla envelope. 'Here's the letter that Lynne Rodgers sent to me. My husband had put it away in a drawer. As I was coming to London, I thought it would be quicker to give it to you than hand it in locally. I meant to drop it in yesterday but got distracted. I reread it. It's total nonsense.'

'Thank you,' Caius said. He looked at the manilla envelope as he tried to grasp the words he wanted to say. 'Why was your daughter removed from St Ursula's? We heard it was because the staff had worked out what was going on with Peter Simpson-Bamber's arrangement. Is that true?'

'St Ursula's? Why do you ask?' Cassandra looked startled at this policeman who knew so much.

'We are also looking into the Eliza Chapel case. Peter's unusual arrangement came up in our investigation.'

'No. I'm sure there were rumours though. Callie has his nose, it's fairly obvious if they stand next to each other that they are related. No, it was me. I pulled her out. I didn't want to send her there in the first place, but tightwad Pete insisted. It was clearly a second-rate school.'

'So that's why? You just thought it was crap.'

'No, well, yes, I did think it was inadequate, but I made my mind up after the end-of-year parents' day. You know what those tedious days are like, demonstrations, piano recitals, flower arrangements in marquees and piddly little glasses of cheap cava. Awful, so dull, but when I saw that young man, I put my foot down. There was something off in how he was looking at her from across the marquee that I didn't like. He was in his twenties. I insisted that Callie be removed from St Ursula's – all of the girls looked a little grey as it was, and Callie complained about it constantly. I told Peter that if he didn't, I'd go to the press about his illegitimate love child and drag up the Symington & Chase business again. I always thought there was the smallest chance that Peter had stolen the money and wouldn't want the attention, so I'd kept that one in my back pocket for real emergencies. He moved Harriet at the same time too. He liked that sibling discount. That awful girl had pinned Callie down and cut a big chunk of her hair off over that boy too – he'd given Callie a chocolate bar or something silly and Harriet didn't like not being the centre of attention. I was not pleased about it. Callie had to get a bob so it would grow out evenly. It didn't suit her.'

'Harriet chopped off Callie's hair because she was jealous of the attention that Callie was getting from Henry Chadwell.'

'Bored schoolgirls – he was the only young man of their "social standing" that they saw all year – but still there was something off with him that I really did not like. He had that glint in his eyes – like a dead shark or something.'

★　★　★

'Did Ruth Miller know that Halloween was Iona Chadwell's birthday?' Caius asked. Matt and Amy had come up to the incident room after finishing with Callie. 'If so, then she probably wondered whether Henry Chadwell would have come back from London to see her.'

'But he wasn't interviewed at the time, so we can assume that he didn't,' Matt said.

'I'm not so sure about that,' Caius said, pacing up and down the incident room as he worked out a hypothetical situation. 'I need to speak to Darren and see what he found out about John Chenoweth, the DI on the case originally. Cathy, the cleaner, found the pill in the other dorm room, and she was adamant it was under Beatrice's pillow. Martin was here in London to speak to Beatrice specifically, he wasn't just trying to speak to the girls in Eliza's year. I bet he was going to ask Beatrice whether she had been in a "relationship" with Henry when Eliza disappeared.'

'OK, so we're pretty sure now that Henry Chadwell is a nonce?' Amy said.

'Yeah. Beatrice is locked up in the infirmary overnight with the nurse, so Henry takes his chance with the first girl he can find,' Caius said.

'Eliza,' Amy said.

'Who got up to go to the loo in the night. Something goes horribly wrong. He attacks Eliza. Tries to keep her quiet and uses too much force perhaps. Eliza dies. Henry, maybe with his mother's help, removes the body in the rug and disposes of both. Eliza looked quite slight though, so he might have managed it on his own.' Caius stopped speaking.

'What's wrong?' Matt asked.

'It's Callie. One of the other girls called her Lovely Lippy.'

'It's probably because they were purposefully mispronouncing Calliope, you know what teenagers are like.'

'It's the "Lovely" that's more troubling. Beatrice was the

second choice for the prefects and their pretend cult. I don't want to read too much into a chocolate bar, but I wonder if he was going to try to groom Callie too. Giving the girls sweets and chocolates in a school that practically starved them is a classic grooming technique.'

58

The theatre

Caius was shown back up to the theatre manager's office. He was so annoyed with himself. Beatrice had told him that it was a 'maniac with a St Trinian's fantasy' but he hadn't given her remark proper weight.

Beatrice was already waiting for him. She was biting her nails as she watched a van unload a delivery for one of the shops in Chinatown out of the window when Caius joined her.

'Back again?' Beatrice said. She turned to face him, arching an eyebrow, preparing herself to use wit to volley back whatever he was going to throw at her.

'Yes.' Caius looked her in the eye and he could see that her archness was as false as the set walls downstairs. She couldn't hold his gaze for long so instead she carried on watching boxes being carried out of the van.

'I have some difficult questions to ask you, I'm afraid.' Caius got straight to it. He wasn't sure how else to broach the topic otherwise. 'Did Henry Chadwell give you the pill to take in the weeks running up to Eliza's disappearance?'

Beatrice froze before starting to breathe shallowly. She focused on a spot on the wall and began to regain control. 'He comes to see every play I'm in, you know. Opening night of fucking everything. Sends me flowers to congratulate me on my performance. First thing I did out of drama school, a piddly little scratch night in the upstairs of a pub, and there he is slap bang in the front row. Every single opening night.'

'He's still stalking you?'

'Would you call it stalking? He's not following me home at night.'

'I'd call it stalking.'

'I don't understand why he's still so fucking interested in me.' Beatrice finally looked at Caius. He could see the pent-up resentment she had bubbling up into a fury against the man who had marred her career with his oh-so-subtle power plays. Beatrice looked like she was going to scream. She needed to.

'Do you want to tell me what happened?'

'Henry liked girls. Not women. Girls. We were all infatuated with him. He was some kind of god to us. Girls' schools are odd places. Our parents shut us up away from the corruptions of the outside world. St Ursula's was supposed to turn us into young ladies with accomplishments and matching dinner sets and good marriages to the right sort of man. We were supposed to be trained for estates and shooting parties and ski chalets, diplomatic circles, hunt balls . . . instead we were fair game. Henry, or Harry as he wanted you to call him if he liked you, used to make eyes at Lippy but she wasn't bothered by him. Everyone else was though.'

'And your friend Lippy is Calliope Foster?'

'Yeah, she used to pout when she concentrated. She came to see the show the night Martin Hartley died actually.'

'Yes,' Caius said, trying not to think about that night and the nights it had led to.

'Lippy was pulled out anyway and I guess I was next in line. He'd stolen the pill from his housemate in the shared house he was in in Balham and told me to take them the week running up to Halloween. He'd been working on me, manipulating me. Chocolate bars. Attention. I never went home on the weekends because my parents were usually out of the country, so he'd get

362

me to meet him in town on Saturdays when we were allowed in. He'd take me in his car and then we'd go for walks along a beach where no one would know who we were.'

'Did you tell anyone?'

'No, I was forbidden to.'

Caius couldn't imagine a parent and child having that remote a relationship that they wouldn't tell you something dreadful like this. 'What about the headmistress? Did she know what he was up to?'

'He was as perfect to her as he was perfect to us. She didn't see it. Or she chose not to.'

'What happened the night Eliza disappeared?' He watched her take her rings off and then put them back on. 'All of it this time.'

She closed her eyes as she began her tale. 'Harry came back every year for Halloween for her birthday. He drove up late in the afternoon from London. The witch trial was only allowed to go ahead because it was old Chadwell's birthday and she wanted us distracted so she could enjoy her evening. She gave the teachers a pot of money and they all got drunk in the staffroom.'

That hadn't surfaced in the police report, Caius thought to himself. Iona Chadwell must have covered up Henry's presence too. 'What happened to you that day?'

'I asked Bossy to hit me in games, but to make it look like an accident. I knew that the infirmary had a lock on the inside of the door, you see. They kept large quantities of paracetamol and things like that in there and a girl had broken in and tried to overdose the term before. So all the drugs were locked away in a cupboard, but the door to the infirmary had a Yale lock too. I tripped the catch so that it couldn't be opened without a key.'

'So you knew what he had planned then?'

'Harry had a fantasy about taking one of us in the night.

363

Something about a book he'd read. He told me about it the last time I saw him. I didn't want to take any chances. I'd started to get scared of him by then. He did that thing where he put his hand on the back of my neck so I couldn't move when we were out on the beach. Harry tried to get into the infirmary to get me, but he couldn't because I wouldn't unlock the door. Someone must have told him about my accident in passing. The nurse was there asleep in a side room, but she'd been drinking with the other teachers, plus a couple of sleeping pills and one more glug of whisky to send her off. She didn't hear him rattling the door and trying to speak to me – she was practically unconscious – but he didn't want to risk it.'

'And the sound you heard, what was that?'

'I don't know what it was exactly, but it sounded like a girl. A shriek out on the lawn.' She looked at him.

★ ★ ★

Caius had spoken to the uniformed officers whom Matt had sent to Henry Chadwell's place in Dulwich. They said the place looked empty, no one responded when they knocked on the door, and there was a pint of milk on the doorstep.

'Amy?' Caius said. He was drinking a cup of peppermint tea. His stomach was in knots.

'Yeah.'

'Chadwell's assistant – do you think she told him you'd been in touch?'

'I would have if I were her.'

'Me too. I don't quite get what's going on here. Chadwell knows the police want to talk to him, so he quits his job and goes to ground?' Caius asked.

'Where would Henry go?' Matt asked.

'He wouldn't hide out in his flat, that's for sure,' Amy said. She started searching the Land Registry for any property or land purchased by Henry Chadwell.

'I'll put an alert out for him in case he tries to leave the country,' Matt said.

'I've got something,' Amy said. Caius and Matt huddled around her computer. 'He bought an orchard three years ago in the Oxfordshire countryside. Less than an acre.'

'Why would anyone just buy a random orchard in the middle of the countryside? He paid £45,000 for it. Is there any property nearby? Get it up on Google Maps,' Caius said as Amy zoomed in on the orchard and then the farmhouse it was adjacent to before searching the Land Registry again.

'The farmhouse was purchased in 1978 by one Gerald Chadwell,' Amy said, sitting back triumphantly in her chair.

59

The Court House

Sir Rupert Beauchamp stood on a small platform in the middle of the private dining room of a Marylebone restaurant that he owned. 'I'd like to thank you all for coming here tonight. It gladdens my heart, it lifts my spirits, to be surrounded by others who share my concerns about the appalling rates of violence against women in this country. According to the Office of National Statistics, four hundred thousand women are sexually assaulted in England and Wales every year. Every damnable year. A shocking number, and that is to say nothing of the myriad cases of physical, verbal and online abuse that women receive every day. I've never been scared to walk down my road – I'm a six-foot-three former rower who can handle himself – but every single woman in my acquaintance has confessed to being terrified to go out at night at one time or another; to go jogging along a quiet path with headphones in. It is with this in mind that I thank you again as a patron – and as a proud feminist – for coming here to celebrate the launch of the Juno Foundation. A charity promoting research into misogyny across all areas of British society.'

Rapturous applause erupted from the room – possibly because a small, but not insignificant, number of guests had come because Rupert always served the best champagne, whatever the occasion. Cameras flashed as a photographer for the *Daily Mail* took a picture of Rupert next to a banner for the Foundation – the logo of which was a contorted and disconcertingly sexy female form. Callie lingered in a corner with a drink in hand and a look of quizzical bemusement. She had thought she was going to dinner and instead she was a spectator at this media circus. Tabitha spotted her from across the room and stormed over.

The journalist accompanying the photographer was wearing a leopard print dress. She pounced. 'Sir Rupert, may I ask you a few questions?'

'Just call me Rupert.'

'What motivated you to start up the Juno Foundation?'

'I love women. My mother was one.'

'Oh, Sir Rupert, Rupert, how droll. I hate to bring it up, but there is an elephant in the room . . .'

'Indeed. It's too painful for me to utter a word. I can't talk about it. To lose a good friend like that . . . Clemmie and I, even though we were no longer a couple when she died, were very good friends still. You understand, don't you?'

'I understand, of course I understand,' she said, putting her arm reassuringly on his shoulder. Her editor was going to be ecstatic about this impromptu little interview. Their readers had been enthralled by the 'Hottie on the Heath' case over the summer and poor Sir Rupert Beauchamp, the handsome boyfriend who'd been cheated on, had come out of the coverage as a firm favourite of certain corners of middle England: a depressingly beautiful little project that matronly Mills & Boon readers wanted to work on. It was as if he were the subject of a reupholstery class. They wanted to stop him sagging in the middle and sit on him victoriously.

Rupert gestured for a (purposefully unattractive) woman to come over. Uncle Arthur had thought it was best if he wasn't tempted. 'Have you met Philippa from our Comms team? She has a wonderful, just smashing, info pack telling you all about the Juno Foundation in a much more erudite fashion than I could ever feign. Thank you for coming tonight. It means an awful lot to me. Do excuse me,' he said, practically bowing to the giddy journalist as the photographer turned his attention to snapping the other notables in attendance.

Rupert made small talk with a (very) junior minister that Uncle Arthur had introduced him to before, then a criminal barrister who specialised in the coercive control clause, and finally with an academic who was angling for funding to research the psychological effects of FGM, before the restaurant began to thin out. He looked up briefly and spotted Callie, who he hoped would become a regular distraction, but perhaps not so regular there was a noun for her. Was that true? Did he want something more? Did he even think he was capable of that? Probably not. The press and all the serious guests having departed, Rupert finally paid attention to his date, who unfortunately was being talked at by Tabitha. She had evidently decided that Callie was going to be her new best friend/unrequited crush. Thankfully, Joly hadn't bothered coming because the idea of feminism bored him, so Rupert didn't have to contend with any of their drama, as amusing as it was. He just had to get Tabs to fuck off.

'Hello, you,' Rupert said, kissing Tabitha on each cheek.

'Cracking speech, Rupe. You're rather turning into a statesman,' Tabitha said as she dead-eyed a swirl of smoked salmon as it swam past on the waitress's tray. She was starving.

'Callie, nice of you to come.'

'Thank you for inviting me.' She wasn't grateful to be there, but she really didn't know what else to say. She had initially tried to slip quietly away into the night, but Tabitha had cornered her and now Rupert had finally graced her with his presence. Callie had a few options running around her head as to how to excuse herself from this very odd situation, but she felt paralysed standing in front of Rupert. She decided the best course of action now was to cling to Tabitha and then feign a headache or something and leave quickly. Callie looked around at the room, bewildered. She didn't want Rupert to think she was impressed by it, by him. The restaurant was impressive – there was a full dinner service going on downstairs and a whole raft of staff running around – but she was baffled as to why he had invited her to a charity event in honour of his late girlfriend. Was it a flex? God, what had she got herself into this time? She looked at Rupert. Fuck, he was gorgeous and she was fucking weak.

'What day is it?' Tabitha asked as she rummaged around her bag for her phone as panic gripped her. 'Oh shit, I'm double-booked.'

'Where are you supposed to be?' Rupert asked, hoping it was something urgent.

'At a family dinner intervention thing. Fuck, bye, darlings. Callie, call me. We'll do lunch, and I'll talk you into letting me style your next set of ads,' Tabitha said, then disappeared in a whirl of panic and shiny hair.

Philippa was packing away Juno Foundation paraphernalia and a couple of waiters were collecting glasses. Rupert thanked them all so much for their hard work, before holding the door open for Callie, who felt too awkward to just leave.

'Where are Arthur and Jeremy?' Callie asked, hoping that one of them might appear.

'Busy. They have a family matter to attend to. It's annoying because Arthur was the one who made me set this whole thing up.'

'Made you set it up?'

'What do you want to do now?' Rupert asked.

'Don't you have anything planned?' Callie thought this could

369

work in her favour. If there was no dinner booking, no cocktails, no bouquets of flowers then she could disappear into the night after a small glass of rosé.

'Well . . . I don't know. Dinner?' Rupert, who was usually so sure of himself, hadn't thought she was going to turn up so he hadn't bothered to think too hard about what might happen if she did. 'Do you want to eat here? The food's all right, although a little overpriced if you're paying for it. Or do you fancy a drink? There's a pub on the road behind that isn't usually full of wankers at this time.'

'Let's just go and get a swift half.' She thought this was the politest way to end the whole thing. 'And you can tell me all about your meeting with that literary agent.'

'I hated her. She hated me. We were in the middle of breaking up when she died. In case you're wondering whether I'm hung up on her.'

★   ★   ★

'I'm sorry, that's never happened to me before.' Rupert had never failed to get it up, not even when he'd shagged a girl for a dare at uni.

'It happens to lots of guys all the time. I shouldn't worry about it if I were you. Somehow, we managed to drink almost two bottles of wine in a very short space of time.' This had been a mistake. She should have just left the moment she realised it wasn't dinner but a press junket. Part of her, dominated by wine logic, had thought that if she just shagged Rupert then she'd be clear of Caius but that wasn't the case. They had sat in a corner booth in a pub round the corner from Rupert's restaurant where he proceeded to deliver a monologue about the beauty of something or other – it was classical, something about her name and the muses – during which she'd kept thinking about their first date. She'd zoned out quite early on, but that might have just been the wine. She was going to blame the wine for why she was in his house right now too.

'Do you want me to—?' Rupert began, before Callie cut him off.

'I'm going to go home. I've got an early client fitting tomorrow,' she said, getting out of the bed she'd barely been in.

'Can I see you again?' He sat up in the bed.

'You don't want to do that.' What she really meant was that she didn't want to see him. Callie took her bra from the top of the chest of drawers it had been flung onto a few minutes before.

'No, I do. That is probably the problem. I may actually like you as a person. That doesn't usually happen.'

'Yeah, you look like a fuck and go kinda chap.'

'Oh I am, but I appear to be getting soft in my old age.' Rupert shook his head at the accidental pun he'd just made.

'Can I ask you a question?' Callie looked him dead in the eye but this time finally saw a rather sad-looking shell of a man, isolated and lonely, rather than the hot-blooded god that wine had shown her.

'Yes, I do own a five-hundred-year-old historic house in the Chilterns.'

'Why was Arthur so desperate to set us up? He tried twice.' She wanted to leave but she was so curious that she couldn't not ask.

Rupert decided to be honest for once. His therapist kept getting at him about honesty. 'Arthur thinks I need to practise my social skills – how I relate to women – and he thought you'd be a suitable test subject.'

'How charming.' It was definitely time for her to go.

'By test subject, I mean he thought you were beautiful and intelligent.'

'Right.'

'And I think he was right, and I really want to see you again.' Rupert checked the time on his phone as Callie realised he seemed more sober than she did. 'He doesn't like your parentage though.'

'Me neither.'

'When are you free?'

'I don't think I'm the sort of person that goes on dates any more.'

'Oh come on, you're not that old. You're my age. Your eggs haven't all shrivelled up yet.'

'No, it's not that.' She still hadn't wrapped her head around the evening and it would annoy her not to know the truth. 'Why did you ask me to the launch party of the charity in honour of your dead ex-girlfriend?'

'I have a history, easily searchable, but if this is going to be more than a fly-by-night then I thought you should be aware of it.' He looked earnest.

'Well, I have no intention of ever being the second Mrs de Winter. No housekeepers. No ghosts.'

'And I have no intention of ever marrying you, but it's nice to take a pretty girl to dinner once a week and fuck a few times afterwards. Get your phone out. Read about me now.'

Callie humoured him, putting her dress back on as she waited for an article that she hadn't read previously on the MailOnline to load. She skimmed the text – words like 'lovelorn baronet' and 'wrongfully suspected of murder' jumping out at her – before scrolling ahead to the comments. God, their readers loved him. He was gorgeous and posh but still. In the comments he was being talked about like a romantic hero. Dotty, good friend and society soothsayer, said he was a player and that was obviously true, but Callie had sensed that deep down something was off with Rupert: no one with that much charm could be functioning. She felt silly for not having taken Peter at his word – she was used to not listening to him too closely because there was always a risk of something bordering on a slur slipping out. She started to read the article from the top as Rupert sat naked on the edge of the bed watching her. 'Shit.'

'What?' Rupert demanded.

'The chief investigating officer on the case: is he a relation of yours? You've got the same surname.' It hadn't occurred to her before because Rupert and Caius pronounced Beauchamp differently. She couldn't imagine they were related, but then both of them got her into bed under potentially dodgy circumstances, so they did have that in common. No, Caius and Rupert were different, so different. Rupert's charm was calculated whereas Caius's was accidental and earnest.

'That nasty little creature with a chip on his shoulder. He has it in for me.'

'Has it in for you?' Callie couldn't imagine Caius acting like that, but then, did she even know him? She felt like she knew him well enough to know that he was conscientious and took his job seriously.

'He swore an oath on the Styx that he'd get me one day.' Rupert stood up and put his boxers back on. It was clear he wasn't going to get any.

'Get you? Why? For what?' Callie pressed him. She couldn't believe that Caius would start a random vendetta against an innocent man.

Rupert laughed, or sneered rather, but then he looked at Callie with barely suppressed wild-eyed panic.

'I really should go,' Callie said, moving towards the door.

'Does the article bother you?' Rupert asked. He needed to know if this was his fate now: whether Clemmie's fait accompli was to have made him unfuckable, unlovable.

'I shouldn't have come tonight. I'm sort of seeing someone.'

'No, you're not.' Rupert moved towards her, smirking. He thought it was silly to still be playing hard to get once he'd seen her naked.

'I'm going to go now.' Callie said it more firmly than she meant to as she opened the door to his bedroom.

'If you insist.' He backed away.

'Rupert.' Curiosity had well and truly got the better of her that night and she turned around and looked at him from the doorway. 'The charity is reputation laundering, isn't it?' Callie had heard of it before – a client of hers had a dodgy ex who set up an animal charity to distract from their finances. She could see that whatever Rupert had done was worse than tax avoidance or a drink driving offence. Rupert looked wounded. He looked like he was going to either ashamedly tell her the terrible truth or cry. 'What did you do that was so bad your godfather and his husband forced you to set up a charity?'

'I think you'd better go,' he said quietly, gesturing to the door.

60

Callie's flat

Harriet was outside Callie's flat, periodically yelling into her letterbox so Callie was hiding under her duvet, again. The wine had begun to wear off and after reading about Clemmie's case chronologically in her Uber home, Callie had fallen down a rabbit hole of Caius's past cases. He'd seen a lot of death, a lot of carnage. Lives torn apart and, once, limbs torn from an abandoned torso. The last of the wine gave her the courage to go straight to the source.

You
23.11
Did you really get stood up at the theatre?

Caius
23.12
It was a genuine meet puke
(Screenshots of messages arranging the date with a woman he never contacted again)
I shouldn't joke. How do I delete that?

You
23.12
Quote: It was a genuine meet puke
Would you swear that on the Styx?

Caius
23.13
I would
Funny turn of phrase that

You
23.14
I accidentally googled you

Caius
23.14
Oh dear

You
23.14
Rupert Beauchamp?

Caius
23.14
Do you know him?

You
23.15
Ish
He's the guy who sent me that scarf. The one from the dinner party

Caius
23.15
. . .

Caius called Callie. He didn't want to do this conversation over text. They said the obligatory awkward 'hellos' and Caius repeated that their meeting and her involvement in his cases had been pure coincidence. He told her about his previous run-in with Rupert – minus a few classified details. She told him about her recent run-ins with Rupert and Arthur Hampton – minus the almost sex. They each knew the other was holding something back, but both decided to ignore it.

'Arthur Hampton as in the MP?' Caius asked, feigning ignorance.

'Yeah, I met him at Harriet's engagement party. He works with Peter.'

'I see.'

'So the Clemmie O'Hara case?' Callie couldn't leave it alone. She'd been on holiday in the South of France when the press interest had been at its peak, and she wasn't really one to read tawdry newspapers as it was.

'We had clear evidence that Rupert had attacked someone, a friend, but the charges didn't stick. It really got to me that I couldn't do anything about it . . . because I don't think he's safe for women to be around, if you understand me.'

'Not safe.' Callie couldn't believe she'd put herself in a situation like that, that she could be so intellectually aware of Rupert's dangerous charm and yet so emotionally self-destructive as to put herself in his path.

'How are you holding up?' Caius asked, changing the subject.

'I'm not great.'

'Your parents?'

'Well, there is that. I've spoken to Peter – we're going to have coffee next week.' Callie sighed, thinking about how awkward that was going to be. 'And now I'm wondering whether I should close my millinery business to do something more serious and important, but I don't know what.'

'Are you serious or just in a funk?'

'I don't know.'

'Why don't you find something meaningful to do on the side while you work it out? Volunteering or something.'

'Yeah, maybe.' Callie heard a car outside rev its engine. She peered out of the window and watched as Harriet pulled away in her huge SUV. 'Harriet turned up at my flat twenty minutes ago, but I pretended I wasn't in.'

'Do you want me to get someone to have a word?' Caius asked. He could send a uniformed officer round if needs be.

'No, she'll stop it eventually.' The elephant on the phone call was there poking her with its trunk. 'Do you still like me?' By 'like me' she meant 'almost love me'.

'Yes, I still like you. I like you a lot.'

'I still like you too.'

'Let's take it slow.'

'A snail's pace.'

'Let's meet up once everything has calmed down. I've still got to find Henry Chadwell.' Caius hadn't intended to say that. He had been tempted to ask her if she remembered him being creepy, but he changed his mind. That was an official conversation for Amy to have with her.

'Henry Chadwell? The headmistress's son? Is he your suspect? You know, funnily enough, I heard from him recently.'

'Oh really?'

'I had a message request on Instagram from him after he'd also been at Harriet's engagement party. He asked me out, but I just ignored it. I'll send you a screenshot.'

She put Caius on speakerphone as she captured an image of

Henry's message and sent it to him, before adding hastily, 'But I'm not interested in him, I swear. I'm not trying to make you jealous. I don't like playing games. Shit. I really like you.'

'I really like you too,' Caius reassured her.

THURSDAY

61

A Cotswold farmhouse

Caius had parked up on a grass verge, out of sight of the farmhouse. He had a warrant in his back pocket to search Henry Chadwell's property for traces of Eliza. A team of armed officers was parked opposite, shielded by an ancient oak, as was Barry and his team, ready to search for any signs of a decayed corpse, ancient blood splatter, anything previously corporeal. Matt and Amy were wearing stab vests as they chatted to a guy Amy used to work with during her time busting down the front doors of other sex offenders.

'This guy could be expecting us. He left London and retreated to a rural farmhouse,' Caius said to the team leader. Caius had just been fitted with a microphone. 'He doesn't have any registered firearms, but we can't exclude the possibility that he has an old shotgun. It is the countryside, after all.'

'We've circled round the property and as far as we can tell there's only one entrance, but we can't see into the garden from here.'

'What about the barn?'

'We've got eyes on it. No movement there all morning. But don't worry, we've got it covered.'

'OK. I'll knock first and see if he's amenable.'

'You're all wired up, so just give us the word,' said the team leader.

★　★　★

Caius drove the car up to the front of the house and got out. He could hear chickens. A fat red hen appeared from behind a bush and wandered in front of him, blocking his path to the door. She sat down in front of him and started clucking aggressively.

'Don't mind Gwendoline, she's looking for somewhere to lay,' said a voice. A young woman had followed the hen from the garden. She was slightly built with freckles. She was nervous of him. She scooped the bird up in her arms and avoided Caius's gaze. 'Are you lost? Chipping Norton is twenty minutes down the lane.'

'Bloody hell!' Caius was taken aback. He floundered for a moment as he tried to get back on track with the plan. 'Sorry . . . Umm . . . Madam, I'm looking for Mr Henry Chadwell. Is he here at all?'

'Why?'

Caius took out his warrant card. 'We understand that Mr Chadwell may know something about financial misconduct at his firm.' He was taking a punt here, but Matt's impression that his boss was worried he might leak sensitive info was the only pretence he had to go on.

'Harry,' she called back to the garden where she had come from. She still refused to look him in the eye. Henry Chadwell appeared moments later carrying a chubby-cheeked toddler in his arms. Caius could hear other children playing in the garden.

'Mr Chadwell?' Caius asked.

'Yes. How can I help?'

'May I have a word in private, sir?' Caius asked, flashing his warrant card.

'Of course,' Henry said. He handed the child over to the woman and beckoned for Caius to follow him into the garden. Caius saw two older girls who had been messing about on a swing walk quietly into the house at the sight of him. Henry Chadwell took a seat at the wrought-iron table overlooking the lawn. The leftovers of breakfast were scattered on it. 'What can I help you with?'

Caius introduced himself. 'We've recently become aware of potential illegal activity at your employers'.'

'Have you now? I wouldn't know anything about that. I don't work there any more. If you'll excuse me, we're about to take our annual camping trip.'

'How nice. Is that you, your wife and your three children?'

'We have five children.' He looked proud as he took a sip of tea that he'd left on the table. He didn't offer Caius anything.

'Sorry, I only have a few more questions. Apologies if any of them are sensitive,' Caius said. He put more emphasis on the word 'sensitive' than he meant to, but Henry didn't notice. 'May I ask why you left the company?'

'I couldn't stand it there any more – morally, that is. Three years ago they made a killing by acquiring a company that runs care homes for children being looked after by the state. Local authorities pay them to care for vulnerable children. That company has a 15 per cent profit margin. We IPO'd it last year and walked away with a cool £16 million. I can't abide anyone who takes advantage of vulnerable children.'

'Me neither,' Caius said.

Henry Chadwell stood up as he heard another vehicle drive up to the front of the house.

'Henry Chadwell, you're under arrest for the kidnap of Eliza Chapel,' Caius said, pinning the surprised man down on the wrought-iron table and handcuffing him as he read him his rights. Caius looked up at the house and saw Eliza at the back door; the living, breathing body that he'd asked forensics to search for mere traces of was stood there watching her tormentor be arrested. They heard the armed officers enter the house. Caius glanced at a shock of red on his wrist – he'd managed to smear jam onto his cuff.

62

Chipping Norton Police Station

Eliza Chapel, or rather Eliza Chadwell as she referred to herself, sat on a squeaky black chair with her youngest child in her arms in her local police station. Not that she'd been in Chipping Norton often enough to think of it as local. Not that she'd been anywhere often.

'I'm very sorry, Eliza, but we're struggling to find a record of your children,' said a social worker tasked with finding a foster family to look after the children temporarily.

'There won't be a record. I had them all at home, not the hospital.'

'I see.'

The social worker left and cups of sweet tea and slices of hot buttery toast arrived. Then Eliza was shown briefly to another room where all her children were now waiting for her, before being taken back into the original room for Amy to interview.

'Could you please state your name for the tape?' Amy asked. She felt bloody awful that she'd been pissed off that she'd been put on the 'smaller case' but here she now was, confronted with a living, breathing woman whose death or rather whose life hadn't been enough for her ambitions.

'Eliza Chadwell.'

'And what was your maiden name?' Amy gave her a meek smile, trying to reassure her.

'Chapel, as in a small church.'

'Eliza, how did you get . . .' Amy struggled to find the right verb. Did she want to say how did she get abducted, kidnapped, locked in a farmhouse, trapped in a madman's eighteenth-century rape fantasy? 'Eliza, how did you end up living in the Cotswolds.'

'It's Henry's house. He inherited it when his father died. His parents were divorced so it went to him.'

'And where did you meet Henry?' Amy nodded encouragingly as she asked the question.

'We don't talk about that.' Eliza whispered as she rocked gently in her chair. 'Henry works in finance. He's very important. He has to go all over Europe for business.'

'OK.' Amy wasn't going to be able to be as direct as she normally was. Eliza wasn't going to let her story flow. Instead, Amy was going to have to sift it out from the mud of Henry's ego that Eliza was regurgitating. An egoist like Henry would need to be told about his 'achievements' by Eliza and if she just parroted back his nonsense then he'd be calm and kind to her. 'Eliza, did you attend St Ursula's School?'

'I did, briefly.' Eliza looked around the room. 'Are my children all right in that room?'

'They're perfectly safe.' Amy wanted to reach out and touch her hand to comfort her, but of course she couldn't. 'I'm sure they're being plied with orange squash and as many biscuits as they can eat. Do you want to talk about that Halloween?' Amy asked her gently. 'You can say whatever you want now. Henry isn't here.'

'My parents, are they still alive?' Eliza asked cautiously.

'Your parents are fine. We've called them and they're coming over to see you.' Amy smiled at her. 'Would it be all right if I asked you about what happened on Halloween 2004? I can ask you yes or no questions to begin with if that feels easier for you?'

'Yes.'

'Did Henry come to your dorm room that night?'

'No.'

'Did he find you in the bathroom?'

'Yes.'

'Did he grab you?'

'Yes.'

'Did he do worse than that?'

'No, not then.'

'What do you mean?'

Eliza looked over her shoulder and then turned to stare at the two-way mirror in front of her. She was clearly trying to work out whether Henry was watching her from the other side and this whole episode was really a test of her loyalty.

'It's just my superior officer on the other side of the mirror. The man who came to your house. Henry is locked in a cell. He can't hurt you.'

Eliza looked at Amy, trying to work out whether this was true.

'Do you want to see his cell?'

Eliza looked reluctant at first but then nodded. Amy walked her through the bowels of the station to the holding cell where Henry was being kept. They could hear him complaining from the inside: 'I demand to speak to whomsoever is in charge,' 'You can't just leave me here, I'm a pillar of the community,' 'There's been a terrible mistake.'

Once back in the interview room Eliza briefly adopted a quiet but steely resolve. This was the story that she'd been waiting to tell. That she'd practised in her head over and over again, but now she was here surrounded by police officers and the faintest smell of dust her words failed her.

'Take your time,' Amy said, but she could see that time wasn't the issue here. 'Start with the plainest facts.'

'I got up to go to the toilet. I was washing my hands when I heard something in the corridor. I went out and he was there, just staring out of the window.'

'Did he say anything to you?'

'That he was looking for a pliable muse.'

'Right.'

'I said that I'd be his muse.' Eliza relaxed into her chair, relieved that she was finally telling her story. 'It's so silly. I was trying to sound grown up. We all had crushes on him, you see, and if I was the one he liked then I thought everyone would stop laughing at me all the time.'

'Did he usually wander the halls at night?'

'I don't know. I'd only ever really seen him from afar. He'd help out at big school events sometimes.'

'What happened next?'

'He asked me if I wanted to go for a drive in his car. And I did. No one else had ever been inside it. He took me by the hand and led me down the servants' stairs and past the infirmary. I'd be lying if I said that I wasn't thrilled. We got to the bottom of the stairwell, and he held the door open for me like a gentleman. I could see his car parked on the gravel not too far away. I stepped outside, but it was cold, so I tried to turn back. I was only wearing slippers and a nightie, but he shut the door and grabbed me. I struggled for a bit, but he was so much bigger than me and I froze. I thought someone would hear and come and save me, but nothing. Henry threw me into the back seat and that was it.'

'What do you mean, "it"?'

'The beginning of my new life with Henry.'

'And what was life with Henry like?'

Eliza bit the skin around her thumbnail until it bled.

'It's all right. You've seen him in his cell. He can't hurt you any more.'

Eliza nodded slowly.

'Did you see much of the outside world?'

'There was no TV,' Eliza began, casually listing off her isolation as mere facts. 'There was a radio but he took it away with him when he left. There was no landline. The doors out of the house have locks, but I don't have the keys. The windows have bars. I was allowed into the garden only when he was there. The children. The children are home schooled. Well, they can read at least. The children, God, they just kept coming. I love them I do, but . . .' Eliza started to sob. Amy passed her a tissue from a box on the table. Eliza pulled herself together, she'd rehearsed this. She could tell her story. 'During the week when he was in London working, we stayed inside. I was supposed to keep the curtains shut at the front of the house in case anyone got nosy. Henry bought an orchard, dug a vegetable patch and then last year, a flock of chickens. He said it didn't matter if I stayed out in the garden any more because he'd done it. I was his Pamela and no one was looking for me. He'd saved up enough money from his job and was going to sell his flat. That way he could live "the good life" all the time. He was going to take the bars off the windows and was thinking of letting the children go to school but only if I swore to never say a word about how it all began. If I said anything to anyone when I was out in the world, he'd smother them in their sleep, and it would be my fault.'

★   ★   ★

'All this time, he kept her locked up in a farmhouse in Oxfordshire in some sort of idealised rural rape fantasy. There were fucking

391

chickens.' Caius watched Eliza be comforted by a member of the emotional support team. 'Like a doll wrapped up in tissue paper and not allowed out of the box.'

'Eliza was fourteen when she went missing. It's statutory rape of a minor. Plus, there's Beatrice's testimony. He's not going to see daylight for quite some time,' Amy said. She'd popped her head in after finishing her interview with Eliza.

'I had a quick look around the house and the fucker has a scrapbook of all of Beatrice's playbills and another with press cuttings from society magazines of Callie's hats. It's unbelievably creepy. Both women were at risk this entire time. What if he'd decided to "get rid" of Eliza one day? Callie said he'd asked her out after spotting her at Harriet's engagement party.'

'Have you spoken to Callie?' Matt asked.

'Yeah, I've just sent a support officer around to hers to explain everything that's happened with Eliza and offer to sort out some therapy for her. She was being groomed, after all. Callie may not have realised it, but she came pretty close to being abducted. Beatrice as well. Half the school will probably need anxiety pills.' Caius took out his phone. 'I should let Darren know what's what. He's just texted me to say that he's managed to speak to a cousin of John Chenoweth, the original SIO. Apparently, on his deathbed, he admitted taking money from Iona Chadwell to not mention either the staff's drinking or her son being present, but the family thought he was high on morphine and talking gibberish.'

'But have you spoken to Callie?' Matt pressed. 'Spoken, spoken.'

'Yeah, we spoke last night.'

'And?' Matt raised his eyebrows hopefully.

'I met her by chance, and yet as chance would have it, she's right in the middle of all this mess. I really like her, she says she's still into me, but I've been thinking about it and I can't date her, can I? It's unethical.' Caius gave Matt a weak smile and then stared at his shoes in shame.

'Unethical?' Matt gave Caius a withering look.

'What?'

'I get what you're saying but you did not get into a relation-ship with Callie under false pretences. If she's uncomfortable with it then yes, walk away, but that's not what you just said.'

'But . . .'

'No, you are not a bad guy. Stop it.'

★ ★ ★

Caius looked across at Henry Chadwell. He'd refused a solicitor. He was a proud man, and confident in his ability to walk out of the police station unscathed. After all, he'd got away with it for so long and Eliza always did what he said now that he'd thoroughly instructed her. He was sure he'd be home for lunch.

'Did you abduct Eliza Chapel on 31 October 2004?' Caius asked.

'No comment,' said Henry.

'How did Eliza come to be living with you if not?'

'No comment.'

'How did you come to father five children by her?'

'No comment.'

'Have you been keeping Eliza prisoner in your home?'

'No comment.' It was beginning to dawn on him that he'd been caught. He sat up straight in his chair, trying to muster his remaining dignity.

'What was your undergraduate dissertation on?'

'No comment.'

'I actually know the answer. You wrote about "the fine line between love and male aggression" in *Pamela* and *Clarissa*. You've been enacting a rape fantasy based on two eighteenth-century novels for the last fifteen years. I bet you weren't sure whether Eliza was going to be a Clarissa and resist you or a Pamela who you end up marrying.'

'Let this expiate.' Henry began to panic now that his 'personal philosophy' had been discovered and undoubtedly would be picked over by the unenlightened public. The uninformed masses would not understand. They wouldn't see that he was right, that his method was the only reasonable way to deal with women. Henry sank back into his chair and refused to utter another word, not even another 'no comment' as he resolved to do the decent thing.

★ ★ ★

'What does that even mean?' Amy asked. She and Matt were watching Caius trying to interview Henry through the two-way mirror.

'It's the line that Lovelace says in *Clarissa* before he dies of the wounds he sustained in a duel,' Matt said. He'd googled it quickly. 'I'll tell the duty sergeant to put him on self-harm watch.'

63

The Police Station

'You've solved your pet case then,' Arthur Hampton said. He'd called just as Caius got back from the Cotswolds to oversee the search of Henry's Dulwich flat. 'It's broken on the BBC.'

'Have you got a couple of unpopular bills to bury on page twenty-six then?' Caius couldn't help himself. He had temporarily forgotten about Robert Symington and Lynne Rodgers, but Hampton had brought the woolliness of the case back into focus.

'I'll let you have that one because I'm assuming you feel triumphant.'

'How can I help you today?'

'Where are you in the Symington & Chase case?'

'You've got what you want. Simpson-Bamber is going to be embroiled in a messy and very public divorce. His political credibility is over and whatever threat he posed to you has passed. He's tabloid fodder now.'

'Are you very sure he didn't do it?'

'By "it", do you mean any combination of stealing the fund, killing Lynne and even killing Robert? I'm never sure unless I have hard evidence, but I don't think he did any of those things,' Caius said, noticing a brown envelope on his desk with his name on it.

'Call me when you have an actual viable suspect.' Hampton hung up.

'Something concrete,' Caius said to himself. He wasn't sure where the Symington & Chase investigation was going to go next. No one seemed to have minded Lynne much but there were a lot of people that had a potential motive if they thought she did in fact have the pension fund – the whole factory floor, for starters – and Robert even more so. The wife and the lover: both would have been hurt by Robert's affair with Lynne and both Jane and Cassandra seemed to be women who held grudges, but for this long? He couldn't see it. They'd both moved on with their lives. Either of them being angry enough after all these years to follow her down a towpath and shove her into the Thames felt extremely unlikely. Then there was the colleague: Peter didn't steal the money to set up his business – Caius had seen the bank statements and the paperwork from the sale of Jane Simpson-Bamber's parents' house – so there was no need to cover his tracks and kill Lynne, the only other person who might have known if Peter had indeed stolen the fund. None of them had a good enough reason to kill Lynne and all of them had alibis. Caius stared at the whiteboard where Matt had been tracking the case. Something wasn't quite right, but he couldn't put his finger on it. Caius picked up the brown envelope that Cassandra Hunstanton had given him again. He'd prioritised chasing down Henry Chadwell over reading it. He put on a pair of gloves and began opening the envelope when his desk phone rang.

'Hello, DI Caius Beauchamp,' he said absent-mindedly.

'Hi, this is Kim from the housing department at Richmond Council, I'm ringing about a complaint you made against the landlord of 16 Mermaid Court.'

'Yes, it was really damp in there. A lot of black mould. I don't think it was fit for human habitation.' Caius put the letter down.

'Did you happen to take any pictures of it?'

'I didn't, sorry.'

'That's all right, we'll send a health inspector around this week to corroborate your account. Mr Stephenson, the landlord, has already agreed to a course of damp proofing. He said that his previous tenant hadn't informed him of the extent of the problem.'

'OK, cheers.' Caius hung up and finally began to read the letter. Lynne apologised profusely and repeatedly for the affair and the pain this must have caused Cassandra. Then Lynne laid out her tale of abandonment, poverty, pain and deep remorse. Caius read and reread the last paragraph aloud to himself, before reading it to Matt over the phone.

'"I know that Robert is dead. I now know for sure that he was murdered. I suspected as much. I couldn't believe that he'd abandon me like that, but for myself I cannot go on living this misery. I can't live any more in the shadow of Robert's crime and our affair. I leave this world giving you the truth and the power to decide what to do with it because I cannot bear to. I thought Harold was my friend, and yet he made my life this misery."'

64

The Police Station

'More questions, detective?' Harold Stephenson asked.

'Yes, just the one,' Caius said. He'd sent uniform to collect him. 'Harold, where were you on the night of Friday 29 August?'

'At home, like always.'

'Were you with anyone?'

'No.'

'I don't like being lied to, Harold.' Caius looked at him and saw an old man who didn't like lying either. 'Now I'm going to have to ask you all manner of questions. Like, do you own many properties?'

'A couple of flats. I bought my first one cheap after the house price crash in the early nineties. I had some spare cash and there's nothing safer than houses.'

'Do you vet your tenants? Do you meet them in advance?' Caius asked. This whole charade was frustrating. Harold knew what he was getting at, but he was refusing to play along.

'I don't really care as long as they prove they can pay the rent,' Harold said, staring at the wall to the right of Caius's ear.

'Were you aware that you were renting out 16 Mermaid Court to Lynne Rodgers?'

Harold shrugged.

'Do you expect me to believe that a man like you, a proud man, a union man, would just take it on the chin that a weak man like Robert Symington would steal from the workers?'

'What are you trying to say, detective?' Harold said. He was offended.

'I'm trying to say that I thought you were principled.' Caius took a sip of water. He needed to calm down. 'What were your real movements the day that Robert Symington went missing?'

'I can't remember now.'

'I think you remember killing him,' Caius said, waiting for a reaction that never came. 'Did you do it at the factory?'

Harold said nothing so Caius started piling the questions on top of him, hoping the guilt-laden weight of them would squeeze out the truth. 'Did you mean to do it? When did you realise that something was up? Did you confront him? When did you realise that he'd seduced the nice secretary? Were you good friends with her before that? Did you have feelings for Lynne? Were you close? Is that why she asked you for help when she came back to the UK, and you let her one of your flats? But when did she realise that you weren't the person she thought you were? Did she confront you that Friday evening along the river?' Caius sat back in his seat. Every question had been a chip from Harold's facade. 'Lynne had had a drink that night. She'd been sober for quite a while and yet she felt so compelled to drink, like she needed either courage or numbing. Did she confront you about what you did?' This wasn't working and Caius needed to change tack. 'You're getting on, Harold, you may as well get it off your conscience.'

'I don't like these questions. I'm not a bad person.' But Harold knew he'd been discovered. There was no point in pretending any more. 'I didn't see Lynne that evening.'

'But you saw her recently?' Caius leaned forward.

'I did.' Harold leaned back in his chair and laughed. He was liberated by finally being caught. 'My old mum did go to the hospital that day, but I didn't go with her. No one ever bothered to check that. They took me at my word. Probably just rang up and confirmed that she'd been in.'

'Then what really happened?'

'It's a relief, you know. A blessed relief to tell the truth after all this time.'

'What happened to Robert Symington, Harold?'

If Harold was going to tell the truth he was going to do it in his own time, and not be pushed by this uppity young detective. He relaxed into the story of his crime. He'd wanted to tell someone, someone impartial, for a very long time. 'I loved Lynne. I know I was twenty years older than her, but that doesn't matter when you have feelings like I did. I was trying to build up the courage to ask her for a drink but then one night I saw them together in the factory after hours. It was only me and a couple of the girls working overtime and I'd stepped outside for a cigarette. The back door to the shop floor was overlooked by the offices and I saw them kiss through the window. I wasn't going to do anything. He'd discard Lynne soon enough like he did with all the other women he cheated on his wife with. There were quite a few, I'd say. Robert was fast with the ladies. I knew he had his eye on a couple of the younger girls who worked there. It's partly why I always stayed late with them. Robert wouldn't have tried anything if I was there. I even saw him with that designer he sacked Dickie for once too. Getting out of her fancy car looking all smug. Lynne wasn't Robert's sort. She was raised right. I figured I could let it fizzle out and then appear when the time was right and sweep up the broken shards from the floor. I was getting on. I just wanted a bit of stability, to settle down. A nice woman, it's all I wanted. I'm a nice guy.'

'So what made you change your plan?'

'I could tell something was different – there was something in the way he was carrying himself. Then I heard Robert talking to her about them going to Brazil in the stairwell. He kept reassuring her that he could get hold of a lot of money easily. It wasn't lit well, and I waited at the bottom. They thought no one could hear them. Something snapped. I waited until the next morning to confront Robert. I'd noticed that he'd been coming into the factory earlier and earlier for the last couple of weeks, so I got the bus there when it was just him. Later on, I realised he was trying to set up his pension swindle without anyone noticing. I waited for him in the car park and confronted him about Lynne. He was supposed to be catching the flight in a couple of hours so I knew that was it. I tried to talk to him. I tried to be reasonable. He was arrogant. So entitled. I punched him. Just one glancing blow, and that was it. He hit his head on the kerb, but it started raining and the blood washed away. Rain in July, I never thought I'd be grateful for it.'

'What did you do next?'

'His car keys were in his pocket. I shoved his body into the boot and drove off into the countryside. It's amazing what you can do when put in a spot. I didn't think I'd be capable of it. Dumped him in some woods out near Watford and then abandoned the car with the keys in the ignition. Someone must have just driven off with it. Took it to a chop shop and then didn't want to admit they'd stolen it when the news of Robert's disappearance came out the following week. I turned up late that day. No one questioned me. Why would they? I told everyone the day before that I might be in late because I was taking my old mum to see the specialist. And I was going to. I called her up from a payphone on the way and said something had come up at work, so my sister went with her instead. I bought a couple of maps with cash the next day and left the receipt in his office to explain away the missing car.'

'Where were you on the evening of Friday 29 August?' Caius asked, just to remove any lingering doubt.

'I was at home.'

'Did you kill Lynne Rodgers?'

Harold, who until now had stated everything about Robert's death as fact, began to mull over the great romantic vagaries, the great fiction of his life and how it might have been if the story had only gone a little differently. 'I may as well have done. I told her the truth that afternoon. I'd gone round to look at the flat. I hadn't been there for years, you see. She cloistered herself. Refused to live much of a life in penance for the time that she lived a little too much. Lynne hadn't told me about the black mould. She thought she deserved it like it was a mark on her soul, so I told her what happened. I thought it would help her. I'm a fucking idiot. We should have had a nice life together, me and her. Nice detached house, two children, a holiday to Spain every year. We would've been happy together. I deserved it.'

'Did Robert deserve it?' Caius asked Harold once he'd terminated the interview.

FRIDAY

65

The Herakleion Club

The same identikit hostess who had greeted him before led Caius back to the red dining room. Arthur Hampton was peering past the velvet curtains when Caius arrived and barely acknowledged him entering the room. Whatever was going on outside was more important than the conversation they were going to have inside. 'I have a matter to quickly take care of. Please, excuse me.'

As Hampton left the room a wine waiter appeared and held out a tray with a glass of whisky for Caius which he gladly took. He was worried he was going to develop a taste for it. He looked at the paintings briefly before curiosity got the better of him and he peered out of the window at whatever had spirited Hampton away. Caius saw a very drunk Rupert wobbling about on the pavement opposite as a blacked-out car pulled up and Hampton put him in it. He hadn't noticed before that their hair was the same sandy blond colour. The car sat motionless outside the club and Hampton clearly asked the driver to wait for him. He watched Hampton disappear back into the building.

'Just a spot of bother at the Treasury,' Hampton said, coming back into the room. 'But when isn't there? Well, two cold cases in as many days, how impressive.'

'Both had an element of flukiness to them,' Caius said.

'Coincidences, or flukiness, are when it becomes obvious that we are fated for something more.'

'I'm not a hero.' Caius took a sip of his whisky. 'I wouldn't have thought you were a man who believed in fate or predestination. You're far too active.'

'A man has to go out into the world and make it his, but there comes a point where one has to realise that they have or have not curried favour. That there sometimes is a lady in a lake.'

'Life is a grand quest then?' Caius asked.

'It is.' Hampton downed the rest of his glass. 'Your missing schoolgirl was living the good life in the Cotswolds?'

'Abducted, brainwashed and forbidden from leaving the property under threat of violence. She told a social worker that she hadn't been to the dentist since 2004. They did keep chickens though, if that's what you meant.'

Hampton ignored his remark. 'And Robert Symington was killed by one of his mistresses' jealous suitors.'

'I got a call just as I came out of the tube that forensics have found his body. A scenic picnicking spot in Hertfordshire. The money is still lost somewhere in an unknown bank account in the British Virgin Islands though.'

'I'm not sure what can be done about the money.' Hampton paused for a moment and then as if to dismiss Caius's concern: 'This girl you found . . .'

'Eliza.'

'What will happen to her?'

'Eliza and her children are being looked after by social services at the moment. It'll take a lot of adjustment.'

'And this Henry Chadwell has been formally charged?'

'Yes, with kidnap and with statutory rape of a minor. We are expecting other women to come forward. He used that school as a personal hunting ground.'

'I'm used to hearing such things in the abstract.' Hampton was disturbed by the vile reality of the predilections of other men. The crime was too close to home for him.

Caius looked around at the impossibly opulent room – a room, a setting, a class of people to which he did not belong – and settled his gaze firmly on Hampton. 'Why me?'

'What do you mean?'

'Why me? Why my team? You could have got Special Branch to look into Robert Symington's disappearance if you wanted, or any other major crimes unit. There are whole teams who specialise in cold cases. Why mine?'

Hampton, who Caius suspected could never look apologetic, began speaking with his usual assured brightness. 'I'm afraid I meant to stay for dinner tonight, but events have occurred that mean I can't. I'm deeply sorry. It's frightfully rude of me to drag you here on a Friday night and then abandon you.'

'The Treasury, eh?'

'Yes, the Treasury.' Hampton needed to leave, but he didn't think it was fair to, not yet, not when the boy was asking the right questions. 'In answer to your question, I ask you another. What do you know of your father's family history?'

'My dad was born and raised in Notting Hill and his parents are both Jamaican. My nan's dead now. Dementia. My grandfather got married a little late in life. He'd been in the RAF in the war, but he doesn't talk about it.'

'Is that all your grandfather has said about his family?'

'He's cagey. I would be if I left home seventy-odd years ago. The man's in his late nineties, he probably doesn't want to dwell on such things.'

'You and your father need to have that conversation with him.' Hampton drained the last of his glass as he got to the real reason he had asked Caius here. 'I have a proposal for you: I send the odd case your way when I need it looking into and in return you can investigate anything that takes your fancy. Cold cases, whatever. Quid pro quo. Even things that you would not normally be permitted to investigate – if you understand my meaning – and by that, I mean any case. You will carry on your normal duties, of course.'

'Anything?' Lydia, his poor sister, flashed through Caius's mind as he tried to suppress his feelings.

'Yes.'

'Let me think about it.' Caius didn't think it was possible to be entertaining such an idea and yet, Lydia.

'Of course.' Hampton picked up a small brown paper package tied up with twine that had been waiting on a marble-topped sideboard. He handed it to him, encouraging Caius to open it. 'Just a small token of my appreciation.'

Caius unwrapped the gift – a first edition of *A Room with a View*. 'Thank you.'

'Now you have no excuse to not read it,' Hampton began. He continued to talk about Forster but Caius wasn't listening.

Caius looked down at the copy of the book and then up at Hampton. Callie had told him that Jeremy was Rupert's god-father, but he now suspected there was more to it. More 'family drama' in the words of Abi, his podcasting uni friend. Something in the way that Hampton stood there talking about novels made it so very obvious. He couldn't believe he hadn't noticed the likeness before. Hampton was Rupert's father. Caius could feel a ball of anger in his belly. It was Hampton who had frustrated his efforts in the summer. Something worse though was beginning to form: shame. He couldn't believe that he'd begun to be taken in by him. Caius had almost come to respect Hampton, or at least thought that he might be a necessary evil rather than an out-and-out villain.

'What is it?'

Caius wanted to broach the subject of why he was chosen to

look into Lynne's case politely, but he knew Hampton would be too adept at brushing him off. He wasn't going to let that happen again. 'I've spent the last couple of weeks thinking about principles and morals. Primarily, was taking this case from you the right thing to do? There was always a niggle at the back of my head – "why me?" But now I see that I have an original sin.'

'My goodness, what a weighty topic and one so absolute. You and I need to have a proper conversation to clear up any misunderstandings, but just not this evening.'

'I am not in the business of misunderstandings.'

'All right then. Say your piece. I can see that you're itching to.'

'I won't do this again. I cannot. You are asking me to compromise my morals. I will not be a stooge that props up a system that lets Rupert Beauchamp off on a rape charge.'

'Now calm down, Caius.' Hampton was deeply unpleased at the mention of Rupert and his crime.

'His guilt is plainer than the nose on my face.'

'He's been to rehab. He's seeing a psychiatrist. He's deeply remorseful for taking things a little too far.'

'A little too far?'

Hampton, who so far had been nothing but smoothness itself, was rumpled. 'Did it occur to you that I could have made you disappear? I've done it before. Discredit you. I could have had your career ended. I've done worse things than that.'

'Make me disappear like you made Hereward and Yannis disappear in the summer?'

'I've done it before,' Hampton repeated firmly. 'But I didn't, because you are meant for something else, young Galahad. I've been watching you for quite some time. It was providence that you were the one to find that ghastly girl.'

'What do you mean?'

'Like I said, I've been watching you for some time, your grandfather the war hero, and your father the property developer. Breeding will always out. Then of course your poor sister. You were interning for an MEP in Brussels when she died, and then you changed course totally. I admire you for that.'

'What has my family got to do with any of this?'

'It is your "original sin" to have been born a Beauchamp. Speak to your grandfather and then we shall talk again.' Hampton checked his watch, aware that he'd been longer than he said he would. 'My only sin is making sure that my family, my line survives. My country too. There is a great upheaval coming and it is the duty of people like us to see this island through it. This will be your sin too. It is our burden and our duty.'

Caius, sick of all Hampton's cryptic answers, his deflections and rhetoric, agreed to meet him in a few weeks to discuss his offer again. Caius just wanted to leave now, but he did have one more matter of business. 'I was, am, dating his daughter.'

'Whose daughter?'

'Peter Simpson-Bamber's daughter, Callie. She told me about your little dinner party experiment.'

'Ah, you're the lucky chap. She's a very pretty girl, quick too.' Hampton smiled to himself. That explained the bluster. Caius was a stag rutting with Rupert over Callie. Oh to be young, thought Hampton.

'Can you keep her out of it, out of the media frenzy? It's going to hit the papers any day now, right? I know the tabloids go wild for an MP's love child story, but she hasn't done anything wrong.'

'I can't promise a thing, I'm afraid. You know how the press are. If I were you, I'd use this as a good excuse to take any extra holiday you have left and hide out in a lovely little hotel in the country somewhere eating room service.'

Caius looked at Hampton and Hampton looked at him. Caius knew that Hampton had laundered Rupert's reputation in the press. He could do it again on a smaller scale. Hampton capitulated.

'I can suggest that young Calliope is merely referred to in passing as a "celebrated society milliner" or something like that and that no one tries to hassle her for her side of the story.'

'Thank you.'

'Not at all,' Hampton said as he shook Caius's hand. They had a gentleman's agreement now. 'I'm looking forward to working with you again.'

66

Notting Hill

Caius texted Callie to say that his dinner plans had fallen through last minute and was she free for that drink? She texted him the address of a friend's and told him it was chill if he came. Caius wasn't so sure. He would have preferred to have just found a quiet corner of a pub for their great reconciliation. But she insisted. He'd felt self-conscious dressed up in Hampton's stupid suit as he caught the tube over. He was desperate to see her, to see if the spark he thought was there was still alight.

'I think I'm outside.' Caius hadn't wanted to knock directly on the front door in case Callie wasn't the one to answer, so he'd messaged her to come outside instead. It was only round the corner from what had been his grandparents' house before his grandfather had moved to a nursing home closer to his flat. His father had subsequently refurbished the house and let it out to some oil billionaire. Caius didn't want to think about the money that had been made.

The front door swung open. Callie stood in the doorway wearing the dress she'd worn on their first date. 'Hello.'

'Hello.'

'Do you want to come in? We're about to have pudding.'

'In a minute.'

'Ah, you want to talk.' She had wanted to pretend that nothing had happened – that he was a constant in her life.

'Yes.'

'I didn't sleep with him. I promise I didn't.'

'I don't care about that,' Caius said. It wasn't worth thinking about.

'I have a bit of a self-destructive streak.'

'We've all eaten a whole carrot cake in one sitting before. You'd just met your dad who you've actually known for most of your life. Your best friend started harassing you and you had to deal with your delightful mother. That's enough to make anyone do something a little out of character.' Caius shuffled his weight around. 'I want you. I really really want you. But I don't think it's the right thing to do under the circumstances.'

Callie was trying to work out why he was being so reluctant. Her involvement in his work had been a pure coincidence. 'Is this about Henry Chadwell? I barely remember him. I know you're worried because he had a thing about me, but you wouldn't be saying this if I'd almost been knocked over by a bus fifteen years ago, would you?'

'That's not the point I'm trying to make.' Caius kept thinking about what might have happened if she had gone to meet up with Chadwell after he DMed her. 'I don't want to take advantage.'

'I chased you.' She played with his lapel and took in his smell. 'I gave your colleague my card. I want you too.'

Caius brushed a stray lock away from the side of her cheek as she stepped closer to him. They looked at each other. They were doing this, they were going to be a 'them', a 'we' and an 'us'. They kissed. A passing car bibbed its horn. 'Waaaaheeeey.'

'How are you feeling about . . . well . . .' Caius asked. He still had his arms round her waist.

'Everything? I don't rightly know. My "father" wants to meet up for dinner now, not just coffee. I think he's going to try to take me to Disneyland Paris to make up for all those lost childhood memories. A certain sort of man abandons the child

413

he raised like that. As far as he's concerned Harriet is a stranger now, and instead he's chucking all this attention at me – the child he knew for sure was his but couldn't be bothered to raise in any emotional sense.'

'There's a genetic ruthlessness there, isn't there?' Caius rubbed her arm. 'Are you and Harriet talking now?'

'No, God, no. She's furious with me and I'd already more or less ended our friendship. Plus, Inigo keeps calling to discuss "exit strategies" from their engagement and I can't be involved in any of it. The richly woven rug of normalcy has been pulled out from underneath her. I feel for her though. It's going to be a tough couple of months considering she also quit her job the other day.'

Caius cleared his throat and started saying what he had gone there to say. 'I don't want you to think that I'm taking advantage of you. If you want to take things slowly. If you want to take a break from whatever this is, then I understand.' Caius smiled weakly and then stared at his shoes.

'You look really hot dressed up like that. Where's this jacket from?'

'Gieves & Hawkes, I think.'

'You look a bit James Bondy.'

'They'd never let me play him.'

'Because of your ethnicity?'

'No, because I'm not an actor.'

'Where were you? A charity gala?' She kissed him.

'I was supposed to be meeting a colleague of sorts for dinner, but he changed his plans at the last minute.' He hesitated for a moment. 'I was meeting Arthur Hampton.'

'You know him too?' Callie was confused, she didn't think the two of them would naturally meet socially.

'Unfortunately. He was the one who put me onto the Symington & Chase case.'

'That's weird.'

'It's very weird. I just thought I should tell you.'

Callie nodded. She liked honesty.

A woman with the confidence and hair of a trust fund came to the door. 'Hello, darling, I'm Dotty,' she said, throwing her arms around Caius, almost wrestling him into the house. 'I've heard so much about you. Come in, we've got sticky toffee pudding.'

'My favourite,' Caius said, recovering from her determination in the hallway. He thought to take his shoes off but then realised there were no other pairs there. Callie came in behind him and stole a hug, before shoving him into the open-plan kitchen. The back wall had been extended and replaced with glass overlooking a tiny garden.

'Everyone, this is Callie's boyfriend Caius. He's a detective in the Met.'

Caius was aware that he might well be the only person there with an actual job and not a hobby they got paid a pittance for. All the eyes around the table were watching him with intense interest – he was a curiosity, a novelty.

All except one pair, which were simultaneously terrified and thrilled to see him. Caius flashed Nell a quick smile. She reciprocated it, but he could see there was a sadness beneath the veneer.

'Caius, this is my long-suffering husband Georgie, and this is Casper, Nell, Tommy and Hester.'

'Hello, everyone,' Caius said, taking the spare seat next to Callie. 'Apologies for my get-up. I was supposed to be at a thing.' All the other men were wearing niche trainer brands and Patagonia.

'Caius,' Georgie began. He looked like he had had a few and

was going to ask about dead bodies or grime or weirdly conflating the two. 'Have you ever shot anyone?'

'No. Fortunately not, but I once was shot at. It grazed past my arm. I'm in a Major Investigation Team so we occasionally get quite a few wrong 'uns.'

'Have you ever tasered someone?' Georgie asked.

'Yes.'

'All right, Georgie, eat your pudding,' Dotty said as she brought the sticky toffee pudding in and set bowls in front of her guests. She put a large bowl of syrupy stodge swimming in double cream in front of Caius. 'He was raised by wolves; he has no manners.'

'It's all right. Most people have questions.' Caius ate a spoonful of his pudding. It was delicious. 'What do you do, Casper?'

'I'm a sculptor. I'm inspired by the Arte Povera movement of the sixties and seventies.'

'I see,' said Caius, who didn't see. That had just been words to him.

'This piece,' he said, showing Caius a picture on his phone of a pile of what he thought was junk, 'is made entirely of things I found on the towpath in Haggerston.'

'Cool.' Caius was going to have to google Arte Povera later.

'I was walking down there one day and saw a dead crow. Its torso ripped open. Red guts smeared over feathers so black and glossy they were almost green. If you can understand that. It was probably a fox, maybe a particularly vicious cat. I'm trying to recreate that image, that visceral, gut-churning quality for an installation I have next year in Florence.'

'How fascinating.'

Casper turned inwards thinking about his piece but then remembered himself and his surroundings. 'This is delicious, Dotty.'

'Where are you on drugs?' Georgie asked.

'What do you mean?' Caius asked.

'What do you think about current drugs laws?' Georgie clarified.

'They don't really work. We'd almost be better off if some classes were entirely legal but highly regulated, like alcohol,' Caius said, realising they were closer to that being a reality than he'd considered and that actually maybe Hampton was right to an extent. 'It'd end stop and search which can only be a good thing.'

The table nodded along. Caius doubted that any of them had ever been stopped and searched despite their clear drug habits.

'Excellent,' Georgie said, patting the top pocket of his shirt.

★ ★ ★

Dinner over, an LP by an obscure alternative electronic band was playing on the record player, Tommy and Hester were having an argument in the garden about their dog, Georgie and Casper had disappeared – probably to do a line or three – and Callie had been dragged off upstairs by Dotty, probably to gossip about him. Caius and Nell were left together on the sofa. They avoided talking about the summer, and Rupert and the rape.

'That's one hell of an engagement ring,' Caius said, taking in the sapphire on her finger which was likely the cause of Rupert's apparent breakdown.

'Casper's grandfather is responsible for a literal quarter of Sweden's economy so . . .' Nell said, before telling him that she and Alex broke up a couple of months ago and she and Casper had an honest chat this week about their past behaviour and potential future.

'You probably shouldn't wear that out and about.'

'I figure that it looks so ridiculous people will think it's costume and leave me alone.'

'My sincerest congratulations to you both.'

'Thanks. We've been going out for seven years on and off. We can't keep doing that for eternity.'

'No, I suppose you can't.'

★ ★ ★

'You seemed to get on well with Casper's girlfriend,' Callie said, grasping Caius's hand tightly as they walked down Dotty's road.

'Yeah. I've actually met her before.'

'Dotty said she was at university with Rupert.'

'Yeah.' Caius looked up at the sky. It was a clear night, but there were no stars, just streetlamps and neon shop signs. He squeezed Callie's hand as they stopped at the bus shelter. 'What shall we do tomorrow?'

'Another country house?'

'I do need to get my money's worth from my National Trust membership.'

'If it's clear we can take a picnic.'

Caius flagged the bus down. 'That sounds wonderful.'

SATURDAY,
TWO WEEKS LATER

67

Caius's flat

Caius looked out of the window at the yellowing leaves on the trees. Autumn had finally begun to make itself known. He poured himself a glass of water; he'd gone to the pub last night with Matt and Amy and had got in quite late. He and Matt had been discussing taking an evening class on homebrewing, and Amy had corralled them into joining her and Fi's pub quiz team. Caius had picked his grandfather up in his car from his nursing home for lunch. Pops took his hat off and put it on the table. It was a grey trilby with a green feather in the ribbon. He was wearing a suit, as he always did. He was immaculate in the details of his dress. Caius had never seen him without a tie pin.

'Make yourself at home,' Caius said to his grandfather, who promptly made himself comfortable at the oak dining-room table that Callie had found for him on a resale site for a steal. They'd play dominoes on it later.

'Are you decorating?' Pops asked, nodding at the splodges of paint on the walls. His voice still had a sweet-sounding Jamaican cadence. Thinking about it, Caius couldn't ever really remember his grandfather speaking much patois. The patois that pitter-pattered his childhood had been his grandmother's chastises. 'I like the yellow.'

'Yeah, the place needs sprucing up.' He'd been spurred into action by Callie staying over. An enterprising young journalist had doorstopped her for a comment at her place earlier in the week. They sent her a written apology the following day, so Hampton had been true to his word. 'What have you got there?'

'It's a photo album. I thought you were a detective.'

'Let's have a look then,' Caius said, sitting down next to him.

'Are you not going to offer to make me a cup of tea?' asked his grandfather. He had his hands placed firmly on top of the album as if he were forcing its contents, its memories back. Trying to keep them safely between the yellowing sheets.

'We're out of milk. Callie, the girl I told you about, just popped to the shops to get some. But it is after midday. Would you prefer a whisky?' Caius had developed a taste for it after his trips to The Herakleion and had bought himself a bottle.

'A little one. I don't like your beard; you look like a scruff. What are you cooking? Last time it was just cornmeal with an Italian name.'

'Roast chicken.' Caius poured his grandfather a generous glass and paused for a moment as he tried to work out the best way to phrase his next question. 'Pops, who are the Beauchamps? Were they the plantation owners who enslaved our ancestors?' This was always the assumption that Caius had logically made.

Pops shook his head. 'I've never shown these to anyone, not even your grandmother,' his grandfather said, carefully unwrapping the first picture, a family portrait. They were all smartly dressed. Caius recognised his grandfather as a child but he was shocked by the appearance of his great-grandfather. 'This is my father, his name was Hector Beauchamp. He was English.'

'I didn't know your dad was white,' Caius said, recognising features of his grandfather's and father's faces in Hector's. A dimple here, a smile, the shape of a brow. There was something in the fundamental carriage of all three men, a genetic pride that carried through in their posture that was undeniably the same.

'He was a gentleman. He came to Jamaica in the twenties as a colonial administrator, married my mother and never left. His family didn't approve, and they never spoke to him again.' Pops flicked through more pictures of him and his parents. A picture of Caius's great-grandfather in his uniform taken before he nearly bought it at the Somme. Formal studio pictures. His grandfather in Passchendaele shorts outside a large white house with a small chubby baby enmeshed in a trailing white dress and bonnet.

'Who's the little one?'

'That was my little sister Hebe. She died of the measles when she was two.'

'I'm sorry. That's so sad.'

'That's how it was then. No vaccinations.' Pops snuck a sip of whisky. 'My father was a well-educated man. He could read Ancient Greek. He spoke French and German fluently. He was a brilliant batsman. He used to read me the *Iliad* as a bedtime story. He died in 1938 – his lungs hadn't been good after being gassed in the Great War – and on his deathbed he told me to get in touch with his family, that they'd help me get set up. When I came to England to fight the Nazis, I wrote to them. I didn't get a response. After the war I found out where my uncle lived. It was a big house in the country, not too far from London though. I have never been so rudely treated. I was wearing my uniform and my medals but still no respect. He said I was a disgrace to the family name, so I decided then and there to not pronounce it their way but the French way. I put it out of my mind and tried to pretend it never happened.'

'Did your uncle happen to live in a house called Frithsden Old Hall out in the Chilterns?' Caius asked, realising what Hampton had been saying about 'lines'.

'You've been there?'

'Yeah. You know the big murder case I was working on in the summer?' If Rupert was a Hampton and not a Beauchamp, then

Caius's grandfather was a baronet and one day so would he be. The house was his grandfather's, and so was the vast amount of property all over London. All of Hampton's comments about 'noblesse oblige' and calling him 'a knight errant' were less of a personality quirk and more of a fact now. Caius couldn't get his head around the wealth, and certainly not around the responsibility that his family's position now entailed. He sat back in his chair and tried to work out how he would explain all this madness to his dad.

'I don't pay attention to your nasty work—' his grandfather began, but was interrupted by the doorbell.

Caius got up and let Callie in. She noticed something was off with him but he reassured her it was nothing serious and he'd explain later.

'Pops, this is my girlfriend, Calliope. Callie, this is my grandfather, Big Caius. I was named after him. Didn't make him like me any better though.'

'O sing, goddess,' he said, standing up in the presence of a lady. 'You are far too beautiful to be taken out by this scruff.'

Acknowledgements

There are a huge number of people who I need to say thank you to, first and foremost among them is my husband Ben for all his support and then to the rest of my family.

I'd like to say thank you to my editors Sara Helen Binney, Libby Marshall and J. Edward Kastenmeier and to the wonderful team at Faber, especially Louisa Joyner, Phoebe Williams, Hannah Turner and Rachael Williamson. I would also like to thank my agent Jon Wood and Safae El-Ouahabi.